The Landscapes of the Sublime, 1700–1830

Also by Cian Duffy

CULTURES OF THE SUBLIME (*ed. with Peter Howell*)
SHELLEY AND THE REVOLUTIONARY SUBLIME

The Landscapes of the Sublime, 1700–1830

Classic Ground

Cian Duffy
*Reader in English Literature, St Mary's University College,
Twickenham, UK*

© Cian Duffy 2013

All rights reserved. No reproduction, copy or transmission of this publication may be made without written permission.

No portion of this publication may be reproduced, copied or transmitted save with written permission or in accordance with the provisions of the Copyright, Designs and Patents Act 1988, or under the terms of any licence permitting limited copying issued by the Copyright Licensing Agency, Saffron House, 6–10 Kirby Street, London EC1N 8TS.

Any person who does any unauthorized act in relation to this publication may be liable to criminal prosecution and civil claims for damages.

The author has asserted his right to be identified as the author of this work in accordance with the Copyright, Designs and Patents Act 1988.

First published 2013 by
PALGRAVE MACMILLAN

Palgrave Macmillan in the UK is an imprint of Macmillan Publishers Limited, registered in England, company number 785998, of Houndmills, Basingstoke, Hampshire RG21 6XS.

Palgrave Macmillan in the US is a division of St Martin's Press LLC, 175 Fifth Avenue, New York, NY 10010.

Palgrave Macmillan is the global academic imprint of the above companies and has companies and representatives throughout the world.

Palgrave® and Macmillan® are registered trademarks in the United States, the United Kingdom, Europe and other countries.

ISBN 978–1–137–33217–2

This book is printed on paper suitable for recycling and made from fully managed and sustained forest sources. Logging, pulping and manufacturing processes are expected to conform to the environmental regulations of the country of origin.

A catalogue record for this book is available from the British Library.

A catalog record for this book is available from the Library of Congress.

Typeset by MPS Limited, Chennai, India.

for my parents, and for Lisbet

Contents

Acknowledgements	viii
Introduction: In Search of 'Classic Ground'	1
1 'We had hopes that pointed to the clouds': The Alps and the Poetics of Ascent	28
2 'A volcano heard afar': Vesuvius, Etna and the Poetics of Depth	68
3 'The region of beauty and delight': Reimagining the Polar Sublime	102
4 'The lone and level sands': Romanticism and the Desert	135
5 'My purpose was humbler, but also higher': Thomas De Quincey at the Final Frontier	174
Notes	191
Bibliography	220
Index	228

Acknowledgements

More people have contributed to the making of this book than I could possibly hope to enumerate; without their scholarship, assistance and general encouragement it would have been very much the poorer. Thanks for specific inputs, and for discussions dotted up and down libraries and conferences over the past few years, are due to: Christophe Bode, Jack Donovan, Kelvin Everest, Peter Kitson, Nigel Leask, Rolf Lessenich, Ann Mellor, Frank Erik Pointner, Michael Rossington, Sharon Ruston and Clifford Siskin. Thanks also to Sophie Ainscough, Benjamin Doyle and Paula Kennedy at Palgrave, and to my anonymous reader, who helped to move the book considerably beyond its first conception. Thanks, too, to my copy-editor, Monica Kendall, for her unerring eye. The scholarship and companionship of colleagues at St Mary's have also been integral to the history of this book: thanks to Peter Dewar, Michael and Pauline Foster, Richard Mills, Michelle Paul, Caroline Ruddell, Brian Ridgers, Allan Simmons, Russell Schecter and especially to Peter Howell, whose work on *Cultures of the Sublime* added greatly to my sense of what I was trying to achieve in this book, and to how I might achieve it. Much of the research and writing for Chapters 3, 4 and 5 was done in the West Reading Room of the Royal Library in Copenhagen and I want also to express my gratitude to all the staff there for their friendly and professional assistance. Tak skal i have. The love of my parents, constant throughout the years, can never adequately be acknowledged. To Lisbet I am grateful, as Shelley might put it, for 'more than ever can be spoken'.

Material from Chapter 1 of this book has already been published in the 'Introduction' to Cian Duffy and Peter Howell (eds), *Cultures of the Sublime* (Basingstoke: Palgrave Macmillan, 2011), and is reproduced here by kind permission of Palgrave Macmillan. Every effort has been made to trace rights holders, but if any have been inadvertently overlooked the publishers would be pleased to make the necessary arrangements at the first opportunity.

Introduction: In Search of 'Classic Ground'

> whereso'er I turn my ravish'd eyes,
> Gay gilded scenes and shining prospects rise,
> Poetic fields encompass me around,
> And still I seem to tread on classic ground;
> For here the Muse so oft her harp has strung
> That not a mountain rears its head unsung,
> Renown'd in verse each shady thicket grows,
> And ev'ry stream in heavenly numbers flows.
> – Joseph Addison, *A Letter from Italy* (1701), ll. 9–16

At the beginning of the twenty-first century, popular interest in the wild places of the world shows no sign of abating.[1] Debates about climate change, and catastrophic natural events, such as the eruption of Eyjafjallajökull in April 2010, or the tsunami which inundated Japan in March 2011, have ensured that extreme natural phenomena remain at the forefront of the popular imagination, and this despite the ubiquitous foreboding of financial apocalypse.[2] Enquiries into the fundamental nature of the physical universe, too, continue to enthral the public – witness the range of popular-science cultural texts dealing with 'the wonders of the universe' and the so-called 'theory of everything', or the intense media interest surrounding the search for the Higgs boson at the Large Hadron Collider.[3] This popular fascination with the 'natural sublime', as it came to be known during the eighteenth century, is not new. However, the cultural history of this fascination needs, now, to be re-examined, because the invention of the 'natural sublime' during the eighteenth century continues to determine our engagement with 'nature' and 'the natural', influencing everything from the price of property in Alpine resorts to debates about the positioning of wind farms in areas of outstanding natural beauty, from the creation of national parks at the expense of indigenous populations to the burgeoning commercialisation of 'pristine' environments or 'unspoiled' travel destinations, and from constructions of the history of Western philosophy to arguments about the canon of 'Romantic' literature.[4] This book traces the beginnings of our extraordinary cultural investment in the 'natural sublime' across a diverse range of areas of enquiry and genres of writing in eighteenth-century and Romantic-period Europe.

Scholarly interest in the place of the 'natural sublime' in the cultural history of Europe and America is not new, and a number of excellent studies of various aspects of that place have been and continue to be written. Books like Jim Ring's *How the English Made the Alps* (2000), for example, or Robert Macfarlane's *Mountains of the Mind: a History of a Fascination* (2003), document for the general reader diverse aspects of the cultural history of the European fascination with the mountainous landscapes which have routinely come to be seen, since the eighteenth century, as synonymous with the 'natural sublime', continuing a tradition that also passes notably through Gavin De Beer's writings about the Alps and the history of Alpine mountaineering in the 1930s.[5] Ring charts the parallel development of the sport of Alpinism and the rise of Alpine tourism in the late eighteenth and nineteenth centuries, while Macfarlane documents the wider history of European attitudes to mountains and mountaineering, from the Renaissance to the present day. Simon Schama's *Landscape and Memory* (1995), for its part, offers to the general reader a broader overview of the place of the 'natural sublime' in the history of European attitudes to a range of different kinds of landscape, including mountains, forests and rivers.

Books like Samuel Holt Monk's *The Sublime* (1935) and Walter Hipple's *The Beautiful, the Sublime and the Picturesque* (1957), on the other hand, ushered in the academic study of the 'natural sublime' as a category within European thought and as a context for eighteenth- and nineteenth-century European literature, a study which has subsequently developed along historicist, new-historicist and critical-theoretical lines.[6] Studies in critical philosophy, like Slavoj Žižek's *The Sublime Object of Ideology* (1989) and Jean-François Lyotard's *The Inhuman* (1991), for their part, continue the investigation of the sublime as a philosophical or aesthetic category, an investigation which has been traced back through Immanuel Kant's *Critique of Judgement* (1790), Edmund Burke's *Philosophical Enquiry* (1757), and a plethora of other eighteenth-century texts, to Peri Hypsous, the first-century AD treatise usually attributed to Longinus.

It is possible to discern within this extensive and valuable body of writing about the 'natural sublime' the existence of a disciplinary lacuna which has opened up between what we might call (for the time being, at least) the 'popular' and the 'academic' or 'critical' approaches to the subject. One consequence of this lacuna is that, for reasons of scope as much as of conception, neither strand of enquiry manages accurately to represent the complexity of the place occupied by the 'natural sublime' in Western and European thought: 'popular' studies often only gesture towards theoretical contexts; 'academic' studies often neglect wider 'popular' perspectives.[7] Conversely, some of the most fruitful accounts of the early history of our fascination with the 'natural sublime' have been those broadly cultural-historical or new-historicist studies which have sought precisely to bridge this disciplinary lacuna between the 'popular' and the 'academic'. Ground-breaking, in this respect, was Marjorie Hope Nicolson's *Mountain Gloom and Mountain Glory* (1959), which traces the surge of interest in the 'natural sublime' during the late seventeenth and early eighteenth centuries to the development of new astronomical instrumentation and, consequently, to a new understanding of and appreciation for the physical universe.[8] Much of Nicolson's study is concerned with the engagement with the 'natural sublime' in those early works of natural philosophy, such as Thomas Burnet's *Sacred Theory of the Earth* (1681), which paved the way for the modern science of geology, and it is on the history of geology, too, that many of the more recent of the cultural-historical approaches to the 'natural sublime' have chosen to focus. Noah Heringman's *Romantic Rocks, Aesthetic Geology* (2004), Ralph O'Connor's *The Earth on Show: Fossils and the Poetics of Popular Science, 1802–1856* (2007) and Martin Rudwick's *Bursting the Limits of Time* (2005) all document different aspects of the place of the 'natural sublime' in the developing genre of geology, and in the remediation of that genre to the general public in non-specialist terms, as both spectacle and commodity.[9] And, most recently, Richard Holmes, in *The Age of Wonder* (2008), has begun to move us beyond the bias of such studies towards matters more or less to do with *mountains* and towards an understanding of the enabling and restricting role of 'wonder' – a concept associated with 'the sublime' within the genre of British philosophical aesthetics since the beginning of the eighteenth century – across a range of different genres of enquiry within natural philosophy during the Romantic period, in activities so ostensibly diverse as ballooning and chemistry.

What emerges from these studies, then, is the idea not only that the practice of natural philosophy during the eighteenth century and Romantic period often involved an encounter with the 'natural sublime', but that that practice actually often amounted to an enquiry *into* the 'natural sublime', and often generated sublime or other aesthetic effects as much as it did factual information. Hence, for example, the confidence with which Joseph Addison, at the beginning of the eighteenth century, in his seminal 'Pleasures of the Imagination' essays, could hail those natural philosophers, 'whether we consider their theories of the earth or heavens', who 'gratify and enlarge the imagination [...] with a pleasing astonishment' by revealing 'the immensity and magnificence of nature'.[10] And 90 years later, the seminal statement of this view for the Romantic period was offered by Adam Smith in his essay on 'The Principles which Lead and Direct Philosophical Enquiries; Illustrated by the History of Astronomy', which Smith composed in the 1750s, but which was only first published in the posthumous *Essays on Philosophical Subjects* in 1795. In this essay, Smith, drawing directly upon descriptions of 'the sublime' within the genre of eighteenth-century British philosophical aesthetics, traces the origins of astronomy, and of natural philosophy more generally, to the reaction of primitive cultures to the 'wonder, surprise, and astonishment' occasioned by the 'natural sublime'.[11]

This book bears out and develops each of these claims about the relationship between natural philosophy and the 'natural sublime' during the eighteenth century and Romantic period. And while it falls more on the 'academic' than on the 'popular' side of the lacuna in approaches to the sublime which I have been describing, I hope here to follow scholars like Heringman, Holmes, Nicolson, O'Connor and Rudwick, both in tracing the origins of that disciplinary chasm, and in suggesting ways in which we might bridge it. Indeed, this is possible not only because the disciplinary lacuna which I have described opened up during the period with which I am concerned in this book, but moreover because the invention of the 'natural sublime' during the eighteenth century and Romantic period actually played a significant role in defining and delineating the wider boundaries of genre and discipline at the precise moment in the cultural history of Europe when those boundaries were in the process of being first formulated. Although we are now familiar, following the work of C. P. Snow, with the idea of a divide between the 'two cultures' of the arts and the sciences, a number of recent studies have shown that no such divide was operative in the late eighteenth century and Romantic period. In his masterful account of 'the reconstruction of geohistory' in the so-called 'age of revolution', for example, Martin Rudwick has shown how the early history of the modern scientific disciple of geology 'entailed and required the deliberate transposition of analogical and metaphorical resources from right outside the sacred boundaries of "Science", namely from the human sciences (*Wissenschaften*) of history and even theology'.¹² Noah Heringman's work, too, has at some length 'the shared set of cultural practices shaping Romanticism and geology'.¹³ And most recently, in *The Earth on Show*, Ralph O'Connor has demonstrated the extent to which, in Britain at least, 'science writing was an integral part of nineteenth-century literary culture – not that science writing and literature enjoyed a fruitful relationship, but that scientific writing *was* literature'.¹⁴ In a different vein, Carl Thompson, too, in *The Suffering Traveller and the Romantic Imagination* (2007), has shown that the persona of the explorer in the eighteenth century and Romantic period – a figure about whom I will have much to say in this book – could be at once a natural philosopher, a semi-professional littérateur, a semi-professional agent of the state, a lone wanderer and a celebrity.¹⁵ A key claim that I make in this book, then, is not just that the place of the 'natural sublime' in the cultural history of eighteenth-century and Romantic-period Europe can only adequately be described in terms of what would now be understood as a multidisciplinary enquiry, but also that the invention of the 'natural sublime' played a vital role in the development of a number of modern disciplines, genres of writing and professional or semi-professional pursuits. Put differently, the invention of the 'natural sublime' during the eighteenth century and Romantic period was an integral part of what Clifford Siskin has described, in *The Work of Writing* (1999), as the development of the new technology of writing. One consequence of this is that we shall repeatedly encounter, in the texts which I consider, appeals to the *imagination* in contexts where, today, such appeals would be considered inappropriate at best, and 'unscientific' at worst. To draw on Ralph O'Connor's terminology, in the eighteenth century and Romantic period there was 'nothing controversial in the idea that scientific ideas could appeal to the imagination', and hence 'science', and a range of other 'practices defined against imagination', could often be 'promoted in literary texts using imaginative techniques'.¹⁶

It is perhaps worth pausing for a moment to note that the claims which I make, in this book, about the place of the 'natural sublime' in the cultural history of eighteenth-century and Romantic-period Europe could arguably also be made about the wider category of the sublime at that time, both in its many experiential and in its many discursive mediations.¹⁷ I have chosen to focus more or less exclusively on the 'natural sublime', here, for a number of reasons, beyond the obvious one of the scope of a single book. First, because of the prominence of the 'natural sublime' across the range of eighteenth-century and Romantic-period engagements with the category of the sublime *per se*: even when the 'natural sublime' itself is not the main object of enquiry, tropes of the 'natural sublime' are often used in or generated by other areas of enquiry.[18] Second, because of the continued prominence of the 'natural sublime' in contemporary popular culture: of all the genres of the sublime which we have inherited from the Romantic period, it is the 'natural sublime' which continues most to determine our perceptions of 'nature' and 'the natural'. And third, because the 'natural sublime' has largely dominated twentieth-century academic histories of the place of the wider category of the sublime in Western and European thought, despite, for example, significant parallel strands of interest in the philosophical, psychological and linguistic mediations of sublime effect in the work of highly influential thinkers like Jacques Lacan and Jean-François Lyotard.[19] It is in engagements with and writings about the 'natural sublime', in other words, that the contours and fractures of our continuing fascination with the wider category of the sublime have been and continue to be most visible.[20]

The academic history of the place of the 'natural sublime' in Western and European thought began to be written, in the twentieth century at least, with Samuel Holt Monk's seminal *The Sublime: a Study of Critical Theories in Eighteenth-Century England*, first published in 1935 and reissued in 1960. Monk was the earliest academic critic to survey the plethora of enquiries 'into the nature and causes of sublime sensation' in eighteenth-century Britain: the body of writing that Peter de Bolla has termed 'the discourse on the sublime'.[21] Monk describes a British tradition which is broadly empirical in its origins and which is, in consequence, dominated by the attempt to explain the sublime as a perceptible property of things rather than as a construction, or attribute, of the mind of the perceiver. However, as Ashfield, De Bolla, Howell and I have all argued elsewhere, it was also Monk who first constructed the narrative which came to inform many of the subsequent academic descriptions of the place of the sublime in the cultural history of Western and European thought which were written during the twentieth century. To put it in Ashfield and De Bolla's terms, Monk was the first to claim 'with some scholarly authority' that the eighteenth-century British empirical enquiry into sublime should be read as a precursor to the transcendental-idealist paradigms of the sublime set out by Immanuel Kant in his 'Analytic of the Sublime', the centrepiece of the *Critique of Judgement*, which describes the sublime as an effect or category of perception rather than as a property of objects.[22] In other words, Monk sees the paradigms of Kant's 'Analytic of the Sublime', following Kant himself, as both accurate and objective, and the British tradition as striving towards that accuracy and objectivity. Hence, for Monk, the most significant of the eighteenth-century British writings about the sublime – foremost amongst them, Edmund Burke's *Philosophical Enquiry*, with its emphasis on the link between terror and the sublime – were those works of philosophical aesthetics which seemed most to anticipate Kant's discussion.

The canon, the narrative and the critical-theoretical bias of Monk's *The Sublime* all came to be adopted, often largely without question, by many subsequent, highly influential academic histories of the place of the sublime in the cultural history of eighteenth-century and Romantic-period Europe, to say nothing at all of the many studies of individual Romantic-period writers. Both Thomas Weiskel's *The Romantic Sublime* (1976) and Neil Hertz's *The End of the Line* (1985), for example, assume largely Kantian paradigms in their discussion of the sublime, while even Philip Shaw's recent casebook *The Sublime* is also informed by the same orthodoxy. Indeed, Nicolson's *Mountain Gloom and Mountain Glory* is almost unique, in the twentieth century, in its cultural-historical approach, which does not present a British empirical tradition driving inexorably towards Kant's *Critique*.

As noted, I and others have elsewhere taken detailed issue with various aspects of the narrative formulated by Monk and its impact, both on subsequent academic histories of eighteenth-century critical philosophy and on influential readings of canonical Romantic-period poetry, and I have no intention to rehearse those discussions in any substance here. Nor do I have any wish to downplay either the importance of Kant's 'Analytic' within the cultural history of 'the sublime' in Western and European thought, or of the remediation of that 'Analytic' in the work of canonical Romantic-period poets like Samuel Taylor Coleridge or William Wordsworth, to say nothing of the prose of Thomas De Quincey, who played a significant role in introducing the philosophy of Kant to a wider British readership. That said, it might be worth recalling, here, Giuseppe Micheli's assessment that 'it is only from around 1830 that one can speak of any substantial influence of Kant's thought in England and of its reception in an adequate way', despite a brief period of attention, in British periodical reviews, in the late 1790s.[23] However, my purpose here is not to reject this genre of engagement with the 'natural sublime', but rather to recover another genre which has until now been largely neglected. Hence, there is one consequence of the 'widely unexamined Kantian appropriation of sublimity' in and by academic histories of the category which I have already begun to interrogate in *Shelley and the Revolutionary Sublime* and *Cultures of the Sublime*, and which I mean to subject to further scrutiny here.[24] This is the idea that the individual's response to the 'natural sublime' is disinterested, to use Kant's terminology, that is, devoid of individually or culturally determined elements, of any sense of use-value or other motivation, or of any ethical or political considerations.

In *Shelley and the Revolutionary Sublime*, I have argued at length that the tendency of academic histories of the place of the sublime in Western and European cultures to read the encounter with the sublime, following Kant, as essentially free from cultural and political bias, has led to persistent misreading and misrepresentation of the various, intensely political remediations of the 'natural sublime' in the poetry and prose of Percy Bysshe Shelley. Building on that earlier work, in *Cultures of the Sublime* Peter Howell and I have argued that within a wide range of engagements with the sublime during the eighteenth century and Romantic period, the encounter with the sublime should be understood less as 'the disinterested transcendence, by the individual mind, of empirical phenomena' than as 'the individual's response to the specific cultural values with which certain empirical phenomena have been, or are capable of being, inscribed'.[25]

This is the argument which I intend further to develop in this book, not only with a view better to reflect the place of the 'natural sublime' in the cultural history of the eighteenth century and Romantic period as I see it, but also to begin to move away from the pervasive empirical/idealist divide which has dominated descriptions of the sublime within both philosophical aesthetics and academic histories of philosophical aesthetics. The central claim of this book, then, is that the encounter with the 'natural sublime' during the eighteenth century and Romantic period – by explorers, by natural philosophers, by tourists, by artists, by antiquarians and by those who were all of these to a greater or lesser extent – was quintessentially *interested*. In other words, that encounter was often a highly determined and highly motivated response to a particular landscape or phenomenon, that is, to a particular species of the 'natural sublime'. In short: when it came to the encounter with 'natural sublime', it mattered what you saw; it mattered who you were and where you were when you saw it; and it mattered why you were there looking at it in the first place.

The title that I have chosen for this book reflects my sense that eighteenth-century poetry provides us with a useful paradigm for understanding this idea of a culturally determined and interested response to the 'natural sublime' in the form of Joseph Addison's concept of 'classic ground'. Indeed, I mean to argue here that the idea of 'classic ground' becomes one of the key paradigms of late eighteenth-century and Romantic-period engagements with the 'natural sublime'. Addison introduces the concept in his *Letter from Italy* (1701), the product of a journey during which he visited the major cities of northern and southern Italy, ascended Vesuvius, sailed to Capri, and ticked many of the other boxes on the already well-established itinerary of the European Grand Tour.[26] In the section of Addison's *Letter* which provides my epigraph to this 'Introduction', Addison deploys the notion of 'classic ground' as a means of explaining the experience of encountering, almost everywhere he went in Italy, not just blank physical features, but spaces whose cultural values were already highly determined, that is, spaces, both natural and artificial, which had already been inscribed with a rich layer of historical and cultural associations. These associations in no small part determined Addison's 'own' response to the scenery, and of course Addison would himself further augment those associations for others with the publication of his *Letter*. '[W]hereso'er I turn my ravish'd eyes,' Addison recalls:

> Gay gilded scenes and shining prospects rise,
> Poetic fields encompass me around,
> And still I seem to tread on classic ground;
> For here the Muse so oft her harp has strung
> That not a mountain rears its head unsung,
> Renown'd in verse each shady thicket grows,
> And ev'ry stream in heavenly numbers flows.[27]

As Peter Howell and I have already argued in *Cultures of the Sublime*, what Addison registers in his concept of 'classic ground', then, is the extent to which it is all but impossible for an educated traveller to have a disinterested aesthetic response to a landscape or an environment which has long possessed a range of specific historical and cultural associations.[28] Of course, by 'classic', Addison in Italy refers quite specifically to the inheritance of classical culture, everywhere in evidence around him. What I want to argue in this book, however, is that Addison's idea of a composite of landscape and cultural value becomes a key paradigm of the encounter with the 'natural sublime' during the eighteenth century and Romantic period. Indeed, 'classic ground' is precisely the term which Mary and Percy Shelley use to describe the areas of the Alps made famous by Rousseau's celebrated novel *Julie* (1761) in their *History of a Six Weeks' Tour* in 1817: a landscape 'peopled with tender and glorious imaginations of the present and the past'.[29] Time and time again in the texts which I consider here, this concept is invoked to characterise the encounter with the 'natural sublime' as involving either a landscape or an environment which already exists as what might be called 'classic ground' in the European cultural imagination, that is, which already possesses a range of culturally determined and topographically specific associations, or which is in the process of becoming 'classic ground', that is, of acquiring the associations which it often continues to possess to this day, of being inscribed upon Europe's cultural map of the world. In the former circumstance, the individual's encounter with the 'natural sublime' is not only conditioned by pre-determined cultural values, but also participates in the perpetuation of those values and expectations. Indeed, as was the case with Addison in Italy, the individual in these cases is often intensely aware of the pressures exerted by the cultural inheritance with which they are confronted: as Carl Thompson has recently reminded us, travel during the Romantic period was increasingly 'scripted' by a 'vast' and growing 'matrix' of related writings.[30] In the latter circumstance, conversely, we shall see that the individual is often troubled precisely by the cultural blankness of the landscape or environment which they encounter and struggles to impose values upon it. Hence, descriptions of the encounter with the sublime in such *terrae incognitae* as the desert or the Arctic often parallel contemporary descriptions, within the genre of philosophical aesthetics, of the relationship between 'the sublime' and 'obscurity', or 'silence', or 'solitude', such as Edmund Burke's in his *Philosophical Enquiry*.[31] It is also arguably in the encounter with landscapes or environments which are in the process of becoming 'classic ground' that developing attitudes to the 'natural sublime' play an even more fundamental role in determining the cultural significance that a given area will come to possess in the European imagination, and that it often continues to possess to the present day.

It is in this sense that I mean to claim here that the invention of the 'natural sublime' during the eighteenth century and Romantic period shaped and continues to shape our fascination with the wild places of the world: the invention of the 'natural sublime' was also the invention, or the reinvention, of the cultural significance of the landscapes and environments where it was encountered. It is also in this sense that the engagement with the 'natural sublime' during the eighteenth century and Romantic period needs often to be seen as a component of a wider political or colonial project. In *The Age of Wonder*, Richard Holmes has demonstrated the frequency with which the encounter with the 'natural sublime' during the eighteenth century and Romantic period took place within the context of enquiries in natural philosophy.

However, as Holmes makes clear, such enquiries were often themselves only part of an underlying process of European colonial, cultural and economic expansion, as for example in James Cook's search for the fabled *terra australis incognita*, which I consider in Chapter 3, or Mungo Park's quest for the Niger, which I discuss in Chapter 4. Carl Thompson, too, has recently shown how 'the information brought back' by such explorers 'was never just a contribution to a growing body of purely scientific knowledge; it was also frequently a means to much more pragmatic ends': explorers like Cook and Park had, in other words, a highly complex relationship with the British imperialism of which they were at once the 'agent' and the 'enabler'.[32] Hence it is very difficult to see the encounter with the 'natural sublime' by such individuals as entirely *disinterested*, as entirely devoid of cultural, ethical or political motivation. Private *financial* motivation, too, is often impressed upon the encounter with the 'natural sublime', or at least upon the remediation of that encounter to the general public. There could be immediate financial benefits for discovery of course: the British Admiralty, for example, offered a substantial reward to anyone who could demonstrate a north-west passage through the Arctic ice to the Pacific, while the growth of organisations like the African Association meant that exploration became at least semi-professionalised. However, published accounts of expeditions were also highly saleable commodities in the late eighteenth century and Romantic period, providing the rush of a vicarious experience of the 'natural sublime' to a reading public saturated with Romance and Gothic fiction, as well as to those soberly seeking intellectual improvement. In *The Earth on Show*, Ralph O'Connor has described the role of economic and intellectual factors in the dissemination of 'spectacular' ideas about the history of the earth to a non-specialist audience in the early nineteenth century. In a similar vein, I draw repeated attention, here, to the extent to which the 'natural sublime' becomes commoditised in and by the nascent publishing industry during the Romantic period.

Hence, within the genres of engagement with the 'natural sublime' which I describe in this book it is not always easy to perceive the autonomy of the individual which is asserted by Kantian descriptions of the aesthetic encounter. The genre I describe is, rather, closer to those elements of the eighteenth-century British genre of philosophical aesthetics in which, to use Ashfield and De Bolla's terms, 'there is a consistent refusal to relinquish the interconnections between aesthetic judgements and ethical conduct', in which 'the aesthetic is constantly called back to other forms of understanding the world'.[33] The underlying methodological assumption of this book, therefore, is that to map the place of the 'natural sublime' in the cultural history of the eighteenth century and Romantic period is to attempt to reconstruct a genre which ranges across the boundaries of what would now be viewed as discrete forms of cultural activity and productivity but which were, then, intimately entwined areas of enquiry with no clearly demarcated borders between them. To focus too exclusively on any one of the many genres of writing or areas of enquiry in which sublime effects are investigated or produced, then, be that philosophical aesthetics, expedition narrative or canonical poetry, is to restrict understanding of the range of the 'natural sublime' as a culturally determined genre, a genre which is continually mediated and remediated through a variety of other cultural texts. Let this not be misunderstood. I have no wish to downplay, here, the influence of the genre of eighteenth- and early nineteenth-century philosophical aesthetics, British and German alike, on the formulation of the category of the 'natural sublime', despite my already stated caveats about the subsequent impact of a particular reading of that genre on our understanding of Romantic-period poetry and, indeed, on our understanding of Romanticism more generally. Nor is it my intention to attempt to offer any kind of corrective reading of any given position within this genre of philosophical aesthetics. What I do intend to describe, however, are different and neglected genres of engagement with the 'natural sublime' in the eighteenth century and Romantic period, genres which in many respects avoid or at least renegotiate the tension between British-empirical and German-idealist approaches which has remained at the core of many academic discussions of the place of 'the sublime' in the cultural history of that period. The genres which I consider here register the 'natural sublime' neither wholly as a property of objects nor wholly as an effect of discourse. Rather, the 'natural sublime' emerges from these genres as the product of the inscription of cultural values upon empirical phenomena, and of the subsequent mediation and remediation of that composite in and by a range of other genres and areas of enquiry. It consists, in other words, in the construction, the perception and the perpetuation of the kind of cultural text that Addison describes as 'classic ground': the amalgamation of physical and imaginative geography.

My aim in this book, then, is to reassess the place of the 'natural sublime' in the cultural history of the eighteenth century and Romantic period with a view to increasing and refining our understanding of both that history and our continuing fascination with the 'natural sublime'. In practical terms, I mean to do this by taking a selection of canonical, and in some cases very well-known, Romantic-period engagements with the 'natural sublime' as a point of entry into the wider generic context of which those engagements originally formed a part. Hence my aim is not so much to generate new readings of canonical texts as it is to generate new cultural histories of various species of the 'natural sublime' during the eighteenth century and Romantic period, and to indicate how familiar Romantic-period texts constitute part of those histories, by replacing the canonical within its wider, cultural-historical context. Very often, this wider context is comprised of cultural texts which had greater contemporary influence than the material now considered canonical, but which have fallen into neglect because they belong to genres which have not routinely been invoked in the context of literary studies or histories of philosophical aesthetics, or because they have been considered only as so many sources for canonical texts, rather than as part of a system of cultural exchange, of mediation and remediation. Some of this material will be familiar, at least to specialists; some of it will not.

I hope, in adopting this methodology, precisely to avoid, insofar as possible, re-inscribing upon the material which I study any versions of those disciplinary boundaries which we have inherited *from* the Romantic period but which were not generally operative, or at least not generally recognised, *during* that period. Ralph O'Connor – noting the recent proliferation of 'poet *x* and science *y*' studies – has cautioned against just such a retrospective imposition of a 'two cultures' model, adding that 'we still have only a vestigial sense of where scientific texts fit into literary history as a whole' whilst 'individual scientific texts have often been treated as *sui generis*, without indicating their relation to other texts of the same literary genre'.[34] Armed with this warning, I intend (again, at least insofar as possible) that the cultural histories of the different species of the 'natural sublime' which I generate here avoid not only the imposition of an overly reductive distinction between 'literature' and other kinds of writing (or between literary texts and their non-literary sources), but also the imposition of an unhistorical distinction between canonical and non-canonical writing.[35]

An important corollary claim of this book, then, is that many of the now non-canonical genres of engagement with the 'natural sublime' which I describe had greater contemporary influence upon constructions of the category than the now relatively well-known works of philosophical aesthetics upon which academic histories of the sublime have typically tended to focus, a claim which Peter Howell and I have already begun to outline in *Cultures of the Sublime*. Hence, as in Nicolson's pioneering *Mountain Gloom and Mountain Glory*, the reader will perhaps find rather less here in the way of attention to eighteenth-century and Romantic-period works of philosophical aesthetics than they might expect to find in a book on the topic of 'the landscapes of the sublime'. My point, however, is precisely that it is not primarily to the genre of philosophical aesthetics that we should turn if we wish fully to understand the construction of the 'natural sublime' as a cultural category, or genre, during the eighteenth century and Romantic period. Or, at its least strong, my claim is that an excessive dependence on the paradigms of eighteenth-century and Romantic-period philosophical aesthetics, be they British or German, can and has led to a restricted or misconstrued description of the place of the 'natural sublime' in the cultural history of the period. In this, I follow, to a certain extent, Noah Heringman's argument that the 'tropological' basis of the sublime is 'precisely' why 'one must look outside theoretical contexts to understand its local and specific meanings'.[36] Having said that, influential, contemporary theoretical constructions of the sublime by figures like Archibald Alison and Edmund Burke – the major proponents, for example, of the links with religious experience, and with terror – are of course mediated in and remediated by the genres of engagement with the 'natural sublime' on which I have chosen to focus here. Put more simply, the travellers and explorers on whose writings I have chosen to focus in this book often show themselves to be aware of, even if they often depart from, the terminology and the paradigms of contemporary philosophical aesthetics.[37] Indeed, while such a project would clearly fall outside the scope of the present study, I have no doubt, either, but that it would be possible to discern in the genre of philosophical aesthetics during the eighteenth century and Romantic period the remediation of the writings about the sublime on which I have chosen to focus here. I do not mean, in this suggestion of a dialectical relationship between these different contemporary genres of engagement with 'the sublime', to reject Peter de Bolla's influential distinction between the discourses of and on the sublime, but only to argue that the boundary between those two discourses is not always, perhaps, so easy to discern. Outside the context of philosophical aesthetics, published enquiries into the 'natural sublime' – for example, speculation about the emotive effects upon a European traveller of an African desert – can also generate sublime effect in the reader of that account: hence, at least in part, the already noted commercial value of such accounts. Throughout this book, however, I will take issue with De Bolla's concomitant suggestion that we can talk about a 'romantic sublime' which is 'less a variant of the eighteenth-century enquiry than a completely distinct discourse which borrows many terms from it'.[38]

Scholars like Nicolson, Schama and Holmes have long since moved us beyond the commonplace assumption that interest in the 'natural sublime' during the eighteenth century and Romantic period was primarily a matter of mountains, although mountainous landscapes were obviously a major focus of that interest, as has again been made evident by the recent attention of Heringman, O'Connor and Rudwick to the place of 'the sublime' in the development of the modern scientific discipline of geology, and in its interaction with a variety of other genres. The species of the 'natural sublime', that is, the landscapes and environments, upon which I have chosen to focus in this book – the Alps, the Italian volcanoes, the Arctic and Antarctic, the deserts of central and southern Africa, and the universe revealed by the new astronomy – are not only those which feature most prominently in the canon of Romantic-period engagements with the 'natural sublime', but also those which seem to me best to illustrate the process by which the encounter with the 'natural sublime' during the eighteenth century and Romantic period is either an encounter with something that might best be described as 'classic ground' or an encounter which constructs 'classic ground', that is, a landscape or environment overwritten with cultural value. Having said this, however, I am of course all too aware that for each of the five species of the 'natural sublime' which I do consider here, there are at least twice as many more which I have not considered, not least amongst them the various landscapes encountered by the likes of Alexander von Humboldt and Aimé Bonpland in South America, or by John Barrow in south-east Asia and China, to say nothing of domestic tourists in North Wales, the Lake District and the Scottish Highlands.[39] And these domestic tourists of course include canonical figures like Samuel Johnson, William Wordsworth, Percy Shelley and John Keats. These territories I leave for other scholars to examine.

Similar restrictions have applied to the range of material which I have been able to consider here. A significant portion of that writing might be classified, broadly, as travel or expedition narrative, although at a time when 'scientific writing *was* literature', to use O'Connor's phrase, such arbitrary boundaries are perhaps as difficult to draw as they are unhelpful to invoke.[40] I have already noted Carl Thompson's reference to the 'vast matrix' of writing by which the expectations of travellers were 'scripted' during the eighteenth century and Romantic period, and even the briefest glance at Tim Fulford's and Peter Kitson's monumental, multi-volume *Travels, Explorations and Empires, 1770–1835* series will give a sense of the extent of contemporary writing about the regions on which I have chosen to focus.[41] There are of course some localised disparities within this body of writing. Areas well known to the European imagination and (increasingly) accessible to travellers – such as the Alps, or the volcanoes of Italy – tended unsurprisingly to generate a greater body of responses than lesser-known and less accessible regions, like the Arctic or the Sahara. Despite these disparities, however, fairly rigorous selection has been necessary to prevent this study running to multiple volumes. In view of the nature of the argument that I wish to make in this book, my rationale, in selecting which material to consider, has been to focus on works which had contemporary prominence rather than works which subsequent academic or popular histories might have brought to prominence. Hence, some of the material covered here will be familiar, while some will not: the writings of James Cook and Mungo Park are relatively familiar; those of Louis Ramond de Carbonnières and Patrick Brydone perhaps less so.[42] Overall, though, I must also rely somewhat on the mercy of dissenting critics not to assume that I have simply chosen to focus on those texts which support the argument that I wish to make at the expense of those texts which do not. Again, my purpose here is not to attempt to knock down the hierarchy of one genre of writing about the sublime and set another in its place. It is only to broaden our understanding of the extent of the genres of the 'natural sublime' in the cultural history of the eighteenth century and Romantic period.

It might be worth pausing again, at this point, to reflect also on the fact that the evidence which I consider here is almost entirely textual, a fact which may strike some critics as surprising if we consider the prominence in Romantic-period popular culture, at least, of representations of the 'natural sublime' by artists like John Martin and Joseph Turner, to say nothing at all of the presence of such representations in dedicated works of natural philosophy. In *Bursting the Limits of Time*, Martin Rudwick has pointed justly to the extent to which the work of literary critics and historians of science tends often still to be 'rooted in *literary traditions* that have little or no comprehension of the place of *visual* imagery in the life and work of most natural scientists, both past and present', and has therefore called for the 'routine' use of imagery in studies not unlike the kind which I am attempting here.[43] Ralph O'Connor, too, has urged that greater attention be paid 'to the aesthetic component of scientific culture'.[44]

True to these arguments, both Rudwick and O'Connor have themselves made compelling use of illustration, and my decision to focus on textual sources here is certainly not meant to downplay the significance of such other genres of engagement with the 'natural sublime', nor of the mingling of textual and visual genres in illustrated books. Nor, however, is that decision entirely motivated by concerns about the scope of a single monograph, or of even-handedness given the plethora of illustrations of, for example, the Alps, compared to paucity of illustrations of the Arctic, to say nothing at all of the Antarctic, which no one had even seen during the Romantic period. My sense, rather, is that the genres of engagement with the 'natural sublime' which I describe here were primarily textual genres, and that the effects they produced were primarily narrative effects: these genres engaged with *imagined* spaces formed of a composite of physical geography and cultural values. O'Connor has noted 'the crucial enabling roles of spectacle and (in particular) of literature' in promoting geological knowledge in the nineteenth century, and that '[i]t was in their literary productions – in books, journals, magazines and newspapers – that these geologists and their followers reached most of their increasingly variegated public'.[45] The same is undoubtedly true of the many explorers, travellers and natural philosophers whose writings I consider in this book: the 'natural sublimes' which they construct, the personae which they construct, are for the most part textual rather than visual phenomena, *imagined* or *culturally determined* rather than empirical. Addison's idea of 'classic ground', which this book takes as its leitmotif, is, similarly, a narrative rather more than a visual concept. And indeed, by the time we reach the end of this book, we will see popularisers like Thomas De Quincey turn explicitly away from visual accuracy in search of marketable rhetorical effect. Hence, whilst some might feel that this study would have been the stronger had it taken more account of contemporary visual representations of the different species of the 'natural sublime' which it describes, I hope that none will feel it significantly the weaker for the lack of them.

Chapter 1 of this book explores some eighteenth-century and Romantic-period engagements with a landscape which has come to typify the 'Romantic sublime', both in academic descriptions and in popular culture: the Alps. I take as my point of entry, here, one of the most canonical of all the Romantic-period engagements with the 'natural sublime': Wordsworth's account of crossing the Alps in Book VI of *The Prelude*. Wordsworth's reconstruction of this episode from his walking tour of Europe in 1790 (a different version had already appeared in his *Descriptive Sketches* of that year) has routinely been considered, since Monk's early reading, as the 'apotheosis' of 'the experience that lay behind the eighteenth-century sublime', as a 'set piece of the sublime', to use Thomas Weiskel's phrase.[46] While not denying

Monk's perception 'that there is a general similarity between the point of view of the *Critique of Judgement* and *The Prelude*', I interrogate the usefulness and the consequences of that claim here by relocating Wordsworth's account of crossing the Alps in the wider, contemporary genre of writing about Chamonix-Mont Blanc.[47] I trace the origins of this genre to the 'discovery' of the area by European travellers in the 1740s, and follow the subsequent incarnations of that genre in the work of, amongst others, Jean-Jacques Rousseau, Marc Bourrit, Louis Ramond de Carbonnières and Horace-Bénédict de Saussure. My claim, in this chapter, is that Chamonix-Mont Blanc is essentially invented as what we might call 'classic ground' on the cultural map of Europe during the eighteenth century and Romantic period, that is, that the area is transformed from a relatively unknown space into a familiar landscape, inscribed with a range of highly specific, culturally determined connotations, many of which it continues to possess to this day. In *Mountain Gloom and Mountain Glory*, Marjorie Hope Nicolson describes the Alps as the primary locus where reverence for God came to be transferred, by a succession of British travellers, to those aspects of the natural world which seemed most to reflect God's grandeur.[48] As I make clear in this chapter, however, the religious discourse which Nicolson describes – prevalent though it is in contemporary British writing about the Alps – is in fact only one facet of the wider, European 'discovery' of the Alpine sublime, and in this sense my analysis confirms and extends Martin Rudwick's account of 'how religious and scientific practices and knowledge claims have interacted' in the period.[49] That discovery, I argue, involved the generation of what I call the 'discourse of ascent', a discourse which links the physical ascent of mountains to a wide variety of ostensibly unrelated forms of elevation: moral, political, epistemological, etc. – as well as religious. It is this wider discourse of ascent, I argue, which is both mediated in and remediated by Wordsworth's account of his Alpine experiences in Book VI of *The Prelude*.

In Chapter 2, I examine a species of the 'natural sublime' which, by the beginning of the eighteenth century, had, by contrast, long been familiar to the European cultural imagination: the Italian volcanoes, Vesuvius and Etna, both quintessentially 'classic ground', famed from antiquity. Marjorie Hope Nicolson's discussion of Thomas Burnet's *Sacred Theory of the Earth* was amongst the first to alert scholars to the place of an engagement with the 'natural sublime' in eighteenth-century speculation about the geological history of the earth.[50] As noted, more recent scholarship, by Heringman, O'Connor, Rudwick and others, has refined our understanding of the integral role played by the 'natural sublime' in the development of the modern scientific discipline of geography, and in the remediation of specialist enquiries into the history of the earth to the general public in popular-cultural texts during the Romantic and Victorian periods. Building on this scholarship here, my argument, in this chapter, is that while eighteenth-century and Romantic-period engagements with the Alpine sublime often generate tropes of ascent, contemporary engagements with Vesuvius and Etna often tend, conversely, to generate tropes of depth. My point of entry into this genre of writing about the volcanic sublime is the now little-known work of Patrick Brydone, whose account of his observations on Sicily and Etna was included in his widely read and (in Britain, at least) highly influential *Tour through Sicily and Malta* (1773). Although Brydone was certainly not one of Rudwick's 'scientific elite', Brydone's account of Etna plays its own small part in the Europe-wide, eighteenth-century debate about the age of the earth and the discovery of what has come to be known as geological 'deep time': the concept which underpins the modern science of geology as formulated (in Britain, at least) in James Hutton's *Theory of the Earth* (1788) and Charles Lyell's *Principles of Geology* (1830–33).[51] However, Brydone's *Tour* also typifies the hybrid nature of engagements not just with the volcanic sublime, but with the 'natural sublime' *per se* during the eighteenth century and Romantic period. Part natural philosophy, part travel guide, part philosophical aesthetics and part commercial product, Brydone's *Tour* does not fit comfortably within any of the disciplinary categories which were to emerge during, and which we have inherited from, the Romantic period. Hence, perhaps, why it has been mostly neglected by subsequent histories of those categories: the genre of writing which Brydone's *Tour* exemplifies does not really exist today. But it is precisely this hybridity of Brydone's *Tour* which flags up the fact that it was not only the nascent science of geology which was influenced by eighteenth-century and Romantic-period engagements with the volcanic sublime. Rather, those engagements also generate tropes of depth which enable and shape contemporary descriptions of the human mind and of diverse modes of consciousness, providing the late eighteenth century and Romantic period with a potent, pre-Freudian vocabulary for expressing, for example, concepts of repression, typified in Byron's well-known characterisation of 'poetry' as 'the lava of the imagination, whose eruption prevents an explosion'.[52] Once again, then, the engagement with the volcanic sublime emerges from my reading here as a process which not only ranged across what would now be perceived as the borders of discrete disciplines and areas of enquiry, but which was also instrumental in the formulation of those boundaries. Hence, to adapt O'Connor's terms, the enquiry into the sublime was central to the contemporary 'debate about what kinds of language were appropriate to communicating knowledge about nature'.[53]

Chapters 3 and 4 focus on landscapes and environments which were essentially unknown to European travellers at the start of the eighteenth century: the Arctic and Antarctic, and the deserts of central and southern Africa. At the beginning of the eighteenth century, these regions were not only 'a blank space' on Europe's physical and cultural maps of the world, as the English translator of Christian Frederick Damberger's *Travels in the Interior of Africa* put it in his preface in 1801, but also largely blank spaces in the European imagination.[54] As such, the place of engagements with these species of the 'natural sublime' in the European imagination during the eighteenth century and Romantic period in many respects parallels Edmund Burke's ideas about the link between vastness, solitude, and mental and physical privation, and the sublime, in his *Philosophical Enquiry*, just as it also prefigures the subsequent remediation of 'the sublime' during the twentieth century, in the works of Lyotard and Lacan, as the sign of the unpresentable and the inhuman. The physical and cultural emptiness of these places challenges and defies both representation and interpretation. Hence, the engagement with these landscapes by European explorers throughout the eighteenth century and Romantic period exemplifies the process by which the contemporary encounter with the 'natural sublime' involved the construction of 'classic ground', the inscription of cultural values on environments and features – or, as in these cases, the often-failed attempt to claim imaginative as well as territorial possession of landscapes and environments which proved as inimical to the imposition of European cultural values as they were hostile to human settlement. A parallel genre of engagement with these places is sometimes also visible, in which indigenous cultures – such as the Inuit described by John Ross in Greenland, or the Moors encountered by Mungo Park and James Bruce in North Africa – must be effaced from European accounts of the landscape, or somehow incorporated into that landscape, precisely in order to facilitate this pseudo-Burkean aesthetics of sublime emptiness.

Building on works like Francis Spufford's *I May Be Some Time: Ice and the English Imagination* (1996) and Eric Wilson's *The Spiritual History of Ice: Romanticism, Science, and the Imagination* (2003), Chapter 3 examines a selection of eighteenth-century and Romantic-period engagements with the Arctic and the Antarctic, with what we might call the 'polar sublime'. Spufford, in particular, has already begun to describe a 'kind of polar history, largely uncharted; an intangible history of assumptions, responses to landscape, cultural fascinations, aesthetic attraction to the cold regions', and linked this 'history' to interest in the sublime, and it is this 'history' which I mean further to develop here – and indeed it is exactly this kind of history which this book, as a whole, attempts to generate for the different species of the 'natural sublime' which it considers.[55] Spufford's work is concerned primarily with the place of the polar ice in the cultural history of the Victorian and modern periods, with the context for and the legacy of the expeditions of Scott and Shackleton. My purpose here is to backdate the 'imaginative history of polar exploration' which Spufford identifies to its origins in the eighteenth century and Romantic period.[56] I take the Antarctic sequence of Coleridge's *The Rime of the Ancyent Marinere* (1798) and the Arctic frame narrative of Mary Shelley's *Frankenstein* (1818) as my point of entry into the constructions of the polar sublime generated in and by the writing of figures like James Cook (whose 'farthest south' record, established in 1774, remained unbroken for almost 50 years), John Ross and William Edward Parry. Both the *Ancyent Marinere* and *Frankenstein* reveal not only the continuing public fascination with the polar regions, but also the extent to which the genre of the polar sublime that developed in the writings of Cook and others in the mid-eighteenth century had quickly become embedded in the popular imagination. Both the *Ancyent Marinere* and *Frankenstein* configure the polar regions as inhuman absences. Both register the desire to claim these spaces for the European imagination by inscribing cultural values upon them, that is, by reconfiguring them as 'classic ground', a desire which of course parallels and complements the wider contemporary desire for the commercial and political exploitation of these regions, and which continues to mark engagements with these environments to the present day. Both the *Ancyent Marinere* and *Frankenstein* also turn around the narrative of heroic failure which would come to dominate British engagements with the polar sublime for almost a century after the disaster of Franklin's expedition in 1845.[57]

Following a track laid out by Richard Holmes in *The Age of Wonder* and Carl Thompson in *The Suffering Traveller*, Chapter 4 takes Percy Shelley's well-known sonnet 'Ozymandias' (1818) as its point of departure for an examination of the European engagement with the sublime of the desert during the eighteenth century and Romantic period, by explorers such as John Barrow and François Le Vaillant in

South Africa, and such as Mungo Park and James Bruce in the central and southern regions of the Sahara.[58] The chapter traces in these European engagements with the sublime emptiness of African desert the attempt to inscribe cultural values upon landscapes which proved as resistant to the imposition of European aesthetic categories as they did to European colonisation, a resistance which I argue is figured for many writers in the dreaded desert wind: the simoom. Hence, the story of European engagements with the sublime of the desert during the eighteenth century and Romantic period emerges from this chapter as in many respects parallel to that of contemporary engagements with the polar sublime: both involve ultimately unsuccessful attempts to claim these territories for the European imagination by reconfiguring absence as 'classic ground'. Building on work by Alan Liu and Carl Thompson, I suggest, in the latter part of this chapter, ways in which we might read Wordsworth's well-known 'Dream of the Arab' from Book V of *The Prelude* alongside Bruce's account of his harrowing journey through the Sahara in his *Travels to Discover the Source of the Nile* as texts which epitomise the tendency of the eighteenth-century genre of engagement with the sublime of the desert to figure the desert as inimical to European cultural subjectivity. The chapter concludes with a brief coda tracing the remediation of this Romantic remediation of the sublime of the desert in the mid-nineteenth century through Richard Francis Burton's widely read account of his experiences of the deserts of Saudi Arabia in his *Personal Narrative of a Pilgrimage to Al-Medinah and Meccah* (1855).

I return in Chapter 5 to astronomy: the area of enquiry to which Marjorie Hope Nicolson traces the upsurge of interest in the 'natural sublime' in late seventeenth- and early eighteenth-century England, in *Mountain Gloom and Mountain Glory*. Nicolson traces that upsurge to the advances in optical instrumentation which made newly visible the wonders of the universe. Astronomy enjoyed something of a second renaissance during the period covered by this book, again due to technological advances in optical instrumentation. In the last quarter of the eighteenth century, the technical and observational work of William and Caroline Herschel – whose story has recently been retold by Holmes in *The Age of Wonder* – was to revolutionise both the theory and the practice of astronomy, leading to the discovery of Uranus in 1781, and to new hypotheses about the nature and dimensions of the observable universe, effectively ushering in the modern, scientific discipline of astronomy. These developments in astronomical knowledge constitute an important context for a number of Romantic-period poems such as, for example, Percy Shelley's *Queen Mab* (1813), which interrogates the ontological and political implications of the 'indefinite immensity of the universe'.[59] In the final chapter of this book, however, I focus not on a Romantic-period poetic engagement with the astronomical sublime, but on a post-Romantic essay: Thomas De Quincey's 'System of the Heavens as Revealed by Lord Rosse's Telescopes'.

First published in *Tait's* magazine for September 1846, De Quincey's essay was composed well after the accepted, chronological high-water mark of the canonical Romantic period, and at a moment when astronomy had securely been established as a discrete, and at least semi-professional scientific discipline. Following John Barrell's lead in *The Infection of Thomas De Quincey*, the essay has often been read in relation to a psycho-sexual profile constructed out of readings of De Quincey's autobiographical writings, or in relation to broader 'Romantic' concerns about the nature and implications of subjectivity. Some recent, broadly new-historicist studies have also traced the discursive context of De Quincey's essay – ostensibly a response to John Pringle Nichol's *Thoughts on Some Important Points Relating to the System of the World* (1846) – in contemporary debates about astronomy and cosmology, such as those exhibited in John Chambers's *Vestiges of Creation* (1844).[60] I have already noted the increasing awareness, during the late eighteenth century and Romantic period, amongst authors, publishers and providers of popular entertainments of the potential commercial value of remediating the 'natural sublime' as a saleable commodity. O'Connor's *The Earth on Show* is the seminal account of the remediation of specialist enquiries into the geological history of the earth as both general knowledge and public spectacle during the early nineteenth century. But O'Connor's claim that 'in an age marked by debates over the dangers of imagination and the deceptive allure of cheap romances and sensation novels, geology was marketed as the key to true facts which were nonetheless more marvellous and sensational than fiction' might apply just as well to the contemporary popularisation of astronomy.[61] Here, I read De Quincey's 'System of the Heavens' as exemplary of the process by which the astronomical sublime is remediated as commodity within the popular-culture industry, a process which Wordsworth's poem 'Star-Gazers' allows us to trace back to at least 1807, some 40 years earlier. De Quincey, standing, like O'Connor's popular(ising) geologists, between 'self-styled "experts"' and 'a non-specialist public, whose identity and constitution varied', offers the reader of *Tait's* a vicarious encounter with the 'natural sublime' which remediates the experience of the astronomer at the telescope, substituting rhetorical effect for physical spectacle (and scientific accuracy).[62] Reflecting both De Quincey's long-standing interest in astronomy and no less long-standing need to write for money, the essay thus reflects De Quincey's sense of the 'natural sublime' as a saleable commodity. My argument, then, is that De Quincey is not only involved in the remediation to a general readership of specialist scientific knowledge, after the fashion of the works by Nichol and others to which his essay is ostensibly a response. Rather, De Quincey is also involved in remediating the 'natural sublime' as a commercial product, available for consumption by the general public. In this sense, I read De Quincey's essay as exemplary of a tradition which we have inherited from the Romantic period and which finds its latest expression in the plethora of popular-science cultural texts engaging with 'the wonders of the universe'.

Before turning now in earnest to the beginning of the story that I want to tell in this book – that is, to Chamonix, in the 1740s – there is one other aspect of the engagement with the 'natural sublime' during the eighteenth century and Romantic period which I want to pause, briefly, to consider, but which falls essentially outside the main scope of my discussion here.

As scholars from Monk and Hipple onwards have noted: the engagement with the 'natural sublime' during the eighteenth century and Romantic period often comprised an interrogation and negotiation of questions concerning individual identity, or subjectivity: put simply, speculation about the dynamics of an individual's response to the 'natural sublime' necessarily involved speculation about the nature of the individual *per se*.[63] This speculation is as apparent, for example, in the physiological arguments of Edmund Burke and David Hartley and their contemporaries in the eighteenth-century genre of British philosophical aesthetics as it is in Kant's claim that 'true sublimity must be sought only in the mind of the judging subject', and indeed it continues to inform more recent configurations of the sublime in the works of Lacan and Lyotard.[64]

Many of the genres of engagement with the 'natural sublime' which I consider in this book also have a direct bearing upon contemporary constructions of the individual. Almost by definition, the encounter with the 'natural sublime' in the landscapes and environments on which I have chosen to focus took place, to a greater or lesser extent, at some remove from the familiar domestic space of the individual(s) involved. By extension, that encounter often tended to involve a very particular kind of – usually, though not always, male – individual. A great deal of valuable scholarly work has been done on eighteenth-century and Romantic-period configurations of the persona of the traveller, of the distinction between travel and tourism, on the metaphor of travel or journey, on the rise of commercial tourism and on the figure of the explorer, a term which Carl Thompson suggests acquired its modern meaning during the Romantic period.[65] Richard Holmes, too, has recently drawn our attention to the extent to which 'the idea of the exploratory voyage, often lonely and perilous, is in one form or another a central and defining metaphor of Romantic science'.[66]

What I want to draw to brief attention here is the extent to which the remediation of the encounter with the 'natural sublime' to the general reading public, through the cultural texts on which I have chosen to focus, similarly tends to generate a very specific construction of – again, usually male – subjectivity. Ralph O'Connor has recently shown how the 'literary productions' of geologists like Adam Sedgwick and William Buckland, in the early nineteenth century, were 'performances', how such writers set about 'inscribing themselves into their writing'.[67] Both Nigel Leask and Carl Thompson have also drawn attention to the various ways in which the literature of travel and exploration, during the eighteenth century and Romantic period, involves 'performative and rhetorical' elements of 'self-promotion', even self-fashioning, to use a Stephen Greenblatt phrase.[68] Thompson considers 'the Romantic traveller' to be 'defined to a great extent by his desire to shape both his image qua traveller, and to some extent his actual travelling, according to paradigms drawn from the misadventurous strands of contemporary travel writing'.[69] Clearly, many factors lay behind this 'self-promotion', not least amongst them the prospect of financial gain from compelling narrative. Whatever the motivation, however, one effect of the remediation of the encounter with the 'natural sublime' to the general public through many of the cultural texts which I consider in this book is that the sublime which the individual describes becomes implicated with their own persona through the act of description. Their presence in the landscape becomes part of the cultural associations which that landscape is in the process of acquiring, but the sublime of that landscape also becomes associated with the individual who encounters it. Hence, what we get in these various cultural texts – in the remediation of Horace-Bénédict de Saussure, James Cook, Mungo Park or James Bruce – is a new perspective on the genesis of the still-potent trope of the 'sublime', 'Romantic' hero, as male subject tested, proved and improved by an encounter with the sublime other. What we also get is a new perspective on the ways in which the genre of philosophical aesthetics – British and German alike – might come to locate 'the sublime' within perceiving subjects rather than perceived objects.

Hence, while such an enquiry clearly falls outside the scope of the present volume, it would no doubt prove fruitful to pursue in more detail the dialogue established between the genres of engagement with the 'natural sublime' which I consider here and the other, contemporary genres of writing which generate issues of subjectivity, not least among them the various works of philosophical aesthetics which investigate the wider category of 'the sublime'. I do, however, want briefly to mention the role of contemporary constructions of gender in this process, not just because of the importance of such constructions to engagements with 'the sublime' during the eighteenth century and Romantic period, but also because of the role which such constructions have played in subsequent feminist criticisms of 'Romanticism' more generally. As noted, the encounters with the 'natural sublime' which I describe in this book – perhaps unsurprisingly, given the cultural-historical context – tended to involve a male subject encountering a sublime object which is often (though by no means always) gendered as female, as in, for example, the frequent remediation of the Arctic and the Antarctic as beautiful but implacable goddesses. For this reason, many of the genres of engagement with the 'natural sublime' which I consider in this book are susceptible to the kinds of criticism levelled at a masculine Romanticism by contemporary figures like Mary Wollstonecraft and Mary Shelley, and which have been charted and extended in the twentieth century by scholars like Ann Mellor in *Romanticism and Gender* (1993) and Barbara Freeman in *The Feminine Sublime* (1995). A detailed examination of the interaction between contemporary constructions of gender and the genres of engagement with the 'natural sublime' which I consider here is clearly beyond the scope of this book. However, as an indication of what critical territories might lie in that direction, I offer, in Chapter 3, a brief discussion of the intermixture of some eighteenth-century British constructions of gender with contemporary remediations of James Cook's engagement with polar ice.

My purpose in drawing attention to this intermixture of contemporary constructions of gender – to say nothing at all of contemporary constructions of social class – in both the encounter with the 'natural sublime', and in the remediation of that encounter to the general public, is to alert us once again to the dangers of applying any one set of overly restrictive paradigms to the scholarly approach to the place of the 'natural sublime' in the cultural history of the eighteenth century and Romantic period. My aim in this book is rather to identify the engagement with the 'natural sublime' as a cultural phenomenon which ranged across even as it helped to define the boundaries of genre and discipline which demarcate the modern Western and European episteme. It is neither helpful nor ultimately possible, I think, to talk about 'the eighteenth-century sublime' or 'the Romantic sublime'. One can only talk about what Peter Howell and I have already begun to identify as the various 'cultures of the sublime' which formed part of the wider cultural history of the eighteenth century and Romantic period, and which continue to shape our cultural history to the present day. It is, therefore, only the beginnings of some of those cultures which I intend to examine here.

1
'We had hopes that pointed to the clouds': The Alps and the Poetics of Ascent

> However wonderful what I have advanced may appear, I shall not want evidences of its truth, and shall only find those incredulous, who have never ascended above the plain.
> – Louis Ramond de Carbonnières, 'Observations on the Glacieres and the Glaciers'[1]

The quotation in this chapter's title is taken from William Wordsworth's description of crossing the Simplon Pass in Book VI of *The Prelude*, long considered one of the defining episodes of Romantic-period writing.[2] Wordsworth's refashioning of this moment from his tour of the Alps in 1790 has become, in Alan Liu's terms, 'one of a handful of paradigms capable by itself of representing the poet's work'.[3] More than half a century after Samuel Holt Monk described the same lines as the 'apotheosis' of 'the experience that lay behind the eighteenth-century sublime', Book VI of *The Prelude* also remains the favoured literary paradigm of the 'Romantic' encounter with the natural sublime, a so-called 'set piece of the sublime', as Thomas Weiskel puts it.[4] Wordsworth's apostrophe to the imagination – that 'awful Power' which recovers the mental 'prowess' initially 'usurped' by the 'soulless image' of Mont Blanc – is routinely said to coincide with the Kantian model of the sublime that many twentieth-century historians of the discourse on the sublime have identified as the theoretical goal of eighteenth-century British enquiry into sublime effect (*The Prelude*, vi, ll. 592, 594, 611, 527–8). Hence, for example, Monk's seminal suggestion 'that there is a general similarity between the point of view of the *Critique of Judgement* and *The Prelude*'.[5]

Recent critical commentaries on Wordsworth's work have re-examined Book VI of *The Prelude* and offered a number of different interpretative contexts for its address to the imagination. Liu's rereading of the passage in *Wordsworth: the Sense of History*, for example, suggests that the struggle for primacy which Wordsworth dramatises in *Prelude* VI is not so much a struggle between the individual imagination and the natural world as it is a struggle between the individual imagination and historical process.[6] The vocabulary of Wordsworth's apostrophe to the imagination, Liu suggests, records a specific engagement with Napoleon's crossing of the Alps in 1800, en route to defeat the Austrians at Marengo. Wordsworth is thus testing the imagination, or poetic power, against political power, rather than against a material nature. This explains, Liu concludes, why Wordsworth's first account of his Alpine tour, in his *Descriptive Sketches* of 1793, does not contain any comparable address to the imagination: because Wordsworth's actual antagonist in the apostrophe to the imagination, Napoleon, had not yet crossed the Alps.

Readings such as Liu's undoubtedly illuminate the contextual and discursive richness of Wordsworth's texts. However, they do not – they are not intended to – interrogate the adequacy of the Simplon Pass episode as a paradigm of the 'Romantic sublime', defined, following the paradigms of Kant's 'Analytic', as an ultimately transcended conflict between the individual imagination and something outside the self, be that nature or history. We can begin to interrogate that adequacy, however, by returning to the most obvious, and the most curiously overlooked, interpretative context for Book VI of *The Prelude*: the extensive European cultural engagement with the Alps during the long eighteenth century, and particularly with the valley of Chamonix, in Haute Savoie, site of some of the most dramatic Alpine landscapes in Europe, and of the highest mountain in Western Europe, Mont Blanc.

In *Mountain Gloom and Mountain Glory*, Marjorie Hope Nicolson documents at length the manner in which the Alps, in particular, functioned during the eighteenth century as the locus where a succession of anxious British travellers came gradually to transfer the affective responses traditionally evoked by the idea of God, to those aspects of the physical universe which seemed most to partake of the qualities of their supposed creator: in short, the Alps became, according to Nicolson's analysis, a figure of the grandeur of God, and the locus for the secularisation of religious attitudes. Leaving aside, for a moment, the fact that Nicolson's study is more or less exclusively concerned with *British* engagements with the Alps (a focus shared, for example, by Jim Ring and Robert Macfarlane), and more or less unconcerned with descriptions of the 'natural sublime' within contemporary philosophical aesthetics, part of my argument in this chapter is that the religious responses which Nicolson describes are in fact only a single strand of a much wider contemporary genre of engagement with the Alpine sublime, which Nicolson neglects, and that these religious responses are conditioned, at least in part, by a dialectical relationship with that wider engagement. My purpose in this chapter is to chart the contours of that wider engagement. My argument here is that eighteenth-century exploration of the Alps, and, again, of Chamonix-Mont Blanc in particular, generates something which I want to call the 'discourse of ascent': a discourse which consistently correlates the physical ascent of the Alps with a variety of ostensibly unrelated forms of elevation: moral, political, epistemological, aesthetic – as well as religious.

Obviously, this 'discourse of ascent' has some important precursors in Renaissance writing, notably in Petrarch's 'Ascent of Mont Ventoux', in which Petrarch records having gained not only moral and spiritual insight during his ascent, but also having acquired a new perspective on his own subjectivity. This discourse also parallels and complements contemporary formulations of the link between height or elevation and the sublime with eighteenth-century philosophical aesthetics, such as Burke's discussion of height in his *Philosophical Enquiry*. Despite these precursors and parallels, however, the point that I wish to make about the 'discourse of ascent' is that it is locally and culturally specific, generated in response to a quite precise geographical region, and encoded with quite specific cultural values: it is quintessentially of and about the Alps, and the Alps alone. It is this culturally and geographically specific discourse of ascent, then, rather than works of philosophical aesthetics, which I want to suggest constitutes an alternative, and ostensibly more immediate, context for understanding Romantic-period engagements with the Alpine sublime, not least amongst them Wordsworth's famous apostrophe to the imagination in Book VI of *The Prelude*.

'For whom is Switzerland a remarkable country?': discovering the Alpine sublime

In his popular and influential epistolary novel *Julie, ou, la Nouvelle Héloïse: Lettres de Deux Amans Habitans d'Une Petite Ville au Pieds des Alpes* (1761), unnoticed by Nicolson, Jean-Jacques Rousseau equates the physical ascent of the Alps, a landscape still relatively unfamiliar to mainstream European culture at the time, not simply with aesthetic gratification or scientific discovery, but with the achievement of an elevated *consciousness*. Writing to his lover from the Upper Valais, in the twenty-third letter of the first part of *Julie*, Rousseau's protagonist, St Preux, recalls:

> Here it was that I plainly discovered, in the purity of the air, the true cause of that returning tranquillity of soul, to which I had been so long a stranger. The impression is general, though not universally observed. Upon the tops of mountains, the air being subtle and pure, we respire with greater freedom, our bodies are more active, our minds more serene, our pleasures less ardent, and our passions much more moderate. Our meditations acquire a degree of sublimity from the grandeur of the objects that surround us. It seems as if, being lifted above all human society, we had left every low, terrestrial sentiment behind; and that as we approach the ethereal regions the soul imbibes something of their eternal purity.[7]

This specific passage, not simply Rousseau's claim, echoes throughout eighteenth-century and Romantic-period writing about the Alpine sublime. Helen Maria Williams, for example, quotes it in full in her *Tour in Switzerland*, while G. W. Bridges both paraphrases and quotes it in his *Alpine Sketches* (1814). By the second decade of the nineteenth century, the refrain is virtually clichéd. 'Nothing is better calculated to *exalt* the imagination and improve the feelings of man,' according to Henry Coxe's widely used *Traveller's Guide in Switzerland* (1816), than 'the towering and majestic Alps of Helvetia'.[8]

Rousseau's influential correlation of physical ascent with bodily and mental elevation actually originates in the published records of the earliest European expeditions to the Alps, and to Chamonix-Mont Blanc in particular, the 'general' opinion to which he refers in the passage quoted. To Wordsworth's striking claim that our seemingly innate taste for mountainous landscapes actually originated in the seventeenth century, we can add the fact that the valley of Chamonix, the scene of so many Romantic-period engagements with the Alpine sublime, was only discovered by mainstream European culture in the mid-eighteenth century. 'Incredible as it may appear', Ebel's *Traveller's Guide through Switzerland* noted in 1818, by which time Chamonix was well established as a premier attraction on the European Grand Tour, 'this valley so singularly interesting, in which is seen the highest mountain of the old world, was entirely unknown till the year 1741'.[9] As Ebel suggests in answering the opening question of his *Guide* – 'for whom is Switzerland a remarkable country?' – the European discovery of Chamonix-Mont Blanc had been multivalent:

> every individual who knows how to derive some enjoyment from the contemplation of nature, or who is desirous of acquiring a rich store of the most lively images, or of the most innocent gratifications; he likewise, whose breast labours under affliction, or whose cares require consolation, who is in need of being roused and fortified, may remain assured that he will find [...] whatever he may wish for.[10]

In the second half of the eighteenth century, in other words, the 'singularly interesting' valley of Chamonix came to be identified as a site of immense scientific importance, as a 'rich store' of 'lively images' for the artist, as a locus of 'fortification' and 'consolation' for the physically or emotionally 'afflicted', and as the destination of choice for those simply seeking 'some enjoyment from the contemplation of nature'. In other words, Chamonix-Mont Blanc was in the process of being transformed from a landscape unknown to European culture into 'classic ground', as the Shelleys pointedly called it in their *History of a Six Weeks' Tour* (1817), into a landscape overwritten with a range of cultural values and expectations, centring around the promise of 'gratification'.[11] And from the outset, the European perception of these Alpine 'gratifications' was inextricably linked with the idea, the practice and the image of *ascent*.

Ebel dates the European discovery of Chamonix to 1741, the year of the earliest (recorded) British expedition to the region, by William Windham and Richard Pococke, the latter on his way home from the three-year journey around the Middle East which later provided the subject for his influential *Description of the East* (1743–45).[12] Windham and Pococke left Geneva on 19 June 1741 and reached Chamonix three days later. Windham's record of the scenes they discovered there, in his *Account of the Glacieres, or Ice Alps, in Savoy* (1744), effectively originates the tropes that will become conventional in Romantic-period engagements with the Alpine sublime: the tension between the desire to provide credible narrative and the difficulty of describing incredible landscape in sober terms; the tension between the evidently impoverished locals and the perception, or the *wish* to perceive their society as idyllic, etc.[13] Hence, for example, while Windham registers his desire to provide reliable witness of Chamonix in the language of natural philosophy, 'in the plainest Manner, without endeavouring to embellish it by any florid Description', he also acknowledges the inherent difficulty of describing the glacial landscape, admitting that he is 'extremely at a Loss how to give a right idea of it'.[14] Similarly, while Windham observes that the local population, 'as in all Countries of Ignorance', is 'extremely superstitious', he also affirms that they 'are a very good sort of People, living together in great Harmony; they are robust, live to a great Age, and have very few beggars among them'.[15]

Alongside these clear discursive similarities, however, there are also, of course, a number of significant differences between Windham's *Account* and the major Alpine-travel narratives of the Romantic period. It is, for example, immediately apparent just how much Windham and Pococke felt that they were venturing into the unknown, into an 'unfrequented Part of the world': in addition to their scientific apparatus, the expedition went heavily armed, a precaution which Windham advises his readers to follow should they ever plan to visit the valley themselves.[16] Beyond the sense of potential danger, however, what is most striking in Windham's *Account*, notwithstanding the local traditions which he describes, is the extent to which mid-eighteenth-century Chamonix was a landscape almost entirely unknown to mainstream European culture, a landscape largely devoid of familiar literary or historical points of reference.

By the end of the early nineteenth century, as Marjorie Hope Nicolson points out, visitors to the Alps 'self-consciously anticipated the "sublime" experience'.[17] William Wordsworth, of course, tells us in *The Prelude* that he was disappointed by his first sight of Mont Blanc: 'a soulless image on the eye / That had usurped upon a living thought / That never more could be'.[18] This 'disappointment' has often been read, following Monk, in relation to Kant's paradigms of the sublime, in which the mind must redress an initial loss of balance. Such comparisons are no doubt valid. But to read Wordsworth's 'disappointment' exclusively through the lenses of philosophical aesthetics is to miss an alternative genre of engagements with the Alpine sublime by which his expectations had been conditioned, by which that 'living thought' had been constructed and determined. And moreover, Wordsworth's experience was far from representative of contemporary encounters with Mont Blanc. Compare, for example, Helen Maria Williams's account of her first sight of 'that solemn, that majestic vision, the Alps' in her *Tour in Switzerland*:

> how often had the idea of those stupendous mountains filled my heart with enthusiastic awe! – so long, so eagerly, had I desired to contemplate that scene of wonders, that I was unable to trace when first the wish was wakened in my bosom.[19]

William Hazlitt, too, was more than satisfied by his first, long-anticipated encounter with the Alps: in his *Notes of a Journey through France and Italy* (1826), Hazlitt affirms of his first sight of the Grande Chartreuse that 'it was a scene dazzling, enchanting, and that stamped the long-cherished dreams of the imagination upon the senses'.[20]

What Williams and Hazlitt and numerous other Romantic-period commentators on the Alps make clear, however, is not simply that Romantic-period travellers to the Alps 'self-consciously anticipated the "sublime" experience', as Nicolson puts it, but rather that they went equipped with a plethora of cultural references through which those 'stupendous mountains' could be mediated and interpreted. In other words, by the end of the early nineteenth century, the Alps had become 'classic ground', as we have seen Mary and Percy Shelley described it in the preface to their co-authored *History of a Six Weeks' Tour* (1817), using Addison's phrase, a landscape richly imbued with a range of historical, literary, political and other culturally specific associations. The exponential growth in this range of associations (which would eventually include the Shelleys themselves, and the much mythologized *Frankenstein* summer) is best exemplified in the development of the Alpine guidebook. Thomas Martyn's *Sketch of a Tour through Switzerland* (1788), for example, outlines an itinerary, provides useful information about accommodation, currency, taxes, local culture, etc., and appends a brief account of Horace-Bénédict de Saussure's successful ascent of Mont Blanc in 1787.[21] In 1816, however, Henry Coxe's encyclopaedic *Traveller's Guide in Switzerland* provides not only local information and up-to-the-minute speculation in natural philosophy, but also glosses virtually every spot on its suggested itinerary with literary references (to the works of Gibbon, MacKenzie, Rousseau *et al*.), effectively telling its readers not simply where to go, but also what to think and feel when they got there. Martyn, by contrast, makes absolutely no mention of Rousseau, despite extended discussions of locations (Clarens, Meillerie, Vevey, etc.) made famous by *Julie*.

By identifying Windham and Pococke as the discoverers of Chamonix-Mont Blanc, then, Ebel's *Traveller's Guide* does not point simply to their importance as geographical explorers, but also indicates their role as the inaugurators of the European cultural investment in the Alps which would become such a marked feature of the Romantic period, and which finds continued expression in hiking, mountaineering, skiing and sightseeing tourism today. My argument in this chapter is that this cultural investment was inextricably linked to the idea of *ascending* the Alps. The original basis of this link is readily apparent from the two letters which comprise Windham's *Account*. Windham closes the first letter by noting that 'a Man of Genius might do many things which we have not'. Peter Martel, author of the second letter, takes up this challenge and climbs an unnamed nearby peak to get a better view of things.[22] 'I got to the top', Martel tells Windham:

> to observe the Angle of Position of the Glacieres, with respect to Geneva, which I found to be 158 Degrees precisely. I looked down on all the Objects about us with great Pleasure; the Prospect put me in mind of that fine Plan which you have seen in our Publick Library [at Geneva], for the Plain below, seen from this high Mountain, at first sight gives one the same idea. 'Tis wonderful to see [...] In a word, all the Pains I took to clamber up this Mountain were sufficiently recompensed by a Prospect so beautiful and so uncommon.[23]

Martel's contribution and the *Account* itself close, then, with a clear indication that the explorer, or natural philosopher, can only acquire detailed knowledge of the Alps by ascending their summits. The key to a systematic understanding of the landscape, Martel affirms, is a better view of it, a more elevated view; the higher you climb, the more you see and understand; an increase in altitude equates with an increase in knowledge. But Martel also emphasises the aesthetic payoff of a higher point of view: an increase in altitude equates not only with an increase in understanding, but also with a more impressive view; essentially, the higher you climb, the more sublime it gets. Martel's correlation of altitude and insight (epistemological and aesthetic) is at the heart of the discourse of ascent which is generated by eighteenth-century engagements with the Alps, and it sets the trend for travel and exploration in the Alps for decades to come, effectively inaugurating a kind of altitude-race: a quest for ever-higher ground which would culminate with the first successful attempt of Mont Blanc itself. Some 60 years after the publication of Windham's *Account*, travellers were still registering the same overlap between epistemological, aesthetic and physical elevation: in his influential *Illustrations of the Huttonian Theory of the Earth* (1802), for example, John Playfair affirmed that the attempt by the natural philosopher in the Alps to 'discover [...] the works of nature' by climbing 'in the midst of the scene' could only succeed after 'he has recovered from the impression made by the novelty and magnificence of the spectacle before him'.[24] With their 'hopes that pointed to the clouds', William Wordsworth and his fellow 'mountaineer' Robert Jones had clearly bought into this same trend when they set out to cross the Alps in August 1790 (*The Prelude*, vi, ll. 587, 323).

Hence, as Charles Marie de La Condamine noted in his *Journal of a Tour to Italy* (1763), Windham's *Account* seemed 'calculated rather to excite than to satisfy curiosity'.[25] That said, the next significant expedition to Chamonix-Mont Blanc took place over 20 years after Windham's journey, led by a man who would later reach the summit of Mont Blanc itself: the famous Swiss naturalist Horace-Bénédict de Saussure, whose Alpine career is discussed later in this chapter. Five years after Saussure's first visit, however, another Swiss – the artist and explorer Marc Théodore Bourrit – conducted a lengthy survey of the Chamonix region, publishing his *Description des Glacières de Savoye* in 1773, with an influential English translation appearing two years later, and boasting an impressive list of subscribers, including William Beckford, Edmund Burke, Catharine Macaulay, Joshua Reynolds and Horace Walpole.[26]

Bourrit opens, and to some extent seeks to justify the publication of his *Relation of a Journey to the Glaciers of Savoy*, by noting that despite the efforts of earlier travellers, the area still remained 'almost wholly unknown to strangers'.[27] However, Bourrit's narrative also makes clear the extent to which the Savoyard Alps are in the process of becoming 'classic ground', as the Shelleys would put it 40 years later. Bourrit does not simply reference the earlier expeditions by Windham and Saussure. Rather, he consciously treads in their footsteps, offering 'a sparkling libation to the honour' of Saussure at the 'very spot' on the Mer de Glace where his expedition rested, and recalls, on discovering a rock on which Saussure had inscribed his name, how he had constantly felt 'the ideal presence of the writer' in the landscape.[28] This, again, is exactly the dynamic which Addison sought to explain through the concept of 'classic ground' in his *Letter from Italy*: the inscription of cultural values upon the physical features of landscape.

Bourrit himself contributes significantly to the inscription of Chamonix-Mont Blanc on the cultural map of Europe. His *Relation of a Journey* is the first text to describe in detail the key sites – e.g., the Nant d'Arpenaz, the Bossons Glacier, the Mer de Glace, the source of the Arve – which would become the key *sights* of the Alpine Grand Tour, thereby delineating an itinerary which many tourists still follow to this day. However, Bourrit also takes up and develops the correlation between altitude and insight formulated by Windham and Martel, and which I am suggesting is at the heart of the discourse of ascent generated by eighteenth-century writing about the Alpine sublime. Following the lead of Martel and Saussure, Bourrit's *Relation of a Journey* records that after his team had made a 'general survey of the Glaciers', the expedition decided to 'spend the rest of our time in examining the construction of each of them particularly'.²⁹ 'For this purpose', Bourrit affirmed, 'we ascended *Montanvert* [Montenvers].'³⁰ The reward of attaining the summit was immediate. Once again, we find an insistent correlation of altitude and insight, of physical ascent and advances in natural philosophy. 'A single glance over all these Glaciers together', Bourrit says of his view from the summit of Montenvers, 'seemed to throw a light upon their correspondence and extent.'³¹

Bourrit, like Martel before him, also affirms that the 'fatigues' and 'difficulties' of ascent are 'rewarded' not only by greater understanding of the landscape, but also by a heightened impression of 'the beauties displayed' in the landscape.³² Indeed, Bourrit's *Relation of a Journey* opens with a general account of these 'beauties', noting the 'singular emotion which the sight of this country excites in the mind, from the prodigious height of the mountains', the 'elevated, awful feelings of the soul' which it 'produces'.³³ This is also, of course, the language of philosophical aesthetics, the language used by figures like Addison and Burke to describe the link between 'height' and the sublime, and it will have become conventional by the late eighteenth century and Romantic period. But it is also the language of Rousseau's *Julie*, a language with a specific, local resonance. What is particularly striking about Bourrit's *Relation of a Journey*, however, is not simply the perception that 'elevated' landscape 'produces' an 'elevated' state of mind, although the terminology of that perception is instructive in itself. Rather, it is Bourrit's insistence that the intensity of these 'elevated' feelings is directly related to the physical altitude of the perceiver: once again, the claim is that the higher you go, the more sublime it gets. Hence, Bourrit recalls of the view from the summit of Montenvers that while the sight of the higher, surrounding peaks 'from their foot, was a most ravishing sight', he was still 'strongly agitated' by a 'longing attention' and 'restless inclination' to 'attempt at least to set a foot upon their heads'.³⁴ Proceeding with 'determined resolution' higher up the glacier itself, Bourrit's expedition gets its reward, which Bourrit himself, with the eye of an artist, describes at some length:

> what a picture was before us ! we were surprised to a degree of transport, and incapable of expressing our admiration, but by frequent acclamations [...] we beheld a spacious icey plain, entirely level; upon this there rose a mountain all of ice, with steps ascending to the top, which seemed the throne of some divinity. It took the form moreover of a grand cascade, whose figure was beyond conception beautiful, and the sun which shone upon it, gave a sparkling brilliance to the whole: it was as a glass, which sent his rays to a prodigious distance.³⁵

Some two pages later, Bourrit reaches a kind of pause, affirming that 'new beauties still continued to delight us, astonished as we were'.[36] However, even this 'astonished' halt is momentary: continuous new discoveries in scenery and natural philosophy seem possible. Eventually, for Bourrit, the pursuit of the Alpine sublime becomes *itself* sublime, an irresistible scramble up the mountainside in search of ever greater experiences. 'The valley on our right was ornamented with prodigious Glaciers', Bourrit continues, as even the syntax grows frantic:

> that shooting up to an immeasurable height between the mountains, blend their colours with the skies which they appear to reach. The gradual rise of one of them, induced us to conceive it practicable to ascend it; and such is the engrossing nature of these objects, that they seem to efface every other idea. We are no longer our own masters; and it is next to impossible to stop the impulse of our inclinations [...] such a point of elevation (beyond which no mortal whatever had yet gone) would not only present Mont Blanc to us under a new form, and with new beauties, but that in short, looking towards the south, we should have a picture of all Italy before us as in a Camera Obscura. It was thus the wildness of the imagination prompted us to think the project possible, and we were in full enjoyment of our reverie, when a horrid noise from the very same Glaciers put an end to this delightful dream.[37]

With the return of 'Reason', then, with Bourrit's realisation that any further ascent 'would require our stay all night upon this frozen valley, which was absolutely impossible, from the want of fewel only', the 'fancied picture' dissipates.[38] But Bourrit's account of the almost irresistible lure of the untrodden Alpine summits, of an 'engrossing' ascent simultaneously enabling advances in natural philosophy (a 'new' perspective on Mont Blanc, 'all Italy [...] in a Camera Obscura') *and* gratifying the 'wildness of the imagination', would shape the course of European thinking about the Alps. Ascent emerges from Bourrit's work as the key to successfully engaging with the mountains.

Bourrit's *Relation of a Journey* was also largely responsible for first situating that 'astonishing mountain', Mont Blanc, on Europe's cultural map of the Alps, and at the heart of the discourse of ascent.[39] In his account of the Alpine sublime in the 'Preliminary Discourse' of his *Relation of a Journey*, Bourrit suggests that 'Mont Blanc especially [...] produces a sensation which is very difficult to explain [and which] no tongue whatever is capable of describing and conveying justly to others'.[40] After his first visit to

Chamonix in 1767, Saussure had offered a substantial reward to anyone who could discover a viable route to the summit of Mont Blanc. In the 'Preliminary Discourse' of his *Relation of a Journey*, Bourrit suggests that 'it is certainly a very great mistake [...] in any person, to suppose it possible for him to ascend Mont Blanc', although Bourrit would himself subsequently try and fail to do just that on three separate occasions, spurred on by that same 'restless inclination'.[41] Notwithstanding his assertion of the 'absolute impossibility of ascending to its summit', however, it is nevertheless Bourrit's *Relation of a Journey* which first holds out to the European reading public the tantalising prospect of the view from the top of Mont Blanc: describing that 'magnificent prospect of a chain of mountains' visible at Chamonix, Bourrit wonders aloud in a footnote 'what would it be then if we could ascend to the summit of Mont Blanc?'[42]

British interest in Chamonix-Mont Blanc, at least, was further stimulated by the publication, in 1779, of the first edition of William Coxe's *Travels in Switzerland*. Coxe, who had been one of the original subscribers to the English translation of Bourrit's *Relation of a Journey*, had already published respected accounts of his travels in Germany, Poland and Russia. Coxe visited Chamonix for the first time in 1776, and returned in 1779, 1785 and 1786. His three-volume *Travels* was destined to become one of the most influential guides to the region, with revised editions appearing until 1809, and counted William Wordsworth amongst its readers. Interestingly, in this respect, Coxe's *Travels* frequently register frustrated expectations. In his description of the Grindelwald Glacier, for example, Coxe admits that he was 'somewhat disappointed, and that a nearer view of the glacier has not sufficiently compensated for the fatigue and trouble of the expedition'.[43] Coxe attributes this repeated pattern of 'expectation' and 'disappointment', which clearly anticipates Wordsworth's account of how 'the soulless image' of Mont Blanc 'usurped upon a living thought / That never more could be', to the increasing proliferation of 'turgid accounts' and 'exaggerated descriptions' which, he claims, 'led' him 'to expect more than could be reached'.[44] Here again, then, we have an alternative to the Kantian paradigm for contextualising Wordsworth's disappointment with the Alpine sublime. However, Coxe's description of Chamonix is the sole exception to this pattern of expectation and disappointment. Recalling his expedition to the Bossons Glacier, for example, Coxe affirms, in a markedly un-Wordsworthian formulation, that 'having proceeded about an hour, we were astonished with a view far more magnificent than imagination can conceive; hitherto the glaciers had scarcely answered my expectations, but now they far surpassed them'.[45]

Despite his enthusiasm for Chamonix, however, Coxe's deadpan condescension is often painfully evident in the *Travels*. On first 'breathing the air of liberty' in Switzerland, for example, where 'every person [...] has apparently the mien of content and satisfaction', Coxe is moved to admit that he 'could almost think, for a moment, that I am in England'.[46] And it was precisely this kind of condescension which occasioned a further key intervention in the history of the discourse of ascent: the publication of Louis Ramond de Carbonnières's 'Observations sur les Glacieres et les Glaciers'. The 'Observations' originally formed part of the extensive editorial commentary in Carbonnières's 1781 French translation of Coxe's *Travels*, which was, in fact, less a 'translation' than an often sharply critical interrogation of the English original.[47] English translations of the 'Observations' were included in subsequent editions of Coxe's *Travels*, and a second English translation was published by Helen Maria Williams as an appendix to her *Tour in Switzerland* in 1798.

The initial textual debate between Carbonnières's editorial apparatus and Coxe's *Travels* represents a nascent struggle for ideological or cultural possession of the Alps, with Carbonnières, the local editor, challenging the disengaged foreigner on virtually every point. This struggle would take on a new geographical immediacy in the years following the French Revolution, and also inform, to an extent, the controversy which surrounded the first successful ascent of Mont Blanc (which I discuss later in the chapter). However, Carbonnières's 'Observations' also significantly expanded the parameters of the discourse of ascent. While writers like Martel and Bourrit formulate a correlation between physical ascent, advances in natural philosophy and aesthetic gratification, Carbonnières effectively proposes a whole new consciousness 'above the plain'.[48]

Carbonnières's 'Observations' respond specifically to Coxe's description of the glaciers around Chamonix-Mont Blanc. Carbonnières questions both Coxe's account of the formation of these glaciers and his consistent denial of the 'melancholy [...] fact' that they appeared to be perpetually increasing and 'tending to insulate the more temperate valleys which they enclose'.[49] Carbonnières bases his critique of Coxe on the same correlation between altitude and understanding which we have traced in the works of Windham, Martel and Bourrit, making a distinction, in the second paragraph of the 'Observations', between the level of understanding available to those (like Coxe) who are satisfied with 'contemplating these mountains' from the valley, and those (like Carbonnières himself) who actually 'scale' them.[50] The 'Observations' as a whole insist upon this distinction, correlating the journey of a 'mind of genius' to 'discover the periods and fix the epochs' of the 'history of nature' with the ascent of the mountains, from the 'shores of the sea' to 'the highest points'.[51] Carbonnières's argument, then, is that he knows better than Coxe because he has actually ascended the mountains in pursuit of advances in natural philosophy and aesthetic insight, while Coxe has merely gazed up, like a tourist, from below. Carbonnières closes his 'Observations' with this same emphasis on the benefits of ascending the Alps, linking an elevated position not simply to advances in natural philosophy and heightened aesthetic pleasure, but now also to elevated *consciousness*. 'However wonderful what I have advanced may appear', Carbonnières insists:

> I shall not want evidences of its truth, and shall only find those incredulous, who have never ascended above the plain. I call these to witness, who have scaled some of the heights of the globe; is there a single person who did not find himself regenerated; who did not feel with surprise, that he had left at the feet of the mountains, his weakness, his infirmities, his cares, his troubles, in a word, the weaker part of his being, and the ulcerated part of his heart? Who amongst them but will acknowledge that at no moment of his life, in the age even of his warmest passions, in the midst of circumstances which have given the greatest force to his imagination, he has never felt himself so disposed to that kind of enthusiasm which kindles great ideas![52]

With its sustained insistence on the intellectual, aesthetic, physical and psychological benefits of ascending 'above the plain', Carbonnières's 'Observations' is one of the key statements of the eighteenth-century discourse of ascent. Readily available into the early decades of the nineteenth century through the numerous editions of Coxe's *Travels* and Williams's *Tour in Switzerland*, the 'Observations' helped to open the range and shape the course of Romantic-period engagements with the Alpine sublime. It may also, as I suggest later in this chapter, have exerted a specific influence on Wordsworth's account of crossing the Alps in Book VI of *The Prelude*.

Eighteenth-century European interest in Alpine ascent reached its high point in the mid-1780s, with the first successful ascents of Mont Blanc. After his first visit to Chamonix in 1760, Saussure had offered a substantial reward to anyone who could discover a viable route to the summit, an offer he would frequently repeat over the coming decades. The first recorded attempt to claim this prize took place in 1762, when a group of local hunters failed to find an approach by Montenvers or the Bossons Glacier.[53] Interest in the summit intensified from the mid-1770s, driven less by the temptation of Saussure's money than by Mont Blanc's increasing grip on the European imagination, with early editions of Coxe's *Travels* speculating that Mont Blanc might actually be the highest peak in the 'ancient world', even 'the Atlas of the Globe', and with Bourrit's *Relation of a Journey* holding out the prospect of the ultimate view from the top.[54] At least 18 unsuccessful attempts took place between 1775 and 1784, three of which involved Bourrit, who was accompanied on one occasion by Saussure himself. A major breakthrough occurred on 8 June 1786, when two expeditions left Chamonix simultaneously, climbing via different routes to the Dôme du Goûter (4304 metres), and then proceeding together to the Vallot rocks (4362 metres). In rapidly deteriorating weather, one of the group, the local crystal hunter Jacques Balmat, became separated from the others, who were forced to descend without him. When he returned from his night alone on the mountain, Balmat claimed to have discovered a route to the summit of Mont Blanc, known today as the *Ancien Passage* ('old route'). Twentieth-century historians of Alpinism have questioned Balmat's claim, pointing to the inconsistencies between his various accounts of this discovery.[55] What is beyond doubt, however, is that exactly two months later, on 8 August 1786, Balmat and a local doctor, Michel-Gabriel Paccard, who had already attempted the ascent in 1775 and 1784, reached the summit of Mont Blanc via the *Ancien Passage*.

As with Tenzing's and Hillary's first ascent of Mount Everest in 1953, controversy broke out almost immediately over which of the two men was the first to reach the summit. On 20 September 1786, Bourrit published his *Lettre sur le Premier Voyage fait au Sommet du Mont Blanc*, a deliberate pre-emptive strike against Paccard's own advertised *Premier Voyage á la Cime de la Plus Haute Montagne de l'Ancien Continent, le Mont Blanc*, which in the event was never actually published. Bourrit gave the honour of the first ascent to Balmat, and in terms far from flattering to Paccard: the bourgeois doctor had been terrified and exhausted by the climb, Bourrit claimed in a narrative that was evidently calculated to appeal to a nascent democratic and Romantic sensibility, and only managed to reach the summit through the energy and persistence of the intrepid peasant, Balmat.

As the first available account of the successful ascent in 1786, Bourrit's narrative was quickly disseminated across Europe and gained widespread acceptance, despite the fact that the 1789 edition of Coxe's *Travels* suggested (diplomatically) that both men had reached the summit together. Hence Paccard's star would increasingly drop below the Alpine horizon, to such an extent that John Ruskin's 1833 poem 'Evening at Chamouni' could easily conflate Balmat's initial discovery of the summit route with the actual ascent. Having 'braved' the 'stormy' night 'on the Goûter's height', Ruskin suggests, 'heroic Balmat' awoke to find 'the untrodden summit stood / Accessibly beside him'.[56] Again, we get a clear sense here of the ongoing cultural struggle for ideological or imaginative possession of the Alps. Immediate European interest in the Balmat–Paccard controversy was short-lived, however. By the end of August 1787, another Alpine hero had captivated the public imagination, effectively and to some extent designedly eclipsing all his predecessors: Horace-Bénédict de Saussure.[57]

On 21 August 1786, Paccard had tried and failed to repeat his earlier ascent. The following day, an expedition led by Saussure was also forced to turn back. On 5 July 1787, however, Balmat, who had been commissioned by Saussure to consolidate the *Ancien Passage* route, reached the summit for a second time. Less than one month later, on 3 August 1787, Saussure, led by Balmat, followed the same route to the summit, where he remained for four-and-a-half hours, conducting numerous experiments and observations. Saussure's account of this ascent, his *Relation Abrégée d'un Voyage à la Cime du Mont Blanc en Août 1787*, was published in Geneva almost immediately after his return, and was subsequently included, along with accounts of his five previous attempts on Mont Blanc and extensive other Alpine journeys, in the final volume of his *Voyages dans les Alpes* (1796). Swift publication helped to ensure that Saussure's ascent was celebrated across Europe, and English translations of his *Relation* were widely disseminated in journals and travel guides, including Martyn's aforementioned *Sketch of a Tour through Switzerland* (1788).[58]

As Martin Rudwick points out, Saussure's account of his ascent, which counted James Hutton amongst its many avid readers, made a signficant contribution to the development of the nascent science of geology. However, my concern here is rather with the immediate cultural impact of Saussure's engagement with Mont Blanc than with his wider place in the history of the science of geology. Saussure's *Relation* is actually one of the first texts of the discourse of ascent which emphasises the physical hardships of Alpinism. Saussure reveals that he had initially suffered 'great uneasiness' on attaining the summit that he had so long desired to reach.[59] Indeed, Saussure's *Relation* draws an explicit parallel between learning to cope with this 'uneasiness' and learning to deal with ethical or existential dilemmas, describing a kind of moral mountaineering in a passage which looks forward to the role of vertigo and nausea in twentieth-century existentialist philosophy, and which echoes, at least in part,

Petrarch's account of his ascent of the rather lower Mont Ventoux. 'This rule of conduct [...] appears to me applicable in moral as well as natural cases,' Saussure affirms: 'if you cannot bear the sight of the precipice and accustom yourself to it, give up the enterprise, for [...] this sight, if taken unawares [...] may prove your destruction'.[60] Taken as a whole, however, Saussure's *Relation* effectively sums up, for the Romantic period, the correlation between physical ascent, advances in natural philosophy and aesthetic gratification which we have been tracing in eighteenth-century engagements with Chamonix-Mont Blanc. Recovering from his 'painful ascension' to the summit, Saussure affirms that he began 'to enjoy without regret the grand spectacle'.[61] 'A light vapour suspended in the lower regions of the air, concealed from my sight the lowest and most distant objects', he recalls, 'but I did not much regret this loss':

> what I had just seen and what I saw in the clearest manner, is the whole of all the high summits of which I had so long desired to know the organisation. I could hardly believe my eyes, it appeared to me like a dream, when I saw placed under my eyes those majestic summits [...] I seized their relation to each other, their connection, their structure, and a single glance cleared up doubts that years of labour had not been able to dissolve.[62]

From the highest point in Western Europe, then, Saussure vindicates for the reading public the distinction between the mountaineer and the tourist, between those who merely contemplate the mountains and those who actually ascend them, gaining, in the process, epistemological, existential and aesthetic insights denied to even the most industrious of those who remain below.

The promptness with which Saussure published his *Relation* suggests that he was chary of his own reputation in the wake of the Paccard–Balmat–Bourrit controversy, and it must be said that Saussure effectively downplays the previous successful ascents, noting only in passing that:

> diverse periodical works have informed the public, that last year in the month of August, two inhabitants of Chamounie, Mr. Paccard a physician, and Jacques Balmat, the guide, attained the summit of Mont Blanc, which till then had been deemed impossible.[63]

Certainly, the immediate and widespread dissemination of the *Relation* ensured that Saussure's ascent quickly eclipsed his predecessors in the public imagination, and indeed long continued to eclipse them: hence, for example, the dramatic sculpture of Balmat and Saussure in the centre of Chamonix, which was commissioned to commemorate the centenary of Saussure's ascent, even though it was actually the *third* time that the mountain had been successfully summited. Saussure had already been a high-profile figure before his successful ascent of Mont Blanc. Following it, he was lionised by Europe's savants, natural philosophers and littérateurs. Alessandro Volta, no less, summed up the mood in his 'Omaggio al Signore di Sossure, per la sua salita alla cima del Monte Bianco' (1787). 'I will ascend just there', Volta's intrepid figure of Saussure affirms, 'where Nature sits enclosed in a thick veil, / And I will reveal her beautiful new forms.'[64] Entirely forgetting Balmat and Paccard, Volta concludes his 'homage' by suggesting that Mont Blanc should be renamed 'Monte Sossure' (l.189).

Spurred on by Saussure's high-profile achievement, attempts on the summit of Mont Blanc became more common around the turn of the century as the concept of Alpinism as a sport began to develop.[65] Describing his own successful ascent of Mont Blanc in 1827, for example, John Auldjo attributed his inspiration for the climb to Saussure's *Relation*: 'who that has read the interesting account which the indefatigable De Saussure has given us', Auldjo asks, 'but must have felt an inspiration to emulate him and his intrepid guides?'[66] In fact, by the time that Percy Shelley described Mont Blanc as 'remote, serene, and inaccessible' (l. 97) in his eponymous poem of 1816, no less than eight expeditions had successfully reached the summit, two of them British, and one including a local Savoyard woman. So popular did the idea of an ascent become, that Ebel's 1818 *Traveller's Guide*, registering the poor chances of a clear view from the summit, felt obliged to warn its readers that:

> no one therefore ought to expose himself to the dangers, fatigue, and considerable expense, which an excursion to Mont Blanc renders indispensable, allured by the deceitful expectation of enjoying prospects of extraordinary magnificence.[67]

The implication, of course, is that any of the *Guide*'s well-to-do readers could now realistically contemplate making just such an 'excursion'. Today, of course, the summer ascent of Mont Blanc by the so-called ordinary route has become a staple of adventure tourism, attracting hundreds each year.

Clearly, guidebooks like Ebel's played a considerable role in creating and sustaining this desire for a summit view. Indeed, while eighteenth-century guidebooks were largely content to reproduce or paraphrase published accounts of attempts on, or successful ascents of, 'the long wished for summit of Mont Blanc', in the 1810s and 1820s guidebooks began to transform the representation of Alpine ascent by offering their readers first-person narratives of ascent, based on details taken from published accounts of actual ascents.[68] What we have in such narratives is, in effect, the commoditisation of the 'natural sublime', the same realisation of the saleable value of the 'natural sublime' that would inform the development of mainstream Alpine tourism. Numerous examples of this practice could be adduced, but Samuel Glover's *Description of the Valley of Chamouni* is typical.[69] Instead of merely describing the ascent of Mont Blanc, Glover, having enjoined his readers to 'prepare with renovated steps, to tread the path to the summit', leads them through a four-page first-person narrative, a vicarious – or what we might today call a virtual – ascent to the summit of the 'gigantic mountain, to which "many are called, but few are chosen"'.[70] Towards the end of the Romantic period, in other words, the ascent of Mont Blanc was effectively being transformed into a commodity, available in virtual form to those without the financial and physical resources to attempt an actual ascent. Such, indeed, was the contemporary fascination with the idea of ascending Mont Blanc, that it even found its way into books written for children: an anonymous novella of 1823, *The Peasants of Chamouni*, concludes with a lengthy, admonitory account of a disastrous attempt on the summit in August 1820, when three guides had died during an avalanche.

Sometimes, of course, the reality of an actual ascent fell rather short of expectations. We have already noted Coxe's and Wordsworth's Alpine disappointments. To this list we might add William Hazlitt's honest admission, in his *Notes of a Journey*, that during his traverse of the Col de Balme, between Martigny and Chamonix, 'we had a mule, a driver, and a guide [and] I was advised [...] to lessen the fatigue of the ascent by taking hold of the *queue of Monsieur le Mulet* [the tail of Mr Mule], a mode of travelling partaking as little of the sublime as possible, and to which I reluctantly acceded'.[71] By the end of the eighteenth century, however, the discourse of ascent had become a key component of the European cultural investment in the Alpine sublime, with the correlation of altitude and insight forming the dominant trope of a range of Alpine genres and disciplines.

'I raise my head, awhile bowed low': the view from the valley

In his *Relation*, Saussure records that when he reached the summit of Mont Blanc for the first time, his 'first looks were fixed on Chamounie where I knew my wife and her two sisters were, their eyes fixed to a telescope following our steps'.[72] Volta picked up on this recollection in his 'Omaggio', imagining the excited reaction ('transport') of the crowd which had gathered to view the successful ascent, and wondering 'why wasn't I / Even a part of the crowd of spectators?' (ll. 111, 92–3). The celebration of Saussure's spectacular achievements, which Volta responds to, participates in and perpetuates in his 'Omaggio', forms part of what I described in the introduction to this book as the process by which a new understanding of individual subjectivity is generated out of a range of Romantic-period engagements with the 'natural sublime'. Saussure, having ascended Mont Blanc, becomes himself a sublime figure, a new kind of 'Romantic' hero, defined by the sublimity of his achievements and set, in this case literally, far above the adoring masses. It is not only within the context of philosophical aesthetics, then, that engagements with the 'natural sublime' give rise to new, 'Romantic' ideas about subjectivity. And as the Paccard–Balmat–Saussure controversy also makes evident, this new kind of celebrity is not only premised upon actual achievements, but also stage-managed through careful control of publication and information flow, through the creation of persona-as-brand. As we shall see, this dynamic recurs again and again in the mediation and remediation of the figure of the Romantic explorer of the landscapes of the sublime. To return to Volta, however, his regret also flags up for us the dichotomy at the heart of the discourse of ascent between those who merely contemplate the mountains and those who actually ascend them. The virtual ascents offered by some nineteenth-century guidebooks constitute an attempt to compensate those individuals who could not, for whatever reason, actually ascend 'above the plain' themselves, as Carbonnières put it. However, such compensatory, virtual ascents constitute only one of a number of discursive strategies which seek, precisely, to renegotiate the value-laden opposition between the view from the summit and the view from the valley which is at the heart of the discourse of ascent. We can begin to approach the importance of such renegotiations for literary engagements with the Alpine sublime during the Romantic period, by returning to one of the most familiar aspects of eighteenth-century British writing about the natural sublime: religion.

As Marjorie Hope Nicolson long ago pointed out, religious feeling pervades much of eighteenth-century British literary engagement with the Alps.[73] By the end of the eighteenth century, Mont Blanc had become the primary focus of the religious response to the natural sublime, as is evident from one of the Romantic period's best-known examples of it: Samuel Taylor Coleridge's 'Hymn Before Sunrise, in the Vale of Chamouni' (1802). However, while examples of religious responses to the Alpine sublime are relatively common in British eighteenth-century and Romantic-period writing, the trope is almost entirely absent from the mainstream of the discourse of ascent that I have been describing, that is, from works by figures like Windham, Martel, Bourrit, Carbonnières and Saussure. Of course, this absence is not altogether surprising, given the basis of the discourse of ascent in nascent scientific and specifically geological enquiry into the Alps, which posed increasingly troublesome questions for received, Biblical accounts of creation. What works like Coleridge's 'Hymn' and its innumerable counterparts make clear, however, is that the religious response to the Alpine sublime described by Nicolson depended for its success precisely upon the repudiation of the idea of actually ascending the Alps, a practice which religious responses consistently figure as hubristic and invasive, if not downright sacrilegious. In other words, while the discourse of ascent privileges the view from the top over the view from the valley, the rhetoric of the religious response to the natural sublime depends precisely upon the idea that the highest summits are inaccessible. One is reminded of Edmund Burke's suggestion that 'heathen' religions often enhanced the affective power of their 'idols' by keeping them in places inaccessible to direct scrutiny.[74]

Accordingly, the standard position of the speaker in religious writing about the Alps is not on a peak looking down, but in the valley looking up: that is, the viewpoint of the tourist. So Coleridge, who had not even visited Chamonix when he adapted his 'Hymn' from its German source, enthuses to the 'sovran Blanc': 'I raise my head, awhile bowed low / In adoration, upward from thy base / Slow travelling with dim eyes suffused with tears'.[75] The speaker in Helen Maria Williams's 'Hymn Written among the Alps', published in her *Tour in Switzerland*, must also 'raise' their 'gaze' to 'loftier summits' in order to 'see' the 'hand divine' – and this despite the fact that Williams says she composed her 'Hymn' *amongst* the Alps during a walking expedition, when her companions were busy examining rock formations: a neat encapsulation of the tension between the various modes of contemporary engagement with the Alpine sublime, between natural philosophy and the Book of Genesis.[76] Contemporary prose expressions of the religious response to the Alpine sublime are likewise predicated upon the view from the valley. Ann Radcliffe's novels, for example, consistently position their pious protagonists at the foot of the mountains, looking up in religious rapture towards the summits.

Nor is the religious response to the Alpine sublime predicated only upon the view from the valley. Rather, those responses also consistently repudiate the very possibility of the summit views extolled by the discourse of ascent. To put it more precisely, eighteenth-century and Romantic-period religious responses to the Alpine sublime seek to conserve the idea that the highest summits, and especially the summit of Mont Blanc, are *inaccessible*. I have italicised the term *inaccessible*, because it has a considerable pedigree within the discourse of ascent. In his *Relation of a Journey*, for example, Bourrit twice refers to the summit of Mont Blanc as 'inaccessible', while Saussure's *Relation* likewise records his initial conviction that the summit was 'inaccessible'.[77] After the successful ascents of Mont Blanc in the 1780s, the term *inaccessible* quickly drops out of the discourse of ascent. However, the trope of the *inaccessible* summit persists for decades in religious responses to the Alpine sublime. As late as 1824, for example, nearly 40 years after the first ascent of Mont Blanc, Alaric Watts eulogises 'the vast and searchless height' of Mont Blanc in his poem 'Chamouni: a Sketch on the Spot'.[78]

The rhetorical strain involved in maintaining the trope of the *inaccessible* summit in the wake of the high-profile ascents of Mont Blanc is clearly visible in a number of eighteenth-century and Romantic-period responses to the mountain. Thomas Whalley's poem 'Mont Blanc' (1788), for example, was written almost a year after Saussure's successful ascent, and over two years after the summit was first reached by Balmat and Paccard. However, Whalley still apostrophises Mont Blanc, 'greatest thou the works of God among', as if it had *not* been summited at all, asking:

> What foot shall sully with its tread
> The spotless honours of thy head?
> What sacrilegious eye profane
> The awful secrets of thy reign?[79]

In a similar vein, Samuel Glover's ultra-pious *Description of the Valley of Chamouni*, which seeks to figure Mont Blanc as a sacred space safe from the 'sacrilegious' claims of 'atheistical' natural philosophers, resorts to describing the summit, paradoxically, as 'almost inaccessible'.[80] Nor is it only religious responses to the Alpine sublime which continue anachronistically to deploy the trope of the *inaccessible* summit. Percy Shelley's avowedly atheistic 'Mont Blanc', for example, supports its figuration of the mountain as the locus of an unidentified natural 'Power' by describing the summit as 'remote, serene, and inaccessible', and this despite the fact that Shelley was demonstrably aware of the achievements of 'the naturalist' Saussure before he wrote the poem.[81] Byron's necromancer Manfred similarly identifies 'the tops / Of mountains inaccessible' as the 'haunts' of the 'spirits' governing 'the unbounded Universe'.[82] In sum, then, the ability of eighteenth-century and Romantic-period poets and novelists to figure Mont Blanc or other high Alpine summits as the emblem or locus of some transcendent agency apparently depends upon those summits remaining physically, or at least conceptually, inaccessible – and, therefore, symbolically potent. John Ruskin's 'Evening at Chamouni' might thus be said to stand at the conclusion of a tradition when it reminds the reader how Jacques Balmat awoke from that solitary night on the Dôme de Goûter to discover that 'the untrodden summit stood / *Accessibly* beside him'.[83]

'Mont Blanc, the king of mountains': the Alps and the politics of ascent

A hierarchical relationship between summit and valley, similar to that at the heart of religious responses to the Alpine sublime first studied by Nicolson, also informs the competing political appropriations of the Alps by eighteenth-century and Romantic-period writers. In Britain at least, in the decades following the French Revolution, political appropriations of the Alps are predominantly conservative, and effectively complement the pious tone of writing about the Alpine sublime by figuring the mountains, and especially the Mont Blanc massif, as the image of an ideal monarchy. Thomas Whalley's 'Mont Blanc' exemplifies this conservative genre. 'See with what grandeur to the skies / The monarch Mountain lifts his brow', Whalley enthuses:

> While crowding round the vale below,
> His vassal Alps in tow'ring order rise;
> And, watchful of his regal nod,
> His mighty pleasure seem to wait,
> As 'twere the mandate of a God!
> Sublime in his imperial state,
> From 'midst the splendours of his throne,
> He looks with sovereign favour down,
> Smiles their prompt service to approve,
> Awaits their homage, and accepts their love.[84]

By the time that mainland Europe reopened to British travellers after the Napoleonic Wars, this conservative mountain-monarch trope has become so familiar in British writing about the Alps that it is possible for Henry Coxe's *Traveller's Guide* (1816) to propose as uncontested an

Alpine nomenclature which is quite specifically British. Describing the Mer de Glace above Chamonix, Coxe suggests that it is:

> eight leagues in length, and one in breadth; and, on its margin, rise pyramidical rocks, called *needles* [*aiguilles*], whose summits are lost in the clouds; they are also denominated *the Court* of their august Sovereign *Mont Blanc*, who glitters on the opposite side in stately repose, and being far more elevated than her attendants, veils in the heavens, which she seems to prop, a part of her sublime and majestic beauties.[85]

Phrases like 'they are also denominated' represent as uncontested a nomenclature which effectively remediates the Alpine sublime in the comforting image of a well-ordered state. This 'courtly' nomenclature certainly complements the religious tone of many British eighteenth-century and Romantic-period engagements with the Alpine sublime: just as the Mont Blanc massif images the relationship between creator and creation, so too does it image the socio-political incarnation of that same divine order, with monarch-summit reigning over aristocratic court and plebeian plain. However, the 'courtly' nomenclature deployed by Henry Coxe and so many other British eighteenth-century and Romantic-period writers on the Alpine sublime also evidently responds to the contestation, within the ideology of the French Revolution, of the supposedly natural order of monarchical society. To put it more precisely, figuring the Mont Blanc massif in the image of an ideal monarchy effectively remediates arguments, like Burke's, in his *Reflections on the Revolution in France*, that the political status quo in Britain was 'the happy effect of following nature'.[86]

As noted, this 'courtly' nomenclature is ubiquitous in British Romantic-period writing about the Alps: Henry Coxe's *Guide* echoes, almost verbatim, Mariana Starke's description of Mont Blanc in her *Letters from Italy* (1815), and even the radical William Hazlitt could describe Mont Blanc, in his *Notes of a Journey*, as 'the King of Mountains'.[87] However, this conservative mountain-monarch trope was by no means the only operative political appropriation of the Alpine sublime. In fact, the mountain-monarch trope responded not only to contemporary interrogations of the supposed natural order of monarchical society, but also to a long-standing European tradition of eulogising the Alps as a bastion of republican virtue and democratic mores. This tradition had its roots in the profusion of eighteenth-century European responses to the political history of Switzerland, from the libertarian exertions of William Tell, Werner

Stauffacher, Walter Fürst and their successors, to the contemporary state of the cantons. In Britain, at least this tradition of valorising Swiss mountain liberty arguably originates with Joseph Addison's allegorical 'dream' of the 'happy region' among the Alps 'inhabited by the Goddess of liberty', published in the 20 April 1710 number of *The Tatler*. Rousseau's description of the democratic society of the Upper Valais in *Julie*, 'where the same freedom reigns in homes as in the republic, and the family as the image of the State', also played a key role in shaping this perception: writing in 1816, over half-a-century after the publication of *Julie*, Henry Coxe could still confidently assert that 'the amiable manners of the Swiss [...] are so well known, and have been so ably depicted by Rousseau, in his "Nouvelle Helois" that they need no further encomium'.[88]

A systematic survey of the various European interpretations of the relationship between the Alpine landscape and democratic politics of Switzerland is clearly beyond the scope of my discussion here. However, we might take as representative the fact that the idea of a link between the Swiss landscape and Swiss liberty was the one thing about which William Coxe and Ramond de Carbonnières agreed, even if the cantons did ultimately remind the Englishman of home. In fact, the perception of a causal relationship between environment and society is central to most eighteenth-century eulogies of Swiss liberty, which consistently move beyond the simple notion of Switzerland as an Alpine 'Temple of Liberty', to use Helen Maria Williams's phrase, and towards a representation of the country as an environmental and social utopia. Consider, for example, George Keate's apostrophe to Switzerland in his popular 1763 poem *The Alps*:

> Thrice happy regions, could we mount the wind
> And post around the Globe, where should we find
> A calmer dwelling? While destructive War,
> With Discord leagu'd, rings her infernal peal
> And fires the mad'ning Crowd, thy Vallies hear
> No sounds but those of Peace; secure the Swain
> Bears plenty to his fields, nor fears a foe
> Shall reap the harvest
> [...]
>   Here reigns *Content*,
> And Nature's child *Simplicity*, long since
> Exil'd from polish'd realms. Here ancient Modes
> And ancient Manners sway; the honest Tongue
> The Heart's true meaning speaks, nor masks with guile

> A double purpose: Industry supplies
> The little Temp'rance asks; and rosy Health
> Sits at the frugal board. – If banish'd hence,
> Be *Luxury*, and all the *finer Arts*
> Which swell her train, say, Tenants of these Climes,
> What lose ye?[89]

Nor was it only Switzerland which was thus eulogised. Peter Martel, for example, had written to Windham in 1741 about the 'great Harmony' enjoyed by the 'good' people of Chamonix, and almost a century later Samuel Glover would offer as evidence that 'mankind may yet be wise' the 'fact' that in the valley of Chamonix, 'during a century, a law-suit was unknown!!!'[90] In his *Alpine Sketches* of 1814, G. W. Bridges went so far as to claim that 'among the Alps alone, are found men, rustic without being ferocious, civilised without being corrupted. Our peasants in England are not to be compared with them' (although William Coxe would surely have disagreed).[91] 'Here', Byron's Manfred concluded of the Alps, 'the patriarchal days are not / A pastoral fable'.[92] Set against the backdrop of reports about the seemingly idyllic societies which James Cook and Joseph Banks had discovered in the Pacific, the cultural potency of this view of Switzerland becomes apparent.

As Keate's and similar encomia make clear, then, eighteenth-century and Romantic-period writing about Alpine society routinely blends Rousseau-esque arguments about the virtue of uncivilised man with an emphasis on the causal relationship between the sublime landscape and the sublime politics of the Alps: and again, a constrast might be noted here between this austere, sublime virtue, and the heavily sexualised (depiction of) Tahitian and Hawaiian society. In this respect, such writing parallels Johann Joachim Winckelmann's influential arguments, in his *Geschicte der Kunst des Alterthums* (1763), about the relationship between classical Greek culture and the environmental conditions of the eastern Mediterranean. And just as eighteenth-century and Romantic-period travellers to Greece were often disappointed by the reality of the Greek society which they found there, so, too, was the image of an Alpine utopia often shattered by first-hand acquaintance with the situation on the ground, for all that Rousseau might have written in *Julie*. Even so ardent a disciple of the Alpine 'spirit of freedom' as Helen Maria Williams, for example, was forced to admit that:

> the truth is, that the inhabitants of the democratic Cantons of Switzerland are under the dominion of a power far more absolute

than that exercised by the privileged classes of the great Cantons. This power is superstition [...] no other part of Switzerland is so unenlightened.[93]

Likewise, despite the popular image of the Alpine 'swain' enjoying perpetually 'rosy Health', to adopt Keate's phrase, visitors to the high Alpine valleys routinely record that large numbers of the population suffered from goitres and mental illness, a consequence of the heavy mineral content of the local water, and of inbreeding. William Coxe, for example, observes that 'the inhabitants of this part of the Valais are very subject to goitres, [...] idiocy also remarkably abounds among them', and then adds for good measure that 'the uncleanliness of the common people is disgusting beyond expression'.[94] Writing from the shores of Lac Leman in July 1816, Percy Shelley similarly noted that 'the children here appeared in an extraordinary way deformed and diseased. Most of them were crooked and with enlarged throats.'[95] Even the sympathetic Williams had found these health problems 'a spectacle of disgust'.[96] Clearly, Romantic-period disappointments with the Alpine sublime were not restricted to Wordsworth's failure to be impressed by Mont Blanc. The increasing remediation of the Alps as 'classic ground', and the concomitant range of expectations created in would-be travellers, perhaps inevitably provoked the occasional disillusionment.

Despite the often sobering political and environmental reality of the Alps, however, British eulogies of the Alpine 'temple of liberty' also continued well into the Romantic period, and gained added force following the outbreak of the French Revolution. Indeed, cross-party British condemnation of the two French occupations of Switzerland during the Revolutionary and Napoleonic Wars was registered, at least in part, within precisely this eulogistic tradition. In *France: an Ode* (1798), for example, written after the French invasion of Switzerland, Coleridge condemns what he represents as a French attack on 'the bloodless freedom of the mountaineer'.[97] The Switzerland Coleridge imagines in the poem is explicitly and entirely Alpine: he hears the 'loud lament' of 'Freedom' from 'icy caverns', 'mountain snows' and 'stormy wilds', rather than from the cities of Geneva, Lausanne and Berne.[98] Wordsworth's 'Thought of a Briton on the Subjugation of Switzerland', written during the second French occupation of Switzerland in 1807, similarly laments that 'Liberty' has been 'driven' from its 'Alpine holds', once again portraying a Switzerland of 'mountains and torrents' rather than cities.[99]

Despite the frequent contemporary identification of the French as the 'cruel foes' of Switzerland's 'patriot race', however, defenders of both the Revolution and, later, of Napoleon, often invoke the discourse of ascent as a means of valorising the political achievements of France.[100] In her *Tour in Switzerland*, for example, Helen Maria Williams praises the 'sublime effort which effected the French Revolution' by comparing that 'sublime effort' to the ascent of a mountain, in terms which appear to recall Carbonnières's account of the progress of 'a mind of genius', which I discussed earlier in this chapter.[101] 'Like the traveller', Williams writes:

> who from the scorching plains, climbs the rocks that lead him to the regions of eternal snow, and finds that in the space of a few hours he has passed through every successive latitude, from burning heat to the confines of the frozen pole, the journey of months; so the human mind, placed within the sphere of the French revolution, has bounded over the ruggedness of slow metaphysical researches, and reached at once, with an incredible effort, the highest probable attainments of political discovery.[102]

For Williams, in this passage, the 'mighty [...] principles' of the French Revolution are the political equivalent of Saussure's enlightening view from the summit of Mont Blanc: a 'political discovery' to match his contribution to natural philosophy. The achievement of this political summit ('the highest probable attainments') explicitly recalls Saussure's account of his ascent: 'an incredible effort' which overcame 'at once' the limitations of 'slow metaphysical researches'.[103] 'I seized their relation to each other', Saussure had affirmed of the peaks visible from the summit of Mont Blanc, 'their connection, their structure, and a single glance cleared up doubts that years of labour had not been able to dissolve'.[104] Ascent is revolutionary, and, following Williams, revolution is an ascent. Numerous comparable loci of interaction between the discourse of ascent and European reactions to the French Revolution could be adduced had I space here to do so. Throughout the Romantic period, however, the most potent political focus for the discourse of ascent was, undoubtedly, Napoleon Bonaparte.

Napoleon's career intersected with the discourse of ascent at two key moments. Although Napoleon was in Egypt during the first French occupation of Switzerland in 1798, when Brune plundered the country, Napoleon led the second occupation in 1802. The following year, Napoleon's Act of Mediation proclaimed a new constitution for the renamed Helvetic Confederation, and won broad popular approval from the Swiss, albeit doing nothing to assuage British concerns about

French foreign policy. An ambitious construction programme followed the Act, notably including the opening up of the major Alpine passes, and of the Simplon Pass in particular. An initially sceptical Swiss populace evidently feared the economic impact of newly normalised trade relations, but relented as the long-term financial benefits became apparent. A decade later, however, a generation of British Romantic writers remained to be convinced about this particular inscription on the 'classic ground' of the Alps. Lord Byron, for example, on discovering that Napoleon had 'levelled part of the rocks of Mellerie', a key location in Rousseau's *Julie*, while 'improving the road to Simplon', observed that although 'the road is an excellent one [...] I cannot quite agree with a remark which I heard made, that "la route vaut mieux que les souvenirs ['the road is better (that is, more useful) than the memories']"'.[105]

The event which placed Napoleon at the heart of the discourse of ascent, however, was neither the new Helvetic constitution nor the new roads over the Alps. It was, rather, one of Napoleon's most daring military gambles: the tactical crossing of the Alps in May–June 1800 in order to surprise Austrian forces in northern Italy. By early 1800, France had lost to the Austrians almost all the Italian territories captured in 1796–97: only Genoa remained under French control, and it was heavily besieged, and finally surrendered on 4 June 1800. In mid-May 1800, while thick snow was still lying on the high passes, Napoleon led his entire Interior Army, some 40,000 troops, across the Alps, suffering significant loss of equipment en route. Napoleon was hoping to trap the Austrians between his Interior Army and General Masséna's troops at Genoa. In the event, Genoa had fallen to the Austrians before Napoleon arrived in Italy. On 14 June, however, Napoleon destroyed the numerically superior Austrian army at Marengo. Stunned and demoralised, the Austrians immediately, and arguably unnecessarily, sued for peace in Italy, eventually ceding all but Venice to the French. At a stroke, Napoleon had transformed the balance of power in Europe. On his return to France, he was made First Consul for life.

I have already discussed Liu's influential account of the impact that Napoleon's crossing of the Alps had upon Wordsworth's apostrophe to the imagination in Book VI of *The Prelude*. In fact, it would be difficult to overstate the wider legacy of Napoleon's Alpine campaign to the discourse of ascent in the Romantic period. By crossing the Alps en route to victory at Marengo, Napoleon had effectively repeated Hannibal's earlier conquest of Italy, and hence Coleridge was certainly not the only Romantic-period writer to identify the First Consul as a latter-day Hannibal. Reactions to Hannibal's achievement had played an important role in the development of the discourse of ascent during the eighteenth century. In his influential 'Observations', for example, Carbonnières had described Hannibal's invasion of Italy as another instance of that dichotomy between those who contemplate and those who ascend the Alps which he places at the heart of the discourse of ascent. 'Whilst the Romans were contemplating these mountains', Carbonnières writes:

> Hannibal scaled them. He found, as he had conjectured, that the whole of their surface was not covered with snows, and was led by their savage, but free inhabitants, across their wild pasturages, hidden amidst the masses of rocks, and the Romans discovered that they were not invincible.[106]

In thus characterising Hannibal's crossing of the Alps, Carbonnières's 'Observations' effectively correlate physical ascent not simply with advances in natural philosophy and aesthetic gratification, as Martel and Bourrit had done, but also with *political* achievement. This was doubtless the hint taken by Carbonnières's translator, Helen Maria Williams, in her account of the achievements of the French Revolution, and it would also set the tone for the inscription of Napoleon's crossing of the Alps within the discourse of ascent.

Hence William Hazlitt, writing about Napoleon's achievement in his *Notes of a Journey*, stresses that his readers should not 'imagine that crossing the Alps is the work of a moment, or done by a single heroic effort [...] they are a sea, or an entire kingdom of mountains'.[107] 'It gives one a vast idea of Buonaparte', Hazlitt continues:

> to think of him in these situations [that is, amidst the 'lofty mountains' and 'horrid abysses' of the Alps]. He alone (the Rob Roy of the scene) seemed a match for the elements, and able to master 'this fortress built by nature for herself'. Neither impeded nor turned aside by immoveable barriers, he smote the mountains with his iron glaive, and made them malleable; cut roads through them; transported armies over their ridgy steeps; and the rocks 'nodded to him, and did him courtesies'.[108]

Here, Hazlitt celebrates not only Napoleon's Alpine achievements, but also figures Napoleon as the agent of revolution, as a latter-day freedom fighter in the tradition of the highlander Rob Roy, as the scourge of the *ancien régime*: in Hazlitt's portrait, the Alps, which had so often been figured as an image of the religious and political orthodoxy, are reclaimed for a democratic politics and do 'courtesies' to the First Consul of Revolutionary France. Of course, by the time that Hazlitt arrived in the Alps, three years after Napoleon's death, this heroic image was also difficult to sustain. Hence, perhaps, the allusion to Titania's speech in *A Midsummer Night's Dream* (III.i.169), in which she instructs her courtiers to honour the hubristic Bottom, currently sporting an ass's head: 'Nod to him, elves, and do him courtesies'. Napoleon as hero, or Napoleon as the fool of fortune? With the benefit of hindsight on Napoleon's career, Hazlitt, it seems, could not ultimately choose between these alternatives.[109] But it was through the discourse of ascent that Hazlitt could best register Napoleon's 'heroic' Alpine achievements.[110] 'Anyone who is much of an egoist', Hazlitt writes, 'ought not to travel through these districts':

> his vanity will not find its account in them; it will be chilled, mortified, shrunk up; but they are a noble treat to those who feel themselves raised in their own thoughts and in the scale of being by the immensity of other things, and who can aggrandise and piece out their personal insignificance by the grandeur and eternal forms of nature![111]

Hazlitt's account of the chilling or mortifying effects of the sublime here parallels similar descriptions in contemporary philosophical aesthetics, though, once again, the context here is both geographically and culturally specific. And eschewing this pervading sense of human 'insignificance' in the face of the Alpine sublime, Napoleon 'alone' seemed to Hazlitt 'a match for the elements' in this 'world of wonders', a kind of political Saussure, a sublime 'Romantic' hero aggrandised by association with the sublimity of the landscape and his engagement with it.[112] Hazlitt's own crossing of the Col de Balme, grasping 'the *queue of Monsieur le Mulet*', must indeed have seemed 'mortifying' in comparison to this heroic Alpinist. But Hazlitt's 'vanity' need not have been excessively 'chilled': notwithstanding Jacques-Louis David's heroic vision of *Napoleon Crossing the Alps* – showing Napoleon on horseback, with the wind from the valley, the wind of history, driving him onwards – Napoleon had actually crossed the Alps on a mule.

For Helen Maria Williams, on the other hand, writing before Napoleon's Alpine campaign in 1800, but after Napoleon had driven the Austrians out of Switzerland and back across the Tyrol in 1797, precipitating their withdrawal from the war against Directorate France, it was not simply as a 'modern Hannibal' that Napoleon was to be praised. 'Buonaparte', she enthuses:

> it is not Buonaparte scaling the Alps, and chasing the imperial eagle back to its haunts, after tearing from its beak its choicest prey, that claims the transport of admiration; his acts of valour have been unequalled [...] but these are not his loftiest honours [...] what swells the heart with reverence, is not the hero standing in the breach, it is the benefactor of his race converting the destructive lightning of the conqueror's sword into the benignant rays of freedom, and presenting to vanquished nations the emblems of liberty and independence entwined with the olive of peace.[113]

And yet despite these caveats, it is through the discourse of ascent that Williams sums up Bonaparte's 'glory', drawing precisely upon the association of the mountain sublime with revolutionary politics. 'Nor do we wonder', Williams affirms:

> to find associated with such a mind [...] what excites in my heart, some emotion of national pride, that sympathy with the elevated sentiments, the pathetic sublimity of Ossian: Ossian, the companion of his [that is, Napoleon's] solitary hours, who seems to raise him above this terrestrial region.[114]

Created by James McPherson on the basis of his research into the historical culture of the Scottish Highlands, the fictitious warrior-bard Ossian was introduced to the British reading public in the early 1760s as the author of two epic poems, *Fingal* (1762) and *Temora* (1763), which portray third-century Scotland as the locus of a mountain republic, as sublime in its polity as in its scenery.[115] By concluding her paean to Napoleon with a reference to his taste for Ossian (the fictional bard of Scotland's sublime Highlands), then, Williams reaffirms for the Romantic period the link between Napoleon's achievements and the 'elevated sentiments' of the mountaineer, the correlation of the mountain sublime with political enlightenment.

'Ere these matchless heights I dare to scan': the poetics of ascent

The scope of Napoleon's achievement as the 'modern Hannibal' assured him a place alongside Saussure at the heart of the discourse of ascent: that body of writing about the Alps which correlates the physical ascent of the mountains with other, ostensibly unrelated forms of elevation, and which I am arguing was central to the construction of the Alps as 'classic ground' on the cultural map of Europe in the eighteenth century and Romantic period. At the beginning of the nineteenth century, then, Saussure's achievements in natural history on the summit of Mont Blanc and Napoleon's military achievement on the St Bernard Pass, each an epoch-making event, effectively dominated the cultural horizon of the Alps, and constituted a backdrop against which most contemporary British engagements with the Alpine sublime (at least) needed to situate themselves. I have already considered the representational dynamics of two such engagements: the religious and political remediations of the Alpine sublime in eighteenth-century and Romantic-period writing, both of which, as we have seen, are intensely, and sometimes uncomfortably, aware of these high-profile ascents. In the final section of this chapter, I want to examine a third mode of engagement with the Alpine sublime: the development during the eighteenth century and Romantic period of something I want to call the *poetics of ascent*, a poetics which valorises the imaginative effort involved in representing the Alps as the equivalent, and, often, as the apotheosis, of an actual, physical ascent to their summits. The valorisation of the imagination within this poetics is in some respects comparable to the paradigms of the sublime drawn up by Kant in his 'Analytic', and indeed to the paradigms of some eighteenth-century British works of philosophical aesthetics. But context is important: this is a poetics generated in and by engagements with the Alps, and hard to miss by contemporary travellers increasingly steeped in writing about the area.

An example might be useful at this point. George Keate opens his popular poem *The Alps* (1763) with an invocation to 'Fancy, parent sweet / Of ev'ry Muse', saying that

> with joy *I'd tread*
> *Thy steps* o'er hill and vale, *with thee ascend*
> The craggy summit of yon Mountains bound
> In ever during Frost.[116]

Some four hundred lines later, Keate closes the poem with a renewed invocation: 'Here, Fancy, my conductress, let us rest, / Enough our toil, for we have trodden paths / New to the muse'.[117] The poetic narrative contained between these two invocations, Keate's lengthy survey of

Europe's 'proud Eminence', is thus figured as itself a kind of Alpine expedition, on which 'Fancy' guides ('conducts') the poet and his readers through 'this wild scene of Nature's true sublime'.[118] 'I' would 'tread *thy steps* [...] *with thee ascend*' Keate says to 'Fancy' before the journey; 'let *us* rest', 'for *we* have trodden' he later concludes. In Keate's poem, in other words, an effort of the *imagination* stands in for the physical effort of climbing the Alps: an effort of the imagination which delivers for the reader (at least in part) the same elevation, the same aesthetic gratification, as an *actual* ascent.

It is precisely this paradigm of vicarious Alpine ascent, via the agency of the imagination, which I want to identify as the key component of what I am calling the poetics of ascent. In fact, this paradigm becomes an increasingly marked feature of eighteenth-century poetry about the Alps. We have already noted, for example, Thomas Whalley's ambivalence in his 1788 poem 'Mont Blanc' about Saussure's actual ascent to the summit of the mountain. However, Whalley explicitly configures his own poem as a vicarious ascent, asking the mountain's 'pardon' if 'presumptuous *thought*':

> With fear and admiration fraught,
> Thy sacred solitudes assail,
> And turns, with trembling hand, aside,
> A little turns, the solemn veil,
> By mighty Nature form'd to hide
> The mysteries high of a many a birth,
> That makes the wonder of the pride
> Of weak, short-sighted man, on earth.[119]

The standard dichotomy between the view from the valley and the view from the summit in the religious response to the 'natural sublime', the dichotomy between 'earth' and the 'high' 'sacred solitudes' of the mountains, is sustained here. However, while Whalley configures his poem as a less invasive, more respectful version of Saussure's actual ascent, the implicit parallel is clear: Whalley's poem effects in imagination precisely the same unveiling as Saussure's actual climb, remediating and commoditising the encounter with the 'natural sublime' which is available to the natural philosopher for the general reader.

Throughout the Romantic period, poetic engagements with the Alps, and with Mont Blanc in particular, continued to evoke this trope of the vicarious ascent in imagination. In the second part of his 1822 poem *The Alps: a Reverie*, for example, James Montgomery, seated on the shores of Lake Geneva, exhorts his 'spirit' to 'take thy stand' on the summit of Mont Blanc and 'spread':

> The world of shadows at thy feet;
> And mark how calmly, overhead,
> The stars like saints in glory meet:
> While in the solitude sublime,
> Methinks I muse on Nature's tomb,
> And hear the passing foot of Time
> Step through the gloom.[120]

For Montgomery and his readers too, then, an effort or ascent of the *imagination* ('spirit') takes the place of the physical effort of climbing Mont Blanc. And this effort of the imagination delivers the same payoff as an actual ascent, the same sublime awareness of the 'passing foot of Time', a substitution neatly encapsulated in Montgomery's pun on the word 'muse' as both a poetic and a perceptual verb. After all, Montgomery's imaginative ascent of Mont Blanc precisely recasts Saussure's actual ascent, echoing the Alpinist's recollection that 'the repose and profound silence which reigned in this vast extent [...] inspired me with a sort of terror; it appeared to me as if I had outlived the universe, and that I saw its corpse stretched at my feet'.[121] And finally, like Keate before him, once Montgomery's 'spirit' has done its work, he notes his safe return to the shores of Lake Geneva. 'Safe on thy banks again I stray,' he affirms, 'the trance of poesy is o'er':

> And I am here at dawn of day,
> Gazing on mountains as before;
> For all the strange mutations wrought
> Were magic feats of my own mind.[122]

The vicarious ascent ('magic feats of my own mind') completed, Montgomery's perspective returns to the conventional religious viewpoint on the Alpine sublime: the view from the valley. The reader has been granted a vicarious engagement with the 'natural sublime' which is offered as equivalent to the experience of one who had actually ascended the Alps. This is the 'natural sublime' for sale, available for consumption in polite drawing rooms across the country. But it is also a vindication of the scope of the imagination to go beyond the restrictions of experience.

Nor is the poetics of ascent limited, during the Romantic period, to conservative or non-canonical engagements with the Alpine sublime.

Conversely, that poetics is at the heart of one of the Romantic period's best-known engagements with the Alpine sublime: the third canto of Byron's extremely popular *Childe Harold's Pilgrimage* (1816). The Alpine sections of *Childe Harold* III mediate and remediate the eighteenth-century discourse of ascent in a number of ways. The canto as a whole, for example, deliberately sets the history of Alpine republican and democratic virtu against the prevailingly conservative tone of contemporary remediations of the Alpine sublime. Byron rejects the mountain-monarch topos by comparing the major players in this republican history ('the high, the mountain-majesty of worth') to the mountains themselves: they are 'like yonder Alpine snow, / Imperishably pure beyond all things below'.[123] Stanza 113, which glances both at the rise and fall of Napoleon, and at Byron's own problematic relationship with celebrity ('I have not loved the world, nor the world me'),[124] similarly compares the hardships and rewards of human achievement with the hardships and rewards of Alpine ascent, echoing the parallel drawn in Saussure's *Relation* between Alpine and existential vertigo. 'He who ascends to mountain-tops', Byron writes, interrogating the unquestioned valorisation, in the discourse of ascent, of the view from the summit, 'shall find':

> The loftiest peaks most wrapt in clouds and snow;
> He who surpasses or subdues mankind,
> Must look down on the hate of those below.
> Though high *above* the sun of glory glow,
> And far *beneath* the earth and ocean spread,
> *Round* him are icy rocks, and loudly blow
> Contending tempests on his naked head,
> And thus reward the toils which to those summits led.[125]

Actually, says Byron, it's tough at the top (as the expression goes), and he would later repeat these sentiments in the first canto of *Don Juan*:

> what is the end of fame?
> 'tis but to fill a certain portion of uncertain paper:
> Some liken it to climbing up a hill,
> Whose summit, like all hills, is lost in vapour.[126]

In addition to these various mediations and remediations of the eighteenth-century discourse of ascent, the Alpine sections of *Childe Harold* III also deploy a poetics of ascent, blurring the distinction between an actual and an imagined Alpine itinerary. At the precise moment when Byron shifts the focus of *Childe Harold* III from Waterloo to the Alps, he pauses to discuss Morat (Murten), the site of the Swiss victory over the invading Burgundian duke, Charles the Bold, in 1476. Hence, this moment simultaneously introduces to the canto both a new political and a new geographical topos. However, the terms of Byron's pause are instructive. 'But ere these matchless heights I dare to scan', Byron says of the Alps, 'there is a spot should not be pass'd in vain'.[127] This pause is instructive because what Byron does, after describing the 'patriot field' of Morat, is, precisely, to 'scan' the Alps: to 'survey' the mountains but also, in a telling pun on 'scan', to inscribe the mountains in verse.[128] In other words, the epistemological and aesthetic payoff of an actual Alpine itinerary is again remediated as commodity through the vicarious representation of that itinerary. Childe Harold's travels figure Byron's own, and of course we should remember that no small part of *Childe Harold*'s popularity was based on its thinly disguised autobiographical basis. At the end of *Childe Harold* III, with much of the initial 'dare' successfully met in his four hundred lines on the Alps, Byron returns to re-enforce for the reader the overlap between the imagined and the actual ascent of the Alps, between the Childe's crossing and his own. Anticipating 'Italia', both his and the Childe's next destination, and speaking now in the first person, Byron affirms that:

> The clouds above me to the white Alps tend,
> And I must pierce them, and survey whate'er
> May be permitted, as my steps I bend
> To their most great and growing region, where
> The earth to her embrace compels the powers of air.[129]

The reader, anticipating the next canto, joins Byron and the Childe on this journey. Indeed, glancing ahead to Rome's 'imperial hill', that 'fount at which the panting mind assuages / Her thirst of knowledge', Byron is evidently also whetting the reader's appetite for the next canto, and hinting at the final, definitive unmasking of the Childe, by blurring the distinction between his own and the Childe's crossing of the Alps.[130]

An exhaustive description of the impact of the discourse of ascent on the many poetic engagements with the Alpine sublime during the Romantic period is clearly beyond the scope of this chapter; indeed, such a project would require a book of its own. However, we can begin to appreciate the implications of that discourse for received descriptions of a 'Romantic sublime' grounded in philosophical idealism by returning to Wordsworth and his fellow 'mountaineer', Robert Jones, high up on the Simplon Pass in 1790.[131] On a walking tour of the Alps in the late eighteenth century, Wordsworth and Jones were following what had already become, in James Buzzard's apt phrase, 'the beaten track' to modern European tourism.[132] Indeed, it is now generally accepted that the pair followed an itinerary laid out in the 1789 edition of William Coxe's *Travels*.[133] The point that I wish to make here is not so much that there is anything wrong with reading Wordsworth's apostrophe to the imagination, following Monk, in terms of the paradigms of Kant's 'Analytic of the Sublime'. My point is rather that affording the 'Analytic' privileged status as the defining Romantic-period account of the sublime runs the risk of missing the other contemporary genres of engagement with the 'natural sublime' of which Wordsworth was undoubtedly aware, and to which he might have been responding. Rather than reading Wordsworth's apostrophe to the imagination as a versification of Kant's 'Analytic of the Sublime', then, I want to see what happens if we read that apostrophe as an engagement with what I have been calling the discourse of ascent. To do this, I will look at the putative relationship between Wordsworth's poem and a key text of that discourse: Carbonnières's 'Observations on the Glaciers'.

Wordsworth had certainly read Carbonnières's 'Observations' before he composed *Descriptive Sketches* (1793), his first verse account of the tour of 1790, because he acknowledges his debts to 'M. Raymond's interesting observations annexed to his translation of Coxe's Tour in Switzerland'.[134] His continued awareness of the text is confirmed by a letter to Henry Taylor of 26 December 1823, in which he accuses Byron of having, in the third canto of *Childe Harold's Pilgrimage*, 'taken an expression' from Carbonnières's description of Schaffhausen and 'beaten [it] out unmercifully into two stanzas which a critic in the *Quarterly Review* is foolish enough to praise'.[135]

In the final section of the 'Observations', Carbonnières describes the effect on the spectator of the sublime glacial landscapes above Chamonix. 'Everything' about this 'immense chaos of mountains', he writes, 'concurs to make our meditations more profound; to give them [...] that sublime character which they acquire, when the soul, taking that flight which makes it contemporary with every age, and co-existent with all beings, hovers over the abyss of time.'[136] This characterisation certainly echoes Rousseau's description of St Preux's experience in the Upper Valais, in *Julie*. However, Carbonnières's vocabulary and imagery also anticipate Wordsworth's account of the rise of the imagination, out of 'the mind's abyss', to recover the 'glory' that the 'soul' had previously 'lost' to the 'soulless image' of Mont Blanc, and to reveal that 'our destiny, our nature, and our home / Is with infinitude'.[137] Carbonnières then concludes the 'Observations' by formulating his own apostrophe to the 'Imagination', registering the impossibility of ever arriving, via rational enquiry, at any idea of the enormous geological time-scale implied by this landscape:

> In vain would reason strive to count by years. The solidity of these enormous masses, opposed to the accumulation of their ruins, startles and confounds all its calculations. Imagination seizes the reins which Reason drops, and in that long succession of periods, catches a glimpse of the image of eternity [...] Thus, our most extended ideas, and our most elevated and noble sentiments, have their origin in the wanderings of the imagination; but let us forgive its chimeras, for what would there be great in our conceptions, or glorious in our actions, if finite was not, through its illusions, continually changed into infinite, space into immensity, time into eternity, and fading laurels into immortal crowns![138]

The encounter with the Alpine sublime 'startles and confounds' the 'reason', but the 'imagination' redresses the balance. Parallels with Kant's 'Analytic of the Sublime' are clear, but again the context here is geographically and culturally specific, and the registers are entirely distinct in their insistence on the usefulness, and the complexity, of the aesthetic response. My claim would be, then, that in this passage, Carbonnières provides a clear alternative, and, from a contextual point of view, more obviously relevant and accessible, antecedent for Wordsworth's apostrophe to the imagination as the agent of the mind's 'prowess' in the encounter with the Alpine sublime. Just as Wordsworth's account of that encounter identifies the 'imagination' as the 'strength' and 'greatness' of a human mind whose 'home / Is with infinitude', so, in Carbonnières's account, it is the 'imagination' which transforms 'finite [...] into infinite, space into immensity, time into eternity, and fading laurels into immortal crowns', an image surely not lost on the author of *The Prelude*. However, Carbonnières's heavily qualified apostrophe to the imagination is neither idealist nor idealising. Rather, with its conviction that we are indebted to the 'wanderings' and 'chimeras' of the imagination for 'our most extended ideas [...] our most elevated and noble sentiments', Carbonnières's apostrophe is closer to David Hume's scepticism about the limitations of rationalism ('calculation'), closer to Hume's vindication of the imagination as the only faculty of the mind capable of going beyond the limitations of sensation towards the formulation of general hypotheses about the world.[139]

Read against this backdrop, the 'rise' of the 'imagination' in Book VI of *The Prelude* might be said to compensate not only for Wordsworth's political 'hopes', which had been frustrated by Napoleon's usurpation, but also for Wordsworth's frustrated Alpine 'hopes', for those 'clouds' which he and Jones had failed to reach, for that ultimate, unattained view from the top, for the 'classic ground' which had failed to live up to its billing. By redressing the mind's defeat by the 'soulless image' of Mont Blanc, the 'rise' of the imagination in *Prelude* VI amounts to a conquest of the Alps which is the equivalent of Saussure's conquest of Mont Blanc, or, following Liu's reading, of Napoleon's conquest of the St Bernard Pass. Indeed, the verbal and imagistic topography of the apostrophe, which describes how the imagination 'rose' out of 'the mind's abyss' to 'break through' the 'vapour' which 'enwraps' the 'lonely traveller', and to 'reveal' the hitherto 'invisible' world, is unmistakably indebted to the physical experience of mountaineering, of breaking through cloud at the summit. Arguably, then, Wordsworth's apostrophe to the imagination, that 'set piece' of the 'Romantic sublime', is neither idealist nor idealising: rather, its registers are personal, historical, political and, above all, *Alpine*. Arguably, the apostrophe is premised upon what I have been calling a *poetics of ascent*: Wordsworth figures the rise of the imagination, precisely, as the apotheosis of his own disappointing ascent of the Simplon Pass. The larger point, then, is not that Carbonnières's 'Observations' may constitute a previously unrecognised influence on Wordsworth's account of the role of the imagination in the encounter with the 'natural sublime' in Book VI of *The Prelude*. Because Carbonnières's 'Observations' are only one text which I have selected as representative of a much wider genre of engagement with the Alpine sublime. Hence, the point is rather the extent to which traditional claims of a 'general similarity' between Kant's and Wordsworth's 'point of view' on the 'natural sublime' elide any sense of the relationship between Wordsworth's text and the various other contemporary genres of engagement with the 'natural sublime' from which it emerged, of which it forms a part, and to which it responds. The consequence of this elision is to limit both the interpretation of Wordsworth's text and to restrict critical understanding of the diversity of the genres of engagement with the 'natural sublime' in Romantic-period culture.

2
'A volcano heard afar': Vesuvius, Etna and the Poetics of Depth[1]

> It is strange, you will say, that nature should make use of the same agent to create as to destroy; and that what has only been looked upon as the consumer of countries, is in fact the very power that produces them.
> – Patrick Brydone, *A Tour through Sicily and Malta*[2]

By the time that Windham and Pococke 'discovered' the valley of Chamonix in June 1741, the Italian volcanoes, Vesuvius and Etna, had long been 'classic ground', familiar landmarks on the cultural map of Europe. In his *Voyage to Sicily and Malta, in the Years 1700 and 1701*, John Dryden, son of the poet, and one of the earliest of the eighteenth-century English travellers to the region, reminded his readers that Etna was 'famous from all antiquity for its vomiting up fire'.[3] Aeschylus, Diodorus Siculus, Pindar, Thucydides and many other classical authors mention eruptions; Greek and Roman myth recounts that Zeus imprisoned the monster Typhon beneath the mountain; the Roman emperor Hadrian is supposed to have climbed to the summit in AD 125 in order to watch the sunrise; the third-century Greek historian Diogenes Laërtius records the tradition that the philosopher Empedocles, a native of Sicily, lived near the summit and finally committed suicide by jumping into the crater; etc., etc.[4] Writing towards the end of the Romantic period in his *Sketches of Vesuvius*, John Auldjo similarly reminds his readers that the 'celebrated' Vesuvius, 'the burning mountain', had 'allured the curious and learned, in all ages and from all countries'.[5] Foremost amongst the 'curious and learned' of ancient history was, of course, the Roman naturalist and statesman Pliny the Elder, whose death during the eruption of Vesuvius in AD 79, the eruption which destroyed the cities of Pompeii and Herculaneum, is described in his nephew's *Epistulae*, a canonical text in schools and universities throughout the eighteenth century and Romantic period.

At the beginning of the eighteenth century, European perceptions of Vesuvius and Etna continued to be mediated, more or less exclusively, through these classical sources: travel to the volcanoes was uncommon and Sicily, in particular, was virtually a *terra incognita*. During the course of the eighteenth century, however, the cultural significance of Italy's 'classic' volcanoes was entirely transformed by the testimony of the burgeoning number of travellers to Sicily and Campania. As was the case during the 'discovery' of the Alps, the ascent of Etna and Vesuvius became an increasingly prominent component of this travel, and actually formed the focal point of many such journeys: in his *Tour through Sicily and Malta*, for example, Patrick Brydone describes the ascent of Etna as 'one of the greatest objects of our expedition', while Joseph Addison, in his *Remarks on Several Parts of Italy*, says, of his ascent of Vesuvius, that 'there is nothing about Naples, nor indeed in any part of Italy, which deserves our admiration so much as this mountain'.[6] One key difference between Alpine and volcanic ascents also emerges from eighteenth-century writing about Vesuvius and Etna, however: while Alpine ascents tended to be motivated primarily by the desire to see the view *from* the summit, ascents of Etna and Vesuvius were much more likely to be motivated by the desire to look *into* the crater. Hence, while we have seen that eighteenth-century engagements with the Alpine sublime generate tropes linking ascent with expansion (of natural philosophy, of aesthetic pleasure, etc.), engagements with the volcanic sublime more usually generate tropes linked to *depth* and *eruption*.

The link between depth and the sublime was something of a commonplace in eighteenth-century British works of philosophical aesthetics. Hence Edmund Burke, to take just one representative example, suggests, in Part I, Section VII, 'Of Vastness', of his *Philosophical Enquiry into the Origin of our Ideas of the Sublime and the Beautiful*, that 'depth' is perhaps 'the most powerful cause of the sublime' of all the forms of spatial 'extension' which he considers, noting that he is 'apt to imagine [...] that height is less grand than depth; and that we are more struck at looking down from a precipice, than looking up at an object of equal height'.[7] However, the engagement with depth within eighteenth-century and Romantic-period writing about the volcanic sublime goes well beyond the questions of spatial depth to which discussions in philosophical aesthetics were largely, though not entirely, confined. In fact, the generic link between the volcanic sublime and the idea of *depth* is generated in the mid-eighteenth century by those enquiries in natural philosophy which would pave the way for the emergence of the modern, scientific discipline of geology. Spatial depth is only one facet of this link. Temporal depth is another.

In his masterful study *Bursting the Limits of Time*, Martin Rudwick has described in comprehensive detail how the emergence of the modern scientific discipline of geology was made possible by the 'reconstruction', during the late eighteenth and early nineteenth centuries, of the 'highly eventful narrative' of the 'deep or prehuman history' of the earth, that is, by the discovery of so-called *deep time*.[8] The working out of this new 'conceptual space', of the idea that the earth was immensely old, was a process which transcended national boundaries, despite the ongoing Revolutionary and Napoleonic Wars: 'even when the cosmopolitan culture of the late Enlightenment was replaced by the often nationalist cultures of the early Romantic period', Rudwick argues, 'the outlook of those who worked in the natural sciences remained *in practice* highly international'.[9] Indeed it was precisely this 'pervasive internationalism', in Rudwick's view, which enabled the working out of 'a reliable geohistory'.[10]

The study of volcanoes, and of Etna and Vesuvius in particular, played a key role in this process: in the discovery of so-called 'deep time', or in 'the *historicisation* of the earth itself', to use Rudwick's phrase.[11] Arguments about volcanoes, by savants and natural philosophers like William Hamilton (1731–1803), in his *Campi Phlegraei* (1766) and *Observations on Mount Vesuvius* (1772), Georges-Louis Leclerc, Comte de Buffon (1707–88), in his *Les Époques de la Nature* (1778; volume 20 of his monumental *Histoire Naturelle*), James Hutton (1726–97) in his *Theory of the Earth* (1788) and Georges Cuvier (1769–1832) in his *Theory of the Earth* (1813), were all instrumental in the rejection of the so-called 'Mosaic Chronology': the claim, based on the Biblical chronologies of James Ussher (1581–1656), in his *Anales Veteris Testamenti, a Prima Mundi Origine Deducti* (1650) and *Annalium Pars Postierior* (1654), that the earth had been created in October 4004 BC. Hence, through these enquiries in natural philosophy, the visible sublimity of the volcanic landscape came to signify for the Romantic period what John Playfair, the populariser of Hutton's theories, would later describe, drawing on Buffon's potent image, as the sublime 'abyss of time' involved in the geological history of the earth.[12]

However, just as enquiries into the 'historicity of the earth' transcended the boundaries of national identity, so also they ranged across the boundaries of what would now be seen as entirely discrete disciplines or areas of enquiry. Marjorie Hope Nicolson was amongst the earliest scholars to draw to our attention the many and various interactions between engagements with the 'natural sublime' and the history of the earth sciences during the eighteenth century and Romantic period, as well as to the pre-disciplinary nature of such interactions. More recently, Martin Rudwick has shown how the early history of geology 'entailed and required the deliberate transposition of analogical and metaphorical resources from right outside the sacred boundaries of "Science", namely from the human sciences (*Wissenschaften*) of history and even theology'.[13] Part of my intention in this chapter is further to consider the extent to which a reverse 'transposition' also proved to be the case, with the developing earth sciences providing the late eighteenth century and Romantic period with a potent set of paradigms for exploring a variety of ostensibly unrelated phenomena. As discussed in the introduction to this book, Noah Heringman and Ralph O'Connor have documented in considerable detail 'the shared set of cultural practices shaping Romanticism and geology': hence, again, O'Connor's perception that in the early nineteenth century 'scientific writing *was* literature', that 'literature was central to the business of science popularisation', and that 'science, a group of practices defined against the imagination, was promoted in literary texts using imaginative techniques'.[14]

This pre- and interdisciplinary interaction between the earth sciences and areas of enquiry or cultural activity which would now be considered entirely unrelated meant that engagements with the volcanic sublime were not restricted, during the eighteenth century and Romantic period, to enquiries in natural philosophy and philosophical aesthetics. Conversely, as advances in natural philosophy across Europe provided new insight into the subterranean and eruptive dynamics of volcanoes, thereby changing the place of the volcano in the European imagination, sublime volcanic processes came increasingly to be deployed as figures within a wide range of ostensibly unrelated areas of enquiry, and for a wide range of ostensibly unrelated modes of 'the sublime'. That is to say that enquiries into the volcanic sublime within the context of natural philosophy enable and facilitate (at least in part) a number of other, ostensibly unrelated genres of enquiry, and become part of a wider contemporary 'debate', to use O'Connor's phrase, 'about what kinds of language were appropriate to communicating knowledge about nature'.[15] Volcanic imagery is common, for example, in the republican iconography of the French Revolution, and, in the decades following the Revolution, volcanic processes are repeatedly used by apologists and critics alike to figure the dynamics of revolutionary political change. Significant modes of this genre of engagement with the volcanic sublime include the use of volcanic eruption to figure political violence, and the use of subterranean volcanic processes to figure both the action of covert political societies and the hidden build-up of popular political resentment, or other revolutionary energies. Volcanic imagery also comes increasingly to be used during the late eighteenth century and Romantic period, almost to the point of cliché, to provide a potent, pre-Freudian vocabulary for figuring a range of existential and psycho-sexual topoi, for exploring concepts of repression, creativity and mental illness, and for representing the dynamics of the public mind and the individual unconscious. My aim in this chapter is to begin to outline these various mediations and remediations of the volcanic sublime.

'That venerable and respectable father of mountains': Etna and the age of the earth

Throughout the eighteenth century and Romantic period, Etna was widely considered to be the *oldest* volcano in the world, 'the most ancient, and perhaps most considerable, volcano that exists', as William Hamilton put it in his influential *Observations on Mount Vesuvius, Mount Etna, and Other Volcanoes*.[16] Buffon, in his *Histoire Naturelle*, had gone even further, suggesting, as Henry Swinburne phrased it in his *Travels in the Two Sicilies*, that Etna was 'a primitive mountain, that is, a protuberance existing as such from creation'.[17] Hence, although the bulk of European volcanology during the period focused on Vesuvius, speculation about the age and origins of the less well-known and less frequently visited Etna played a key role in answering three fundamental questions about the history of the earth. First: were volcanic mountains in fact permanent and essentially unchanging features of the earth's surface, existing since the beginning of time, as Buffon and others suggested, or did they develop over the course of time? Second, and by extension: what role did volcanic activity play in shaping the surface of the earth? Third, and arguably most significant: what implications did this role have for speculation about the likely age of the earth?

When John Dryden junior arrived in Sicily in the winter of 1700–1, these questions had yet to be raised. Dryden's intention to climb the '30 miles, all up-hill' from Catania to the summit of Etna was prompted, rather, by the desire to follow in the legendary footsteps of Hadrian and Empedocles.[18] To his disappointment, however, Dryden found that it was 'impossible' to reach the summit at that time of year because of 'the vast quantity of snow already fallen all on the top', 'the season being now advanced too far in the winter'.[19] Dryden was the first of the eighteenth-century English travellers to Sicily, and although his *Voyage* remained unpublished until 1776, more than 70 years after his death, it nevertheless anticipates some of the key tropes of eighteenth-century engagements with the volcanic sublime. Dryden is the first to draw attention, for example, to the striking co-existence of fire and ice on the upper reaches of the volcano: 'it is a wonder', he writes, 'to see so much snow remain unmelted near so much flame and smoke'.[20] This 'wonder' would become a consistent refrain of visitors to Sicily. In his *Travels in the Two Sicilies*, for example, Henry Swinburne, whose attempt to reach the summit of Etna was thwarted, like Dryden's, because of 'deep and dangerous' snow which made 'all farther progress impracticable', offers a 'distant survey' of exactly this same 'awful scene' which he 'had not the power of visiting'.[21] Similarly, in his *Tour*, Patrick Brydone, who actually made it to the summit, also registers his 'astonishment' at seeing 'in perpetual union, the two elements that are at perpetual war':

> an immense gulf of fire, forever existing in the midst of snows which it has not power to melt; and immense fields of snow and ice forever surrounding this gulf of fire, which they have not power to extinguish.[22]

By extension, and as European familiarity with the Alps and the Italian volcanoes developed in tandem, travellers would increasingly compare the lava flows of both Etna and Vesuvius with the glacial ice of the Alps. These comparisons bore, as we shall see, not only upon questions within natural philosophy about the role of lava, water and ice in shaping the surface of the earth, but also lent themselves to an ever-broadening range of remediations.

Dryden also draws attention to the apparent risk-reward calculation that he suggests has been performed by the local Sicilian population. Noting that it is 'not a little to be admired how those people will venture to live and build so many villages all about Mount Etna, considering the many and often eruptions', he concludes that the 'extreme' fertility of the volcanic soil persuades the population 'to live there in continual fear and trembling' rather than to abandon 'so fruitful a soil'.[23] While Dryden's suggestion that the Sicilian peasantry actually have a *choice* about where to live is, perhaps, insouciant, these remarks might nevertheless be said to stand at the head of a protracted debate which continues across Europe throughout the eighteenth century and Romantic period – ranging from natural philosophy through political theory and agronomy – about whether volcanism is ultimately a force for good or for ill.

The posthumous publication of Dryden's *Voyage* was prompted, as the editor's preface explains, by the appearance, in 1773, of Patrick Brydone's *Tour through Sicily and Malta*.[24] Brydone, a Scot, had travelled extensively in Europe, including a protracted stay in Switzerland, during which he had performed a series of electrical experiments in the Alps which later earned him the recognition of the Royal Society. Brydone is an interesting figure within the eighteenth-century genre of engagement with the volcanic sublime, and I have chosen to focus on his *Tour* in the first section of this chapter for a number of reasons. For one thing, Brydone has not played a significant part in the academic histories of the development of the earth sciences during the eighteenth century which have so far been written: he receives only brief, passing notice, for example, in Rudwick's *Bursting the Limits of Time*, because he was not one of 'the scientific elite' upon whom Rudwick chose to focus his attention.[25] But my decision to focus on Brydone's *Tour* here is not the result of caprice, nor of the desire simply to find untrodden territory to explore. Nor do I mean to claim, for that matter, that Brydone made a significant contribution to the development of the earth sciences which has, for some reason, been elided from subsequent academic histories of those sciences. That said, Brydone's omission from canonical histories of science is, at least in part, a consequence of the emergence of disciplinarity and the effect of this process on the manner in which the history of science has been written. Brydone's *Tour* is not a work of science, nor even really a work of natural philosophy, and thus has not formed a part of the canon of science writing. But Brydone's *Tour*, and its speculations about Etna, did have considerable contemporary reach. The *Tour* was widely read and helped Brydone gain election to the Royal Society; it also made him something of a minor celebrity, in Britain at least, and a figure of some notoriety: both Samuel Johnson and Thomas De Quincey, for example, allude to Brydone's engagement with orthodox religious ideas about the age of the earth, and indeed De Quincey does so some 60 years later, which suggests a considerable impact upon the public imagination, even granting De Quincey's taste for recondite sources. And, of course, the *Tour* had continued influence as a travel guide: Samuel Taylor Coleridge, for example, had a copy with him during his Mediterranean travels in 1804.[26] It is precisely this generic hybridity of Brydone's *Tour* which interests me here: part travel book, part natural philosophy, part social and political theory, and part philosophical aesthetics, Brydone's *Tour* exemplifies the extent to which the engagement with the 'natural sublime' during the eighteenth century ranged across the boundaries of what would now be viewed as entirely discrete disciplines or genres of enquiry even as it was instrumental in the construction of those same boundaries.

When Brydone arrived in Sicily in the summer of 1770, European perceptions of the island were still largely dominated by classical literature: 'remember', Brydone tells his readers, 'that I am now in the country of fable [...] this island having given rise to more perhaps, except Greece, than all the world beside'.[27] As Brydone recognises, Etna, 'one of the greatest objects of our expedition', had played a central role in this process: 'call to mind', he continues, 'that Mount Etna has ever been the great mother of monsters and chimeras, both in the ancient and the modern world'.[28] However, Brydone's 'examination' of Etna had actually been preceded by William Hamilton, better known for his studies of Vesuvius, who made the voyage to Sicily in 1769, and hence Brydone is self-consciously manipulating the reader's sense of his journey into the unknown.[29] Hamilton's account of Etna, in a letter of 17 October 1769 written on his return to Naples, was published in the *Philosophical Transactions* of the Royal Society in 1770, and therefore did not immediately reach so far outside the community of savants and natural philosophers as Brydone's *Tour*, which had a much broader readership. Hamilton argues of Etna, as do the *Observations* generally, that volcanic activity rather than water is the primary agent for effecting changes in the surface of the earth. 'After a careful examination', Hamilton suggests, 'most mountains, that are or have been volcanoes, would be found to owe their existence to subterraneous fire.'[30] 'May not subterraneous fire', he concludes, 'be the great plough (if I may be allowed the expression) which nature makes use of to turn up the bowels of the earth.'[31] Hamilton also participates, throughout the *Transactions* and *Observations*, in contemporary speculation about the large time-scale required for volcanic geomorphology: 'Nature acts slowly', he affirms:

> it is difficult to catch her in the act. Those who have made this subject their study have, without scruple, undertaken at once to write the natural history of a whole province, or of an entire continent, not reflecting, that the longest life of man scarcely affords him time to give a perfect one of the smallest insect.[32]

However, Hamilton also remains at least superficially consistent with Biblical ideas about the history of the earth, and, indeed, consistently represents the 'wonderful operations of Nature' as 'intended by all-wise

Providence'.³³ Brydone's *Tour*, conversely, does not shy away from engaging head-on with the troubling questions which the study of Etna raised about the age of the earth and the implication of those questions for anyone wedded to a literal interpretation of Biblical accounts of creation.

Brydone opens his account of 'that wonderful mountain', Etna, by registering the tension that is consistently noted by travellers in the landscapes of the sublime: the tension between the overwhelming physicality of that landscape and the desire to provide credible witness, in the language of natural philosophy, to the sublime scenery.³⁴ In part, this was a practical problem. 'One of my greatest difficulties', Brydone suggests, 'will be the finding proper places to write in [...] I am just now writing on the end of a barrel [...] How can one be methodical upon a barrel! It has ever been the most declared enemy to method.'³⁵ But there were also serious representational difficulties: 'the most moderate account of [Etna]', Brydone affirms, 'would appear highly fabulous to all such as are unacquainted with objects of this kind'.³⁶ The language of natural philosophy seems inadequate to the task at hand. Nor was Brydone himself entirely immune to the 'infection' of the extreme affective response to the volcanic sublime, which he suggests underpins not only the classical myths about the mountain, but also the curious weave of superstition and mainstream Catholicism exhibited by the local population. 'I own I have sometimes envied them their feelings', he admits:

> and in my heart cursed the pride of reason and philosophy, with all its cool and tasteless triumphs, that lulls into a kind of stoical apathy these most exquisite sensations of the soul. Who would not choose to be deceived, when the deception raises in him these delicious passions [...] But if once you have steeled ['the human heart'] over with the hard and impenetrable temper of philosophy, these fine-spun threads of weakness and affection [...] become hard and inflexible.³⁷

For Brydone, then, as for so many other travellers to the landscapes of the sublime, the affective and the 'philosophical' responses to the landscape are incompatible: the enthusiasm, which eighteenth-century British works of philosophical aesthetics consistently identify as a consequence of the sublime, threatens always to destabilise the attempt at rational observation, and Brydone, the sober Scottish philosopher, finds himself seduced by the lure of a primitive, irrational (and Catholic!) emotional response.

Brydone's 'philosophical' interests are evident from the outset of his *Tour* and he quickly sets out his position on two of the key issues in late eighteenth-century and Romantic-period natural philosophy: the debate between Neptunists and Vulcanists about the identity of the main agent responsible for shaping the surface of the earth – was it water (even a Biblical flood) or volcanic fire? – and the debate between Catastrophists and Gradualists about the essential nature of the earth's geological history: did that history involve the gradual operation of processes over time, or was it driven by a series of catastrophic events? Although Brydone identifies 'the examination of mount Etna' as 'one of the greatest objects of our expedition', he begins to speculate on the potential role of volcanic activity in shaping the surface of the earth even before landing on Sicily.[38] His opening account of the voyage from Naples presents the landscape around Naples, seen from offshore, as an almost carnivalesque space:

> an amazing mixture of the ancient and modern [...] Mountains and islands that were celebrated for their fertility changed into barren wastes; and barren wastes into fertile fields and rich vineyards. Mountains sunk into plains, and plains swelled into mountains. Lakes drunk up by volcanoes, and extinguished volcanoes turned into lakes. The earth still smoking in many places; and in others throwing out flame. – In short, nature seems to have formed this coast in her most capricious mood [...] She seems never have gone seriously to work; but to have devoted this spot to the most unlimited indulgence of caprice and frolic.[39]

Vesuvius, 'in the background of the scene, discharging volumes of fire and smoke', is the lord of this apparent misrule.[40] But Vesuvius, paradoxically ('it would require, I am afraid, too great a stretch of faith to believe me'), is the agent of a hidden order.[41] All the apparently chaotic features of the Neapolitan landscape are, Brydone concludes, 'the produce of subterraneous fire'.[42] Drawing explicitly on the 'observations' of William Hamilton, 'our minister here', Brydone reads the Neapolitan landscape as evidence of volcanic processes which ultimately regenerate what they appear to destroy.[43] 'It is strange', he concludes, 'that nature should make use of the same agent to create as to destroy; and that what has only been looked upon as the consumer of countries, is in fact the very power that produces them.'[44] Like Hamilton, then, Brydone identifies volcanism as the primary agent effecting changes to the surface of the earth, and implicitly rejects, or at least downplays, a catastrophist interpretation of the geological history of the earth: 'this part of the earth', Brydone observes of the Neapolitan countryside, 'seems already to have undergone the sentence pronounced upon the whole of it. But, like the phoenix, has risen again from its own ashes, in much greater beauty and splendour than before it was consumed.'[45]

Brydone's account of Sicily and Etna bears out these initial conclusions about the geomorphic function of volcanic activity. Lying off the Sicilian shore, amongst the Aeolian Islands, Brydone describes the continuous eruption of Stromboli, 'the explosions of which succeed one another with some degree of regularity, and have no great variety or duration'.[46] Brydone had heard, at Naples, that 'a new island' had begun to form off Stromboli after a 'violent' submarine eruption, and believed he had 'discovered this island, as we have observed several times the appearance of a small flame arising out of the sea'.[47] 'It is probable', he concludes, 'that Stromboli, as well as all the rest of these islands, is originally the work of subterraneous fire.'[48] Volcanic activity is identified, once again, as the primary agent of geomorphic change.

Once landed on Sicily itself, Brydone and his party set about examining the geomorphic impact of the lava flows from previous eruptions of Etna, noting that there appeared to have 'been eruptions of fire all over this country at a great distance from the summit, or principal crater'.[49] The most striking feature of these flows for Brydone was not so much their extent, however, as their extraordinary *depth*. In some places, Brydone observes, the lava from previous eruptions had 'been covered so deep with earth, that it is nowhere to be seen but in the beds of the torrents. In many of these it is worn down by the waters to a depth of fifty or sixty feet, and in one of them still considerably more'.[50] Before reaching any conclusions about the depth of these lava flows, however, Brydone supplements his own observations with those of his guide: the Catholic priest and observer of Etna, Giuseppe Recupero. Recupero (1720–78), a native of Sicily, had been given a semi-official commission to investigate what Brydone describes as 'a very singular event' which occurred during the 1755 eruption of Etna, when 'an immense torrent of boiling water issued, as is imagined, from the great crater of the mountain, and in an instant poured down to its base, overwhelming and ruining everything it met with in its course'.[51] Recupero's report on this 'event' in his *Discorso Storico sopra l'Acqua Vomita dal Mongibello* (1755) is one of the earliest descriptions of a volcanic lahar, and it won him some standing amongst the community of savants and natural philosophers concerned with volcanoes and their role in the history of the earth. Spurred on by this success, Recupero then began work on a systematic history of Etna, but the result, his *Storia Naturale e Generale dell'Etna*, remained unpublished until 1815, nearly 40 years after his death. It was Recupero who guided Hamilton's expedition to Etna in 1769, but Hamilton made no mention, in the *Transactions* or *Observations*, of Recupero's own speculation about Etna and the age of the earth.[52] So it was Brydone's *Tour* which remediated to the general reading public in Britain (at least) Recupero's conviction that the physical depth of the previous lava flows from Etna meant that the earth must be considerably older than was suggested by the chronologies then endorsed by the Catholic Church, of which Recupero was of course a member.

In Letter VII of his *Tour*, Brydone describes how Recupero brought the group to 'a vault, which is now thirty feet below ground, and has probably been a burial place'.[53] Near this vault, they examined 'a draw-well, where there are several strata of lavas, with earth to a considerable thickness over the surface of each stratum'.[54] 'As it requires two thousand years or upwards to form a scanty soil on the surface of a lava', Brydone continues, paraphrasing Recupero, 'there must have been more than that space of time betwixt each of the eruptions which have formed these strata.'[55] 'But what shall we say', Brydone continues, 'of a pit they sunk near to Jaci [Acireale], of a great depth? They pierced through seven distinct lavas one under the other, the surfaces of which were parallel, and most of them covered with a thick bed of rich earth.'[56] Recupero draws the inevitable conclusion: 'now, says he', Brydone reports, 'if we may be allowed to reason from analogy [...] the eruption which formed the lowest of these lavas [...] must have flowed from the mountain at least 14,000 years ago'.[57]

If accurate, this 'reasoning' would make Sicily more than ten thousand years older than the age of the earth endorsed by the Catholic Church, based on Ussher's chronology which, as we have seen, dated the Biblical creation to just 4004 BC. Fourteen thousand years is hardly a vast amount of time in comparison with Buffon's suggestion, in his *Époques*, that the earth might be as much as seventy-five thousand years old, to say nothing at all of James Hutton's famous conclusion, in his *Theory of the Earth* (1788), that his enquiries into the physical history of the earth revealed 'no vestige of a beginning, – no prospect of an end'.[58] However, Brydone's remediation of Recupero's ideas certainly forges a clear and accessible link for the general reading public between the physical depth of the volcanic landscape and the temporal depth of which that landscape is both figure and evidence: 'what an idea does this give', Brydone enthuses of the layers of lava, 'of the great antiquity of the eruptions of this mountain?'[59] For the devout Recupero, however, this was a troubling prospect, and his response to his own discoveries prefigures the conflict between various genres of natural philosophy and mainstream religion that would rage during the Romantic and Victorian periods. 'Recupero tells me', Brydone records, somewhat sardonically, 'he is exceedingly embarrassed by these discoveries, in writing the history of the mountain':

> that Moses hangs like a dead weight upon him, and blunts all his zeal for enquiry; for that really he has not the confidence to make his mountain so young, as that prophet makes the world.[60]

Nor was this 'embarrassment' simply a matter of Recupero's personal religious beliefs: 'the bishop, who is strenuously orthodox', Brydone affirms, 'has already warned him to be on his guard and not to pretend to be a better natural historian than Moses; nor to presume to urge anything that may be in the smallest degree deemed contradictory to his sacred authority'.[61] Nor, for that matter, was the censure limited to the Italian clergy. James Boswell reports Samuel Johnson asking of Brydone's conclusion about the lava flows, 'shall all the accumulated evidence of the history of the earth – shall the authority of what is unquestionably the most ancient of writings, be overturned by an uncertain remark such as this?', and again later that 'if Brydone were more attentive to his Bible, he would be a good traveller'.[62] Indeed, as late as September 1846, in his essay 'System of the Heavens as Revealed by Lord Rosse's Telescopes', Thomas De Quincey still invokes the challenge offered by Recupero and Brydone to the official position of the Church on the age of the earth, referring the reader to 'Brydone's Travels' and affirming that:

> The canon, being a beneficed clergyman in the Papal church, was naturally an infidel. He wished exceedingly to refute Moses [that is, the Ussher Chronology], and fancied that he really *had* done so by means of some collusive evidence from the layers of lava on Mount Etna. But there survives, at this day, very little to remind us of the canon, except an unpleasant guffaw that rises, at times, in solitary valleys of Etna.[63]

Whatever may have been its contribution to the Europe-wide debate, during the eighteenth century, about the age of the earth, Brydone's *Tour* certainly exemplifies the growing and potentially troubling link, in the public imagination, between the volcanic sublime and the idea of *depth*.

From the depth of Etna's ancient lava flows, Brydone's expedition then turned its attention to the 'high summit' of the volcano itself, 'rearing its tremendous head, and vomiting out torrents of smoke'.[64] The expedition had two main objects in mind when making the overnight ascent: to 'see the sun rising' from the summit of the volcano, a 'motive' which, Brydone reminds his readers, had supposedly also prompted Hadrian and Plato to climb Etna; and, of course, to look into the 'tremendous gulph' of the crater itself, 'so celebrated in all ages'.[65] When the expedition broke through the forests covering the lower slopes of the mountain, they had their first, proper glimpse of the summit, 'still at a great distance'.[66] This 'alarming' 'prospect' initially prompted Brydone to invoke, like so many contemporary writers about the *Alpine* sublime, the trope of the *inaccessible* summit: 'the highest summit', he affirms, 'appeared altogether inaccessible, from the vast extent of the fields of snow and ice that surrounded it'.[67] Led by Recupero, however, and after 'incredible labour and fatigue', the expedition finally reached, 'before dawn', the 'ruins of an ancient structure, called *Il Torre del Filosofo*', then widely reputed to have been constructed and inhabited by the philosopher Empedocles.[68]

Brydone's account of this 'sublime' location deploys the same discourse of ascent, the same correlation of altitude and insight, which we have already discerned in contemporary eighteenth-century engagements with the Alpine sublime.[69] The physical elevation of the *torre*, at 2920 metres above sea level, establishes it, for Brydone, not only as an aesthetically impressive site, but also as a site linked to a wide variety of other, ostensibly unrelated modes of elevation. Recovering from his initial 'astonishment' at the 'sublime objects of nature', Brydone begins by emphasising the potential for observing the night sky from such an elevated position. 'The sky was clear', he writes, 'and the immense vault of the heavens appeared in awful majesty and splendour':

> we found ourselves more struck with veneration than below, and at first were at a loss to know the cause; till we observed with astonishment, that the number of stars seemed to be infinitely increased; and the light of each of them appeared brighter than usual. The whiteness of the Milky Way was like a pure flame that shot across the heavens.[70]

The explanation for this sublime spectacle, Brydone immediately realises, is the physical elevation of the spot on which his party stands: 'we had now passed through ten or twelve thousand feet of gross vapour, that blunts and confuses every ray, before it reaches the surface of the earth'.[71] 'What a glorious situation for an observatory', he concludes: 'had

Empedocles had the eyes of Galileo what discoveries must he not have made!'[72] As with the discourse of ascent generated within late eighteenth-century and Romantic-period writing about the Alpine sublime, then, Brydone's initial observations, from high up on Etna, affirm that physical elevation affords not just a heightened aesthetic awareness of 'the sublime objects of nature', but also (potential) advances in natural philosophy.

Brydone's discussion of the legends connecting Empedocles with the *torre* also invokes the discourse of ascent that we have discerned in contemporary writing about the Alpine sublime. Brydone outlines the various stories about Empedocles, especially Diogenes Laërtius's relatively well-known and less than flattering account, in his *Lives of Eminent Philosophers*, in which he describes how Empedocles, wishing people to remember him as a god who had been taken up to heaven, committed suicide by jumping into Etna's crater, only to have his deception unveiled when the mountain subsequently ejected his brass shoes during an eruption.[73] Brydone himself remains non-committal about whether it was the 'vanity' or 'philosophy' of Empedocles which 'led him to this elevated situation'.[74] However, he confirms of the *torre* itself that 'if there is such a thing as philosophy on earth, this surely ought to be its seat', asserting, once again, the correlation between altitude and insight at the heart of the discourse of ascent:

> the mind enjoys a degree of serenity here, that even few philosophers, I believe, could ever boast of [...] All nature lies expanded below your feet [...] and you still behold united under one point of view, all the seasons of the year, and all the climates of the earth. The meditations are ever elevated in proportion to the grandeur and sublimity of the objects that surround us; and here, where you have all nature to arouse your admiration, what mind can remain inactive?[75]

The echo of Rousseau's seminal account of the Upper Valais in *Julie* (discussed in detail in Chapter 1), in which the physical ascent of the Alps is linked to elevated consciousness, is then made all but explicit as Brydone continues with what amounts to an unacknowledged quotation from Rousseau's novel:

> It has likewise been observed, and from experience I can say with truth, that on the tops of the highest mountains, where the air is so pure and refined, and where there is not that immense weight of gross vapours pressing upon the body, the mind acts with greater

freedom, and all the functions both of body and soul are performed in a superior manner. It would appear, that in proportion as we are raised above the habitations of men, all low and vulgar sentiments are left behind, and that the soul, in approaching the ethereal regions, shakes off its earthly affections, and already acquires something of their celestial purity.[76]

Paraphrasing Rousseau's seminal formulation of a discourse ascent, then, Brydone concludes of *Il Torre del Filosofo* that not only is it a prime location for aesthetic appreciation of the 'sublime objects of nature' and for enquiries in natural philosophy, but also for rising intellectually above 'the little storms of the human passions': 'surely the situation alone', he affirms, 'is enough to inspire philosophy, and Empedocles had good reason for choosing it'.[77] Here, then, we have the antithesis of the link between the volcanic sublime and (Catholic) superstition which Brydone had remarked upon during his account of the influence of Etna on the local population, complementing the theories of French ideologues like Baron d'Holbach and Constantin Volney, who argue that religious belief originates in the reaction of primitive peoples to sublime natural phenomena beyond their comprehension. Religion, it seems, as in contemporary engagements with the Alpine sublime, is a matter for those in the valley; philosophers seek the summits.

Brydone's account of the 'highest summit' of Etna is itself a seminal account of the 'awe' and 'horror' of the volcanic sublime, combining the 'unbounded extent of the prospect' from such 'immense elevation' with the 'prospect' into the crater: 'a bottomless gulf, as old as the world [...] discharging rivers of fire, and throwing out hot burning rocks'.[78] Brydone's vocabulary here evidently draws on seminal descriptions of the 'natural sublime' within the tradition of British philosophical aesthetics, by figures like Joseph Addison and Edmund Burke. However, Brydone's experience on the summit also avoids any trace of Wordsworthian disappointment: reality, in this instance, exceeds imagination; the 'classic ground' of Etna's summit exceeds its billing. 'Here', Brydone affirms of the summit, invoking the familiar idea of the inability of language adequately to mediate the effect of the sublime: 'description must ever fall short, for no imagination has dared to form any idea of so glorious and so magnificent a scene'.[79] Hence Brydone, like so many other travellers to the landscapes of the sublime, emphasises the tension between the overwhelming affective power of this 'scene' and the desire to observe and to describe the landscape within the terms of natural philosophy: 'the senses', he writes, 'unaccustomed to the sublimity of such a scene, are bewildered and confounded, and it is not till after some time, that they are capable of separating and judging of the objects that compose it'.[80] The 'absolutely boundless' view from the summit, however, effectively defies this analytical process of 'separating and judging', 'so that the sight is everywhere lost in the immensity'.[81] And finally confronted with 'the great mouth of the volcano' itself, Brydone concedes not only that this 'tremendous gulf' exceeds imagination, but that the language of the imagination, the language of the sublime, which he had earlier dismissed as 'deception', is the only means through which it can even be attempted to be mediated:

> we beheld it with awe and horror, and were not surprised that it had been considered as the place of the damned. When we reflect on the immensity of its depth, the vast cells and caverns whence so many lavas have issued; the force of its internal fire, to raise those lavas to so vast a height [...] the boiling of the matter, the shaking of the mountain, the explosions of flaming rocks, etc., we must allow that the most enthusiastic imagination, in the midst of all its terrors, hardly ever formed an idea of hell more dreadful.[82]

So, for Brydone, the 'tremendous' spectacle of Etna's active crater can only be mediated through the language of the sublime ('awe', 'horror'), that is, through the language of the 'enthusiastic imagination', a key descriptor within eighteenth-century British philosophical aesthetics for the emotional response to the 'natural sublime'.[83] And this is not simply because a more sober terminology for describing volcanic activity had yet to be formulated within the nascent science of geology. Rather, by exceeding even the scope of the imagination ('we must allow that the most enthusiastic imagination [...] hardly ever formed an idea of hell more dreadful'), the volcanic sublime emerges from Brydone's *Tour* as what might most appropriately be described as an eruptive force, capable of breaking through and breaking down established systems of representation. As late as 1819, for example, by which time Sicily was relatively well known to European travellers, and the modern science of volcanology was relatively well established, Richard Hoare, in his *Classical Tour through Italy and Sicily*, affirms of Etna's 'stupendous' crater that 'it would be an impracticable task either to express my feelings, or to paint its horrors':

> even the glowing colours in which a Dante and a Milton have depicted the infernal regions of fire and tempest, would convey a

very inadequate idea of the crater [...] vast unfathomable abyss [...] incessantly vomiting forth a thick volume of smoke, mixed with flames.[84]

'Imagination itself', Hoare concludes, after some three pages of this rapture, 'cannot figure a more complete scene of desolation.'[85] For these travellers, at least, the reality of the volcanic sublime exceeds the expectations engendered by its place in the cultural imagination of Europe, a place which these texts themselves are instrumental in transforming.

In Brydone's *Tour*, the eruptive, affective power of the volcanic sublime is evident even in the records which Brydone makes of the experiments which he performed upon the summit. These ostensible documents of natural philosophy fall consistently back upon tropes of 'astonishment' more appropriate to the eighteenth-century British discourse on the sublime. Consider, by way of example, Brydone's account of attempting to determine the height of Etna by measuring barometric pressure at the summit, as Saussure would do on Mont Blanc. 'I own', he affirms, 'that I did not believe we should find Etna so high. I had heard indeed that it was higher than any of the Alps, but I never gave credit to it: How great then was my astonishment to find that the mercury fell almost two inches lower than I had ever observed it on the very highest of the accessible Alps.'[86] Brydone's closing remarks on Etna continue in this same vein, effectively blurring the distinction between 'philosophy' and 'imagination': 'indeed', he concludes, 'the philosopher and the natural historian have found, in the real properties of this mountain, as ample a fund of speculation, as the poets have done in the fictitious'.[87]

Brydone's *Tour* accordingly exemplifies the extent to which, throughout eighteenth-century engagements with Etna, the volcanic sublime is consistently linked to tropes of eruption and of depth, but also to potent images of natural renewal and generation. The eruptive force of the volcanic sublime always threatens to exceed or to overwhelm representation, while simultaneously figuring temporal depths equally beyond imagination and directly conflicting with the official position of the Church upon the natural history of the earth. However, as natural philosophers develop greater understanding of the role of volcanic processes in shaping the history of the earth, the sense of the destructive power of the volcanic sublime comes increasingly to be linked with an understanding of its potential for renewal and regeneration, on both a local and a global level. This is the paradox at the heart of eighteenth-century engagements with the volcanic sublime: the 'strange' truth, as we have seen Brydone put it, 'that nature should make use of the same agent to create as to destroy; and that what has only been looked upon as the consumer of countries, is in fact the very power that produces them'.[88] And precisely this paradox would provide a potent and subtle metaphor for Romantic-period writing about political change and artistic creativity.

'This astonishing convulsion of nature': Vesuvius and the spectacle of eruption

Vesuvius – located just outside Naples, the symbolic goal of the eighteenth-century Grand Tour – received a good deal more attention from eighteenth-century and Romantic-period travellers than the rather less accessible Etna. There were seven significant eruptions of Vesuvius during the period covered by this book – in 1707, 1737, 1760, 1767, 1794 (when the town of Torre del Greco was destroyed) and 1822 – all of which were described and studied in detail by Grand Tourists and natural philosophers alike. The rediscovery, in the mid-eighteenth century, of the ancient cities of Pompeii and Herculaneum, which had been buried during the AD 79 eruption of Vesuvius, further evidenced, for the eighteenth century and Romantic period, the sublime power of volcanic activity. As with contemporary writing about Etna, however, it was the crater of Vesuvius, even when not in a state of eruption, which became the primary signifier of this power, so that, once again, the volcanic sublime is linked not just to tropes of eruption, but also to tropes of *depth*.

It was no less a figure than Joseph Addison – the framer of the concept of 'classic ground' – who offered the eighteenth-century British reading public one of its earliest, contemporary views into the crater of Vesuvius. As we have seen, Addison says of Vesuvius, in his *Remarks on Several Parts of Italy*, that 'there is nothing about Naples, nor indeed in any part of Italy, which deserves our admiration so much as this mountain'.[89] Addison's account of his ascent to the crater of Vesuvius emphasises the 'very troublesome' terrain near the summit: 'it is very hot under the feet, and mixed with several burnt stones and cakes of cinders [...] a man sinks almost a foot in the earth, and generally loses half a step by sliding backwards'.[90] Many subsequent travellers would echo these difficulties: Swinburne, for example, warns those who want to look into 'the gloomy abyss' of the crater that 'it is impossible to give a just idea of the fatigue of this climbing', while Thomas Martyn, similarly, affirms that the ascent is 'very fatiguing' because 'you sink up to the knees, and go two steps backwards for every three that you set'.[91]

Having struggled to the top, Addison's description of the crater itself, which was not then in a state of eruption, focuses almost entirely on its depth:

> shelving down on all sides, until above a hundred yards deep, as near as we could guess [...] this vast hollow is generally filled with smoke: but, by the advantage of a wind that blew for us, we had a very clear and distinct sight of it [...] The bottom was entirely covered [...] we could see nothing like a hole in it.[92]

Addison's conclusion that it might actually have been possible for his party to 'then have crossed the bottom' of the crater 'and have gone up on the other side of it with very little danger' finds a distorted echo, in 1813, when Joseph Forsyth concludes that the sublimity of the then-quiescent and heavily touristed Vesuvius was an 'exhausted subject' because even 'Ladies, as I read in the Hermit's Album, go down to the bottom of the crater'.[93] By the middle of the eighteenth century, however, the literal and figurative depth of the crater had become a recurring trope in writing about Vesuvius. In his *Journal of a Tour to Italy*, for example, the well-known French explorer Charles Marie de La Condamine, who made the ascent of Vesuvius on 4 June 1755, focuses his account of that ascent almost exclusively on the view into the crater. 'I went close up to the edge of the crater', he writes:

> in a place where it was most accessible, and which appeared to me to be the steepest on the inside. There I laid me down on my belly, and stretched my head forward, in order to examine the inside of this gulf [...] I could see down to the depth of forty toises [80 metres] or more, and I perceived therein a large arched cavity [...] I caused great stones to be thrown into this cavity, and counted by my watch twelve seconds, before the noise of their rolling ceased to be heard.[94]

Equally, while Addison himself never actually witnessed an eruption of Vesuvius, it was Addison's *Remarks* which offered one of the earliest eighteenth-century British *imaginings* of what an eruption *might* look like, prefiguring many of the paintings and dioramas that would go on show in London in the late eighteenth century and Romantic period.[95] And this imagining, too, is as much concerned with the depth of the crater as with its eruptive potential. 'During the late eruptions', Addison says of the crater:

> this great hollow was like a vast cauldron filled with glowing and melted matter, which, as it boiled over in any part, ran down the sides of mountain [...] In proportion as the heat slackened, this burning matter must have subsided within the bowels of the mountain [...] and formed the bottom which covers the mouth of that dreadful vault that lies underneath it.[96]

This colourful imagining of an eruption as the 'boiling over' of a 'vast cauldron' (an image possibly echoed in Swinburne's later, playful reference to Vesuvius as a 'volcanic kettle') sets the trend for eighteenth-century and Romantic-period engagements with Vesuvius by explicitly correlating tropes of eruption and depth. As in contemporary descriptions of Etna, it was the 'dreadful vault' of the crater of Vesuvius which became the primary signifier of its eruptive potential.

At the beginning of the eighteenth century, the most prominent, first-hand account of that potential was Pliny the Younger's letter to Tacitus, in which he describes the devastating AD 79 eruption which buried the cities of Pompeii and Herculaneum. Pliny witnessed this eruption, during which his famous uncle 'perished' along with 'whole peoples and cities', from a safe distance, at Miseno, on the opposite side of the Bay of Naples.[97] His account is as remarkable for the 'terrific' scene it describes as for the eye for detail with which it is described.[98] The first sign of the eruption was the appearance, in the afternoon, of 'a cloud of very unusual size and appearance' rising above the volcano: 'I cannot give you a more exact description of its figure', Pliny writes, 'than by resembling it to that of a pine-tree, for it shot up to a great height in the form of a trunk, which extended itself at the top into several branches.'[99] At this point, Pliny says, his uncle left for the town of Stabia, which was much closer to Vesuvius, in order 'to be able to make and dictate his observations upon the successive motions and figures of that terrific object'.[100] The eruption continued for the remainder of the day, and, after nightfall, Vesuvius could be seen 'blazing in several places with spreading and towering flames'.[101] By the following morning, so much cloud and ash had been dispersed into the atmosphere that 'a deeper darkness prevailed than in the most obscure night'.[102] It was on this morning, Pliny writes, that his uncle collapsed and died while observing the ongoing eruption from the beach near Stabia; Pliny attributes the death to 'some unusually gross vapour' emitted from the volcano, noting that his uncle's collapse had been preceded by increased 'flames, and a strong smell of sulphur'.[103]

Most educated Europeans would have been familiar from their schooldays with Pliny's description of the devastating AD 79 eruption, and its place in the eighteenth-century imagination was significantly augmented by the rediscovery, in the middle of the century, of the ruins of Pompeii and Herculaneum. Both Johann Joachim Winckelmann's *Critical Account of the Situation and Destruction by the First Eruptions of Mount Vesuvius, of Herculaneum, Pompeii and Stabia* (1771) and John Chetwode Eustace's *Classical Tour through Italy* (1813), for example, contain extended reimaginings of Pliny's account. Eustace's *Classical Tour*, the standard contemporary guide to Italy, which went through numerous editions, and which had clearly been written with an eye on the saleability of spectacle, offers a particularly lurid vision of the 'awe, expectation, and terror' which must have struck the population 'while the earth was rocking under their feet [...] while the country was deluged with liquid fire, and the whole atmosphere loaded with ashes and sulphur'.[104] But even more sober descriptions of what Forsyth describes as 'the present monumental solitude of Pompeii' raised troubling questions about the place of humans in the natural history of the earth: how could the new claims by natural philosophers about the regenerative role of volcanic activity in the history of the earth be reconciled which such appalling human loss?[105] 'Perhaps the whole world does not exhibit so awful a spectacle as Pompeii', Mariana Starke concludes in her *Letters from Italy*: 'and when it was first discovered, when skeletons were found heaped together in the streets and houses, when all the utensils, and even the very bread of the suffocated inhabitants were discernible – what a speculation must this ill-fated city have furnished to a thinking mind!'[106]

Contemporary eyewitness accounts of major eighteenth-century eruptions of Vesuvius similarly tend to emphasise not just the sublime eruptive power of the volcano, but also the disruption to the *social* order caused by a significant eruption. Prominent amongst such accounts by British writers are William Hamilton's lavishly illustrated *Campi Phlegraei: Observations on the Volcanoes of the Two Sicilies* (1776) and its *Supplement to the Campi Phlegraei: Being an Account of the Great Eruption of Mount Vesuvius in the Month of August 1779* (1779), and Brooke's description of the June 1794 eruption, which destroyed Torre del Greco, in his *Observations on the Manners and Customs of Italy* (1798).[107]

Hamilton signals a figurative link between volcanic and political eruption early in the *Campi Phlegraei* when, arguing for the likely pervasiveness of volcanic activity across the globe, he refers to a letter from Horace-Bénédict de Saussure, in which the famous Swiss natural philosopher says of Rome that 'this famous City, which has undergone so many political revolutions, rests upon a soil, which long before its foundation, had experienced the greatest physical revolutions'.[108] Hamilton's account of the eruption of August 1779, which he witnessed from the harbour at Naples, formulates an analogous, figurative link between volcanic and political eruption. While Hamilton states his intention to avoid 'poetical description [and] flowery style' in reporting the eruption, he ultimately cannot avoid hyperbole in attempting 'to convey [...] at least a faint idea of a scene so glorious, and sublime, as perhaps may have never before been viewed by human eye':

> In an instant a fountain of liquid transparent fire began to rise, and gradually increasing arrived at so amazing a height, as to strike every one, who beheld it, with the most awful astonishment: I shall scarcely be credited [...] that to the best of my judgement the height of this stupendous column of fire could not be less than three times that of Vesuvius itself.[109]

As in Brydone's account of Etna, then, the volcanic sublime threatens to exceed the 'simple' or 'plain' representation required by the natural philosopher. But Hamilton also emphasises the no less sublime disruption to the social order occasioned by the eruption. In his *Campi Phlegraei*, Hamilton had already recorded of the significant eruption of Vesuvius in October 1767 that:

> The confusion at Naples this night cannot be described; his Sicilian majesty's retreat from Portici added to the alarm; all the churches were opened and filled [...] the prisoners in the public jail attempted to escape [...] the mob also set fire to the Cardinal Archbishop's gate [...] in the midst of these horrors, the mob, growing tumultuous and impatient, obliged the Cardinal to bring out the head of Saint Januarius [the patron saint of Naples], and go with it in procession.[110]

Hamilton's account of the eruption of August 1779 records a similar effect, with the sublime spectacle of volcanic eruption triggering the no less sublime spectacle of social insurrection:

> The populace of this great city began to display its usual extravagant mixture of riot, and bigotry, and if some speedy, and well-timed

precautions had not been taken, Naples would perhaps have been in more danger of suffering from the irregularities of its lower class inhabitants, than from the angry volcano.[111]

Nor let it be thought that Hamilton, the British envoy to the court of Naples, was particularly or unusually sensitive to the potential for popular political unrest occasioned by volcanic activity. In his discussion of the eruption of Vesuvius in June 1794, during which 'the rich and beautiful city of Torre del Greco' was destroyed by lava, Brooke perceives exactly the same relationship between volcanic activity and social unrest.[112]

Brooke carried official dispatches to Hamilton at Naples, and was familiar with the diplomat's writings about Vesuvius, which he describes as having 'great merit'.[113] Like Hamilton before him, while Brooke states his intention to provide a 'plain and interesting narrative' of the 'sublime' spectacle of the eruption, he quickly lapses into hyperbole:

> the dreadful roar of the convulsed mountain vomiting volcanic matter from many wide gaping furnaces; a river of vivid lava gliding one mile across the mountain; and its destructive fall in a blazing cascade, half a mile in breadth, while inflammable matter was darting round the mountain in a variety of shapes, formed a combination of awful circumstances.[114]

These 'awful circumstances', Brooke felt confident, could nevertheless be safely considered as the 'wonderful operations of divine order'.[115] As with the religious responses to the Alpine sublime described by Nicolson, then, it was still possible to bring the volcanic sublime within the pale of mainstream religious belief. Far less easy to account for was the 'disagreeable' sight of the 'affrighted inhabitants' of Naples, the 'votaries of fear' who 'had formed themselves into parochial processions [and] bawled their wild and idolatrous hymns [and] worked themselves into a frenzy'.[116] Closer inspection of these 'numerous processions' revealed to Brooke that they were 'composed chiefly of females with dishevelled hair, whose voices were disagreeably hoarse'.[117] There is an unmistakable and instructive echo, here, not only of classical descriptions of maenads during the Dionysiaca, but also of Burke's influential imagining of revolutionary violence, in his *Reflections on the Revolution in France*, where he describes the 'procession' in which the French royal family was taken from Versailles to Paris on 6 October 1789, 'amidst the horrid yells, and shrilling screams, and frantic dances, and infamous contumelies, and all the unutterable abominations of the furies of hell, in the abused shape of the vilest of women'.[118] In Brooke's as in Hamilton's (far more influential) response to Vesuvius, then, volcanic eruption and political instability are closely linked, and while both men are apparently able to relocate the sublime eruptive power of the volcano within a perceived 'divine order' (to use Brooke's phrase), the political instability occasioned by volcanic eruption resists such easy classification. This same link between volcanic and political eruption would leave a significant legacy to the iconography of Romantic-period writing about political change.

'The lava of the imagination': some Romantic remediations of the volcanic sublime

In *The Earth on Show*, Ralph O'Connor has drawn attention to the role of Byron's poetry in bringing speculations by natural philosophers about the history of the earth to a wide readership outside the community of natural philosophers in early nineteenth-century Britain, particularly through *Cain*, published in 1821, in which Byron engages directly with Cuvier's *Theory of the Earth*.[119] In the thirty-sixth stanza of the thirteenth canto of *Don Juan*, published two years after *Cain*, in December 1823, Byron breaks off, in mid-line, to offer a characteristically ironic reflection on the extent to which volcano-imagery has become 'a commonplace' of Romantic-period writing (l. 282). 'Shall I go on?', he asks of the image:

> No!
> I hate to hunt down a tired metaphor:
> So let the often used volcano go.
> Poor thing! How frequently, by me and others,
> It hath been stirred up till its smoke quite smothers! (ll. 284–8)

The image that Byron abandons here involves the conflict between 'snow' and 'lava' at the summit of a volcano, and, as we have seen, this conflict was indeed a recurring trope in eighteenth-century writing about Etna (*Don Juan* XIII xxxvi, ll. 282–3). During the late eighteenth century and Romantic period, however, it had also become something of a 'common-place' to compare the old lava flows around Vesuvius with frozen water, and, in particular, with the glaciers in the Alps. In his *Classical Tour*, for example, Eustace describes one of these old flows as 'like the surface of a dark muddy stream convulsed by a hurricane, and frozen in a state of agitation', while Percy Bysshe Shelley told his friend Thomas Love Peacock, in a letter sent from Naples on 23 December 1819, that Vesuvius was, 'after the Glaciers, the most impressive exhibition of the energies of nature I ever saw. It has not the immeasurable greatness, the overpowering magnificence, nor, above all, the radiant beauty of the glaciers; but it has all their character of tremendous and irresistible strength.'[120] In his 1832 *Sketches of Vesuvius*, John Auldjo, who had previously summited Mont Blanc, similarly affirms that 'the field of lava in the interior of the crater' of Vesuvius:

> might be likened to a lake, whose agitated waves had suddenly been petrified; and, in many respects, it resembles the *mer de glace*, or level glaciers of Switzerland, although in its origins and materials so very different [...] in the sea of ice, the white, dazzling surface is relieved by beautiful tints and various shades of blue and green; in its simulachre of stone, the bright yellow and red of the compounds of sulphur and the metals interspersed with the pure white of the muriate of soda, afford a pleasing contrast to the brown and melancholy hue of the lava.[121]

This particular account of the similarities between Italian lava and Alpine ice is, in fact, an instructive example not just of the extent to which lava and glacial ice were routinely compared during the Romantic period, but also of the extent to which advances in understanding of the volcanic sublime by natural philosophers routinely overlapped with, and augmented, the aesthetic response to a 'scene [...] which almost baffles description'.[122] Exactly this same overlap had been evident in many of the plates illustrating Hamilton's *Campi Phlegraei*: plate XII, for example, depicts the spectacular and devastating outflow of lava from the lower slopes of Vesuvius during the December 1761 eruption, but the stated 'object' of this sublime depiction is 'to show that those who have asserted that the seat of the fire is always towards the summit, or not lower than the middle of the volcano, have been very ill informed'.[123] As so often, natural philosophy and philosophical aesthetics are combined in popular remediations of the volcanic sublime.

What Byron's quip in *Don Juan* about 'common-place' volcanic imagery also reveals, however, is the extent to which *lava*, in particular, had come to fascinate the public imagination of the late eighteenth century and Romantic period. It was Addison's *Remarks* which had offered the eighteenth-century British reading public one of its earliest, contemporary views of the old lava flows around Vesuvius: 'this looks at a distance like new-ploughed land', Addison writes, 'but as you come near it, you see nothing but a long heap of heavy disjointed clods lying upon one another', again suggesting simultaneously both destruction and fertility.[124] Addison, like many tourists and natural philosophers after him, is intrigued by the structure of the extinct flow, and seeks to explain it:

> there are innumerable cavities and interstices among the several pieces, so that the surface is all broken and irregular [...] This, I think, is a plain demonstration that these rivers were not [...] so many streams of running matter [...] I am apt to think therefore that these huge unwieldy lumps that now lie upon one another [...] remained in the melted matter rigid and unliquified.[125]

Almost one hundred years later, travellers and tourists were still echoing Addison's initial description. In his *Classical Tour*, for example, Eustace says that the old lava around Vesuvius 'resembled long stripes of new ploughed land', an image which had come to possess far greater significance for Eustace's generation than it had for Addison's because of advances in understanding, by natural philosophers, of the role played by volcanic activity in the history of the earth.[126]

Despite extensive contemporary interest in the appearance, the structure and the geological implications of extinct lava flows, however, it was, of course, molten lava which primarily fascinated the public imagination of the late eighteenth century and Romantic period. These 'fountains' and 'rivers' of 'liquid fire' (to borrow some of Shelley's phrases) could be commoditised, to a certain extent, for the curious and the wealthy, as evidenced, for example, by plate XXXVIII of Hamilton's *Campi Phlegraei*, which shows Hamilton himself lecturing near an active lava flow to some of the Neapolitan nobility.[127] For the most part, however, molten lava represented, for the late eighteenth century and Romantic period, one of the most impressive examples of the overwhelming and uncontrollable power of nature, and the quintessential symbol of the volcanic sublime.

The destructive potential of this power was re-enforced, not only by the rediscovery, in the mid-eighteenth century, of the cities of Pompeii and Herculaneum, but also by the destruction of the town of Torre del Greco by lava erupted from Vesuvius in 1794: in his *Classical Tour*, published more than 20 years after the event, Eustace described the 'still [...] shattered houses, half-buried churches, and streets almost choked with lava [...] the depth of the destructive torrent is in some places five-and-twenty feet'.[128] Felicia Hemans's poem 'The Image in Lava' (1827), for example, engages directly and emotively with this human cost of volcanic activity. The poem responds, as a note to the title explains, to 'the impression of a woman's form, with an infant clasped to the bosom, found at the uncovering of Herculaneum'.[129] The poem is ostensibly positive (and potentially radical) in affirming that such 'mournful' but 'immortal' monuments of 'human love' outlast 'the proud memorials' raised 'by conquerors of mankind': the 'image' in lava 'survives' while the 'mighty' city of 'renown' has been destroyed (ll. 41, 37, 11–12, 39–40). Despite this ostensible moral, however, the poem as a whole leaves the reader rather with an inescapable impression of the 'strange, dark fate' and 'fiery tomb' which 'fearfully' overwhelmed both 'temple and tower [and] woman's heart' (ll. 17, 115, 10, 5–7). Hemans's poem is also notable, in respect of this impression, for its apparent lack of fidelity to the details of archaeology and natural philosophy: Hemans would surely have been familiar with the many accounts of the destruction of Herculaneum (such as Winckelmann's *Critical Account*) which affirm that the city and its inhabitants were overwhelmed by pumice and ash rather than lava, and which describe a gradual rather than a sudden process. Even Eustace's *Classical Tour*, which offers arguably the most lurid account of the final moments of Pompeii and Herculaneum – when 'the earth was rocking [and] the mountain bellowing [and] the country was deluged with liquid fire and the whole atmosphere was loaded with ashes and sulphur' – slips in almost as an afterthought that while 'it is generally supposed that the destruction of this city was sudden and unexpected [...] this opinion seems ill-founded'.[130]

While the considerable advances in the understanding of the volcanic sublime made by natural philosophers during the eighteenth century might not have impacted on Hemans's poem about the destruction of Herculaneum, however, these advances certainly did equip the late eighteenth century and Romantic period with a potent vocabulary for figuring the sublimity encountered in and generated by the investigation of ostensibly unrelated areas of enquiry. The figurative use of lava had always been present in eighteenth-century writing about the volcanic sublime, for example in William Hamilton's anxiety that the continued adherence to theoretical 'systems' of natural philosophy that were unverified by 'self experience' would progressively 'heap error upon error', like the accumulation of a lava flow.[131] But increased understanding of the regenerative potential of even the most apparently catastrophic volcanic eruption enabled late eighteenth-century and Romantic-period writers to remediate the volcanic sublime as a particularly effective figure for a number of processes whose often invisible operations could result in sudden, spectacular consequences, and whose apparently destructive or traumatic effects might conceal hidden or long-term benefits. Foremost amongst these processes were the operations of the human mind, and the dynamics of political change.

Byron's well-known definition of 'poetry' as 'the lava of the imagination, whose eruption prevents an explosion', to take a relatively familiar example, highlights the remediation of the volcanic sublime to figure what would now be called, in a rather more limiting sense, psychological processes. This definition, which Byron offers in a letter to his future wife, Annabella Milbanke, on 29 November 1813, is often said to anticipate subsequent, Freudian descriptions of the relationship between repression, the unconscious and artistic creativity, to say nothing at all about the provenance of those descriptions in eighteenth-century and Romantic-period models of the mind.[132] The point, however, consists precisely in the relationship between Byron's description of the creative process and the contemporary ideas in natural philosophy by which that description is enabled: that the build-up of magma in a volcano could result in significantly different eruptive outcomes. 'Poetry', in this sense, emerges from Byron's description not simply as a (potentially therapeutic) means of self-expression, but as an art form which has (potentially) immense destructive and/or transformative potential, both for the individual poet and for their audience, as O'Connor has recently shown in his attention to Byron's remediation of Cuvier's theories, in *Cain*, 'as a gift from Lucifer'.[133] Hence, Byron's remediation of the volcanic sublime is not simply a colourful or 'Romantic' image, which can be read as an anticipation of subsequent psychological theory. Rather, Byron's remediation is a sophisticated description, enabled in part by contemporary natural philosophy, both of the means through which poetry might be produced and of the nature and the possible impact of poetry itself.

We might also remember, here, Samuel Taylor Coleridge's letter to Joseph Cottle of September 1814, in which Coleridge invokes his recollections of the crater of Etna to figure the 'impenetrable' 'darkness' of opium addiction and spiritual crisis, problems apparently without solution:

> I recollect when I stood on the summit of Etna, and darted my gaze down the crater; the immediate vicinity was discernible, till lower down, obscurity gradually terminated in total darkness. Such figures exemplify many truths revealed in the Bible. We pursue them until, from the imperfection of our faculties, we are lost in impenetrable night.[134]

As with Saussure's comparison of the head for heights needed in mountaineering with the ability safely to negotiate ethical dilemmas, then, for Coleridge, the 'impenetrable' depths of the volcanic crater can successfully embody the no less impenetrable 'darkness' by which the mind, in despair, is capable of being confronted.

Byron and Coleridge might actually have taken a hint for their descriptions from Germaine de Staël's widely read novel *Corinna; or, Italy* (1807), which contains an extended and multifaceted engagement with the volcanic sublime. In Chapter IV of Book XIII, Corinna, the Italian poetess of the title, performs an improvisation on the landscape around Naples. In the second stanza of this improvisation, Corinna apostrophises volcanic activity and makes an explicit link between poetry and volcanic fire understood, in the terms of natural philosophy, as at once a destructive and creative force:

> Fire, the devouring life which first creates
> The world which it consumes, struck terror most
> When its laws were least known. – Ah! Nature then
> Revealed her secrets but to Poetry.[135]

The nature of the cultural link between poetry and a primitive response to the volcanic sublime which Corinna suggests, here, is made explicit in Chapter I of Book XIII of the novel, which describes Corinna's visit to Vesuvius with the self-exiled Scottish peer, Lord Nelvil. In a passage which is heavily indebted to speculation during the French Enlightenment about the origins of religious belief in the reaction of primitive peoples to the natural sublime, *Corinna* suggests not only that the conventional cultural images of hell are based on the volcanic sublime, but also that the very idea of hell probably originated in the reaction of primitive cultures to a landscape so apparently 'hostile to all that breathes'.[136] 'All that surrounds volcano', the novel affirms of Vesuvius:

> recalls the idea of hell, and the descriptions of the poets are, doubtless, borrowed from this spot. It is here that we can form an idea of a malevolent power opposing the designs of Providence. In contemplating such an abode, we ask ourselves, whether bounty alone presides over the phenomena of creation, or whether some hidden principle forces nature, like man, to acts of ferocity.[137]

This passage reveals not only the extent to which increased understanding of volcanic activity led to the secularisation of the classical, religious connotations of the volcanic sublime, but also, as these traditional connotations were called into question, to the emergence of a new and increasingly diverse range of mediations and remediations of the volcanic sublime.

François Gérard's celebrated painting *Corinne au Cap Misène* (1819), for example, takes up and extends the connection between poetry and the volcanic sublime which Corinna herself suggests in the moment which Gérard depicts. The painting – which shows Corinna improvising, with her eyes raised, in front of a rapt audience, while, in the background, a vast plume of smoke rises from Vesuvius – suggests an explicit, if unexplained comparison between these ostensibly diverse outpourings of energy: both are creative, both are 'natural', and both are potentially destructive. Indeed, in this respect, Gérard's canvas is comparable to Byron's definition of 'poetry' as 'the lava of the imagination', which of course Gérard could not have known, although his representation of Lord Nelvil has a decidedly Byronic look about it!

Staël's own account of Corinna's and Nelvil's visit to Vesuvius, however, displays a number of these new remediations of the volcanic sublime. Staël's description of the molten lava flows that Corinna and Nelvil witness, for example, draws upon descriptions of lava flow by natural philosophers to offer a kind of moral parable which uses lava flow as a figure for the slow but inevitable onslaught of mortality, in a strategy which recalls the parallel which Saussure drew between mountaineering and morality.[138] 'We hear, as we approach it', the novel affirms of the lava, 'a little sparkling noise, which terrifies us the more from its being light and trifling, from cunning seeming to unite with strength':

> thus the tiger steals with slow and measured steps upon his prey. The lava creeps along without hastening or losing a moment; when its passage is opposed by a wall, or an edifice of any kind, it stops, and accumulating its black and bituminous waves, swallows up, in its burning torrent, the obstacle that resisted it. Its progress is not so rapid, that men may not escape it; but like Time, it reaches the imprudent and the aged, who, seeing it approach, heavily and silently, imagine themselves secure.[139]

Staël's account of Vesuvius also emphasises the centrality, to remediations of the volcanic sublime, of the 'terrifying' combination of hidden, subterranean activity with devastating eruptive potential. 'The wind is heard and seen', she writes, 'in the whirlwinds of fire from the gulf whence proceeds the lava. We feel terrified at what passes in the bowels of the earth, which secret storm causes to tremble beneath our feet.'[140] And as with Byron's later definition of poetry, Staël's account of this sublime combination of obscure depth and eruptive power remediates the volcanic sublime as a figure for the operations of the human mind: Lord Nelvil reads the 'terrible', 'infernal' landscape before him not as an image of hell but as an image of his own mind ravaged by the psychological trauma of guilt, of 'the remorse that preys upon the heart [...] of that dreadful thought – *irreparable* !'[141]

Staël's use of lava flow as a figure for the slow but inevitable onslaught of mortality may itself echo Brydone's account of the destruction of Catania when lava, erupted from Etna in 1669, 'scaled the walls' of the city.[142] 'It must have been a noble sight', Brydone observes, rather disingenuously:

> The walls are 64 palms high (near 60 feet), and of a great strength; otherwise they must have been borne down by the force of the flaming matter which rose over this height, and seems to have mounted considerably above the top of the wall before it made its entry; at last it came down, sweeping before it every saint in the calendar, who were drawn up in order of battle on purpose to oppose its passage; and marching on in triumph, annihilated, in a like manner, every object that dared to oppose it.[143]

The political undertones of Brydone's account of the destruction of Catania – the 'flaming' lava 'triumphs' over and 'annihilates' the symbols of a superstitious Catholicism – is in keeping with the general political tone of his *Tour*, which, for example, also frequently contrasts the political and religious oppression endured by the population of the 'luxuriant' Sicily with the republican freedoms enjoyed by the inhabitants of 'barren' Switzerland.[144] Political concerns, conversely, are largely absent from Staël's remediation of lava flow in *Corinna*. However, as we have already noted, there was a clear tendency, in eighteenth-century writing about volcanic activity, to link the volcanic sublime with popular political instability. In the years following the French Revolution, this tendency develops and extends as writers and artists on both sides of the English Channel begin consistently to appropriate the volcanic sublime as a figure for the spectacular politics of revolution, and, in particular, as a figure for both the horrors and the transformative potential of political violence.

A number of recent studies have examined the use of volcanic imagery in the iconography of the French Revolution itself, notably

Mona Ozouf's *Festivals and the French Revolution* and, more recently, Mary Miller's '"Mountain, Become a Volcano": The Image of the Volcano in the Rhetoric of the French Revolution'.[145] Miller's detailed and impressive survey describes two distinct phases in the use of such imagery. In the years before and after the Reign of Terror, Miller suggests, volcanic imagery had predominantly negative connotations, with the volcano functioning both 'as a symbol for the supposed instability and self-destructiveness of the revolutionary regime [and] as an ambiguous, threatening symbol of potential violence and disruption'.[146] The potential for obscure, subterranean volcanic processes to produce a catastrophic eruption largely without warning was a key trope of this salutary use of the volcano as a figure for the hazards of revolution, as in the example which Miller cites from Honoré-Maxime Isnard, who compares 'the current state of Europe [in January 1792]' to 'the menacing tranquillity of Etna': 'silence reigns on the mountain, but open it up suddenly and you will find an abyss of fire, torrents of lava that are preparing the next eruptions'.[147] What is absent from these remediations of the volcanic sublime, conversely, is any understanding drawn from natural philosophy of the potential long-term benefits of apparently catastrophic volcanic eruptions, that is, any sense of the potential long-term rewards of revolutionary violence. During the Terror itself, however, it was precisely this same problematic awareness of the potential long-term benefits of catastrophic volcanic activity which underpinned the transformation of the volcano, within Revolutionary iconography, from a figure of warning to a figure for the simultaneously purgative and regenerative force of Terror.[148]

Miller's survey of the use of volcanic imagery in the iconography of the French Revolution confirms the cultural-historical trend that we have been charting in this chapter: the increased understanding of volcanic processes generated by natural philosophers during the eighteenth century underpins the various and varying political remediations of the volcanic sublime during the Revolution, enabling the remediation of the volcano both as an image of destruction and as an image of (albeit catastrophic) regeneration. Indeed, as Miller suggests, the use of such imagery during the French Revolution forms part of the wider dialogue in the period between natural philosophy and various other forms of understanding and representing the world that we have been describing: natural philosophy informs political iconography, but political iconography also impacts upon natural philosophy.

There has been some investigation of the extent to which this dialogue between the natural and the human sciences continues in English

Romantic-period writing about political change, such as Geoffrey Matthews's and my own discussion of the role of the volcanic sublime in the political poetry of Percy Bysshe Shelley.[149] While a systematic description of the widespread remediation of the volcanic sublime in Romantic-period writing about political change is clearly beyond the scope of my discussion in this chapter, I hope to have outlined some of the many genres of that mediation, with their common tropes of *eruption* and *depth* inherited from eighteenth-century natural philosophy and travel-writing.

3
'The region of beauty and delight': Reimagining the Polar Sublime[1]

> Lands doomed by Nature to perpetual frigidness; never to feel the warmth of the sun's rays; whose horrible and savage aspect I have not words to describe. Such are the lands we have discovered; what then may we expect those to be, which lie still farther to the South?
> – James Cook, *A Voyage towards the South Pole and Round the World* (1777)[2]

The public fascination with the Arctic and the Antarctic during the late eighteenth century and Romantic period will be familiar enough to most readers of Romantic-period literature from the prominent role played by the polar regions in two of the period's best-known works: Samuel Taylor Coleridge's *Rime of the Ancyent Marinere* (1798) and Mary Shelley's *Frankenstein* (1818).[3] This contemporary fascination with the poles can be explained, at least in part, as Peter Kitson has observed, by the fact that throughout the Romantic period, the Arctic and the Antarctic remained two of the least-known parts of the world and hence could typify for the European imagination 'the otherness of sublime nature'.[4] In this respect, the place of the polar regions in the European imagination complements descriptions within eighteenth-century British philosophical aesthetics, by figures like Edmund Burke, of the role of the obscure or the hidden in generating sublime effect.[5] As Eric Wilson puts it in *The Spiritual History of Ice*, 'of all the landscapes in nature, those that are frozen are perhaps the most sublime. The reason: the blankness of ice.'[6] However, the unknown-ness of the poles is only part of the story to be told here because while it is true that no European explorer reached the North or the South Pole until the twentieth century, it is also true that by the start of the Romantic period, European literature had long been replete with speculation and sheer excitement about what and who might eventually be discovered there. This speculation ranged from classical and medieval myths about the Hyperboreans and Antichthones to seventeenth- and eighteenth-century theories about undiscovered paradises in ice-free polar seas: witness Walton's confidence, in *Frankenstein*, that he would discover, in the Arctic, a 'region of beauty and delight [...] a land surpassing in wonders and in beauty every region hitherto discovered on the habitable globe'.[7] Hence, whilst the geographical Arctic and Antarctic remained largely unknown during the Romantic period, both regions had some status as 'classic ground' in the European imagination, as environments overwritten with a range of geographical specific values and associations.

As Eric Wilson in *The Spiritual History of Ice* and Francis Spufford in *I May Be Some Time: Ice and the English Imagination* have begun to show, the cultural history of the polar regions during the late eighteenth century and Romantic period is the history of the transformation of the place that the Arctic and the Antarctic occupied in the European imagination.[8] In essence, it is the history of the reimagining of the polar sublime. This reimagining was driven by the surge in exploration of the polar regions during the eighteenth century. Some of this exploration was ostensibly conducted for the advancement of natural philosophy, as, for example, with James Cook's attempts in 1772–74 to discover a southern continent in the Antarctic, the so-called *terra australis incognita* which influential figures like Joseph Banks and Alexander Dalrymple, the first hydrographer of the British Admiralty, had argued must exist. Other voyages had a more obvious commercial motivation, such as the numerous attempts by Constantine Phipps and the others sent by the British Admiralty to discover the long-fabled Northwest Passage through the Arctic ice to the Pacific Ocean. But of course, as so often in the landscapes of the sublime, natural philosophy and imperial expansion went hand in hand, and what Carl Thompson remarks of the experiences of Park and Bruce in Africa is equally true of contemporary engagements with the polar regions: the exploration of the far North and the far South was 'never just a contribution to a growing body of purely scientific knowledge', and anyone engaging with the polar regions was to a greater or a lesser extent an 'agent', and a would-be 'enabler', of imperialism.[9] What these numerous voyages did discover, however, was an almost indescribable emptiness: in the high northern and southern latitudes, where many had imagined undiscovered island paradises and uncorrupted natural societies, explorers like Cook and Phipps found only frozen seas and icy wastes, what Cook described as 'lands doomed by Nature to perpetual frigidness [...] whose horrid and savage aspect I have not words to describe'.[10] The discovery of the true polar sublime, then, was the discovery of absence, the discovery of the *inhuman*: no new continents were found, no passage through the Arctic seas, only silent, frigid emptiness. Hence, while areas like the Alps or the Italian volcanoes were in the process of becoming 'classic ground' during the eighteenth century and Romantic period, in the process of acquiring new cultural associations, contemporary European encounters with the Arctic and the Antarctic served conversely to strip away rather than to augment the cultural associations which the polar regions had acquired in the European imagination. The reality of the polar sublime was hostile not only to human life, but even to the imagination itself. To adopt the terminology of Kant's 'Analytic of the Sublime', polar ice proved arguably the most potent example, for the eighteenth century, of 'the inadequacy of the imagination' that is revealed by the initial engagement with the 'natural sublime'.[11] Hence, whilst I will agree, in this chapter, with Wilson's claim that the Romantic generation 'are among the first poets, essayists, and novelists to embrace ice', I will part company from Wilson's subsequent assertion that the Romantics saw the polar ice as 'a *positive* – not neutral or negative – fact and symbol: as a unique manifestation of the principle of *life*'.[12]

Building on the work of Spufford, Wilson and others, this chapter examines the cultural history of the polar sublime during the eighteenth century and Romantic period, tracing that history across a range of texts which still remain relatively unknown within both academic and more popular discussions of the place of the 'natural sublime' in the period, but which had a contemporary influence that extended far beyond that of many of the texts now considered canonical.[13] As I have said in the introduction to this book, my aim in this chapter is to extend the 'imaginative history of polar exploration' which Spufford has begun to describe, 'a history of assumptions, responses to landscape, cultural fascinations, aesthetic attraction to the cold regions', by charting the early moments of that history in the eighteenth century and Romantic period.[14] I take as my point of entry into this particular genre of engagement with the 'natural sublime' those two emblematic remediations of the Antarctic and the Arctic: *The Rime of the Ancyent Marinere* and *Frankenstein*. Much interesting scholarly work has already been done to document Coleridge's and Shelley's debts to particular expedition narratives, or to specific theories about the polar regions, most recently by Wilson, who reads Coleridge's poem as a kind of interiorisation of the polar expedition narrative, in which the 'Mariner's violence toward the

Antarctic whiteness [...] results from tyrannical desire to impose upon Life his dream of control'.[15] My purpose in this chapter, however, is not so much to maintain this familiar opposition between canonical text and non-canonical source as it is to describe and to relocate these canonical texts within the wider contemporary genre of engagement with the polar sublime of which the original comprised a part, and by which the public was 'continually pestered', as the German naturalist Johann Reinhold Forster, who had sailed with Cook in 1772–74, put it with characteristic acerbity in his *History of the Voyages and Discoveries Made in the North* (1786).[16] As part of that wider genre, both the *Rime* and *Frankenstein* exemplify the ongoing, 'Romantic' attempt to remediate the emptiness that had been found in the polar regions; in essence, the attempt to reclaim that emptiness for the imagination. Both texts also anticipate the way in which that emptiness would eventually be remediated in the mid-nineteenth century, when a series of disastrous British expeditions, like Franklin's last in 1845, made it possible for the British, at least, to reimagine the Arctic and the Antarctic as a theatre of the tragic-heroic defeat of hubristic aspiration, a figuration which is central to the remediation of the polar regions in both the *Ancyent Marinere* and *Frankenstein*. From this reimagining would come the idea, still potent today, of the British polar explorer as Romantic hero, partaking of the sublimity against which he matched himself: as key a component of the enduring cultural legacy of Shackleton and Scott, for example, as it is absent from the legacy of the pragmatic and successful Amundsen.

'The ice was all around': the *Ancyent Marinere* and the Antarctic

William Wordsworth's claim that he suggested the Antarctic sequence of the *Ancyent Marinere* to Coleridge after reading George Shelvocke's *A Voyage round the World by Way of the Great South Sea* (1723) has been well documented by commentators on the poem.[17] 'I had been reading in Shelvocke's *Voyages* [how] while doubling Cape Horn, they frequently saw albatrosses in that latitude,' Wordsworth wrote: '"Suppose", said I, "you representing him as having killed one of these birds on entering the South Sea, and that the tutelary spirits of these regions take upon them to avenge the crime."'[18] In fact, as commentators have since recognised, Wordsworth's 'suggestion' was drawn in its entirety from Shelvocke's extended account of his experiences at 60°S in October 1719. The passage begins with Shelvocke's description of the death of a crewman,

William Camell, who fell from the rigging when his hands became too numbed by the cold for him to hold on any longer. Shelvocke then continues to affirm that:

> The cold is certainly much more insupportable in these than in the same Latitudes to the *Northward* [...] In short, one would think it impossible that any thing living could subsist in so rigid [perhaps a telling slip for 'frigid'?] a climate; and, indeed, we all observed, that we had not the sight of one fish of any kind, since we were come to the Southward of the streights of *le Mair* [between Tierra del Fuego and Staten Island] nor one sea-bird, except a disconsolate black *Albitross*, who accompanied us for several days, hovering about us as if he had lost himself, till *Hatley* (my second Captain), observing, in one of his melancholy fits [a known symptom of scurvy], that this bird was always hovering near us, imagin'd, from his colour, that it might be some ill omen. That which, I suppose, induced him the more to encourage his superstition, was the continued series of contrary tempestuous winds, which had oppress'd us ever since we had got into this sea. But be that as it would, he, after some fruitless attempts, at length, shot the *Albitross*, not doubting (perhaps) that we should have a fair wind after it.[19]

The essentials of the albatross-episode from the *Ancyent Marinere* are all present in this passage, apart, of course, from the arbitrariness attending the killing of the bird in Coleridge's poem, for which act no rationale is given by poet or speaker, and which consequently provides fertile ground for the speculation of readers and critics alike.

In his seminal study of Coleridge's use of source material in *The Road to Xanadu*, John Livingstone Lowes was the first to document the extent to which Coleridge borrowed the details of the entire Antarctic sequence of the *Ancyent Marinere* not just from Shelvocke's *Voyage*, but from a range of seventeenth- and eighteenth-century writings about both the Antarctic and the Arctic, also including Samuel Purchas's *His Pilgrimage* (1613), Frederick Martens's *Voyage into Spitzbergen and Greenland* (1694), David Cranz's *The History of Greenland* (1767), Constantine Phipp's *A Voyage towards the North Pole* (1774) and James Cook's *A Voyage towards the South Pole and Round the World* (1777). Critics following Lowes have broadened this palette even further, such as in Jonathan Lamb's reading of the *Marinere* as a poem about scurvy, Sarah Moss's account of Coleridge's engagement with Hans Egede's *Description of Greenland* (1745) and Wilson's reading in *The Spiritual History of Ice*.[20]

The combined effect of this scholarship has been to give a comprehensive picture of Coleridge's reliance on source material for nearly every detail of the Antarctic sequence of the *Ancyent Marinere*, a picture which complicates not only Wordsworth's claim about the origins of that sequence in *his* reading, but which also complicates various 'Romantic' assertions about originality, creativity and oral culture in *Lyrical Ballads* more generally. While this source-hunting has been illuminating, however, it has also tended to distort the relationship between the Antarctic sequence of the *Ancyent Marinere* and the wider eighteenth-century and Romantic-period genre of engagement with the polar sublime which is both mediated in and remediated by Coleridge's poem. The emphasis on discovering Coleridge's sources for the *Marinere* has established an arbitrary and historically inaccurate dichotomy between a canonical poem and its now largely unfamiliar sources, a dichotomy which not only obscures the contemporary influence of Coleridge's source texts, but which also effectively detaches Coleridge's poem from its most immediate cultural context in the contemporary genre of engagements with the polar sublime. We can begin to use the *Marinere* as a point of re-entry into that genre, however, by returning to the text to which Wordsworth first linked the Antarctic sequence: George Shelvocke's *Voyage round the World*.

Shelvocke's journey on the *Speedwell*, which is now remembered mainly on account of its connection with the *Ancyent Marinere*, was neither a voyage of exploration nor of commerce, but a privateering expedition against Spanish possessions in South America, sponsored by the English government during the War of the Quadruple Alliance (1718–20). In his account of the early part of the expedition, Shelvocke describes how his ship, like the Ancyent Marinere's, was 'driven' unintentionally far to the south by 'the most severe storms': 'prodigious seas, much larger than any I ever saw', and 'winds reigning [...] tempestuously without intermission'.[21] Once again, it was in these high southern latitudes that Shelvocke and his crew encountered the albatross destined to be immortalised in Coleridge's poem. But the *Ancyent Marinere* is also indebted, in more general terms, to the image of the polar sublime that Shelvocke presents in his *Voyage*. He describes the 'extremity' of cold which had 'cas'd the masts and every rope with ice' and 'continual misty weather, which laid us under hourly apprehensions of falling foul of Islands of ice [...] and many alarms by fog banks, and other false appearances', as well as 'continual squals of sleet, snow and rain, and the heavens were perpetually hid from us by gloomy dismal clouds'.[22] Beyond the extremity of the physical environment, however, Shelvocke also lays repeated emphasis on the isolation felt by the crew as they ventured into the terrifyingly unknown. 'I must own', he affirms of their time at 61°S:

> that this navigation is truly melancholy, and was the more so to us, who were by ourselves without a companion [Shelvocke had lost touch with his escort vessel, the *Success*, early in the voyage], which would somewhat have diverted our thoughts from the reflection of being in such a remote part of the world, and as it were, separated from the rest of mankind to struggle with the dangers of a stormy climate, far distant from any port to have recourse to, in case of the loss of masts, or any other accident; nor any chance of receiving assistance from any other ship. These considerations were enough to deject our spirits, when we were sensible of the hourly danger we were in.[23]

The link between solitude or isolation and the sublime is often drawn within eighteenth-century British philosophical aesthetics, and both Shelvocke's description of the harsh physical environment and his sense of extreme isolation, off-the-map in a hostile, icy ocean, pervade the Antarctic sequence of the *Ancyent Marinere*.[24] But despite its resonance with contemporary descriptions of the sublime within the genre of philosophical aesthetics, Shelvocke's image of the polar sublime is signally not the image which the eighteenth century had inherited from classical and medieval speculation about the polar regions, nor indeed would it become the dominant image of the Antarctic sublime until at least half-a-century after Shelvocke published his *Voyage*. The version of the Antarctic sublime which the *Ancyent Marinere* remediates was, in other words, the product of some 50 years of recent cultural history.

As Eric Wilson observes in *The Spiritual History of Ice*, eighteenth-century Europe inherited a complex vision of the polar regions from classical, medieval and Renaissance speculation about the Arctic and the Antarctic.[25] The terms Arctic and Antarctic derive from the ancient Greek words *arktikos* and *antarktikos*, and of the Antarctic, in particular, early eighteenth-century Europe actually possessed little more factual knowledge than did classical geographers and philosophers like Strabo, Aristotle and Ptolemy; the continent itself was not even sighted by Europeans until 1820. The Greek term *antarktikos* means 'the opposite of the Arctic', of which region Greek culture did have some limited, first-hand knowledge, and which was named for its proximity to *arktos*: the constellation Ursa Major, or the 'Great Bear'.[26] Classical Greek geographies of the Antarctic, conversely, remained wholly speculative. As Wilson points out, however, two consistent strands of thought can be discerned: first, the idea that the northern and southern hemispheres were essentially mirror images of each other, an idea signalled in the etymology of *antarktikos* as the 'opposite' of the Arctic; second, and less prevalent, the idea that the actual poles were the seat of hidden terrestrial paradises, forever cut off from the known world by the hostile environment surrounding them.[27]

Clearly, few in the eighteenth century would still have believed in the fantastic and monstrous creatures with which the classical and medieval imaginations had peopled the Antarctic. However, the classical idea of the southern hemisphere as the mirror of the northern persisted long into the eighteenth century in the form of the influential hypothesis that a large, undiscovered southern continent must exist to counterbalance the known landmasses of the northern hemisphere: the so-called *terra australis incognita*. One of the most influential of the many proponents of this theory in Britain was the Scot Alexander Dalrymple (1737–1808), who would become, in 1795, the first hydrographer of the British Admiralty.[28] Noting that 'we continue ignorant, so far as to absolute experience, whether the southern hemisphere be an immense mass of water, or whether it contains another continent', Dalrymple argued, in a series of publications including his *Account of the Discoveries Made in the South Pacific Ocean* (1767) and *An Historical Collection of the Several Voyages and Discoveries in the South Pacific Ocean* (1770–71), that:

> it has been commonly alleged, and perhaps not without good reason, from a consideration of the weight of land to water, that a Continent is wanting on the South of the Equator, to counterpoise the land on the North, and to maintain the equilibrium necessary for the earth's motion. On a view of the two hemispheres this will appear obvious.[29]

On the basis of this 'strong presumption', Dalrymple offered eighteenth-century British readers sublime vistas of 'totally undiscovered, valuable and extensive countries' lying below Africa and South America, the discovery of which could do for Britain what the discovery of South America had done for Spain and Portugal.[30] 'There can be no object more interesting to a maritime and commercial state', Dalrymple affirmed, in the introduction to his *Historical Collection of Voyages*, without even the slightest nod towards the potential for disinterested advances in natural philosophy:

> than *discovery* of *New Lands*, to invigorate the hand of industry by opening new vents for manufactures, and by a *New Trade* to increase the active wealth and naval power of the country.[31]

'Upon such grounds', Dalrymple sums up, 'there can be no object more important than discoveries in the South Sea.'[32]

As Dalrymple's frequent invocation of the records of earlier voyages in the Southern Ocean as part of the titles of his own published works makes clear (many are translations from the Spanish, etc.), his speculations were supported by a range of sixteenth- and seventeenth-century accounts, many of them rather less than reliable, as it turned out. But Dalrymple's theories sparked widespread interest. A commentator in *The Annual Register* for 1777, for example, observed that Dalrymple's 'opinion' had 'prevailed, and was so well supported by philosophical reasoning, and inferences drawn from analogy, that the existence of a vast continent [...] became generally believed'.[33]

There was conflicting evidence, of course: the testimony of some of those, like Shelvocke, who had sailed the Southern Ocean and found nothing. But in fairness to him, Dalrymple was not overly wary of presenting this evidence either. In his *Collection of Voyages, Chiefly in the Southern Atlantick Ocean* (1775), for example, he included transcripts from the journal kept by Edmond Halley during a voyage in 1699–1700 made to chart variations in compass activity across the earth's surface, the results of which were published in Halley's *General Chart of the Variation of the Compass* (1701). Halley's ship reached 52°S in the Atlantic and, in the transcripts published by Dalrymple, Halley describes impenetrable mists and extreme cold, to which the sunshine offered 'no abatement', leading him to conclude that 'for ought appears this Climate is what Horace means when he says, *Pigris ubi nulla Campis – Arbor aestiua recreatur Aura*'.[34] Moreover, what Halley and his crew initially took for undiscovered land turned out, on closer inspection, to be 'nothing else but one body of Ice of an incredible height', during the approach to which 'another Mountain of Ice began to appear on our Leebow':

> We got clear; God be praised: this danger made my men reflect on the hazards we run, in being alone without a Consort, and of the inevitable loss of us all, in case we staved our ship, which might so easily happen amongst these Mountains of Ice in the Fogs which are so thick and frequent here.[35]

The sublime prospect of discovery is thus transformed into a terrifying encounter with a hostile, inhuman waste, an entirely different kind of sublime.

Despite this kind of first-hand testimony to the contrary, however, Dalrymple's hypothesis of an Edenic *terra australis incognita* sparked not just popular but also official interest. As the *Annual Register*'s commentator observed, 'this new world naturally became an object of consideration with the maritime and commercial powers who hold possessions in America and has [...] excited, by turns, the spirit of enterprise and discovery, in the Spaniards, Dutch, English, and French'.[36] In a series of letters to the Prime Minister, Frederick North, in July and August of 1772, Dalrymple urged that an 'expedition' should be sent 'without delay' in search of the *terra australis incognita* in order to ensure England's territorial claim.[37] Dalrymple, who had considerable experience serving in the East India Company, proposed leading this exhibition himself, and drew up detailed plans, costings, and even a schedule of no less than 34 'fundamental and unalterable laws' to form the basis of civil society in the new colony.[38] The situation had become urgent, in Dalrymple's opinion, when unsuccessful English attempts to locate the southern continent, by John Byron (in 1764–66) and Philip Carteret (in 1766–69), were followed by the news that Yves-Joseph de Kerguelen Trémarec had discovered and claimed for France, in February 1772, what he believed to be the tip of a large Antarctic landmass, which he named 'La France Australe'. Kerguelen Trémarec, who did not actually set foot on this new land, returned to France immediately to announce his discovery, and made a pre-emptive and, as it turned out, entirely fictional, report to Louis XVI, in which he claimed to have discovered a continent whose resources would rival South America: a personal imagining entirely in keeping with high-profile contemporary engagements like Dalrymple's.[39] Inspired by this report, Louis XVI sent Kerguelen Trémarec back the following year, with three ships and the materials to found a colony. When Kerguelen Trémarec discovered the truth – that what he had supposed to be a new continent was in fact only the island group which now bears his name, and that far from a polar paradise, it was a desolate, uninhabited wilderness – he returned, disappointed, to France, where he was promptly court-martialled and imprisoned.[40] When James Cook later made landfall at the same islands during his third voyage, in December 1776, the bleak environment which he found prompted him to dub them the 'Desolation Islands', although he subsequently decided to rename them in honour of their discoverer.

It was James Cook, too, who amongst his many other accomplishments finally shattered for the eighteenth century the dream of an Antarctic paradise and revealed, in its place, a sublime, inhuman waste. Cook had demonstrated during his first voyage around the world on the *Endeavour*, in 1768–71, that if the fabled *terra australis incognita* did indeed exist, then it must lie to the south of New Zealand, which he had circumnavigated and charted. Dalrymple's petitions and publications were instrumental in the Royal Society's decision to commission James Cook to search for the *terra australis incognita* on his second voyage, on the *Resolution*, in 1772–75.[41] The *Annual Register*'s review of Cook's *Voyage towards the South Pole* recalls the anticipation which surrounded this attempt 'to penetrate as far as it was possible towards the Antarctic pole', invoking as a comparison such 'splendid and extraordinary events as attended the discoveries of Columbus, de Gama, and other early navigators'.[42] But the outcome of Cook's voyage proved very different, and decisively transformed European perceptions of the Antarctic sublime.

Cook's expedition crossed the Antarctic Circle twice during the winters of 1772–73 and 1773–74 – becoming the first Europeans known to have done so – and, on Sunday 30 January 1774, Cook's ship reached 71°10'S, just 120 km from the Antarctic coast.[43] But Cook did not sight Antarctica: all he discovered was an empty ocean and ice which finally impeded his progress towards the south. Cook's discovery of this Antarctic 'nullity', as *The Annual Register* called it, was transmitted to the eighteenth-century reading public through a profusion of different sources.[44] The earliest record of Cook's experiences, however, is the journal kept by Cook himself during the voyage. Although this journal was not made available to the public in its original form until many years after Cook's death, it provided the basis for a number of contemporary accounts, including Cook's own *Voyage towards the South Pole* (1777), in which Cook follows his journal very closely. It also provides an interesting control against which to test the ongoing remediation of the Antarctic sublime, not least Cook's own remediation of what he had found.

Cook's journal is, in the main, a practical record of latitudes, longitudes, atmospheric conditions and navigational manoeuvres – a far cry, in other words, from the 'Romantic', and I use the word advisedly, treatment which his expedition would later receive. Where Cook does make reference to the numerous 'Mountains of Ice' which his ship encountered, these references are also, in the main, of a procedural nature, as in, for example, Cook's entry for Friday 18 December 1772:

> Dangerous as it is sailing a mongest the floating Rocks [icebergs] in a thick Fog and unknown Sea, yet it is preferable to being intangled with Field Ice under the same circumstances. The danger to be apprehended from this Ice is the geting fast in it where beside the damage a ship might receive might be detain'd some time. I have heard of a Greenland Ship lying nine Weeks fast in this kind of Ice.[45]

However, Cook does also, on rare occasions, acknowledge the affective power of this bleak, inhuman environment. In his entry for Wednesday 24 February 1773, for example, Cook affirms of the ice that:

> great as these dangers are, they are now become so familiar to us that the apprehensions they cause are never of long duration and are in some measure compencated by the very curious and romantick Views many of these Islands [of ice] exhibit and which are greatly heightned by the foaming and dashing of the waves against them and into the several holes and caverns which are formed in the most of them, in short the whole exhibits a View which can only be discribed by the pencle of an able painter and at once fills the mind with admiration and horror, the first is occasioned by the beautifullniss of the Picture and the latter by the danger attending it.[46]

The combination of 'admiration and horror' which Cook describes as the effect of the Antarctic environment had, of course, been a staple component of descriptions of the sublime within eighteenth-century British philosophical aesthetics since Addison's seminal 'Pleasures of the Imagination' essays, and that combination had also been explored at length by Burke in his *Philosophical Enquiry*. Hence, it is hardly surprising that it was precisely these 'curious and romantick Views', with their ability to inspire 'admiration and horror', the mainstays of technical descriptions of the sublime, which would be taken up and expanded by subsequent, high-profile accounts of Cook's expedition – including, to a certain extent, Cook's own *Voyage towards the South Pole*.

British philosophical aestheticians and French ideologues alike had also long emphasised the role of the imagination in the response to the 'natural sublime', with rationalists on either side of the Channel, in particular, viewing the imaginative response to the 'natural sublime' with distrust, and as a source of everything from primitive superstition to mainstream religious belief. Cook's account of the Antarctic sublime in his journal similarly foregrounds the activity of the imagination in responding to the harsh environment. Indeed, Cook describes precisely that tendency of the imagination, which marks the accounts of so many of the travellers to the landscapes of the sublime, to try to reconfigure the affective power of the extreme environment in a more comforting form: in this case, to populate the Antarctic emptiness. In Cook's entry for Saturday 26 December 1772, for example, when Cook's 'drunken crew' were recovering from their Christmas celebrations, Cook observed of the loose field ice that 'it appeared like Corral Rocks [and] exhibited such a variety of figuers that there is not a animal on Earth that was not in some degree represented by it'.[47] Nor, however, does Cook neglect to mention the numerous actual fauna which his ship encountered, noting, for example, on 12 January 1773, that 'Mr. Forster [Johann Reinhold Forster, discussed below] shott an Albatross [...] Some of the Seamen call them Quaker Birds, from their grave Colour.'[48] The eighteenth century was clearly not a good time to be an albatross in the Antarctic.

Concerning the main object of his expedition, however, his search 'after those imaginary Lands', Cook remains consistently sanguine.[49] Noting the 'general received opinion that Ice is formed near land', Cook acknowledged that the icebergs and field ice which they encountered 'must' indicate 'land in the Neighbourhood'.[50] However, Cook remained convinced that the extent of the surrounding field ice must of necessity render any such land unapproachable, and that even could it be approached, it must be a frozen waste rather than the polar paradise imagined by Dalrymple and others. At 67°15'S, on 18 January 1773, Cook records that 'the Ice was so thick and close that we could proceed no further [...] from the masthead I could see nothing to the Southward but Ice, in the whole extent from East to WSW without the least appearance of any partition'.[51] And at 71°10'S, on Sunday 30 January 1774, Cook was confronted with field ice which 'extended East and West in a straight line far beyond our sight [...] The Clowds near the horizon were of a perfect snow whiteness and were difficult to be distinguished from the Ice hills whose lofty summits reached the Clowds [...] In this field we counted Ninety Seven Ice Hills or Mountains, many of them vastly large.'[52] 'I should not have hisitated one moment in declaring it my opinion', Cook concludes, 'that the Ice we now see extended in a solid body quite to the Pole':

> I will not say it was impossible anywhere to get among this Ice, but I will assert that the bare attempting of it would be a very dangerous enterprise and what I believe no man in my situation would have thought of. I whose ambition leads me not only farther than any other man before me, but as far as I think it possible for man to go, was not sorry at meeting this interruption, as it in some measure relieved us from the dangers and hardships, inseparable with the Navigation of the Southern Polar regions.[53]

Here, then, Cook offers us an early example of what Carl Thompson describes, in the context of nineteenth-century exploration of the interior of Africa, as the 'hugely influential tradition in British exploration, a tradition whereby defeats and setbacks in the field can be almost as triumphant as victories'.[54] Here, too, is an early instance of the persona of the explorer as Romantic hero, partaking of the very sublime which they encounter and remediate to the general public. Later Cook would tell the charming story of the young George Vancouver, after whom the city would be named, who climbed out of the bowsprit of the *Resolution* to be the farthest man south before the ship tacked back towards home.

John Hawkesworth, the man who had been commissioned by the British Admiralty to provide the official, and, as it turned out, highly controversial edition of Cook's journals from his first voyage, had died in 1773, and so Cook, who had anyway been dissatisfied with Hawkesworth's account of the *Endeavour* voyage, edited his own journals from the *Resolution*, publishing the result in 1777 as *A Voyage towards the South Pole and Round the World*. The account which Cook provides of the Antarctic in his *Voyage* is, for the most part, extremely faithful to his journal: most of the journal entries reappear with only minor, cosmetic alterations, such as the standardisation of the spelling and grammar, and the suppression, for example, of the reference to the 'drunken crew' in Cook's entry for 26 December 1772. What is very interesting, however, is the way in which Cook remediates, in his *Voyage*, his original journal entries for 30 January 1774, in which he describes his experiences at 71°S, and for 6 February 1775, in which he offers his final observations on the question of the *terra australis incognita*.

In both these remediations, Cook, in his *Voyage*, augments the sublimity of the scene described in the corresponding journal entry. Cook's remediation of his journal entry for 30 January 1774, for example, affirms of the field ice which blocked the *Resolution*'s passage at 71°S, that 'ninety seven ice hills were distinctly seen within the field, besides those on the outside; many of them very large, and looking like a ridge of mountains rising one above another till they were lost in the clouds'.[55] Compare this with Cook's original journal entry, which records only that 'the Clowds near the horizon were of a perfect Snow whiteness and were difficult to be distinguished from the Ice hills whose lofty summits reached the Clowds'.[56] A subsequent reference, in Cook's journal entry for 30 January, to 'numberless and large Ice Hills' is similarly remediated, in the *Voyage*, as an encounter with 'prodigious ice mountains'.[57] What is taking place here, then, is not simply the augmentation of the sublimity that Cook encountered in the Antarctic, but also the remediation of that sublimity in the more recognisable form, for the general reader, of the *Alpine* sublime.

The cumulative effect of these remediations is certainly to enlarge in the imagination of a reading public already steeped in descriptions of the 'natural sublime' the magnitude of the barrier which prevented the *Resolution* from sailing further south in January 1774, perhaps, in part, to counter any implication that Cook had turned back too soon – both Cook's journal and his *Voyage* emphasise that all the officers agreed this course of action, and the other first-hand accounts of the expedition (discussed below) confirm this. Whatever its origin, the augmentation of the Antarctic sublime in Cook's remediation of his journal entries would be continued and extended by the many subsequent remediations of Cook's own *Voyage*.

It was Cook's *Voyage towards the South Pole*, too, which provided the late eighteenth century and Romantic period with what was destined to become the definitive contemporary reimagining of the Antarctic sublime, in Cook's remediation of his journal entry for 6 February 1775, in which he offers his final opinion on the question of the *terra australis incognita*. 'I firmly believe', Cook affirms, 'that there is a track of land near the pole which is the source of most of the ice that is spread over Southern Ocean.'[58] However, he concludes, in a passage certainly not without its hubris:

> the greatest part of this southern continent (supposing there is one) must lie within the polar circle, where the sea is so pestered with ice that the land is thereby inaccessible. The risque one runs in exploring a coast, in these unknown and icy seas, is so very great, that I can be bold enough to say that no man will ever venture farther than I have done; and that the lands which may lie to the South will never be explored. Thick fogs, snow storms, intense cold, and every other thing that can render navigation dangerous, must be encountered; and these difficulties are greatly heightened, by the inexpressibly horrid aspect of the country; a country doomed by Nature never once to feel the warmth of the sun's rays, but to lie buried in everlasting snow and ice. The ports which may be on the coast, are, in a manner, wholly filled up with frozen snow of a vast thickness; but if any should be so far open as to invite a ship into it she would run a risque of being fixed there for ever, or of coming out in an ice island.[59]

Here, then, Dalrymple's vision of an Antarctic paradise is transformed decisively into a vision of an icy, inhuman wasteland. This Antarctic 'nullity' is the legacy that Cook's *Voyage* transmits to late eighteenth-century and Romantic-period engagements with the polar sublime. However, what that *Voyage* also transmits, as I have already said, is a vision of the explorer as Romantic hero, a persona inscribed in the mind of the reader with the sublimity which he describes and remediates. And this persona, with its varying incarnations in the travellers to the landscapes of the sublime, surely impacts upon contemporary descriptions, within the genre of philosophical aesthetics, of the relationship between subjectivity and sublimity, and not least, perhaps, upon Immanuel Kant's assertion, in his 'Analytic', that 'true sublimity must be sought only in the mind of the judging subject'.[60]

Two further widely read, first-hand accounts of the *Resolution*'s journey to 71°S appeared in the wake of Cook's own. Written by men with considerable experience in natural philosophy, both share Cook's sanguine tone and both insist upon the same conclusion about the fabled *terra australis incognita*: *if* an Antarctic continent does exist, then it will be an inaccessible, ice-bound waste. However, both of these accounts also display the continuing remediation of the Antarctic sublime: the process by which an inhuman waste, devoid of signification, is reimagined and thereby to an extent reclaimed, as the theatre of heroic defeat.

In 1778, the German naturalist Johann Reinhold Forster published his *Observations Made during a Voyage round the World*.[61] Forster, who, with his son Georg, had sailed on the *Resolution* after Joseph Banks withdrew from the expedition, was by all accounts a garrulous companion. In his *Observations*, however, he shows himself susceptible to the affective power of the Antarctic environment, and reveals that now familiar tension between the affective response to the landscapes of the sublime and the desire to describe those landscapes within the terms of natural philosophy. Of the 'immense masses of ice' which the *Resolution* encountered in the high southern latitudes, Forster recalls, returning us to the idea of an actual sublime which exceeds the expectations generated by cultural texts read in advance:

> I must confess, that though I had read a great many accounts on their nature, figure, formation, and magnitude [in descriptions of Greenland and the Arctic], I was however very much struck by their first appearance. The real grandeur of the sight by far surpassed anything I could expect; for we saw sometimes islands of ice of one or two miles in extent, and at the same time a hundred feet or upwards above water [...] But the enormous size of these icy masses is not the only object of our astonishment, for the great number of them is equally surprising [...] We observed stupendous large and high

islands [...] formed in the most strange manner into points, spires and broken rocks. All this scene of ice extended as far as the eye could reach.[62]

For Forster as for so many other travellers to the landscapes of the sublime, then, the reality of the landscape exceeds expectation: it is more impressive than Forster expected on the basis of the 'great many accounts' which he had read: hence, again, the individual's response is both *interested* and culturally determined. On the question of the existence of the *terra australis incognita*, however, Forster confirmed that 'no vestige' had been found, noting in addition that 'there is one circumstance more, which surely most evidently proves, that there is no land in those latitudes, which are still capable of vegetation [...] in all the Southern seas there is no drifting wood to be met with'.[63] Once more, dreams of a polar paradise congeal into a sublime, inhuman emptiness.

A similar trajectory informs Anders Sparrman's account of the *Resolution*'s journey in his widely read *A Voyage to the Cape of Good Hope, towards the Antarctic Polar Circle, and round the World* (1785). Sparrman, a Swedish naturalist who joined the *Resolution* at Cape Town in the autumn of 1772, shows himself less susceptible than either Cook or Forster to the affective power of the polar sublime, and recurs frequently to the 'hardships' of spending such extended periods in 'excessively cold latitudes, continually surrounded with ice'.[64] Of the *Resolution*'s first crossing of the Antarctic Circle, for example, Sparrman records, with a characteristic lack of enthusiasm, that:

> How disagreeably we passed the remainder of the summer in this hemisphere, may be gathered from this, that we made our way through floating islands of ice, sometimes as big as mountains, till we came to lat. 67°10'; so that we are, and probably shall continue to be, the only mortals that can boast the frozen honour (as I may call it) of having passed the Antarctic polar circle. An hundred and twenty-two days, or something more than seventeen weeks, were elapsed without our having been able to see land.[65]

Even the nightly 'spectacle' of the aurora australis failed to lighten Sparrman's mood, which was possibly influenced by scurvy: he remarked only that it was 'the same as the northern lights', although many others felt it differed greatly.[66]

One year later, inside the Antarctic Circle for a second time, Sparrman was homesick and lamenting the 'meagre' Christmas celebrations onboard the *Resolution*.⁶⁷ His remarks on achieving 71°S, however, while similarly unimpressed, are telling: 'we now penetrated into the southern regions as far as we could go [...] we were prevented by the ice from putting in execution the scheme we had fondly formed of hoisting the British flag in a sixth part of the world, or even in the southern pole itself'.⁶⁸ Ice again frustrates the polar dream. But Sparrman explicitly acknowledges the political component of that dream: the sublime inhumanity of the Antarctic environment destroys an imperial ambition, as it would do again and again in the future, until that destruction became itself remediated as a kind of triumph – the very same remediation, I will argue, that informs both the Antarctic sequence of the *Ancyent Marinere* and Walton's failure to reach the North Pole in *Frankenstein*. Hence, the encounter with the Antarctic sublime impacts not just upon constructions of individual subjectivity, but also upon constructions of national subjectivity. Ironically in respect of the former, and despite George Vancouver's efforts on the bowsprit, the unhappy Sparrman might actually have been the farthest man south: he was in the rear cabin when the *Resolution* tacked about and headed north on 30 January 1774.

From these three first-hand accounts of the *Resolution*'s time in the Antarctic Circle, then, emerge elements that would become central to late eighteenth-century and Romantic-period engagements with the polar sublime: the encounter with a vast, inhuman emptiness which rendered void all previous attempts to imagine it; and the subsequent attempt to reimagine these same psychological, cultural and political defeats, in more positive terms, as heroic failures. Indeed, Alexander Dalrymple himself arguably anticipated this latter strategy in the introduction to his *Historical Collection*, published before Cook's second voyage, when he affirmed that 'those heroes who went in search of *New Lands* [...] must *ever* remain in the *first rank* of *heroes*'.⁶⁹ Here again: the explorer of the landscapes of the sublime remediated as sublime Romantic hero, partaking of the sublimity which he confronts.

Public engagements with the reports of the *Resolution*'s achievements in the Antarctic were, of course, numerous. However, I hope that two such responses will serve, here, to illustrate how the remediation of the Antarctic sublime by Cook, Forster and Sparrman was taken up and extended by the wider genre of engagement with the polar sublime during the late eighteenth century and Romantic period. The first example is the aforementioned review, in *The Annual Register* for 1777, of Cook's *Voyage towards the South Pole*. This review pays a great deal of attention, of course, to the speculation about the *terra australis incognita*, to which Cook's expedition had put an effective end. 'It is now evident', the review affirms, 'that no such continent, as was supposed, exists in the Southern Pacific Ocean. That there may be a continent within the Antarctic Circle, and perhaps extending to the pole, seems not improbable; but if there be, nature has most effectively guarded it from human enquiry.'[70] Like one of the primitive idols described by Burke in his *Philosophical Enquiry*, then, for *The Annual Register*, at least, the sublimity of the South Pole depends, at least in part, upon its *obscurity*, from its being impervious to 'human enquiry'. What is striking about the review, however, is the speed with which it moves immediately to compensate for this disappointment – a disappointment impacting on both natural philosophy and imperial ambition – by emphasising the heroic effort that Cook's crew had made in the face of the extreme conditions of the Antarctic sublime:

> It is now generally known, that the severity of the climate in the high southern latitudes, so far exceeds what is experienced under equal parallels in the northern latitudes, as scarcely to admit of comparison. Yet such was the industry and spirit, the contempt of toil, danger, and cold, shewn by our present navigators, that they penetrated at three different periods within the Antarctic polar circle, and, at the last time, advanced to a latitude of 71degrees 10minutes south; which was probably a much nearer approach to the southern pole, than any mortal had ever ventured before.[71]

Hence, *The Annual Register* effectively remediates the defeat of Cook's expedition by the Antarctic sublime as a heroic struggle against appalling conditions, matching the heroic sublimity of their character ('the industry and spirit, the contempt of toil, danger, and cold') against the sublimity of the environment. Accordingly, *The Annual Register* further enlarges the immensity of the obstacles by which Cook and his crew were confronted, remediating Cook's own remediation of his journal entry for 30 January 1774 in his *Voyage towards the South Pole*:

> Their progress was at length stopped by an apparently boundless tract of solid ice, which [...] carried the appearance of a vast continent. It exhibited a level margin to the open sea, from whence it rose gradually, at first into smaller hills, and at length into stupendous mountains of ice, which ascended in great ridges one above another to the south, until their tops were lost in the clouds. It is said, that no known part of the northern seas produce any phenomena at all equal, or even approaching in point of magnitude, and as a natural wonder, to these prodigious ice mountains.[72]

Dalrymple's vision of a polar paradise has thus definitively been replaced with an explicitly sublime vision of a 'stupendous' frozen 'continent', without parallel in the known world. But the disappointment of natural philosophy and imperial expansion is more than compensated for by the heroism with which Cook and his crew struggled with the inhuman environment. From *The Annual Register* too, then, the reader gets that potent vision of the travellers to the landscapes of the sublime as Romantic heroes, intrepid individuals whose achievements partake of the very sublimity against which they struggled.

I have already suggested the possibility that such visions of the explorer-as-Romantic-hero impacted upon contemporary investigations of the relationship between sublimity and subjectivity within the genre of philosophical aesthetics, British and German alike, even as such visions might themselves have been informed by investigations in philosophical aesthetics. I want to pause, now, in order briefly to consider the potential relationship between the idea of the explorer-as-Romantic-hero and contemporary constructions of the relationship between *gender* and the sublime. Anne Mellor in *Romanticism and Gender* (1993) and Barbara Freeman in *The Feminine Sublime* (1995) blazed something of a trail in documenting the extent to which 'the sublime' and 'the masculine' were interlinked in eighteenth-century and Romantic-period writing, building on similar criticisms by Mary Wollstonecraft and Mary Shelley of what would now be called a 'Romanticism' dominated by the valorisation of masculine idealism. Burke's *Philosophical Enquiry* offers a case in point in this instance (as in so many others): for Burke, 'the sublime' is linked to the masculine and 'the beautiful' to the feminine. So pervasive, indeed, has this strand of criticism become within academic engagements with the place of 'the sublime' in the cultural history of the eighteenth century and Romantic period, that it is almost something of a cliché, now, to draw attention to the intermixture of contemporary constructions of 'the masculine' with constructions of 'the sublime'. That said, responses to the achievements of Cook in the Antarctic do reveal precisely that same intermixture, and I want briefly to consider these, here, in order to illustrate what insights such 'theoretical' responses to the genres of engagement with the 'natural sublime' on which I have chosen to focus in this book might be capable of yielding. Without wishing to seem naively 'Freudian', then, it could be said that the language through which *The Annual Register* remediates the engagement of Cook's encounter with the Antarctic environment is susceptible to a sexualised reading: Cook's expedition 'penetrated' as far towards the frozen South Pole as possible; an Antarctic continent would be 'fruitless'; and the desired object itself, the South Pole, remained taboo, impervious to 'human enquiry'. It is (just) possible to argue, then, that *The Annual Register* not only remediates Cook's expedition as Romantic heroes, but also remediates their encounter with the Antarctic wilderness as a test of manhood. Within the second of the responses to the achievements of the *Resolution* in the Antarctic that I want to consider here, however, this remediation is much more visible.

Anna Seward's *Elegy on Captain Cook* was written in 1780 shortly after the news of Cook's death in Hawaii had reached England. In a strategy familiar from Renaissance writing about the 'new world', Seward's *Elegy* represents the Antarctic as a beautiful (and willing) woman, and Cook's journey to 71°S is remediated as the failure of a heroic Englishman to bed this 'Goddess' – but it's not his fault![73] Seward's Antarctic 'Goddess' beckons Cook 'with outstretch'd hands' and 'points the ship its mazy path, to thread / The floating fragments of the frozen bed'.[74] Cook, meanwhile, remains undaunted by the terrors around him ('While o'er the deep, in many a dreadful form, / The giant Danger howls') and 'stands' 'firm on the deck', whilst 'round glitt'ring mountains hears the billows rave, / And the vast ruin thunder on the wave – Appal'd he hears'.[75] It is not 'the terrors of the icy wreck' or 'the giant Danger' which finally thwart this 'firm' Cook from his purpose, however, but rather 'Nature', the Antarctic sublime, which eventually 'draws the circumscribing line', preventing Cook's union with his willing 'goddess':

> Huge rocks of ice th'arrested ship embay,
> And bar the gallant Wanderer's dangerous way. –
> His eye regretful marks the Goddess turn
> The assiduous prow from its relentless bourn.[76]

Again, that 'huge' barrier of 'ice' intervenes between 'the gallant' Cook and his goal. But in this case, disappointment in the Antarctic – the disappointed ambitions of natural philosophy and British imperial expansion – is remediated as *sexual* disappointment: masculine cultural subjectivity is threatened, and in this case defeated, by the 'natural sublime', effectively configuring the 'natural sublime' as something which must be conquered in order for individual and national ambition to be realised. This, in other words, is the attempt to conquer the landscapes of the sublime – by individuals and by nations – remediated in the language of sexual conquest.

Cook's vision of a sublime Antarctic emptiness, and the various subsequent remediations of that vision, constitute the genre of engagement with the Antarctic sublime which Coleridge mediates in *The Rime of the Ancyent Marinere*, and which that poem itself remediates to subsequent Romantic writing, *vide*, for example, Walton's reference to Coleridge's poem in the first chapter of Mary Shelley's *Frankenstein*. As I have already said, Coleridge's specific debts to the details of a range of extant accounts of the Antarctic sublime, including Cook's, have been well documented, although we might add to that list here the fact that Coleridge's ship becomes involved in 'mist' and 'fog' while it leaves the Antarctic, just as the *Resolution* had also been surrounded by 'thick fog' as it tacked back towards the north on 30 January 1774.[77] Arguably the single most significant mediation of this genre of engagement with the Antarctic sublime in Coleridge's poem is, however, the *kind* of Antarctic which is encountered by Coleridge's crew. It might seem like stating the obvious, but it nevertheless needs to be stated: it is *not* Dalrymple's influential imagining of a polar paradise that is encountered by Coleridge's crew, nor any of a range of other accessible imaginings; it is, precisely, Cook's inhuman 'nullity':

> Listen, Stranger ! Mist and Snow,
>   And it grew wond'rous cauld:
> And Ice mast-high came floating by
>   As green as Emerauld.
>
> And thro' the drifts the snowy clifts
>   Did send a dismal sheen;
> Ne shapes of men ne beasts we ken –
>   The Ice was all between.
>
> The Ice was here, the Ice was there,
>   The Ice was all around:
> It crack'd and growl'd, and roar'd and howl'd –
>   Like noises in a swound.[78]

It is this nebulous land of 'Mist and Snow' which the eighteenth-century imagination inherited from Cook's encounter with the Antarctic. It is this sublime, inhuman emptiness which the various responses to Cook's account that I have considered sought to remediate in more familiar, or at least in more favourable, terms. And this is exactly what Coleridge's crew also attempt to do: through their superstitious reaction to the appearance of the albatross and subsequent events, the crew, and the Mariner himself, seek to impose the known, the familiar – in this case, European folk and religious values – upon an environment which defies imagination. We remember Cook and his crew imagining flora and fauna in the shapes of the Antarctic ice. On the 'meta' level, too, this is also what Coleridge himself does in writing the *Ancyent Marinere*: the poem becomes part of the associations which the Antarctic comes to possess in the British imagination, and thereby contributes to the reimagining of the emptiness which Cook had discovered. The writing of the poem by Coleridge is, in other words, part of the process by which the sublime Antarctic void is remediated to the nineteenth century as 'classic ground', as a landscape overwritten with a range of geographically and culturally specific associations. And how exactly does Coleridge remediate the Antarctic sublime? Like some before and many after him: as a theatre of heroic defeat for his explorer-mariner, whose captivating hold over the wedding guest, the figure of the reader in the poem, encapsulates the fascination and the horror that the Antarctic sublime exerts upon the contemporary European imagination. Hence, whether we read the *Ancyent Marinere* as a poem about Romantic attitudes to nature, about religion, about the psychology of guilt or compulsion – and it is, in various ways, a poem about all of these things – we must keep in mind that rather than a canonical text which transcends the circumstances of its creation, it is also part of a much wider contemporary genre of engagement with the polar sublime. And I say *polar* sublime here, of course, because it is also important to remember that Coleridge draws, in the *Ancyent Marinere*, not just upon contemporary engagements with Antarctica, but also upon contemporary engagements with the Arctic, as Sarah Moss has shown.[79] It is to the Arctic that I will now turn in order to consider that other, seminal Romantic engagement with the polar sublime: Mary Shelley's *Frankenstein*.

'The seat of frost and desolation': *Frankenstein* and the Arctic

Although it would also be the early twentieth century before any European explorer reached the North Pole, by the middle of the eighteenth century the Arctic had long been more familiar to the European imagination than the Antarctic.[80] Amongst the most potent imaginings of the Arctic which eighteenth-century European thought had inherited from classical, medieval and Renaissance speculation were the descriptions of Hyperborea and Thule: two semi-legendary landmasses, supposed to lie in the high Arctic. References to Hyperborea – a sublime country believed to lie far north of Greece (literally, 'beyond the north wind'), where a god-like population enjoyed perpetual sunshine – are present in Greek literature from at least the eighth century BC, and, as knowledge of the world developed through the classical and medieval periods, so subsequent writers pushed the putative location of Hyperborea farther and farther to the north, eventually moving it beyond Britain and into the Arctic Circle, decisively off the map and firmly into the cultural imagination, where it remained well into the twentieth century, passing notably, for example, through the works of Madame Blavatsky and Friedrich Nietzsche. Pytheas of Massalia, by contrast, claimed actually to have visited an island called Thule during his voyage around the known part of northern Europe in *c.* 325 BC: a country surrounded by sea ice, some six days' sailing to the north of Britain, where the sun did not set during the summer months.[81] Commentators have variously identified the country which Pytheas describes as Greenland, Iceland, the Orkney Islands and, most consistently, as Norway. During the eighteenth century, however, Thule, like Hyperborea, had become less a geographical term than a sign for an imagined paradise in the far north, the esoteric equivalent of the new Americas that Alexander Dalrymple felt so sure would be discovered in the Southern Ocean. Hence, the Arctic *terra incognita* functioned like its southern equivalent as a kind of blank canvas upon which the European imagination could project sublime territories and beings.

Beyond this legacy of imaginative or speculative engagement with the Arctic which the eighteenth century had inherited from the classical world, however, a good deal of factual knowledge about the far north was also in circulation at the time. Extant historical records revealed to the eighteenth century the existence of Viking settlements in Greenland and Iceland as early as the ninth century AD, while documented attempts by various European powers to discover the fabled Northwest Passage – a viable route through the Arctic ice to the Pacific Ocean – had been ongoing since the sixteenth century. Indeed, British interest in the Northwest Passage – which would shorten the voyage from Europe to Asia, and reduce the dangers associated with navigating the Cape of Good Hope – was given a significant new impetus in 1775, when an Act of Parliament established a prize of twenty thousand pounds for anyone who could demonstrate a viable route. To put this in some kind of context: this prize granted the discovery of the Northwest Passage the same importance as the discovery of the crucial ability to determine the longitude at sea, for which a prize of twenty thousand pounds had been established by the Longitude Act in 1714.

Despite this increasing first-hand knowledge of the Arctic, however, the far north remained shrouded in mystery until the early part of the nineteenth century, when high-profile expeditions like those of John Ross (1818), William Edward Parry (1819–20) and John Franklin (1819–22) began gradually to clarify the geography of the Arctic Circle: and of course Byron, in *A Vision of Judgement* (1822), would later recall Parry's account of an aurora borealis 'seen, when ice-bound, / By Captain Parry's crews in "Melville's Sound"'.[82] Nor indeed was this mystery confined to more esoteric speculation about Hyperborea or Thule, or about what might be found at the magnetic and north poles. More concrete mysteries also presented themselves. What, for example, had happened to the Norse settlements in Greenland: these had thrived for almost six hundred years until contact was lost in the fifteenth century, and virtually no trace of them was found when the Danish missionary, Hans Egede, sought to re-establish contact in 1721 after a number of earlier attempts had been blocked by sea ice. Egede's account of his search for the colony and subsequent 15-year residence as a missionary to the Inuit, in his *Description of Greenland* (1745), offers an extensive and influential account of the geography, flora, fauna and native culture of the country – along with a three-page description of a sea-serpent, thereby exemplifying the curious mixture of the esoteric and the empirical which marks so much of eighteenth-century speculation about the Arctic sublime.[83]

This same mixture of esotericism and natural philosophy is evident in the letters which Walton writes to his sister in the opening chapters of *Frankenstein*, and indeed it is worth remembering at the outset that while a number of Walton's ideas would have been somewhat dated in 1818, they would have had much greater currency in the 1790s, when the novel is set. In the first of these letters, Walton outlines the sublime objectives which motivate his quest for the high Arctic, and reveals his sense of himself in the growing tradition of polar explorer-heroes. Walton's primary objective is to make a significant contribution to natural philosophy, an objective prompted by his belief that in the highest northern latitudes, where 'frost and snow are banished', he will discover a 'calm sea' and 'a land surpassing in wonders and in beauty every region hitherto discovered on the habitable globe': 'its productions and features may be without example, as the phenomena of the heavenly bodies undoubtedly are in those undiscovered solitudes'.[84] In this 'region of beauty and delight' Walton hopes for nothing less than to 'discover the wondrous power which attracts the needle [and] regulate a thousand celestial observations, that require only this voyage to render their seeming eccentricities consistent forever', which would indeed have been an epoch-making contribution to natural philosophy, almost on a par with Frankenstein's goal.[85] 'But supposing all these conjectures to be false', Walton concludes of his belief in the existence of an Arctic paradise and what he may achieve there:

> you cannot contest the inestimable benefit which I shall confer on mankind to the last generation, by discovering a passage near the pole to those countries, to reach which at present so many months are requisite; or by ascertaining the secret of the magnet, which, if at all possible, can only be effected by an undertaking such as mine.[86]

As commentators on *Frankenstein* have long noted, the scope and the hubris of Walton's polar ambitions – not least his conviction that he would discover the Northwest Passage, when so many others had tried and failed, or that he would make 'celestial observations' similar to those made by James Cook and Joseph Banks in Tahiti – put him on a par with Victor Frankenstein himself. Both men seek to 'confer' 'inestimable benefit' on 'mankind', but both are also blinded by their ambition and dangerously heedless of the cost of that ambition in human suffering. In this respect, Walton's eventual decision to heed the request of his crew and retreat from the polar ice in which their ship becomes trapped reflects the moral conclusion which he, and, presumably, the reader, is supposed to draw from Victor Frankenstein's fate. But should we be so comfortably critical of them? Readers of *Frankenstein*, after all, often find something to admire, something of the sublime, in Victor's ambition and situation. And if, in the character of Victor Frankenstein, Mary Shelley remediates the ambiguous type of the 'Romantic' scientist – 'thirsting and reckless for knowledge, *for its own sake and perhaps at any cost*', as Richard Holmes puts it – then surely, in the character of Walton, she also remediates the 'Romantic' polar-explorer-hero whom she would so often have encountered in her reading.[87] Indeed, it is through this pedigree to which Walton aspires that we recover some sense of the status of both men as problematic Romantic heroes, yes, but as Romantic heroes all the same. For whilst, remediated through the popular genre of the mad scientist, Shelley's Victor Frankenstein may look to the reader like a dangerously deluded man, Walton's defeat at the hands of the Arctic sublime places him firmly within the context of the ongoing remediation of the polar sublime as the locus of heroic rather than (or if) deluded failure. Both are Promethean figures, as the subtitle to Shelley's novel makes clear.

In this respect, too, whilst Walton's polar ambitions might at first glance seem fanciful to a modern reader, it is important to remember that just as Victor Frankenstein's attempt to create life engages with a thriving contemporary debate about the nature of organic life which was ongoing while Shelley wrote the novel, so Walton's polar ambitions engage with contemporary speculation about the Arctic, granted, again, that some of his ideas would have had greater currency in the 1790s.[88] As Jessica Richard has put it, this was 'a moment when both the history and the future of polar exploration were subject to increasingly fervent discussion in scientific circles and popular journals in England'.[89] The most striking of Walton's polar ambitions, for example – his conviction that he would discover in the high Arctic a 'region of beauty and delight' surrounded by a 'calm sea', free from ice – seems at first obviously indebted to classical ideas of Hyperborea and Thule, or to Alexander Dalrymple's disproved theories about undiscovered Americas in the Southern Ocean. However, in describing this particular polar ambition to his sister, Walton affirms that his 'trust' in the existence of the Arctic 'region of beauty and delight' is based not upon classical myth but upon the accounts of 'preceding navigators', and reminds his sister that he had, as a young man, 'read with ardour the accounts of the various voyages which have been made in the prospect of arriving at the North Pacific Ocean through the seas which surround the pole', and that 'a history of all the voyages made for the purposes of discovery' had been his 'study day and night'.[90] And by emphasising these debts to 'preceding navigators', Walton is of course, again, seeking to inscribe himself within that same tradition of polar explorers.

As Jessica Richard has pointed out, Walton would most certainly have found support for this theory of an open polar sea in any such 'history' of Arctic 'voyages' because, in point of fact, a considerable number of 'preceding navigators' – amongst them the seasoned explorers Henry Hudson and William Barents – had expressed their confidence that, in the very highest latitudes, the polar seas must be free from ice. One of the most prominent proponents of this theory in eighteenth-century England, however, was the judge Daines Barrington (1727/8–1800), who had been influential both in securing the funding for Constantine Phipps's attempt to discover the Northwest Passage in 1773, and in lobbying for Cook's third voyage, in search of a Northeast Passage from the Pacific, in 1776–79.[91] Barrington published a series of papers on the subject during the 1770s, including *Instances of Navigators who have Reached the High Northern Latitudes* (1774), *Additional Instances of Navigators who have Reached the High Northern Latitudes* (1775), *The Probability of*

Reaching the North Pole Discussed (1775) and *Observations on the Floating Ice which is Found in the High Northern and Southern Latitudes* (1776), and a translation of the Portuguese navigator Franciso Mourelle de la Rùa's search for a Northeast Passage in his *Journal of a Voyage in 1775 to Explore the Coast of America, North of California* (1781); a revised, posthumous edition of *The Probability of Reaching the North Pole* also appeared in 1818, under the rather more circumspect title of *The Possibility of Approaching the North Pole Asserted*, although there is no evidence of a direct link between this edition and *Frankenstein*.

In each of these publications, Barrington collated dubious first-hand testimony from mariners with speculation by natural philosophers about the properties of sea water to conclude not only that the high Arctic seas *must* be open and free of ice, but that certain navigators had already found them to be so. *The Possibility of Approaching the North Pole Asserted*, for example, reports testimony from a number of English sailors, all of whom claimed to have reached latitudes above 83°N, where they encountered 'not a speck of ice', 'a free and open sea', or a 'sea perfectly free from ice, and rolling like the Bay of Biscay', along with 'temperate' or even 'warm' weather – all of which prefigure the 'calm sea' that Walton anticipates.[92]

Barrington's willingness uncritically to accept such dubious testimony – when his sources could have been motivated by greed, search for notoriety, or simply by humour – left him open to accusations of credulity, such as in the poet and satirist Peter Pindar's description of him as 'a man denied by Nature brains'.[93] Indeed, Barrington's blindness in this respect arguably prefigures the blind ambition of both Victor Frankenstein and Walton, both of whom are equally unwilling to listen to dissenting voices. However, Barrington was certainly not alone in advancing arguments drawn from natural philosophy to support the idea of an open polar sea. As long ago as the sixteenth century, for example, William Barents had contended that the perpetual sunshine during the Arctic summer would melt any ice (cp. Walton's contention that 'there [...] the sun is forever visible [...] a country of eternal light').[94] Barrington's *The Possibility of Approaching the North Pole Asserted* extends this kind of thinking, arguing that it cannot 'be contended, that ten degrees of the globe round each Pole were covered with frozen sea at the original creation', because if that had been the case, 'the height of such ice' must now have grown 'excessive, by the accumulation of frozen snow from winter to winter'.[95] In a similar vein, in his *Observations on the Floating Ice*, Barrington had already drawn on a body of eighteenth-century speculation by natural philosophers – also endorsed by James

Cook and Johann Reinhold Forster, amongst others – which asserted that sea water could not normally freeze, and that the ice found in the Antarctic and Arctic seas must therefore originate in fresh water on, or near, land, rather than form a permanent structure over the poles.

Hence, Walton would readily have found in the records of 'preceding navigators' some grounds for 'trust' in the prospect of open polar seas, a prospect which he appears to have combined with classical notions of Hyperborea and Thule, or with Dalrymple's idea of the *terra australis incognita*, to formulate a sublime vision of an Arctic paradise, and a no less sublime vision of himself as explorer-hero, the 'benefactor' of his species. Crucially, however, in accepting this version of the Arctic sublime, Walton would be setting himself in marked opposition to what – even in the 1790s, when *Frankenstein* is set – was increasingly becoming the mainstream view of the Arctic sublime. To put it more precisely, Walton's conviction that he will discover an Arctic paradise at the North Pole arguably implies that he is either unaware of, or simply choosing to ignore, the testimony of those 'preceding navigators' who had discovered a very different kind of Arctic sublime on their failed quests for the Pole or the Northwest Passage: an inhuman, frozen waste like that discovered by Cook in the Antarctic.[96] This, for example, is the version of the Arctic sublime that informs the poet and critic William Lisle Bowles's florid description of the Pole in the fifth book of his *Spirit of Discovery* as 'one torpid blank', a 'frozen waste' of 'desert snows'.[97] Daines Barrington, defending his view of open polar seas, had earlier suggested, in language obviously drawn from contemporary descriptions of the role of the enthusiastic imagination in the encounter with the sublime in contemporary works of philosophical aesthetics, that such bleak poetic descriptions of the Arctic sublime had 'heightened the horrors of these inhospitable regions by all the colouring of a warm and heated imagination'.[98] However, the reality of the Arctic sublime was proving far harsher than any such 'colouring' had anticipated.

As Jessica Richard has observed, Walton's refusal or failure to recognise this other version of the Arctic sublime is one of a number of factors which might have signalled to a reader of *Frankenstein* in 1818 that Walton's polar ambitions were doomed to failure from the outset.[99] Indeed, for Richard, Walton's delusion suggests that *Frankenstein*, which was composed and published in the run-up to John Ross's high-profile Admiralty-sponsored expedition in search of the Northwest Passage in 1818, 'far from simply appropriating a topic of contemporary discussion uncritically, must be counted among those voices that censured the revival of British polar exploration'.[100] I have no wish to dispute this conclusion, which establishes a clear and valuable parallel between the frame and main narratives of *Frankenstein*: both narratives warn against the blind pursuit of an ideal, however well intentioned, regardless of the consequences. However, Richard's reading of the frame narrative also tends to downplay the extent to which *Frankenstein* is not just a critique of a particular kind of male, solipsistic or 'Romantic' idealism, but also a tragedy about the defeat of even the most well intentioned of ambitions if they are ill conceived. With this in mind, what I want to suggest here is that the frame narrative of *Frankenstein* is also an attempt – like the Antarctic sequence of the *Ancyent Marinere* – to remediate the inhumanity of Arctic sublime by inscribing new cultural connotations on the 'torpid blank' which had been discovered there, to use Bowles's phrase. Seen as part of a wider, contemporary genre of engagement with the polar sublime, in other words, the Arctic, in *Frankenstein*, is given significance precisely by the story which it hosts: a story of hubristic, but also tragic, failure – exactly the same kind of story that would come to dominate British cultural engagement with the polar sublime after the loss of John Franklin's expedition in 1845. In short, the frame narrative of *Frankenstein* gives new significance to an Arctic which was in the process of being stripped of the associations which it had acquired in classical and medieval legend, and in the ambitions of more recent natural philosophers, businessmen and politicians alike. The novel, that is to say, participates in the ongoing process of remediating a disturbingly blank space on the map.

The vast majority of the accounts of 'preceding navigators' which Walton might have read in any collection of voyages would actually have described a very different Arctic sublime from the one which he hoped to discover. Yes, there was the 'human' Arctic – with its history of settlement by Europeans, and its indigenous population – that emerges from works like Egede's *Description of Greenland*, as well as David Cranz's *History of Greenland* (1767), Uno von Troil's *Letters on Iceland* (1780) and George Mackenzie's *Travels in Iceland* (1812). And, indeed, this Arctic would also be perpetuated after Ross published his *Voyage of Discovery* in 1819, in which he describes at length his encounters with the Greenland Inuit whom, he suggests, in a revealing inversion of developing European attitudes to the Arctic, 'until the moment of our arrival believed themselves to be the only inhabitants of the universe, and that all the rest of the world was a mass of ice'.[101] Most of those who had actually sailed in quest of the North Pole or the Northwest Passage, though, had found only Bowles's icy 'torpid blank'. Representative amongst these in the years prior to the publication of *Frankenstein* is

Constantine Phipps's expedition of 1773. Daines Barrington had helped to secure the funding for this expedition, and it counted one Olaudah Equiano, no less, amongst its members. Phipps reached approximately 81°N before being halted by field ice, in which the expedition was trapped for almost two weeks. Both Phipps's *Journal of a Voyage undertaken by order of his present Majesty, for making discoveries towards the North Pole* (1774) and Equiano's *Interesting Narrative* (1789) describe this 'dreadful and alarming' experience of the 'uninhabited extremity of the world' at some length, with Equiano concluding in terms which seem to be aimed directly at Barrington, that 'being much farther, by all accounts, than any navigator had ever ventured before [...] we full proved the impracticability of finding a passage that way to India'.[102]

What is evident both from expedition narratives like Phipps's *Voyage* and from more strictly natural-historical descriptions like Cranz's *History*, however, is the simultaneous fascination with the inhumanity of the Arctic sublime and the attempt to remediate that sublimity by inscribing cultural connotations upon the emptiness. Cranz's account of the sea ice around Greenland typifies this dynamic. Cranz introduces these 'astonishing fields and [...] floating *mountains* of ice [...] of monstrous magnitude and form' only immediately to attempt to figure them in recognisable form: 'some of them look like a church, or a castle with square or pointed turrets; others like a ship in full sail'.[103] Here, then, is the Arctic sublime remediated in the comforting form of the emblems of British society and imperial ambition. Fifty years later, in his *Voyage of Discovery*, John Ross reveals a similar process at work. Of his expedition's 'first sight of an iceberg', Ross affirms in language reminiscent of the engagements with the polar sublime in both *The Ancyent Marinere* and *Frankenstein* that:

> Imagination presented it in many grotesque forms: at one time, it looked something like a white lion and horse rampant, which the quick fancy of sailors, in their harmless fondness for omens, naturally enough shaped into the lion and unicorn of the King's arms, and they were delighted accordingly with the good luck it seemed to augur [...] It is hardly possible to imagine any thing more exquisite than the variety of tints which these icebergs display; by night as by day they glitter with a vividness of colour beyond the power of art to represent.[104]

Ross's recollection encapsulates the attempt to remediate the sublime Arctic 'blank' by inscribing cultural – and in this case explicitly imperial – connotations upon it. Ross's crew reimagine their first sight of the Arctic sublime as exactly what they wish it to become: the possession of the king; they take imaginative possession of the iceberg just as they have been sent to take territorial possession of the Arctic. Political meaning is thus inscribed upon an inhuman wilderness, and the Arctic is remediated from a terrifying and ambition-defeating 'nullity' into a signifier of the power of those who could possess it.

The broader, cultural resonance of this language of possession is apparent in the opening lines of *The Arctic Expeditions*, a poem which was written by Eleanor Porden (future wife of John Franklin) just after she had viewed Ross's ships at Deptford as they prepared to depart. 'Sail, sail, adventurous Barks! go fearless forth', Porden writes:

> Storm on his glacier-seat the misty North,
> Give to mankind the inhospitable zone,
> And Britain's trident plant in seas unknown.[105]

Porden remains confident that this attempt to lay siege to the Arctic will succeed where others have failed, and again her confidence is expressed through a language which displays the attempt to remediate the Arctic sublime, to take imaginative or ideological possession of a region which the expedition is trying actually to possess. 'Fear not', she exhorts the expedition, through imagery which would not have impressed Daines Barrington who pleaded for less lurid imaginings of the Arctic sublime:

> Fear not, while months of dreary darkness roll,
> To stand self-centred on the attractive Pole;
> Or find some gulf, deep, turbulent, and dark,
> Earth's mighty mouth ! suck in the struggling bark;
> Fear not, the victims of magnetic force,
> To hang, arrested in your midmost course;
> Your prows drawn downward and your sterns in air,
> To waste with cold, and grief, and famine, there.[106]

In place of these 'strange fancies', Porden acknowledges that the expedition will have to overcome 'real ills [...] not clothed in all the picturesque of fear'.[107] But she remains confident that – unlike Cook's failed attempt to bed the 'goddess' of the Antarctic in Seward's *Elegy* – this expedition is destined to be remembered as 'the men who dared explore the Pole, / On icy seas the lion flag unfurl'd, / And found new pathways to the Western World', as the men who finally vanquished 'The Genius of the North' with 'Britannia's trident'.[108]

I hope, in this chapter, to have provided some overview of the eighteenth-century and Romantic-period genre of engagement with the polar sublime which is both mediated in, and remediated by, the Antarctic sequence of Coleridge's *Ancyent Marinere* and the Arctic frame narrative of Shelley's *Frankenstein*. As part of that wider genre, both texts seek to remediate the inhuman 'nullity' which had been discovered in the high northern and southern latitudes, and to inscribe cultural significance on environments which were proving as hostile to European explorers as they were to the European imagination. However, both texts also stand outside more conservative remediations like Porden's by refusing to imagine an easy conquest of the polar sublime by British imperial ambition. Rather, both remediate the polar sublime not as a locus of triumphant possession, but as the theatre of heroic failure, precisely the connotations which the polar sublime would eventually come to possess in the British imagination for almost a century after the loss of Franklin's expedition in 1845.

4
'The lone and level sands': Romanticism and the Desert

> [T]he disconsolate wanderer, wherever he turns, sees nothing around him but a vast interminable expanse of sand and sky; a gloomy and barren void, where the eye finds no particular object to rest upon, and the mind is filled with painful apprehensions of perishing with thirst.
>
> – Mungo Park, *Travels in the Interior Districts of Africa* (1799)[1]

The quotation in the title of this chapter is taken from Percy Bysshe Shelley's sonnet 'Ozymandias' (1818), arguably the most familiar of the many literary engagements, during the Romantic period, with desert landscape. And that, perhaps, is where I wish to begin this chapter: by remembering that Shelley's sonnet is not just an engagement with *ruin*, not just an engagement with the tyrannical hubris of an Egyptian monarch, but also and moreover an engagement with the desert. The genesis of Shelley's sonnet has been well documented, and a plethora of possible sources for the desert scene which it describes have been suggested, although no single definitive source has been identified, and Kelvin Everest is doubtless correct to point out that Shelley responds to the 'general literary culture' of writing about Egypt rather than to any one specific text.[2] The relationship between the main argument of the poem – the hubris of tyranny – and both Shelley's own political philosophy and the wider eighteenth-century tradition of writing about ruin has also been well documented. What has remained absent from this discussion, however, is attention to the role played by the desert landscape in enabling the cultural and political argument which Shelley makes, a role which the desert also plays in the sonnet that Shelley's friend Horace Smith wrote at the same time and on the same subject, which describes a ruined statue 'which far off throws / The only shadow that the desert knows'.[3]

My point, then, is that these sonnets do not simply remediate a contemporary genre of engagement with the ruins of Egypt, a genre which also comprises, for example, Pococke's *Description of the East* (1743–45), Niebuhr's *Travels through Arabia* (1792), Volney's *Travels in Syria and Egypt* (1787) and *The Ruins; or, a Survey of the Revolutions of Empires* (1792), and Denon's *Travels in Upper and Lower Egypt* (1803). Rather, they also remediate a contemporary genre of engagement with the desert, a genre which comprises Wordsworth's dream of the Arab from Book V of *The Prelude*, to name but one other well-known piece of canonical Romantic-period writing which, like the sonnets written by Shelley and Smith, establishes and investigates an opposition between the sublime of the desert landscape and the scope of human cultural achievements.

Richard Holmes, Nigel Leask and Carl Thompson have all done illuminating work, of late, on various aspects of the careers of arguably the most famous of the British travellers to the deserts of Africa in the eighteenth century, James Bruce and Mungo Park (both Scots, as it happens), and my debts to that scholarship in this chapter will be evident.[4] However, there has been as yet no wider study of the eighteenth-century and Romantic-period genre of engagement with the sublime of the desert, perhaps, at least in part, because desert tends not to feature nearly so prominently as other species of the 'natural sublime', either within the contemporary genre of philosophical aesthetics, or within what has come to be seen as the canon of Romantic-period writing. My purpose, in this chapter, is to begin to outline that genre of engagement with the sublime of the desert. I discern two primary modes within it. The first comprises engagements with what we might call 'cultured' desert: desert landscape which bears the marks, to a greater or lesser extent, of civilisation, that is, desert which is 'classic ground', as in the scenes of ruined statuary which Shelley and Smith describe in their sonnets. Engagements with this type of desert tend to be focused on the Ottoman provinces in the Middle East and North Africa, and, of course, on Egypt. The second mode comprises engagements with what contemporary writers often describe as 'pure' desert: spaces which are essentially unmarked by civilisation or settled societies, at least as far as Europeans were aware or concerned. Engagements with this kind of desert tend to focus on Saharan and sub-Saharan Africa, two regions which remained, during the long eighteenth century, amongst the least-known parts of the world, with 'the map of Africa' still 'disfigured', as the translator put it in his preface to the English edition of Damberger's *Travels in the Interior of Africa*, by 'a blank space entitled *"Parts wholly unknown to Europeans"'*.[5] Like the desert itself, however, the boundaries between these two modes of engagement with the sublime of the desert – with 'cultured' desert or with 'pure' desert – are shifting: there is often considerable overlap between the two, and both share a sense of the desert as the absolute antithesis of culture. Confronting this antithesis can be thrilling, as in Denon's description of the ruined city of Thebes. But it can also be horrifying, as in the engagements with the nullity of the desert in texts so ostensibly diverse as Wordsworth's *Prelude* and James Bruce's *Travels to Discover the Source of the Nile* (1790). Throughout the eighteenth century and Romantic period, however, the desert is consistently constructed as sublime in its capacity physically and psychologically to overwhelm both individual and national subjectivity, an ability witnessed in the recollection from Mungo Park's *Travels in the Interior Districts of Africa* (1799) which serves as epigraph to this chapter. Curiously absent from this genre of engagement with the sublime of the desert, then, is any sustained (Biblical) imagining of the desert as a place of spiritual enlightenment or purification, although that imagining is occasionally remediated in more secular forms. As was the case with contemporary engagements with the polar sublime, however, what does emerge from the published accounts of travellers to these hostile desert landscapes is the persona of the explorer as Romantic hero, partaking of the very sublimity which he remediates to the reader.

'The dreary picture of dead and inanimate nature': the desert and the sublime

As I have already said, the desert is conspicuously absent from the list of species of the 'natural sublime' which are routinely referred to within the genre of eighteenth-century British philosophical aesthetics. This is no doubt in part because, during the long eighteenth century, the 'grandest features' of the 'physical geography' of Saharan and sub-Saharan Africa remained shrouded in 'remarkable [...] obscurity', as the Scots geographer Hugh Murray put it in the preface to his edition of Leyden's *Historical Account of Discoveries and Travels in Africa* in 1817.[6] 'All the interior part', wrote the translator of Saugnier and Brisson's *Voyages to the Coast of Africa* in his preface, 'is filled in our maps with the vague word desert.'[7] Despite, and indeed partly because of, this lack of specific, contemporary information, however, the desert regions of the so-called 'torrid zone' around the equator continued primarily to be known to the European cultural imagination through the writings of classical historians and geographers like Herodotus, Strabo and Diodorus Siculus, the latter one of Shelley's potential sources for the inscription on the statue of Ramses II. Part of this imaginative inheritance from classical writing about the African desert was historical, or pseudo-historical, such as the accounts by Strabo and Herodotus of the conquest of Egypt by the Persian king Cambyses II in 525 BC, during which one of the armies of Cambyses was supposedly overwhelmed and totally destroyed by a sandstorm in the desert: 'while they were taking their morning meal a violent South Wind blew upon them, and bearing with it heaps of the desert sand it buried them under it, and so they disappeared and were seen no more'.[8]

However, much of this classical legacy also hovered on the border between natural philosophy and the fantastical, as in, for example, the reports by Diodorus Siculus of the lethal carnivorous lice, gigantic locusts, spiders, scorpions and snakes which plagued those who entered the deserts of North Africa, as well as the physiological afflictions wrought upon such travellers by the extreme heat, and the terrifying aerial phenomena by which they were sometimes supposed to be pursued across the sands.[9] Indeed, as late as 1801, the English translator of Christian Damberger's *Travels in the Interior of Africa* noted as remarkable that the German had 'travelled over the burning desert of Sahara, noted for its monsters, and deemed an impenetrable barrier between the north and middle of Africa'.[10]

In the chapter on the 'Discoveries of the Ancients' which Hugh Murray added to his edition of Leyden's *Historical Account*, Murray argued that these more fantastical elements of the classical legacy of writing about the desert could be traced to the actual sublimity of the desert landscape, which 'acted powerfully on the exalted and poetical imagination of the ancients' who encountered it.[11] French ideologues like d'Holbach and Volney, and British thinkers like Adam Smith, in his essay 'On the History of Astronomy' (published posthumously, in 1795, in *Essays on Philosophical Subjects*), had all linked the emotional response to the 'natural sublime' to early or primitive religious belief: primitive societies worship natural phenomena which inspire and terrify them. In a similar analysis, and using a description of the sublime which is indebted to Burke's *Philosophical Enquiry*, Murray suggests that the fantastical reports about the desert in classical writing can also be traced to 'the emotions of wonder and curiosity, mingled with terror' that the desert 'inspired always'.[12] The 'immeasurable deserts of sand, and the destruction which had overwhelmed most of those who attempted to penetrate', Murray argues, 'formed, as it were, a fearful and mysterious barrier, drawn around the narrow limits occupied by the civilised nations of this continent [Africa]'.[13] 'Imagination, kept always on the stretch' by the sublime of the desert, Murray continues:

> created wonders even when nature ceased to present them. No part of the interior was ever explored with such precision as to deprive that active faculty of full scope for exertion; and the whole region was in a manner given up to fable.[14]

Murray's emphasis on the role of the imagination in the response to the 'natural sublime' is of course a commonplace of descriptions of the sublime within contemporary philosophical aesthetics, as is the tension, which Murray flags up here, between the imaginative and the rational response to the landscapes of the sublime. Indeed, even Murray's own sober analysis is not entirely immune to this tension: noting that much of the classical 'fable' about the desert 'had generally some basis in truth', Murray goes on to provide, by way of example, a lurid account of the fate of the armies of Cambyses II in the region of 'pure sand', reduced to the 'desperate extremity of devouring each other' before finding 'a grave in the vast ocean of sand'.[15] 'These examples', Murray concludes, again using the language of philosophical aesthetics, 'heightened the mingled sentiment of veneration and terror with which these interior abodes were contemplated. This desert [the Sahara] seemed as a barrier fixed by nature, which she would never permit any mortal to pass with impunity.'[16]

During the eighteenth century, European attempts to breach this sublime 'barrier' and to brave the 'fearful and mysterious' spectacle of what I have described as 'pure' desert tended to occur in the Sahara and in South Africa, mainly because these regions of the African interior were then, comparatively speaking, the most accessible to European travellers. The presence of a well-established and relatively secure Dutch, and then, following the French Revolution, English, colony at the Cape of Good Hope, in particular, made explorations of the desert regions of the South African interior the most feasible for European travellers. Two of the most prominent of such explorations were François Le Vaillant's expeditions to Namaqualand in 1781–84, and John Barrow's travels in the Great Karoo in the late 1790s. Le Vaillant's journeys, described in his *Travels into the Interior Parts of Africa* (1790) and *New Travels into the Interior Parts of Africa* (1796), were the more widely read of the two, with Felicia Hemans, for example, quoting William Howitt's question in his *Book of the Seasons* (1831) in the prefatory note to her poem 'The Flower of the Desert': 'who does not recollect the exultation of Vaillant over a flower in the torrid waste of Africa?'[17] Both Le Vaillant and Barrow, however, evidence the same sense of the relationship between the monotony or homogeneity of 'pure' desert – 'the dreary picture of dead and inanimate nature' – and its sublimity.[18] In this, both remediate the simile used by Diodorus Siculus to describe the Sahara as 'like the sea, where there is no variety of objects, but all on every side waste and desert'.[19] However, both evidently also engage with more recent descriptions, within the genre of philosophical aesthetics, of the relationship between solitude, and emptiness, and the sublime, as in, for example, Edmund Burke's discussion of the relationship between the sublime and 'privation', 'infinity', 'succession' and 'uniformity' in Part II, Sections VI–IX of his *Philosophical Enquiry*. A landscape where, in Burke's terms, the 'eye' is not 'able to perceive the bounds of [...] things', an 'uninterrupted' 'uniformity' which suggests 'infinity', is exactly how Le Vaillant, Barrow and many others remediate the deserts of the African Interior.[20]

Le Vaillant, an employee of the Dutch East India Company, based at Cape Town, made three expeditions into the interior of South Africa in 1781–84. It is curious that Howitt and Hemans should locate Le Vaillant's well-known (by their own accounts) encounter with the flower within a desert context ('in the torrid wastes'), because Le Vaillant himself makes it absolutely clear that he found this flower (a 'magnificent [...] lily seven feet in height') on the comparatively lush 'banks' of the Orange River, near 'a grove of mimosas'.[21] The contrast which Le Vaillant draws is not between the sensuous beauty of the flower and the barrenness of the desert, but rather between the beauty of the lily and the quasi-Gothic scene of a rhinoceros, which his party has shot, being butchered and partly devoured by his native guides.[22] It is during Le Vaillant's attempt to escape from this scene that he discovers the lily, and his suggestion that the plant 'had been respected by all the animals of the district, and seemed defended even by its beauty' stands in sharp relief to his own party's lack of respect for those same animals.[23] In this respect, then, the remediation of the flower incident by Howitt and Hemans is actually closer to the contrast between nullity and profusion described by Anders Sparrman, who had sailed with Cook to the Antarctic (see Chapter 3), when he encountered a man in the Great Karoo 'sleeping under a shady tree, by the side of a perfect beauty, who was clad in a light summer dress':

> no wonder then, that so uncommon and romantic a scene appearing of a sudden in a desert, should immediately chase away all those

images of desolation and wild horror which the savage and dreary aspect of these plains had begun once more to excite in mine and my friend's imagination.[24]

In other words, whether a deliberate revision or simply a failure of memory, the remediation by Howitt and Hemans of the flower episode from Le Vaillant's *New Travels* speaks not only to the moral effect which they wish to draw from that episode, but also to a desire to counter the images of desert nullity which emerge from Le Vaillant's texts, a nullity against which the flower can be marshalled as a comforting and instructive image of fruitfulness, or as a Burkean trope of the beautiful to counterbalance the harsh sublime of the desert. Similarly, Mungo Park's encounter with a flower, to which Howitt refers while discussing the episode from Le Vaillant's *New Travels*, did not take place in the desert: again, the terms of the remediation point to the desire to contrast nullity and profusion in writing about the desert.

Le Vaillant begins his description of the section of the Kalahari that he traversed in the environs of the Orange River by recalling that the locals warned him to expect 'a vast ocean of sand' (that simile from Diodorus Siculus again), with 'no kind of food or refreshment, either for my people or my animals; not the smallest trace of vegetation; not even vegetative earth', where it would be 'impossible to move one step without sinking up to the knees' in sand, and with the added 'risk of being smothered' by flying sand 'upon occasion of the least wind, if we did not perish by thirst, hunger, fatigue, and distress'.[25] Undeterred by this 'terrifying aspect', Le Vaillant affirms – not without bravado – that the sublime of the desert actually encouraged his curiosity: he is lured, not deterred, by the 'natural sublime'. Here, then, we have another glimpse of the persona of the explorer as Romantic hero, motivated by the desire for aesthetic gratification, advances in natural philosophy and imperial ambition:

> The more they [his native guides] persisted in representing the country as extraordinary, the more I was inflamed with a desire of visiting it. I saw there, in my mind's eye, new objects of natural history, discoveries of importance to commerce; and I supposed that it would furnish me with details proper to awaken curiosity, and the more singular as no one before me had ever had an opportunity of becoming acquainted with them.[26]

Hence, in Le Vaillant's expectations – and those he creates in his readers – a sublime prospect of one kind (the 'terrifying' desert known to the locals) gives way to the sublime prospect sought by the European colonial traveller in the landscapes of the sublime: aesthetic gratification, advances in natural philosophy and commercial advantage. This is the explorer as 'agent' and 'enabler' of European cultural expansion, as Thompson puts it in his discussion of James Bruce's quest for the Nile.[27] But it is also an example of how the remediation of the 'natural sublime' through expedition narrative as a facet of the persona of the explorer can come to impact upon descriptions of the relationship between subjectivity and the sublime within the genre of philosophical aesthetics. Where is the 'true' sublime in Le Vaillant's account? In the sublime which he describes? Or in the heroism of the describer?

What Le Vaillant actually encountered in the Kalahari, however, was not the gratification of these sublime expectations, but 'tormenting' and 'insupportable' physical and psychological privation.[28] In addition to the 'excessive heat', Le Vaillant and his party suffered from the effects of the 'saline crystallisation' on the desert surface, 'which, as it lay everywhere dispersed, and was struck upon by the fervid rays of the sun, scorched us by its burning reverberation, at the same time that its reflection dazzled us':

> It was raised around us by the smallest breath of wind: we ourselves also, by the motion necessary in walking, excited thick clouds of it, which flew into our faces, and inflamed our eyes; and, as we were obliged to inspire it in breathing, our nostrils became ulcerated by it [...] Our lips even were attacked by it, and in such a manner that the blood started from them when we made the least effort to speak; so that to pronounce a sentence was next to torture.[29]

As well as causing 'frequent bleedings at the nose and intolerable pains in the head', these extreme conditions also triggered hallucinations ('a confusion of sight and giddiness, or rather a real delirium') and temporary blindness ('our visual faculty was suddenly annihilated, we experienced a temporary loss of sight, and for some minutes remained as it were blind'), and, Le Vaillant believed, caused permanent damage to his 'constitution': 'since that period I have been subject to haemorrhages and head-aches, to which I was before a stranger'.[30] In place of the aesthetic gratifications, discoveries in natural philosophy and commercial edge which he sought and expected, then, Le Vaillant found in the Kalahari only suffering and 'the dreary picture of dead and inanimate nature', the 'horror' of which 'was still increased by the silence which prevailed around' (perhaps another echo of Burke, who had linked silence to 'the sublime'). Hence, Le Vaillant's sublime, culturally determined expectations were trumped by the sublime emptiness of the desert.[31]

In 1798, following his successful participation in the British embassy to China in 1792–94, John Barrow was appointed Auditor General of the British Colony at Cape Town, which had recently been captured from the Dutch. Barrow remained in South Africa until 1804, after the colony was returned to the Dutch, and made a number of semi-official expeditions into the interior. Barrow's description of crossing the Great Karoo, in his *Account of Travels into the Interior of Southern Africa*, dwells less on the physical than on the psychological privations of this journey. But like Le Vaillant, Barrow also traces the sublime effect of the 'arid desert' to the unremitting 'uniformity' of the 'barren' landscape, 'near 300 miles in length from east to west, and eighty in breadth':

> the eye wandered in vain to seek relief by a diversity of objects. No huge rocks confusedly scattered on the plain, or piled into mountains, no hills clothed with verdure, no traces of cultivation, not a tree nor a tall shrub, appeared to break the uniformity of the surface, nor bird nor beast to enliven the dreary waste.[32]

Just as in Burke's claim that 'succession' and 'uniformity' in an object can produce a sublime effect because they 'impress the imagination with an idea of their progress beyond their actual limits', then, so, for Barrow, the sublimity of the Great Karoo arises not from the physical hardships of the environment, but rather from the psychological impact of the 'altogether barren', 'sterile and naked' landscape.[33] The 'eye' is hurried from object to object, seeking but failing to find 'relief' in 'diversity'. Remediating Diodorus Siculus's seminal comparison of the Sahara with 'the sea, where there is no variety of objects', Barrow affirms of the Great Karoo that:

> Not a swell of any sort intervened to interrupt the line of the horizon, which was as perfect as that viewed over the surface of the sea. Here, too, as on that element, the mind was as little distracted by a multiplicity of objects; for in vain did the eye wander in search of tree, or lofty shrub, or blade of grass, or living creature. On every side a wide-spreading plain, barren as its southern boundary the Black Mountains [Groot Swartberg], presented nothing but a dreary waste, 'a land of desolation'.[34]

Barrow's 'eye' is unable to find relief from the sublime uniformity of the desert in any kind of 'multiplicity of objects'. Rather it is confronted and paralysed by nullity, by an absolute lack of signification. Faced with this inability, Barrow tries to restore the balance of the European subject in relation to the sublimity of the desert by appealing to culture, an appeal evidenced not only in his echo of Diodorus Siculus, but also in his invocation of the Biblical trope of the 'land of desolation', as a means of inscribing cultural value upon the emptiness, of reclaiming the horrifying emptiness for the European imagination. And a similar antithesis between desert and culture, a similar attempt to make the desert signify, underpins Barrow's account of finally reaching the other side of the Great Karoo. 'After a journey of nine days over a dreary and barren desert', he recalls, 'the traces of human industry, though in a wild sequestered corner, hemmed in by huge barren mountains, had no less charms than the discovery of land, after a long sea-voyage.'[35] The balance between culture and desert is restored, but only at the moment when the traveller exits the desert.

A similar sense of the relationship between the physical and cultural emptiness of 'pure' desert and the construction of that desert as sublime by European explorers is evident from contemporary accounts of expeditions to the desert regions of North Africa, and especially of the handful of expeditions to the Sahara. Arguably, the seminal such account is James Bruce's description of his torturous journey across the Nubian Desert, in the eastern Sahara, in 1772, on the return leg of his expedition to discover the source of the Nile. I will consider Bruce's account of his experiences in his *Travels to Discover the Source of the Nile* (1790), and its legacy to Romantic-period engagements with the sublime of the desert, later in this chapter. First, however, I want briefly to examine another prominent eighteenth-century engagement with the Sahara: the description offered by Bruce's fellow Scot, Mungo Park, in his account of his first expedition to Africa in *Travels in the Interior Districts of Africa* (1799).

Park made the first of his two expeditions to Africa in 1794–97. He was sponsored by the newly established African Association, which had been established by Joseph Banks and others in 1788, in order to promote British exploration of the continent and, in particular, to determine the course of the Niger and its viability as a trade route. An account of Park's travels written up after his return by Bryan Edwards, the secretary of the African Association, was published in *The Proceedings of the African Association* for 1798. However it was Park's own account, published the following year as *Travels into the Interior Districts of Africa*, which was destined to become one of the most widely read expedition narratives of the late eighteenth century: hence the already noted claim made by Howitt that 'the affecting mention of the influence of a flower upon the mind, by Mungo Park, in a time of suffering and despondency, in the heart of [Africa], is familiar to everyone'.[36]

Park became the first European known to have reached the Niger, and he determined that the river flowed towards the east, and thereby made a significant contribution to European knowledge of the physical geography of Africa. Park also succeeded in the secondary objective of his expedition: to determine the fate of Daniel Houghton, who had preceded him on an African Association commission, and who had died, or had been murdered, in the Moorish kingdom of Ludamar in 1791.[37] In his mini biography of Park in *The Age of Wonder*, Richard Holmes sees the Scotsman as characterised by a 'romantic attitude' to exploration and 'a Romantic belief in his own destiny', and consequently Holmes reads Park's expedition in search of the Niger as typical of the 'exploratory voyage, often lonely and perilous [which] is in one form or another a central and defining metaphor of Romantic science'.[38] In *The Suffering Traveller*, Carl Thompson, conversely, sees Park as a rather different kind of explorer. For Thompson, Park is a 'sentimental' rather than a Romantic figure, and also a semi-professional explorer, sent to collect strategically and commercially useful knowledge about the course of the Niger rather than simply in pursuit of abstract advances in natural philosophy.[39] Hence Park exemplifies, for Thompson, the extent to which 'commercial as much as scientific imperatives underpinned' European expeditions into Africa.[40] These different readings of Park are also visible in the different ways in which Holmes and Thompson interpret Park's apparently famous encounter with the flower: for Holmes, this is a moment of 'pure scientific wonder' (although that wonder is evidently tempered by religious feeling, when Park appeals to the common creator of flowers and Scottish explorers); for Thompson, by contrast, the episode reveals the desire to construct 'the explorer's fundamental innocence and benevolence' against the backdrop of his actual role as 'agent' and 'enabler' of imperialism, with Park's appeal to God in the episode of the flower implying that 'Park is a traveller whose activities are sanctioned by God'.[41]

Neither Thompson nor Holmes is primarily concerned with Park's experience of the Sahara, which of course formed only a prelude to the main object of his expedition, and, as noted, Park's often-mentioned encounter with the flower took place not in the desert but in 'a dark wood'.[42] However, Park's description of the Sahara is indicative of the way that 'pure' desert was coming increasingly to be remediated to the reading public as an immense emptiness, a sublime absence that was hostile both to the individual and to the cultural subjectivity of the European traveller. Park's observations on the Sahara were made during the first six months of 1796, while he himself was held captive in Ludamar, like Houghton before him. Park describes 'almost insufferable' heat ('all nature seemed sinking under it') and 'great scarcity of water [...] felt severely by all the people'.[43] Recalling his inability to procure water, even by begging from those who had it, Park affirms that he 'frequently passed the night in the situation of *Tantalus*'.[44] 'No sooner had I shut my eyes', Park writes of this tormenting thirst, in a passage which is strangely reminiscent of Bruce's account of his disappointment as he stood at the source of the Blue Nile:

> than fancy would convey me to the streams and rivers of my native land: there, as I wandered along the verdant brink, I surveyed the clear stream with transport, and hastened to swallow the delightful draught; – but alas! disappointment awakened me; and I found myself a lonely captive, perishing of thirst amidst the wilds of Africa![45]

Beyond recalling the physical privations which he endured, however, Park, like Le Vaillant and Barrow before him, also traces the terrible psychological power of the desert over the European traveller to the 'dismal uniformity' that 'everywhere presented itself', echoing descriptions within philosophical aesthetics of the link between 'uniformity' (a category used, for example, by Burke in *Philosophical Enquiry*, Part II, Section IX), and 'the sublime'.[46] To convey this 'dismal uniformity' to the reader, Park, like many other travellers to the desert, remediates that familiar simile from Diodorus Siculus, saying that 'the horizon was as level and uninterrupted as that of the sea'.[47] For Park, this sublime emptiness of the desert, its lack of signification, is a psychological privation on a par with, if not exceeding, the physical sufferings caused by the landscape. The Sahara, Park affirms, again remediating Diodorus Siculus, is 'a vast ocean of sand':

> the disconsolate wanderer, wherever he turns, sees nothing around him but a vast interminable expanse of sand and sky; a gloomy and barren void, where the eye finds no particular object to rest upon, and the mind is filled with painful apprehensions of perishing with thirst. 'Surrounded by this dreary solitude, the traveller sees the dead bodies of birds, that the violence of the wind has brought from

happier regions; and, as he ruminates on the fearful length of his remaining passage, listens with horror to the voice of the driving blast; the only sound that interrupts the awful repose of the Desert.'[48]

'Horror': the emotion often associated with the experience of 'the sublime' within eighteenth-century philosophical aesthetics is remediated for the reader from the actual experience of the traveller. This is sensation literature; this is 'horror' for sale. But it is also a literature based in actual experience. Echoing the descriptions by Le Vaillant and Barrow of the deserts of South Africa, as well as descriptions within philosophical aesthetics of the hurrying effects of 'the sublime', for Park the inability of the 'eye' to find 'rest' amidst the 'interminable [...] barren void' of the Sahara parallels the physical privations of the landscape. The lack of signification, the complete erasure of cultural meaning, by which the traveller is confronted, emerges from Park's account as the direct equivalent of the thirst which threatens to kill. The sublime of the desert threatens not only the life, but also the cultural identity, the subjectivity, of the European traveller. At large in such an empty wilderness, confronted with the total erasure of culture, that traveller is the type of the dying bird blown from 'happier regions'. The language of 'the sublime', the language of 'horror', the language of 'the awful', is thus the only language through which the traveller can remediate the inhuman sublime of the desert to the reader who has never left those 'happier regions'.

'Sinking still deeper in the sand': ruin and the desert

An equally complex and troubling negotiation of the relationship between the sublime of the desert and the erasure of European subjectivity, individual and cultural alike, also marks both Percy Shelley's 'Ozymandias' and William Wordsworth's 'Dream of the Arab' in Book V of *The Prelude*. Before turning to those famous Romantic-period engagements with the sublime of the desert, however, I want to consider the other mode of the contemporary genre of engagements with the sublime of the desert, engagements with what I have chosen to call 'cultured' desert. Those engagements focus primarily, though of course not exclusively, on the desert ruins of ancient Egypt.

By the end of the eighteenth century, it had become something of a commonplace to describe the impact of the desert sublime through the inability of the eye to find a focal point in the overwhelming uniformity of the landscape, a description prominent both within philosophical aesthetics and within the accounts of those who had actually travelled in the deserts of central and southern Africa. In his *Travels in Upper and Lower Egypt*, for example, the French naturalist Charles Sonnini describes the 'vast desert of Libya' as a region of 'nothing but drought and horror', an 'immense void', where 'not a plant refreshes with its verdure the weary eye', and where the subjectivity of the European traveller, personal and cultural, is confronted with its own erasure:

> There no road, no path, remains to guide the traveller's course: the impressions of his footsteps are effaced almost as soon as made, and billows of sand, raised by the impetuous winds, sometimes swallow him up.[49]

In his *Travels in Syria and Egypt*, Constantin Volney similarly affirms, again with a nod towards Diodorus Siculus, that 'to paint to himself these deserts, the reader must imagine a sky almost perpetually inflamed, and without clouds, immense and boundless plains, without houses, trees, rivulets, or hills, where the eye frequently meets nothing but an extensive and uniform horizon, like the sea'.[50] And again, what is involved here is not just description for the purposes of advancing understanding, by natural philosophers, of desert landscape; what is also involved is the remediation of the sublime of the desert, to the reader, as commodity.

Beyond this now familiar emphasis on the sublime of the 'boundless' 'uniform' 'sameness' of desert landscape, however, eighteenth-century and Romantic-period writing about Egypt in particular also comprises engagements with what I have chosen to call 'cultured' desert: desert marked by the traces of contemporary or, more frequently, of former civilisations.[51] Shelley's 'Ozymandias', of course, constitutes one such engagement, and while Shelley's highly politicised response to the ruined statue of Ramses II is not, as we shall see, representative of the mainstream of contemporary engagements with the ruin-scattered deserts of Egypt, Shelley's sonnet does remediate a genre which dates back at least a century. Early eighteenth-century engagements with the desert ruins of Egypt, such as Richard Pococke's *Description of the East* (1745), one of Shelley's possible sources for 'Ozymandias', offer comparatively little in the way of aesthetic or moral response to those landscapes, but focus rather more on factual description. Indeed, Pococke says very little about the desert itself, but is almost exclusively concerned with describing antiquities and cultures. In this respect, Pococke's account, and others like it, seems to pre-date a taste for 'the sublime', or at least a sense of the desert as sublime. As the eighteenth century wore on, however, the juxtaposition of desert and culture visible in Egypt became increasingly a topic for aesthetic, political and moral reflection with this last remediating, at least in part, the Biblical tradition of the desert as a place of spiritual enlightenment. This genre of engagement with desert ruins of course partakes in both the wider eighteenth-century engagement with so-called 'ruin sentiment', a genre which has been well documented by scholars like Laurence Goldstein and Ann Janowitz, and in the contemporary engagement with 'the sublime'.[52]

One of the most striking of the many Romantic-period engagements with the sublime spectacle of the ruin-scattered deserts of Egypt is certainly Denon's account of his first view of the ruined city of Thebes, in 1798. Dominique Vivant, Baron de Denon, was one of the leaders of the arts and literature division of the Institut d'Égypte: the group of 154 savants that Napoleon took with him during his invasion of Egypt in 1798–1802 in order to document all aspects of the natural and cultural history of the country. Following the Battle of the Pyramids, on 21 July 1798, Denon accompanied the army of General Desaix, who pursued the remaining troops of the defeated Ottoman governor, Murad Bey, into Upper Egypt. In his *Travels in Upper and Lower Egypt*, Denon recalls the moment, sublime in itself, when the French army, in pursuit of the retreating Egyptian cavalry, crested a hill and saw amidst the desert the ruins of the fabled city of Thebes:

> this illustrious city [...] this abandoned sanctuary, surrounded with barbarism, and again restored to the desert from which it had been drawn forth, enveloped in the veil of mystery, and the obscurity of ages, whereby even its own colossal monuments are magnified to the imagination, still impressed the mind with such gigantic phantoms, that the whole army, suddenly, and with one accord, stood in amazement at the sight of its scattered ruins, and clapped their hands with delight, as if the end and object of their glorious toils, and the complete conquest of Egypt, were accomplished and secured by taking possession of the splendid remains of this ancient metropolis.[53]

As so often for travellers to the landscapes of the sublime, then, for Denon, taking 'possession' in imagination of the sublime ruins of Thebes is an experience equivalent to the 'glorious' elation of actual territorial 'conquest', a dynamic which echoes descriptions, within the contemporary genre of philosophical aesthetics, of the aggrandising effect upon the individual imagination of the encounter with 'the sublime'. Denon, for his part, immediately proceeds to transform this imagined into a more actual 'conquest', in the terms of the Institut at least, by sketching 'this first aspect of Thebes', surrounded by 'the electric emotion of a whole army of soldiers'.[54]

Denon's undeniably potent account of this moment from the Egyptian campaign is, however, just one moment in a much wider contemporary genre of engagement with the spectacle of the desert ruins of Egypt, a genre which consistently links the sublime of that spectacle to the antithesis, or even the *conflict*, visible in the Egyptian landscape between desert and culture. Some engagements with this contrast are largely concerned with aesthetic effects. Consider, for example, Volney's sense, which recalls Burke's distinction between 'the sublime' and 'the beautiful', that the 'contrast' between the 'savage deserts, where the wandering traveller, exhausted with fatigue and thirst, shudders at the immense space which separates him from the world' and the 'fertile' banks of the Nile 'has probably given to the cultivated fields of Egypt all their charms':

> The barrenness of the desert becomes a foil to the plenty of the plains, watered by the river; and the aspect of the parched sands, so totally unproductive, adds to the pleasures the country offers.[55]

In his *Remarks on Several Parts of Turkey: Aegyptiaca*, William Richard Hamilton, who was influential in securing for the British possession of the Rosetta Stone, makes a similar albeit converse argument, observing of the 'landscapes of Egypt' that while 'we regret indeed the want of woods and forests to complete the picture [...] with some aid from the imagination, the eye [...] can derive pleasure even from the contemplation of a desert'.[56] Compare also Sonnini's reaction to the sight of 'herds of antelopes' in the Nubian Desert: 'the groups of living beings exhibited moving scenes, the only ones that could be interesting to us, in the midst of an immense void, and rendered the desert less naked, less frightful, in a word, less desert'.[57] As in descriptions of 'the sublime' with the eighteenth-century genre of philosophical aesthetics, contrast is the key component here, the contrast between desert and its antithesis: culture.

Hence, the thrill experienced by the likes of Denon in his first sight of Thebes is arguably not representative of the mainstream of contemporary engagements with the desert ruins of Egypt, or indeed of engagements with ruin more generally. More frequently, engagements with the contrast between the sublime of the desert and the beauty of culture tend to be sentimental, that is, they tend to remediate that contrast in more sombre terms, less as an occasion for elation, than as a *memento mori*, an occasion for worldly regret and spiritual admonishment. In fact, this more conventional mode of ruin sentiment – in which the fall of past civilisations provides an object lesson to the present – is endemic in eighteenth-century and Romantic-period engagements with the desert ruins of Egypt and the Middle East. Consider, for example, how Carsten Niebuhr laments that 'the famous Sphinx [...] is sinking still deeper in the sand': 'the memory of the authors of these stupendous and fantastic monuments has been lost some thousand years since: the pyramids are visibly decaying, and must perish in their turn'.[58] Indeed, even Denon himself, for all his enthusiasm about the 'magnificent spectacle' of the ruins of Thebes, shows that he was not immune to this kind of 'melancholy'.[59] 'Some vestiges of villages overwhelmed by the sand may be discovered', he affirms:

> nothing is so melancholy to the feelings [...] The ancient Egyptians speak of this encroachment of the sands, under the symbol of the mysterious entrance of Typhon [Seth] into the bed of his sister-in-law Isis, an incest which is to change Egypt into a desert as frightful as those by which it is encompassed.[60]

The idea of the conflict between desert and culture which is embodied in the story of Seth (associated by the Greeks with Typhon) and his attempted rape of Isis, the wife of his brother, Osiris, also informs Denon's account of entering the desert of Upper Egypt while pursuing the retreating army of Murad Bey with General Desaix. 'We were now approaching the desert', Denon recalls, 'which was also advancing to us, for, as the ancient Egyptians express it, the desert is the tyrant Typhon who is constantly invading Egypt.'[61] And this 'invading' 'tyrant' itself, the antitype of Napoleon's would-be conquerors, is described, by Denon, in now familiar terms. Echoing descriptions of 'the sublime' within the genre of philosophical aesthetics, Denon remediates the desert as a landscape of absence, of intense physical and psychological privation:

> a boundless horizon of barrenness, which oppresses the mind by immensity of distance, and whose appearance, where level, is only a dreary waste; and where broken by hills, only shows another feature of decay and decrepitude, whilst the silence of inanimate nature reigns throughout undisturbed.[62]

The 'boundless', 'barrenness', 'immensity of distance', 'silence': these are all key categories within theoretical descriptions of 'the sublime' such as Burke's *Philosophical Enquiry*. And even General Desaix himself was troubled, Denon records, and prompted by the 'melancholy inspired by the scene' to wonder if the sublime, 'inanimate' desert was not 'an error of nature'.[63]

A key mode of the eighteenth-century and Romantic-period genre of engagement with the sublime spectacle of the desert ruins of Egypt is, then, this contrast between absence and plenitude, between desert and culture. Percy Shelley's sonnet 'Ozymandias', for example, depends on precisely this aesthetics of contrast in order to deliver its political message: the futility of the tyrannical Pharaoh's achievements is made visible through the contrast between the 'colossal wreck' of his statue and the 'boundless and bare', 'lone and level sands' by which it is surrounded.[64] And indeed, as has often been noted by commentators on Shelley's poem, in deploying this contrast, Shelley is actually himself remediating another of the most influential of the many eighteenth-century engagements with the sublime spectacle of desert ruins: Constantin Volney's *The Ruins, or, Meditations on the Revolutions of Empires* (1792).

The protagonist of Volney's *Ruins*, a European traveller, the type of Volney himself, is confronted not with the sublime spectacle of the desert-encompassed ruins of ancient Egypt, but with the ruins of the city of Palmyra (Tadmor) in Syria, which Volney had visited during his travels in 1783–85. In his *Travels*, Volney affirms that 'it is universally acknowledged that antiquity has left nothing, either in Greece or Italy, to be compared with the magnificence of the ruins of Palmyra'.[65] Invoking the now familiar idea that the landscapes of the sublime cannot adequately be remediated, Volney suggests that 'the effect of such a sight is not to be communicated'.[66] As if to prove this point, Volney then proceeds to offer the reader a 20-page description, including illustrations and quotations from other sources, of the 'immense' ruins, which are located in an oasis 'separated from the habitable earth, by an ocean of barren sands'.[67]

Hence, Volney's account of the sublime of Palmyra, in his *Travels*, also turns around the contrast between desert and culture, or the remains of culture. So, too, in Volney's *Ruins*, it is this same contrast which enables Volney's argument about tyranny, just as it does in Shelley's 'Ozymandias'. The protagonist of *The Ruins*, evidently a remediation for the reader of Volney himself, 'after three days travel in barren solitude' arrives at 'a most astonishing scene of ruins'.[68] Ascending a nearby hill, 'from which the eye commands at once the whole of the ruins and the immensity of the desert', this contrast between the ruins and the desert ('sometimes turning my eyes towards the desert, and sometimes fixing them on the ruins') provokes, in Volney's traveller, a 'profound reverie' about the nature and the causes of the fall of civilisations.[69] 'What glory is here eclipsed', he asks, 'and how many labours are annihilated! Thus perish the works of men, and thus do nations and empires pass away':

> From whence proceed such melancholy revolutions? For what cause is the fortune of these countries so strikingly changed? Why are so many cities destroyed? Why is not that ancient population reproduced and perpetuated?[70]

By way of an answer to these questions, Volney's traveller is visited by the 'genius of the ruins', an apparition which attributes the fall of civilisations like that of Palmyra to the injustice of their governments. Hence, the contrast between desert and ruin not only affirms the vanity of tyrants, but also warns about the fatal consequences of tyranny and corruption. Nor is this warning confined to the civilisations of the past. 'Who knows', asks Volney's protagonist:

> but that hereafter some traveller like myself will sit down upon the banks of the Seine, the Thames, or the Zuyder Sea, where now, in the tumult of enjoyment, the heart and the eyes are too slow to take in the multitude of sensations; who knows but he will sit down solitary, amid silent ruins, and weep a people inurned, and their greatness changed into an empty name.[71]

Volney's radical remediation of the sublime spectacle of desert ruins, like Shelley's in 'Ozymandias', re-inflects the mainstream of the contemporary genre of engagement with the sublime of desert ruins, which, as we have seen, tends more typically to read such ruins as a *memento mori*, as an occasion for sentimental regret, or spiritual reflection, rather than as a validation of progressive political change. A similar remediation can be discerned in Percy Shelley's poem *Alastor, or, The Spirit of Solitude* (1816), in which the poet-protagonist retraces Volney's journeys through the deserts of Egypt and Syria, and Denon's journey to Upper Egypt, before finally arriving at the 'desert hills' of 'dark Aethiopia', where 'among the ruined temples' he learns 'the thrilling secrets of the birth of time', an allusion to Volney's theories, in *The Ruins*, about the origins of religion in the reaction of primitive peoples to the stars.[72]

The primary mode of the genre of engagement with the sublime spectacle of desert ruins against which both Volney and Shelley are reacting, however, is plainly apparent in the sonnet which Shelley's friend Horace Smith wrote about Ramses II whilst Shelley was composing 'Ozymandias'. Smith's 'Ozymandias' affirms of the 'wonder' occasioned by the spectacle of the ruined statue, in terms which echo Volney's *Ruins*, but which are far less politicised, that:

> We wonder, and some Hunter may express
> Wonder like ours, when thro' the wilderness
> Where London stood, holding the Wolf in chase,
> He meets some fragments huge, and stops to guess
> What powerful but unrecorded race
> Once dwelt in that annihilated place.[73]

In Smith's poem, the ruined statue of Ramses II, and the imagined ruins of London, occasion merely 'wonder', merely regret, without the added dimension of rational enquiry or political agenda. That said, a remediation which supports the status quo is a no less 'interested' remediation of the 'natural sublime' than one which challenges it.

'Alone upon the sands': Bruce's *Travels* and Wordsworth's dream

As we have seen, the eighteenth-century and Romantic-period genre of engagement with the desert sublime repeatedly features a European traveller who is confronted in the landscape by an overwhelming *absence*, an absence which both represents and literally enacts the effacement of European subjectivity, personal and cultural alike. And it is this same confrontation with the erasure of subjectivity, of culture, which lies at the heart of two of the period's most prominent engagements with the sublime of the desert: James Bruce's account of his ordeal in the Nubian Desert, in his *Travels to Discover the Source of the Nile*, and William Wordsworth's 'Dream of the Arab', from Book V of *The Prelude*.

Poetic engagements with what I have chosen to call 'cultured' desert, such as in Percy Shelley's 'Ozymandias' and *Alastor*, are relatively common during the Romantic period. However, poetic engagements with 'pure' desert are rather less so, no doubt, at least in part, because of the ongoing inaccessibility of Saharan and sub-Saharan Africa compared to the exponential increase in military, commercial and private expeditions to the Middle East and to Egypt. The scenario which Wordsworth presents to the reader in the opening of the Arab dream sequence of *Prelude* V, however, is the familiar one from both modes of contemporary engagement with the sublime of the desert: the solitary traveller confronted in the landscape by an overwhelming nullity which threatens the erasure both of individual and of cultural identity.

In the 1805 text of *The Prelude*, Wordsworth describes a dreamer who

> saw before him an Arabian waste
> A desert, and he fancied that himself
> Was sitting there in the wide wilderness
> Alone upon the sands. Distress of mind
> Was growing in him[74]

In the 1850 text, Wordsworth shifts from the third to the first person and removes the reference to Arabia:

> I saw before me a boundless plain
> Of sandy wilderness, all black and void,
> And as I looked around, distress and fear
> Came creeping over me[75]

In both versions, then, the position of the dreamer – 'alone' and in 'distress', confronted with a 'wide', 'boundless' 'wilderness' – is the familiar one from the genre of engagement with the sublime of the desert which I have been describing in this chapter: the genre which comprises the writings of travellers like Park and Le Vaillant, and which also comprises, as I will argue later in this chapter, the harrowing account given by James Bruce of his return home through the Sahara from the source of the Blue Nile. At this point, Wordsworth tells us, the dreamer is reassured by the sudden appearance of 'a man at his side / Upon a dromedary mounted high! / He seemed an Arab of the Bedouin tribes', whom he hopes will serve him as 'a guide / To lead him through the desert'.[76] In the text of 1850, this 'man' is introduced as 'an uncouth shape', but the dreamer's confidence in his abilities as a guide is increased: 'much I rejoiced, not doubting but a guide / Was present, one who with unerring skill / Would through the desert lead me'.[77] The Arab is carrying a 'stone' and a 'shell', which he identifies as Euclid's *Elements*, a metonym of 'geometric truth', and 'something of more worth', which commentators on the dream sequence have tended to identify with poetry, or the arts more generally.[78] These the Arab is attempting to save from an imminent apocalypse, and he hurries away from the dreamer, despite his protestations that he be allowed to accompany him. As the dreamer watches the Arab 'riding o'er the desert sands' (the 'illimitable waste' in the 1850 text) pursued by 'the fleet waters of the drowning world', he wakes 'in terror' to find the book which he had been reading, Cervantes's *Don Quixote*, 'at my side'.[79]

Wordsworth sets the Arab dream sequence within the context of a discussion which he had been having with 'a friend' – Coleridge ('a studious friend' in the text of 1850) – about the impermanence of human cultural productions:

> why hath not the mind
> some element to stamp her image on
> In nature somewhat nearer to her own?
> Why, gifted with such powers to send abroad
> Her spirit, must it lodge in shrines so frail?[80]

Seen in this wider context, the sequence seems an obvious meditation on the same concern: it encodes an apocalyptic anxiety about the transience of human cultural achievements, granted the caveat offered by the figure of Coleridge in *Prelude* V that in expressing 'thoughts like these', Wordsworth 'was going far to seek disquietude'.[81]

The Arab dream sequence has, unsurprisingly, received a great deal of attention from scholars of Wordsworth's writing, although, broadly speaking, such commentaries fit into one of two categories: those which seek to interpret the sequence, and those which seek to discern Wordsworth's possible sources for it, and thereby to interrogate its authenticity as a *dream*. Interpretative readings of the passage, such as Hartman's seminal commentary, tend to focus on what Wordsworth implies about the respective truth claims of science and poetry, and about the role of the imagination in both discourses.[82] A diverse range of putative sources for the sequence has also been proposed, including Genesis, *Metamorphoses*, *Don Quixote* ('the famous history of the errant knight' signalled by Wordsworth himself), Josephus's *History of the Jews*, and *Paradise Lost*.[83] My purpose here is to attempt to move interpretations of the Arab dream sequence beyond this dichotomy between canonical text and non-canonical source(s), and to replace that sequence within the context of the wider contemporary genre of engagements with the sublime of the desert which, I believe, Wordsworth both mediates and remediates in these lines.

We might begin to restore some sense of the relationship between the Arab dream sequence and this wider contemporary genre of engagement with the sublime of the desert by considering Wordsworth's portrait of the Arab himself. Within that genre, European travellers tend more frequently to record encounters with often hostile groups in the desert, rather than with lone individuals, as in, for example, Park's capture by a group of Moors in Ludamar. Wordsworth, conversely, describes a solitary figure, whose sudden appearance is a source of comfort rather than a threat to the dreamer ('much rejoiced the dreaming man'), who believes that the Arab will prove 'a guide / To lead him through the desert'.[84] In this, Wordsworth might have been recalling Charles Sonnini's laudatory and affectionate account, in his widely read *Travels*, of an Arab called Hussein who guided him safely across 'the vast desert of Libya', 'where no road, no path, remains to guide the traveller's course', but 'the Arab, to whom these solitudes are familiar, knows how to traverse them in all directions, without a compass as well as without a path'.[85] 'Memory still paints him in my imagination', Sonnini says of Hussein, who plays a prominent role in the *Travels*, 'walking with tranquillity over these bare plains, where no landmark appears to direct the steps, as devoid of care as if he were in the most nicely planted walk.'[86] Compare, also, Wordsworth's 'uncouth shape' with the description given by Carsten Niebuhr, in his *Travels*, of an optical illusion or 'error of vision' which he experienced in the desert: 'an Arab, whom I saw approaching at a distance, upon a camel, appeared to move through the air, with the gigantic bulk of a tower; although he was travelling along the sand like ourselves'.[87]

Unlike Sonnini's guide who was 'devoid of care', however, Wordsworth's Arab is on an urgent quest, and, towards the end of the sequence, Wordsworth describes how, following the dream, he gradually reimagined this 'Arab phantom [...] this semi-Quixote' as a kind of enlightened 'maniac', whose 'anxiousness' about the transience of culture he 'could share'.[88] 'I to him have given / A substance', Wordsworth writes:

> fancied him a living man,
> A gentle dweller in the desert, crazed
> By love and feeling and internal thought
> Protracted among endless solitudes –
> Have shaped him, in the oppression of his brain,
> Wandering upon this quest, and thus equipped.
> And I have scarcely pitied him, have felt
> A reverence for a being thus employed,
> And thought that in the blind and awful lair
> Of such madness, reason did lie encouched.[89]

In this vision of an individual obsessed by a laudable but ostensibly irrational 'quest', then, Wordsworth transforms the Arab of the dream sequence from the hostile figures of eighteenth-century and Romantic-period engagements with the sublime of the desert not just into 'a gentle dweller in the desert', but into a sublime figure who recalls more than anything else the persona of the European explorer suffering *through* the desert on an ostensibly 'crazed' journey which is nevertheless both credible and laudable in its ambition and its objective. From the Arab who is the master of the desert environment, then, Wordsworth fashions the type of a Mungo Park or a Le Vaillant, who is struggling not to be mastered by it. I do not mean by this to restrict the range of Wordsworth's reference in the character of the Arab: comparisons with Don Quixote, and with a range of Biblical dwellers in the desert, are of course also possible. What I do mean to suggest, however, is that the Arab dream sequence is also, at least in part, a remediation of the contemporary genre of engagement with the sublime of the desert, and, particularly, of the sense of the desert as the locus of the effacement of individual and cultural subjectivity which we have discerned at the heart of that genre. To do this, I want to set Wordsworth's 'Dream of the Arab' alongside arguably the most prominent of all of the eighteenth-century engagements with the sublime of the desert: the account which James Bruce provides of his ordeal in the Nubian Desert.

There is no direct evidence that Wordsworth ever read Bruce's *Travels to Discover the Source of the Nile*, but it seems unlikely that he would not have been familiar with such a widely read and controversial work, and indeed Dorothy Wordsworth's journal records that she and William visited 'the residence of the famous traveller Bruce' during their tour of Scotland in 1803.[90] As Nigel Leask has shown in *Curiosity and the Aesthetics of Travel Writing*, much of the controversy surrounding Bruce's *Travels* concerned not just the Scotsman's claim actually to have located the source of the Nile, but also his account of the time that he had spent, partly as guest and partly as captive, amongst the indigenous population in Abyssinia, which comprised tales of amorous escapades and the consumption of raw beef hacked from live cows.[91] But Bruce's harrowing account of his trek across the Nubian Desert on the final leg of his return journey across Africa had also achieved notoriety both within and beyond the eighteenth-century genre of engagements with the sublime of the desert. No less a figure than Robert Southey, for example, in his review of the posthumous second edition of Bruce's *Travels* (1805), commented that 'in the whole course of our reading, we remember nothing more deeply and lastingly impressive than the journey of Bruce across the desert'.[92]

Potential areas of interaction between various parts of *The Prelude* and various episodes from Bruce's *Travels* have also been flagged up by scholars of Wordsworth's writing. In his seminal rereading of the Simplon Pass episode from Book VI of *The Prelude*, for example, Alan Liu compares the 'grief or despondency' which strikes Bruce at the moment when he believes that he has accomplished the great object of his expedition and discovered the source of the Nile, with the deflation which struck Wordsworth when he 'first'

> Beheld the summit of Mont Blanc, and grieved
> To have a soulless image on the eye
> That had usurped upon a living thought
> That never more could be.[93]

For Liu, both Bruce and Wordsworth find 'at the source of experience' a 'deep emptiness' for which both, somehow, need to compensate.[94] More recently, Carl Thompson has read the persona of the explorer which emerges from Bruce's remediation of his expedition in his *Travels* in apposition to that which emerges from Park's remediation of his experiences on his first journey to Africa in 1794–97. Thompson (complementing Leask's reading) sees Bruce, unlike Park, as 'primarily interested in natural curiosities and wonders, in phenomena and features of the landscape that seem singular rather than typical', rather than details 'obviously useful to contemporary science'.[95] For Thompson, in other words, Bruce's expedition is in effect a pursuit of the exotic or wonderful (as Richard Holmes might put it), that is to say, of 'the sublime'. Thompson develops Liu's sense of a connection between Bruce's account of his disappointment at the source of the Blue Nile and Wordsworth's disappointment in the Alps, noting that Wordsworth's reference to 'the overflowing Nile' in his apostrophe to the imagination at least raises the possibility that 'James Bruce is in his mind'.[96] However, Thompson also points to a potential relationship between Bruce's account of his ordeal in the Nubian Desert and Wordsworth's 'Dream of the Arab': for Thompson, both Bruce struggling back to Europe across the desert and Wordsworth's Arab fleeing across the desert from an apocalyptic wave share 'a mission to rescue from obscurity and preserve from destruction key testimonies of human achievement'.[97] Hence Wordsworth's Arab becomes, for Thompson, 'at some level a reflection of, or a response to, James Bruce'.[98]

This is the suggestion which I want further to pursue here in order to illustrate the extent to which Wordsworth's 'Dream of the Arab' might be seen to mediate and to remediate a wider, contemporary genre of engagement with the sublime of the desert. My argument is that both episodes turn around precisely the same sense of an opposition between desert and culture which I have, in this chapter, been tracing in eighteenth-century and Romantic-period engagements with the sublime of the desert. Hence, my purpose is not so much to argue that Wordsworth must have drawn on the desert episode of Bruce's *Travels* in the 'Dream of the Arab' as it is (again) to move beyond this sense of a dichotomy between a canonical text and its (now) non-canonical source: my point in exploring both texts is to attempt to restore a sense of their common, historical position within a wider genre of engagement with the sublime of the desert, a genre which consistently describes a solitary traveller who is confronted in an inhuman landscape with the erasure of personal and cultural subjectivity.[99]

Bruce's expedition to trace the Nile to its source, which he financed himself, began in June 1768. Just over two years later, on 14 November 1770, Bruce arrived at the source of the Blue Nile, in Upper Ethiopia, and subsequently claimed to have been the first to do so, even though, as he knew, the Jesuit missionary Pedro Paez had almost certainly preceded him by nearly two centuries. After reaching the source, Bruce remained for almost a year in Gondar, then the capital of Ethiopia (or Abyssinia, as it was known to Bruce and his contemporaries), where he observed the various cultural practices which he would so notoriously describe upon his return to London and in his subsequent *Travels*. Bruce eventually began his return journey towards Alexandria in December 1771, arriving just under a year later. The final phase of this journey involved the arduous trek across the Nubian Desert, in November 1771, which Bruce made the subject of the two chapters that were destined to number amongst the most talked-about episodes of his *Travels*.

Bruce's account of his ordeal involves many of the elements which I have in this chapter discerned within the eighteenth-century genre of engagement with the sublime of the desert. Bruce describes the extreme physical privation which his group endured in graphic detail. Early in the crossing, Bruce affirms that 'it was so excessively hot that it was impossible to suffer the burning sun [...] Our eyes were dim, our lips cracked, our knees tottering, our throats perfectly dry, and no relief was found from drinking an immoderate quantity of water.'[100] As their stocks of water dwindled, they were faced with 'that terrible death by thirst', at one point being forced to drink from an oasis littered with dead animals, 'putting a piece of our cotton girdle over our mouths, to keep, by filtration, the filth of dead animals out of it'.[101] They were burned by the sun, and their footwear, too, quickly wore away, becoming 'absolutely useless [...] so that our feet were very much inflamed by the burning sand'.[102] Midway through the crossing, Bruce described his face as 'so swelled as scarcely to permit me to see; my neck covered with blisters' and his 'feet swelled and inflamed, and bleeding with many wounds'.[103] Towards the end, in a 'situation [...] the most desperate that could be figured [...] in the middle of the most barren, inhospitable desert in the world', Bruce could hardly walk:

> The bandage which the Bishareen had tied about the hollow of my foot, was now almost hidden by the flesh swelling over it. Three large wounds on the right foot, and two on the left, continued open, whence a quantity of lymph oozed continually.[104]

Inevitably, Bruce's group were forced to abandon one of their number who, becoming ill, 'refused to continue his journey, or rise from where he lay, so that we were obliged to leave him to his fortune'.[105]

In addition to these hardships, Bruce and his company were also afflicted by some of the even more sublime hazards of the desert environment, which Bruce, with that taste for the exotic noticed by Thompson, describes at some length. On 14 November 1771, Bruce records, in a passage which recalls Edmund Burke's description of the sublime in his *Philosophical Enquiry*, that they were 'at once surprised and terrified by a sight surely one of the most magnificent in the world':

> In that vast expanse of desert, from W. and to N.W. of us, we saw a number of prodigious pillars of sand at different distances, at times moving with great celerity, at others stalking on with majestic slowness; at intervals we thought they were coming in a very few minutes to overwhelm us; and small quantities of sand did actually more than once reach us [...] Eleven of them ranged alongside of us about the distance of three miles [...] leaving an impression upon my mind to which I can give no name, though surely one ingredient of it was fear, with a considerable deal of wonder and astonishment.[106]

The terms of Bruce's description here evidently parallel descriptions of the sublime within the contemporary genre of philosophical aesthetics as a composite of fear, wonder and astonishment. Moreover, just as Edmund Burke had asserted in his *Philosophical Enquiry* that 'terror' only 'produces delight when it does not press too close', so too does Bruce recall that the 'wonder and astonishment' which these 'pillars of sand' had occasioned in his group was entirely effaced, leaving them 'disheartened, and our fear more increased, when we found upon waking in the morning, that one side was perfectly covered in the sand that the wind had blown above us in the night'.[107] Vicarious danger can be productive of the sublime, but actual danger is just dangerous.

Bruce makes a number of observations about the 'effect' of the 'stupendous sight' of the pillars of sand upon those members of his party who were drawn from the indigenous population in Abyssinia, and in so doing he recalls the speculation by thinkers like d'Holbach, Volney and Smith about the origins of primitive religious belief in the reaction to the 'natural sublime'.[108] Upon the first appearance of the pillars, Bruce recalls, the Africans travelling with him made immediate recourse to their 'charms' and their 'prayers'.[109] Indeed, during one particularly impressive display, when the refraction of the sun through the swirling columns of sand gave them the 'appearance of pillars of fire', Bruce reports that the Greeks travelling with him 'shrieked out, and said it was the day of judgment', an Arab that they had entered 'hell', and the Africans 'that the world was on fire'.[110] In such extreme conditions, however, even Bruce himself was not immune to such superstitious reactions to natural phenomena. Later in the desert crossing, exhausted and hungry, Bruce's party encountered a lone antelope. Bruce records that he checked his 'first idea [...] to kill it' – this albatross of the desert – because 'it seemed so interested in what I was doing, that I began to think it might perhaps be my good genius which had come to visit, protect, and encourage me in the desperate situation in which I then was'.[111] Gradually, however, the repeated occurrence of 'the same appearance of moving pillars of sand' throughout the latter stages of Bruce's trek caused his group 'to be somewhat reconciled to this phenomenon, feeling it had hitherto done us no harm'.[112] 'The great magnificence it exhibited in its appearance', he affirms, 'seemed, in some measure, to indemnify us for the panic it had first occasioned'.[113] Aesthetic gratification is enhanced, as in Burke's description of the sublime, by the security of distance and some measure of familiarity.

The apocalyptic 'pillars of sand' which Bruce describes as such a novelty had in fact been noted since antiquity, as in, for example, the account given by Herodotus of the fate of the army of Cambyses II, overwhelmed by 'vast columns of swirling sand'.[114] In his *Remarks on Several Parts of Turkey*, Hamilton also references the description made by Strabo of the temple of Serapis in the Nubian Desert as 'in a very sandy place' where 'columns of sand were frequently raised by the wind, so as to make it dangerous for the passenger; and the heads of the sphinxes were to be seen, the rest of whose bodies was buried beneath the sands'.[115] More recent accounts of these 'pillars of sand' were also available. In his

Travels, for example, Mungo Park describes 'a sand wind' ('the quantity of sand and dust carried before it, was such as to darken the whole atmosphere'), while Le Vaillant recalls 'a terrible whirlwind' in the Kalahari: 'the violence of the wind increased as the sun rose above the horizon; and though the sky was without a cloud, the face of the sun was obscured by the columns of sand'.[116] Saugnier, too, affirms the dangers of this phenomenon, noting that upon its appearance 'the Arabs decamp without delay [because] a single night would be enough to heap fifty feet of sand upon their heads'.[117] However, it was Bruce's description of this 'magnificent' spectacle which would become the defining account within the Romantic-period genre of engagement with the sublime of desert, serving both as an inspiration and as a quest-object for subsequent travellers who would come to desert hoping to witness this species of the sublime. In his *Travels in Africa, Egypt, and Syria*, for example, William George Browne, who cited Bruce's *Travels* as the occasion of his own journey, lamented that although he had witnessed 'a singular appearance, which soon discovered itself to be a column of sand, raised from the desert by a whirlwind' it 'had nothing of the tremendous appearance of the columns of sand described by Bruce'.[118] As so often when the landscapes of the sublime become more familiar to the European imagination, the reality of the 'classic ground' fails to live up to its billing in the growing body of writing about it.

While Bruce and his party did eventually become accustomed to the appearance of these 'pillars of sand', however, and developed the ability to appreciate their magnificence without apprehension, 'it was otherwise', Bruce records, with a second extreme atmospheric phenomenon which they encountered in the Nubian Desert: the dreaded simoom wind.[119] With its power instantly to erase individual and cultural subjectivity, the simoom, or superheated desert wind, would come to embody the sublime of the desert in Romantic-period writing. At the beginning of the eighteenth century, however, the simoom belonged more to the realm of myth than to natural philosophy, and came often also to be confused with the kind of desert 'sand wind' described by Le Vaillant, Park and others. It was Volney, in his *Travels in Syria and Egypt*, who offered one of the first, extended, quasi-scientific descriptions of the '*kamsin*' (= Arabic *khamsin*) or '*poisonous* winds, or, more correctly, *hot winds of the desert*', which combine very high air temperatures with very low humidity.[120] Volney's equivocation over terminology masks the fact that the khamsin and the simoom are actually different phenomena. However, the 'excessive' heat and associated symptoms which Volney describes are consistent with the simoom, and his three-page description moves quickly from the language of natural philosophy to the language of 'the sublime':

> When these winds blow, the atmosphere assumes an alarming appearance [...] The lungs, which a too rarefied air no longer expands, are contracted, and painful. Breathing is short and difficult, and the body consumed by an internal heat. In vain is recourse had to large draughts of water [...] Woe to the traveller whom this wind surprises far from shelter; he must suffer all its dreadful effects, which are sometimes mortal [...] the rapidity of the wind increases the heat to such a degree, as to occasion sudden death. This death is suffocation; the lungs being empty, are convulsed, circulation disordered, and the whole mass of blood driven by the heart towards the head and breast; whence that haemorrhage at the nose and mouth which follows death [...] Extreme aridity is another quality of this wind [...] it withers and strips all the plants, and, by exhaling too suddenly the emanations from animal bodies, crisps the skin, shuts the pores, and produces that feverish heat which is the invariable effect of suppressed perspiration.[121]

The rapid transition from the language of natural philosophy to the language of 'the sublime' in Volney's account bears out the difficulty of providing credible, rational witness to so incredible a phenomenon, a difficulty which we have often seen in the published accounts of the travellers to the landscapes of the sublime: the 'natural sublime' defies remediation in the language of natural philosophy. The same difficulty is visible in Denon's record of his experience of the khamsin during Napoleon's Egyptian campaign. This wind is 'equally terrible', Denon affirms, 'by the frightful spectacle which it exhibits when present, and by the consequences which follow its ravages'.[122] When Denon and his party were 'entirely overcome by a suffocating heat, it seemed as if the fluctuation of the air was suddenly suspended'; they fled to the nearby Nile to escape 'the baneful effects' of the approaching wind, but, despite this precaution, still ended up 'with our eyes smarting, our noses stuffed up, and our throats clogged with dust, so that we could hardly breathe'.[123] Following this experience, Denon, like Volney before him, affirms that he 'could now easily conceive the dreadful situation of those who are surprised with such a phenomenon of nature, when crossing the exposed and naked deserts'.[124]

In his *Account of the Kingdom of Caubul and its Dependencies* (1815), Mountstuart Elphinstone, a British administrator in India, confirmed for the later Romantic period just how 'dreadful' this situation could be: 'when a man is caught in it, it generally occasions instant death. The sufferer falls senseless, and blood bursts from his mouth, nose, and ears. His life is sometimes saved, by administering a strong acid, or by immersing him in water.'[125] For the late eighteenth century and early Romantic period, however, James Bruce was the archetype of just such a traveller who had been 'surprised' by the simoom 'when crossing the exposed and naked deserts', to use Denon's phrase – and who had lived to tell the fantastic tale to the reading public.

Unlike Volney or, later, Denon, Bruce makes no attempt at natural philosophy in his account of the simoom. Rather, he offers a self-consciously spectacular narrative, very much in the style of other flamboyant moments from the *Travels*, and very much in the vein of the emergent persona of the Romantic explorer-hero, whose remediation of himself to the reading public partakes of the sublime which he describes: indeed, as Thompson points out, Bruce is amongst the more significant contemporary instances of that persona. Bruce's party had been warned by their Arab guide, Idris, that if a simoom occurred, they must immediately attempt to protect themselves by lying face down on the sand. On 16 November 1771, Bruce recalls, 'Idris cried out, with a loud voice, fall upon your faces, for here is the simoom.'[126] 'I saw from the S.E.', Bruce writes:

> a haze come, in colour like the purple part of the rainbow, but not so compressed or thick. It did not occupy twenty yards in breadth, and was about twelve feet high from the ground. It was a kind of blush upon the air, and it moved very rapidly, for I scarce could turn to fall upon the ground with my head to the northward, when I felt the heat of its current plainly upon my face. We all lay flat on the ground, as if dead [...] I found distinctly in my breast that I had imbibed part of it.[127]

The experience had severe physical consequences: Bruce 'had nearly lost his voice', which he says he did not fully regain until almost two years later, and his face was 'so swelled as scarcely to permit me to see; my neck covered with blisters'.[128] Nor was this their only encounter with 'the poisonous wind'.[129] Around noon on 20 November, the simoom struck again. This time, however, they had more notice and the wind was less violent. 'My curiosity would not suffer me to fall down without looking behind me,' Bruce writes:

> About due south, a little to the east, I saw the coloured haze as before. It seemed now to be rather less compressed, and to have with

it a shade of blue. The edges of it were not defined as those of the former, but like a very thin smoke, with about a yard in the middle tinged with those colours. We all fell upon our faces, and the simoom passed.[130]

Again, physical consequences ensued: 'we were all taken ill that night', Bruce records, and a camel died.[131]

However, 'the dreadful influence of the simoom' was not limited to physical injuries.[132] After their first experience of the wind, Bruce remembers, 'an universal despondency had taken possession of our people', and Bruce gradually came to identify this 'despondency' as an effect of the simoom, eventually affirming with some confidence that 'the usual despondency that always accompanied it' manifested itself in 'silence, and a desperate kind of indifference about life'.[133] 'It had filled us with fear', Bruce concludes, 'and absorbed the last remnants of our strength.'[134] The encounter with the sublime of the desert, symbolised in the simoom, is thus neither thrilling nor aggrandising for the European subject; it is, rather, an awful reminder of the fragility of subjectivity.

I do not have the space here to consider in detail the extensive legacy left by Bruce's account of 'the dreadful simoom' to the imagery of canonical Romantic-period poetry, but we can begin to get some sense of that legacy if we recall Coleridge's reference, in *Religious Musings*, to the

> sun-scorched waste,
> Where oft majestic through the tainted noon
> The Simoom sails, before whose purple pomp
> Who falls not prostrate dies![135]

Coleridge is indebted here, on almost every point, to Bruce's description, and numerous similar examples could be adduced, including Byron's references to the simoom in *The Giaour*, which cites Bruce's *Travels* as its authority, and in *Don Juan* IV, to say nothing of Southey's enthusiasm in his already mentioned review.[136] And indeed, whilst Wordsworth makes no direct mention of the simoom in his poetry, we might suggest that it is not too far to travel from the description by Bruce of this physically and psychologically devastating wind, with its threat to the personal and cultural subjectivity of the European traveller, to the 'loud prophetic blast' in 'an unknown tongue, / Which yet I understood', 'which foretold destruction to the children of the earth by deluge now at hand', which is heard by the dreamer in *Prelude* VI when he presses the shell that is carried by the Arab to his ear.[137] The simoom emerges from the description given by Bruce as emblematic of the sublime of the desert in its threat to erase the subjectivity of the European traveller and it is of course a very similar anxiety about the fragility of human cultural productions which is at the heart of the drama which plays out in the desert in Wordsworth's 'Dream of the Arab'. And exactly that Wordsworthian anxiety about the erasure of culture – with which Wordsworth engages within the context of the desert, rather than in any other context – is also present in the dénouement of Bruce's account of his ordeal in the Nubian Desert.

On 27 November 1771, Bruce and the surviving members of his party were nearly spent 'amidst the burning sands'.[138] 'We were surrounded', Bruce recalls:

> among those terrible and unusual phenomena of nature which Providence, in mercy to the weakness of his creatures, has concealed far from their sight in deserts almost inaccessible to them. Nothing but death was before our eyes.[139]

Here, then, the 'natural sublime' is not so much a comforting and elevating evidence of the grandeur of 'Providence', as in the religious responses to the Alpine sublime which are described by Marjorie Hope Nicolson in *Mountain Gloom and Mountain Glory*, as it is a cause for profound existential anxiety, a troubling confrontation with the inhuman ('nothing but death'). Even 'in these terrible moments of pain, suffering, and despair', however, Bruce, as a European explorer, returning from an expedition through which he believed that he had made significant discoveries, felt an additional agony that was his alone:

> Honour, instead of relieving me, suggested still what was to be an augmentation to my misfortune; the feeling this produced fell directly upon me alone, and every other individual of the company was unconscious of it.[140]

The problem was that Bruce knew that if he and his party were to have any chance at all of making it out of the desert alive, then they would have to abandon all unnecessary baggage – and this meant leaving in the desert all the sketches, samples, artefacts, maps and notes which Bruce had amassed during his expedition, that is, all of the cultural tools by which Europe might take ideological possession of the territories which Bruce had traversed. All were abandoned, Bruce recalls, 'in an undigested heap, with our carrion camels [...] while there remained with me, in lieu of all my memoranda, but this mournful consideration':

> that I was now to maintain the reality of these my tedious perils, with those who either did, or might affect, from malice or envy, to doubt my veracity upon my *ipse dixit* alone, or abandon the reputation of the travels which I had made with so much courage, labour, danger, and difficulty, and which had been considered as desperate and impracticable to accomplish for more than 2000 years.[141]

In remediating these emotions to the reading public through his *Travels*, Bruce clearly has his eye back on the controversy which surrounded the verbal reports which he made when he first returned to London, the controversy which the *Travels* were supposed to lay to rest.[142] Hence, Bruce is keen to emphasise that the 'despair' which he felt on having to abandon the records of his expedition in the Nubian Desert was not caused by pride, and he takes at the same time the opportunity to attack those 'chicken-hearted critics' who had doubted the reports which he made upon his first return to London.[143] 'I would not be understood to mean by this', Bruce writes, 'that my thoughts were at such a time in the least disturbed with any reflection on the paltry lies that might be propagated in malignant circles.'[144] Rather, Bruce stresses that his 'despair' was occasioned by the *cultural* loss involved in the decision to abandon the records of his expedition in the desert:

> My sorrows were of another kind, that I should, of course, be deprived of a considerable part of an offering I meant as a mark of duty to my sovereign, that, with those that knew and esteemed me, I should be obliged to run in debt for the credit of a whole narrative of circumstances, which ought, from their importance to history and geography, to have a better foundation than the mere memory of any man, considering the time and variety of events which they embraced; and, above all, I may be allowed to say, I felt for my country, that chance alone, in this age of discovery, had robbed her of the fairest garland of this kind she ever was to wear, which all her fleets, full of heroes and men of science, in all the oceans they might be destined to explore, were incapable of replacing upon her brow.[145]

For all Bruce's protestations about his 'despair' not being misunderstood, and for all the benefit of his hindsight on the controversy which had engulfed his claims, an element of egotism is clearly visible here, and not least in the comparison which Bruce draws between his expedition and the achievements of James Cook and Joseph Banks on the *Endeavour* and *Resolution* voyages ('all her fleets, full of heroes and men of science').

In the event, having managed finally to crawl out of the Nubian Desert, Bruce was able briefly to return and to recover the records which he had abandoned, although their testimony made little difference to the scepticism with which his claims were greeted upon his return to London. Despite that reprieve, however, this striking passage from the end of Bruce's widely known account of his trek across the Nubian Desert embodies the tension between the desert and the subjectivity of the European explorer, personal and cultural alike, which I have argued is at the heart of the eighteenth-century and Romantic-period genre of engagement with the sublime of the desert. And it is surely this same tension which lies at the heart of Wordsworth's 'Dream of the Arab', where the desert is again mediated as the locus for exploring anxieties about the erasure of culture. Hence, we might extend Thompson's suggestion that Wordsworth's Arab is 'at some level a reflection of, or a response to, James Bruce', by suggesting that the Arab who plans to 'bury' the 'stone' and the 'shell' (symbols of the sciences and the arts) in the desert sands to preserve them from the coming apocalypse is the exact antitype of James Bruce, forced to abandon his cultural capital in order to survive his trek across the Nubian Desert.[146] So, too, the 'despair' that Bruce feels at the moment when he realises that he must abandon the records of his expedition might be compared to the anxieties about the erasure of culture to which Wordsworth, in *The Prelude*, attributes the origin of the 'Dream of the Arab'. Both Bruce's account of his dream and Wordsworth's account of his anxieties turn, in other words, around the fear of the loss of cultural subjectivity which is at the core of the wider contemporary genre of engagements with the sublime of the desert, of which genre both Bruce's *Travels* and Wordsworth's 'Dream of the Arab' are components. It is not a case of canonical text and non-canonical source, then, so much as a case of varying but related remediations from an underlying genre of engagement with the 'natural sublime', a genre which involves a series of highly determined, and geographically and culturally specific, associations.

Coda

In May 1853, the British explorer Richard Francis Burton left Cairo and set out across the desert towards Suez. Burton, travelling in disguise, with a single local servant, was on his way to becoming only the second non-Muslim European then known to have completed the Hajj: the pilgrimage to Mecca that forms one of the pillars of the Islamic faith.[147] Burton's account of this achievement, in his *Personal Narrative of a Pilgrimage to El-Medinah and Meccah* (1855), won him instant celebrity. However, Burton's description of the desert crossing from Cairo to Suez arguably owes as much to the eighteenth-century and Romantic-period genre of engagement with the sublime of the desert which I have been tracing in this chapter as it does to anything of Burton's own 'personal' experience. This phase of Burton's *Narrative* is, in other words, evidence of the extent to which the desert had become 'classic ground' during the Romantic period, making it all but impossible for subsequent travellers to have any kind of 'personal' experience which did not involve the mediation and remediation of a pre-existent genre.[148] And indeed, Burton's description of the desert remediates not only the Romantic-period genre of engagement with the sublime of the desert, but also aspects of the Romantic-period genre of engagement with the Alpine sublime.

For Burton, the encounter with the sublime emptiness of the desert – an emptiness rendered expected and familiar by previous travellers – is empowering, despite, indeed because of, the threat which that absence poses to individual and cultural subjectivity. 'It is strange', Burton writes, 'how the mind can be amused amid scenery that presents so few objects to occupy it.'[149] 'But in such a country', he continues:

> every slight modification of form or colour rivets observation: the senses are sharpened and perceptive faculties, prone to sleep over a confused shifting of scenery, act vigorously when excited by the capability of embracing each detail.[150]

It is the sensory privation of the desert, in other words – 'the drear silence, the solitude, and the fantastic desolation' – which Burton identifies as key to its sublimity, affording the desert an 'interest [...] unknown to Cape seas and Alpine glaciers, and even to the rolling prairie – the effect of continued excitement on the mind stimulating its powers to their pitch'.[151]

In addition to thus emphasising the physiological elements of the desert sublime, however, Burton, like Park and Bruce and many others before him, also connects the sublime of the desert to the perceived cultural vacancy of the landscape, stressing that 'desert views' are 'by no means memorial', and that 'they arouse because they appeal to the future, not to the past'.[152] Burton never quite clarifies what he means by this 'appeal to the future', but his point seems to be that the psychological potency of desert landscape is focused on the idea of the struggle for survival: 'Man's heart bounds in his breast at the thought of measuring his puny force with nature's might, and of emerging triumphant from the trial.'[153] Here again, then, we have the Romantic idea of the explorer-hero whose persona partakes of the sublimity which he encounters and remediates to the reader. And yet, despite asserting that the desert landscape is 'by no means memorial', virtually all of the examples which Burton gives of this 'measuring' process are taken from accounts of desert ordeals by previous travellers rather than from anything Burton himself experienced:

> Above, through a sky terrible in its stainless beauty, and the splendors of a pitiless blinding glare, the Simoom caresses you like a lion with flaming breath. Around lie drifted sand heaps [...] over which he who rides is spurred by the idea that the bursting of a water skin, or the pricking of a camel's hoof would be a certain death of torture, – a haggard land infested with wild beasts, and wilder men.[154]

Despite the evident physical dangers of the desert environment, then, what emerges from Burton's account – for all his insistence that 'desert views' are 'by no means memorial' – is the suggestion that the mid-nineteenth-century European encounter with the desert sublime involves the traveller 'measuring' themselves as much against a cultural legacy as against a hostile environment. It is the *'sense* of danger', Burton concludes, that 'invests the scene of travel with an interest not its own'.[155] There is an obvious echo, here, of Burke's argument that danger must not be too immediate if sublime affect is to be experienced. But beyond this debt to the eighteenth-century discourse on the sublime, Burton's account primarily depends for its effect upon the reader's awareness of prior eighteenth- and early nineteenth-century writing about the horrors of desert sublime in particular, since Burton himself has no such horrors to offer.[156] Indeed, as if seeming sensible of this shortcoming, Burton concludes the first part of his account of the desert, with telling equivocation, by suggesting that 'the traveller who suspects exaggeration leave the Suez road for an hour or two, and gallop northwards over the sands [to] feel what the Desert *may* be'.[157]

The second phase of Burton's account of his journey across the desert from Cairo to Suez concerns the various oases which he encounters en route. Here, Burton recognises from the outset the place of the desert oasis as 'classic ground' in the European cultural imagination, appending a footnote to his first mention of the word in which he explains that 'nothing can be more incorrect than the vulgar idea of an Arabian Oasis [...] One reads of "isles of the sandy sea", but one never sees them.'[158] Burton's 'personal' account of the oases he encounters – 'some stern flat upon which a handful of wild shrubs blossom while struggling through a cold season's ephemeral existence' – is thus presented as a corrective to the 'vulgar idea' of lush paradises amidst the wastes.[159] However, Burton rejects the conventional, exoticised and often eroticised European vision of the desert oasis only to replace it with another literary trope, this one drawn from the discourse of ascent which I described in Chapter 1, and which dates back to Rousseau's seminal account of the Upper Valais in *Julie*. 'In such circumstances', Burton writes of the oasis:

> The mind is influenced through the body. Though your mouth glows, and your skin is parched, yet you feel no langour [...] your lungs are lightened, your sight brightens, your memory recovers its tone, and your spirits become exuberant; your fancy and imagination are powerfully aroused, and the wildness and sublimity of the scenes around you stir up all the energies of your soul.[160]

Just as St Preux had found a kind of physiological and psychological oasis from his suffering amidst the high Alps in *Julie*, then, so Burton here presents the desert oasis as a similarly invigorating space. And again, as Rousseau had said of the high Alps in *Julie*, in Burton's account of the desert oasis, physiological and psychological invigoration go hand in hand:

> Your *morale* improves: you become frank and cordial, hospitable, and single-minded: the hypocritical politeness and the slavery of civilisation are left behind you in the city. Your senses are quickened: they require no stimulants but air and exercise.[161]

By the end of the passage, Burton moves seamlessly from this description of the salutary effects of the oasis to a renewed encomium to the sublime of the desert environment *per se*, an encomium which is explicitly literary rather than 'personal' in its appeal to the testimony of other European travellers. 'Hence it is that both sexes, and every age,' Burton concludes:

> the most material as well as the most imaginative of minds, the tamest citizen, the most peaceful student, the spoiled child of civilisation,

all feel their hearts dilate, and their pulses beat strong, as they look down from their dromedaries upon the glorious Desert. Where do we hear of a traveller being disappointed by it? It is another illustration of the ancient truth that Nature returns to man, however unworthily he has treated her. And believe me, gentle reader, that when once your tastes have conformed to the tranquillity of such travel, you will suffer real pain in returning to the turmoil of civilisation.[162]

The distance that Burton has travelled in these two pages, from his opening insistence on the struggle and danger of desert travel to this Romantic view of the physiologically and psychologically beneficial effects of the encounter with uncivilised nature, illustrates well what Nigel Leask has called, in a different context, the 'impossibility of personal narrative'.[163] It illustrates, in other words, the extent to which the desert had become, by the middle of the nineteenth century, 'classic ground': a cultural space, a mode of a highly determined genre, rather than the blank physical environment of which it would seem, at first glance, the perfect exemplar.

5
'My purpose was humbler, but also higher': Thomas De Quincey at the Final Frontier

> Of all the phaenomena of nature, the celestial appearances are, by their grandeur and beauty, the most universal object of the curiosity of mankind.
> – Adam Smith, *Essays on Philosophical Subjects*[1]

Adam Smith's essay on 'The Principles which Lead and Direct Philosophical Enquiries; Illustrated by the History of Astronomy' was composed in the 1750s, but not published until the posthumous *Essays on Philosophical Subjects* (1795), edited by James Hutton and Joseph Black. In it, Smith, drawing on technical descriptions of 'the sublime' within the genre of eighteenth-century British philosophical aesthetics, traces the interest in astronomy amongst primitive peoples to the 'wonder, surprise, and astonishment' occasioned by the night sky.[2] 'For Smith then, astronomy, at least in its beginnings, is an enquiry into the 'natural sublime'. As we have seen, in her seminal study of the surge of interest in the 'natural sublime' in late seventeenth- and early eighteenth-century Britain, Nicolson, who curiously does not mention Smith's essay, attributes that interest, at least in part, to technological advancements in optical instrumentation. It was the development of more powerful telescopes, Nicolson argues, which revealed to late Renaissance Europe the existence of a physical universe which was far larger than previously thought. Gradually, Nicolson suggests, the affective responses which had previously been occasioned by reflection on the idea of the divine came to be transferred to this new universe, and eventually to all natural phenomena which seemed to partake of, or were capable of evoking, the idea of the infinite.[3] The 1780s witnessed the beginning of a second such renaissance in European astronomy, which was again driven by technological advances in optical instrumentation.

Amongst its key players were the German émigrés William and Caroline Herschel, and William's son John, whose careers have most recently been described by Richard Holmes in *The Age of Wonder*.[4]

By the time that Thomas De Quincey came to write his essay on 'System of the Heavens as Revealed by Lord Rosse's Telescopes', which was first published in *Tait's Edinburgh Magazine* for September 1846, and again in revised form in the collected edition of De Quincey's works, this second renaissance in European astronomy had not only generated a new understanding of the immensity of the universe, but had also established astronomy as a modern, scientific and at least semi-professional genre of enquiry.[5] In his essay, De Quincey imagines extending an invitation to his reader. 'Now, on some moonless night in some fitting condition of the atmosphere', De Quincey writes, 'if Lord Rosse would permit the reader and myself to walk into the front drawing room of his telescope, then, in Mrs. Barbauld's words, slightly varied, I might say to him, – Come, and I will show you what is sublime!'[6] In default of such 'permission', what De Quincey's essay 'in fact' goes on to 'lay before' the reader is a powerful imagining of the Orion Nebula which William Edward Parsons, the third Earl of Rosse, had recently examined with his state-of-the-art telescope, the so-called 'Leviathan of Parsonstown'. De Quincey's extended imagining of this 'famous nebula', and of Rosse's conclusions about it, form the centrepiece of an essay which offers the reader a range of different perspectives on the 'great [...] mystery of Space' and the 'greater [...] mystery of Time'.[7]

Hence, De Quincey's essay not only participates in the wider contemporary delivery of scientific knowledge to a non-specialist audience, but also anticipates many of the popular-science cultural texts about 'the wonders of the universe' which proliferate today. De Quincey was by no means unique in doing this: after all, his essay is less a response to the scientific work of Rosse than to the popularisation of Rosse's work by John Pringle Nichol, then Regius Professor of Astronomy at the University of Glasgow, in his widely read *Thoughts on Some Important Points Relating to the System of the World* (1846).[8] But it is important to recognise that De Quincey's essay stands at (at least) two removes from its ostensible, scientific source.

Some excellent readings of 'System of the Heavens' have been offered by scholars of De Quincey's work. Joseph Hillis-Miller, Robert Platzner, John Barrell and Robert Lance Snyder have each examined various aspects of the relationship between the essay and the existential and psycho-sexual concerns which they see exhibited in De Quincey's autobiographical writings, the *Confessions of an English Opium-Eater*,

Suspiria de Profundis and *Autobiographical Sketches*.[9] More recently, studies by Jonathan Smith and Alex Murray have traced the debts owed by De Quincey not only to Nichol's *Thoughts* but also to the wider, contemporary genres of astronomy and cosmology in sources as diverse as the work of Robert Chambers and Immanuel Kant, to say nothing of Jean Paul Richter, with an extended adaptation from whose work De Quincey's essay concludes: as Smith points out, the risk of the psycho-biographical approach is that it 'ignores or minimizes' the relationship of De Quincey's essay 'not only to early Victorian science but to early Victorian *culture*, and particularly to its cultural conception of space'.[10]

My concern here is also with the relationship between De Quincey's essay and those wider contemporary genres of astronomy and cosmology of which it forms a part. De Quincey's essay actually consists of a series of remediations from those genres. De Quincey remediates some of Immanuel Kant's ideas about the age of the earth, and some of his own previous engagements with Kant's ideas. He deals similarly with the work of the Herschels, Rosse and Nichol on the Orion Nebula; with some of the cosmological prose-poems of Richter; and with some of his own previous engagements with Richter. And of course, as Jonathan Smith has shown, in the version of the essay which De Quincey prepared for his *Selections Grave and Gay*, De Quincey actually revisits his own essay. I am concerned here, to varying extents, with De Quincey's handling of each of these earlier texts. However, I mean primarily to examine the ways in which De Quincey's 'System of the Heavens' involves the remediation of the engagement with the 'natural sublime' which is generated within the contemporary genre of astronomy. In this respect, my argument follows and extends Ralph O'Connor's claims about 'the crucial enabling roles of spectacle and (in particular) of literature' in popularising scientific knowledge during the early nineteenth century.[11] I make two claims. First: that De Quincey remediates in non-specialist language what he calls, in the revised text of his essay, the 'impressive effect' of 'scientific discussion', thereby making accessible to the general reader of *Tait's* some 'momentary glimpses of objects vast and awful' which would otherwise remain beyond them, both experientially and conceptually.[12] Second, and by extension: that De Quincey offers the reader of his essay a vicarious encounter with 'the natural sublime' which remediates the actual experience of the astronomer at the telescope, by substituting rhetorical effect for physical spectacle. In this respect, De Quincey's essay not only recalls the vicarious Alpine ascents which I have described in Chapter 1, but also parallels the various other forms of contemporary 'virtual tourism' which Ralph O'Connor has described in *The Earth on*

Show. In other words, De Quincey's essay commoditises the 'natural sublime' for the magazine reader.

De Quincey's essay no doubt reflects his long-standing interest in astronomy, and his long-standing involvement in the remediation of specialist astronomical knowledge to the general public: De Quincey had met the astronomer William Rowan Hamilton many years earlier in Edinburgh, and he had published articles on 'Immanuel Kant and Dr Herschel' and on 'The Planet Mars' during his brief tenure as editor of the *Westmoreland Gazette* in 1819.[13] Integral to both of the claims which I am making here, however, is the fact that this personal interest in astronomy is also tempered by the reality that De Quincey's essay was written first and foremost, as was so much of De Quincey's work, for the purposes of earning money, both for De Quincey himself and for the editors of *Tait's*. This pressure to earn is at least in part responsible for the impressive range of De Quincey's essay: since he was probably being paid by the sheet, more essay equals more money. However, De Quincey's essay also registers an awareness, both on his part, and on the part of the editors of *Tait's*, that the 'natural sublime' was a saleable commodity, and, moreover, a commodity arguably more saleable to a general magazine readership than specialist scientific knowledge about the nature of the universe. Again, O'Connor's remarks about the popularisation of contemporary geological ideas are germane here: 'in an age marked by debates over the dangers of imagination and the deceptive allure of cheap romances and sensation novels', astronomy, like geology, could be 'marketed as the key to true facts which were nonetheless more marvellous and sensational than fiction'.[14] Hence, it is not simply *what* De Quincey writes about the 'impressive effect' generated within the genre of astronomy which is of interest to me here, but also *how* De Quincey writes about it. Books like Nichol's *Thoughts* were undoubtedly desirable commercial products as well as instructive texts. But for De Quincey, 'impressive effect' rather than scientific accuracy seems to be the primary concern, and despite the Romantic argument which we shall see that De Quincey offers in its defence, this prioritisation of spectacle over accuracy in his essay is arguably the product of financial motivation.

My point, then, is not just that De Quincey, like Nichol, is involved in the making available to the general public of specialist scientific knowledge. Rather, it is that De Quincey's essay represents the commoditisation of the 'natural sublime', the making available of the 'impressive effect' generated within the genre of astronomy as a commodity which can be purchased and consumed by the general magazine reader without the need either for technical knowledge or first-hand experience, and perhaps even without the desire for these. In other words, and in the terms of the critical vocabulary which De Quincey himself develops elsewhere, 'System of the Heavens' is less concerned with communicating the 'knowledge' which is generated within the genre of astronomy and more concerned with the 'power' generated by that genre.[15] It is in this sense, then, that I mean to locate De Quincey's essay on 'System of the Heavens' within the genre of popular astronomy which we have inherited from the Romantic period, in which the 'impressive effect' generated by astronomical enquiry continues to be commoditised and made vicariously available for consumption well beyond the boundary of the originating scientific genre.[16] No systematic genealogy of this genre of popular astronomy in the eighteenth century and Romantic period – comparable, say, to that which Ralph O'Connor has provided for the contemporary popularisation of geology – has yet been constructed. However, Wordsworth's poem 'Star-Gazers' reminds us that at least in 1807, some 40 years before De Quincey composed his essay, 'show' men in London's Leicester Square had gathered around telescopes 'spectators rude, / Poor in estate, of manners base, men of the multitude'.[17] De Quincey's essay must, then, be seen in this tradition, as an appeal to 'the multitude' rather than to men and women of science: 'Come, and I will show you what is sublime!', says De Quincey the 'show' man.[18]

In *The Age of Wonder*, Richard Holmes, no doubt taking his cue from Adam Smith, has outlined the sense of excitement which marked the second renaissance in European astronomy from its beginnings in the 1780s. The continued presence of that excitement is registered in 'System of the Heavens' through De Quincey's use of the language of 'the sublime' to describe Rosse's work. Rosse's primary achievement, De Quincey affirms, in language at once sublime and pseudo-Biblical, was to have 'revealed' with his telescopes a universe *'immeasurably* beyond the old one which he found', thereby effectively demarcating 'two worlds, one called Ante-Rosse, and the other Post-Rosse'.[19] As Holmes has shown, however, almost 70 years before Rosse began making observations with the Leviathan of Parsonstown, it was the German émigrés William and Caroline Herschel who had begun this second renaissance in European astronomy.

In 1757, the 19-year-old William Herschel, a native of Hanover, had sought refuge in England after the defeat of the Hanoverians at the Battle of Hastenbeck, during the Seven Years' War. Following a successful first career as a musician, Herschel began, in 1774, to conduct and document systematic sweeps of the night sky. Key to the success of these sweeps were the increasingly powerful, reflecting telescopes which William manufactured together with his sister Caroline, who had joined him in England in 1772, with the pair sometimes spending up to 16 hours a day polishing the speculum metal mirrors. Over the next five decades, the Herschels' observations of the night sky produced a series of catalogues comprising over 2500 objects, including stars, nebulae, comets and, of course, the planet Uranus, which William Herschel discovered in March 1781, naming it Georgium Sidorum ('the George star') after George III, then the King of England. This observational work was continued and extended into the mid-nineteenth century by William Herschel's son John, who eventually published his own *Results of Astronomical Observations Made at the Cape of Good Hope* (1847) and *General Catalogue of Nebulae and Clusters* (1864), adding almost 2000 more items to William's and Caroline's lists. In fact, as we shall see, it was one of John Herschel's early sketches of the Orion Nebula, as reproduced in Nichol's *Thoughts on Some Important Points*, which provided the centrepiece of De Quincey's 'System of the Heavens': his lurid 'Description of the Nebula in Orion, as forced to show out by Lord Rosse'.[20]

This second renaissance in astronomy – the direct consequence, as De Quincey put it, of 'Herschel the elder having greatly improved the telescope' – provided the nineteenth century not only with a highly detailed taxonomy of the observable universe, but also with an unprecedented sense of the almost incomprehensible size and age of the universe.[21] 'Herschel,' Nichol records in his *Thoughts*, 'by gradually enlarging his metal discs [the mirrors of his telescopes], passed, by gigantic strides, through regions of the universe to which not even imagination, in its wildest moods, had essayed to penetrate before.'[22] Here, then, Nichol gives us a vision of the astronomer-as-hero, of Herschel as a sublime ('giant', 'striding') Romantic figure whose persona partakes of the grandeur which he encounters. Herschel's instruments, Nichol continues, provided 'majestic revelations' of 'depths apparently fathomless', 'a boundless ocean of space', 'unfathomable Durations', 'abysses' of time comprising 'centuries whose number stuns the imagination'.[23] And the effect of these revelations, Nichol concludes, was that 'the idea [...] of Infinity in its true awfulness, was for the first time dawning upon the Soul'.[24]

Nichol's appeal to descriptions of the sublime within eighteenth-century and Romantic-period philosophical aesthetics (an 'infinity' which 'stuns the imagination', etc.), is instructive. In effect, the new astronomy – driven by the Herschels and carried on by Rosse – emerges from Nichol's *Thoughts*, as ancient astronomy had from Adam Smith's essay, as an enquiry into 'the sublime'. The 'elevation' to which the observations of the Herschels and Rosse 'leads us', Nichol affirms, 'is indeed a dizzy one, far aloft from the usual haunts of human thought'.[25] 'I shrink', Nichol concludes, still drawing on descriptions of the sublime within the genre of philosophical aesthetics, 'below the conception that here – even at this threshold of the attainable – bursts forth on my mind.'[26] Once again, then, Nichol's use of the terminology of philosophical aesthetics effectively configures astronomy, after Herschel, as an enquiry into the sublime, a dizzying and elevating enquiry 'far aloft from the usual haunts of human thought'. However, Nichol's reference to the 'threshold of the attainable' also reveals his conviction, which he voices throughout the early sections of his *Thoughts*, that it would not be possible physically to construct a telescope larger than Rosse's 'Leviathan of Parsonstown', and hence that Rosse's observations with this telescope marked the zenith of what optical astronomy could attain.[27] In other words, Nichol also points here to the technical or technological boundaries of human knowledge. Hence in this sense, too, astronomy after Herschel emerges from Nichol's *Thoughts* as an enquiry into 'the sublime' – that is, into the limits of the possible.

The correlation of technological and epistemological possibility to which Nichol points here is well exemplified in his (and in De Quincey's) reaction to the implications of Rosse's observations for the so-called 'nebular hypothesis'.[28] In France, the mathematician and astronomer Pierre-Simon Laplace, drawing in part upon earlier work by Immanuel Kant, had proposed that stars and planets were formed by the gradual cooling and contraction of nebulous gases. William Herschel, in England, had similarly theorised that all nebular appearances in the night sky could be classified into two types: those which could be resolved, on close observation, as distinct stars, and those which were in fact gaseous matter, out of which stars seemed to be formed. Key to the 'nebular hypothesis', then, was the question of whether the universe was in a steady state or evolving over time, a question with profound implications for conventional Christian descriptions of creation. Rosse claimed to have resolved the Orion Nebula into component stars using his telescopes, thus favouring the steady-state model which was more conducive to the Christian account of creation. Both Nichol and De Quincey accepted Rosse's claims (others, like John Herschel, did not), but both also acknowledged that definitive proof was impossible because of the limitations of optical instrumentation. Both felt that there were necessary limits to what humanity could know – in this case, because it would not be possible to construct a telescope large enough to answer this fundamental question – and hence both appeal to faith to supply the deficiencies of science, as has so often been the case in the encounter with the 'natural sublime'. We are reminded, of course, of Martin Rudwick's description of the many ways in which 'religious and scientific practices and knowledge claims have interacted' in the episteme of the late eighteenth century and Romantic period.[29]

Nichol's understanding of astronomy, after Herschel, as an enquiry into the sublime, is also a key component of De Quincey's essay on 'System of the Heavens'. Contemplating the 'great [...] mystery of Space' and the 'greater [...] mystery of Time' which the new astronomy has revealed, De Quincey suggests that:

> either mystery grows upon man, as man himself grows; and either seems to be a function of the godlike which is in man. In reality the depths and the heights which are in man, the depths by which he searches, the heights by which he aspires, are but projected and made objective externally in the three dimensions of bodily space which are outside him. He trembles at the abyss into which his bodily eyes look down, or look up; not knowing that abyss to be, not always consciously suspecting it to be, but by an instinct written in his prophetic heart feeling it to be, boding it to be, fearing it to be, and sometimes hoping it to be, the mirror to a mightier abyss that will one day be expanded in himself.[30]

As a number of commentators have noted, De Quincey, despite his pseudo-Biblical phrasing, seems close, here, to Immanuel Kant's description of 'the sublime' in his 'Analytic', in which the mind transcends its initial defeat by the sublime object and in the process comes to an elating recognition of its own powers. John Barrell, for example, sees in the passage a 'quasi-Kantian epistemology', while Robert Platzner similarly reads it as an appeal to 'the complex ideology of the Sublime', 'a single and deeply personal act of heightened consciousness and rhetoric, a construct as unstable as it is subjective'.[31]

It is of course precisely this kind of problematic identification of 'the sublime' with the sublime as described within the 'Analytic' of Kant which I have been subjecting to scrutiny throughout this book. In this case, however, De Quincey is known to have been familiar with a range of Kant's work, and of course actually discusses Kant's ideas about the age of the earth, and his own earlier engagement with those ideas, in the opening section of 'System of the Heavens', albeit again, at least in part, for the purposes of filling out those valuable pages. Even having said that, though, De Quincey's sense, here, of the relationship between the immensities of space and time which are revealed by the new astronomy and 'the godlike [...] depths and the heights which are in man' probably originates less in a dialogue with the philosophical aesthetics of Kant than it does in Nichol's ideas about the implications for the Christian religion of the sublime discoveries made by the Herschels and by Rosse. 'If these majestic revelations', Nichol argues:

> not in the mere rudeness & bareness of outward and obvious forms, but instinct with suggestive powers, gleam fixedly on the Soul, how awful its conception of the mysteries within whose lap it lies![32]

For Nichol, in other words, as in many of the religious responses to the sublime examined by Marjorie Hope Nicolson, contemplating the 'mysteries' of the physical universe enables the 'soul' to acquire some 'conception' of the 'awful' (that is, sublime) spiritual order of which it is supposed to be a part. Hence the physicality of the 'natural sublime' is read as both veiling and signifying the immanent. Nichol seeks immediately to cement this point by quoting from Joseph Blanco White's sonnet 'Night and Death' which similarly explores, in the context of astronomy, the relationship between the apparent and the immanent:

> Who could have thought such darkness lay conceal'd
> Within thy beams, O Sun! Or who could find,
> Whilst fly, and leaf, and insect stand reveal'd,
> That to such countless orbs though mad'st us blind!
> Why do we then shun Death with anxious strife?
> If Light can thus deceive, wherefore not Life?[33]

De Quincey's 'System of the Heavens', like Nichol's *Thoughts*, seeks consistently to remediate the mysteries of the physical universe as the guarantor of the mysteries of faith: the repeated references to 'God's Universe', the Biblical phrasing (as in, for example: 'A voice was heard, "Let there be Lord Rosse!"'), and the 'spiritual' context of the 'bravura' from Richter, are just a few obvious examples of the overwhelmingly Christian ontology of De Quincey's essay.[34]

The extent to which both Nichol and De Quincey remediate the scientific theories of the Herschels and Rosse as a moralising and, in De Quincey's case, highly conservative cosmology based on aesthetic *spectacle* rather than on scientific *speculation* is an important element of the story that I want to tell here. What I am primarily concerned with, however, is the extent to which both Nichol and De Quincey *commoditise* the 'natural sublime' for their readership, and with what is gained and what is lost in that process. That De Quincey from the outset conceived the purpose of his essay to be, at least in part, to remediate for the *Tait's* readership the astronomer's encounter with the 'natural sublime' is evident from the invitation which he imagines offering to his reader: 'Come, and I will show you what is sublime!'[35] Hence, the purpose of 'System of the Heavens' is, in this respect at least, to make vicariously available to the reader the experience of the astronomer at the telescope, something that Nichol had also tried to do in his *Thoughts* through the inclusion of numerous detailed (and rather beautiful) plates depicting nebulae and other astronomical phenomena. Unlike Nichol, however, whose main concern was to communicate to the non-specialist reader the knowledge generated by astronomy, and to comment upon the wider cultural significance of that knowledge, De Quincey seems rather more concerned with communicating the 'impressive effect' generated by astronomy, that is, with commoditising the 'natural sublime' for the magazine reader.

The means by which De Quincey seeks to effect this commoditisation are best exemplified in the centrepiece of his essay on 'System of the Heavens': the 'Description of the Nebula in Orion, as forced to show out by Lord Rosse'.[36] The passage has formed the kernel of most scholarly studies of the essay and, as we shall see, it was also controversial during De Quincey's own lifetime. In three lengthy paragraphs, including a 12-line quotation from *Paradise Lost* (a poem routinely invoked in descriptions of 'the sublime' within the genre of philosophical aesthetics), De Quincey extemporises on an illustration of the Orion Nebula from Nichol's *Thoughts*, and remediates the celestial object as an 'abominable apparition', as an anthropomorphic figure conflating Milton's portrait of Death with the stereotypical despot from the popular contemporary genre of the Oriental tale.[37]

John Barrell's influential reading of this passage in *The Infection of Thomas De Quincey* finds, in De Quincey's lurid transformation of the nebula, the index of a number of psycho-sexual anxieties which Barrell argues 'infect' the entire corpus of De Quincey's work.[38] Whatever its relationship with De Quincey's psychopathology might be, however, Jonathan Smith is certainly also right to point out that the presence of 'a representation of the Great Nebula at the heart of De Quincey's essay' also signals De Quincey's engagement with contemporary astronomical debate, because the ability visually to determine the actual composition of the nebula was widely thought to be the most reliable means of verifying or falsifying the nebular hypothesis. Within the context of the argument about commoditisation which I want to make here, however, it is important to recognise the extent to which De Quincey's essay is more concerned with spectacle than with scientific rigour. More precisely, De Quincey's reimagining of the Orion Nebula does not only remediate for the *Tait's* reader the sublime visual spectacle (the 'impressive effect') of the nebula that is available to the astronomer at the telescope. Rather, De Quincey's reimagining of the nebula also enables him to move beyond mere description and towards the *interpretation* of spectacle: De Quincey comments at some length upon the moral significance of 'the horror of the regal phantasma which [the Orion Nebula] has perfected to the eyes of flesh'.[39] In this respect, then, De Quincey goes considerably farther than Nichol, who was for the most part content with outlining the scientific implications of the phenomena illustrated in the lavish plates of his *Thoughts* – rather too much farther, as we shall see that some of De Quincey's contemporaries felt, not least amongst them Nichol himself. In the ensuing debate we see exemplified the same 'repudiation and the cultivation of the imagination' which O'Connor shows to be endemic in the 'literary history' of the earth sciences.[40]

The fact is, then, that De Quincey's account of the Orion Nebula does not just remediate the visual as the textual, or the 'natural sublime' as the 'rhetorical sublime'. Rather, De Quincey entirely (re)imagines the nebula, combining empirical data and culturally determined responses into a composite product which can be had for money by the *Tait's* reader without the need for specialist education or experience. De Quincey acknowledges that his version of the Orion Nebula is a composite image, with overlapping layers of detail drawn from successive observations by the Herschels and Rosse: first William Herschel, then John Herschel with 'his eighteen-inch mirror' in the late 1820s, then John Herschel again 'at the Cape of Good Hope' in the 1830s, 'and finally [...] Lord Rosse'.[41] At no point, in other words, could anyone have looked through a telescope and seen exactly what De Quincey describes: his reimagining of the Orion Nebula is a palimpsest of successive observations, to use a term De Quincey himself might have favoured.[42] In other words, it is not a popularisation of scientific knowledge after the manner of Nichol's *Thoughts*. It is, rather, a spectacular *product*, specifically designed for sale and consumption, with arguably little reference to any 'actual' nebula.

In this composite structure lies the strength and commercial value of De Quincey's remediation of the 'natural sublime' as textual spectacle: his essay offers the reader a product which observational astronomy, the empirical encounter with the 'natural sublime', could never provide, even to a reader with sufficient leisure and capital to pursue the study of astronomy. In this same composite structure, however, lie the weaknesses of De Quincey's reimagining of the Orion Nebula, and it was on these weaknesses that De Quincey's critics were quick to focus.

Those critics were concerned, in the main, with the apparent distance between De Quincey's extemporisation on the Orion Nebula and the 'actual' nebula – and ostensibly with good reason. De Quincey introduces his reimagining of the Orion Nebula as 'a dreadful cartoon, from the gallery which has begun to open upon Lord Rosse's telescope', and titles the passage, as we have seen, as a 'Description of the Nebula in Orion, as forced to show out by Lord Rosse'.[43] In point of fact, however, De Quincey does not describe the 'Nebula' as revealed by Rosse's telescope. Conversely (again, as we have seen), the details which De Quincey describes are drawn from a succession of different observations: at no single point would all the details which De Quincey describes have been visible through a telescope. Nor is that the only liberty which De Quincey takes. As Jonathan Smith first pointed out, the illustration in Nichol's *Thoughts* on which De Quincey's reimagining of the Orion Nebula is ostensibly based is not related to Rosse's work: De Quincey directs the reader 'to Dr. Nichol's book, at page 51', where the illustration (Plate no. VIII) is clearly labelled as 'The Nebula of Orion Figured by Sir J. Herschel' and *not* 'as forced to show out by Lord Rosse'.[44] And to cap things off, De Quincey informs 'the obedient reader' that 'in order to see what *I* see' whilst looking at this illustration they must 'view the wretch upside down', that is, must invert the plate in Nichol's book.[45] So much, then, for any attempt by De Quincey to connect his reimagining of the Orion Nebula with the 'real' nebula visible in the night sky and at the heart of contemporary astronomical debate.

Jonathan Smith has already described in some detail how De Quincey responded, both in unpublished manuscript fragments and in private correspondence, as well as in the revised version of 'System of the Heavens' that was published in 1854, to the criticisms which had been levelled against his handling of the Orion Nebula in the original version of the essay that had been published in *Tait's*. As Smith points out, Henry Bright, commenting in the *Westminster Review* for 1854 on the ongoing unauthorised American reprint of De Quincey's work by the Boston publishers Ticknor & Fields, singled out De Quincey's extemporisation on the Orion Nebula as both exaggerated and scientifically dubious, while Nichol himself urged De Quincey not even to include 'System of the Heavens' in the official collected edition of his works, again citing De Quincey's handling of the Orion Nebula as particularly problematic for its lack of scientific accuracy.[46] I have no wish to go over again, here, ground which has already ably been covered by Smith, and I recommend the reader to consult Smith's illuminating essay for a thorough account of De Quincey's various engagements with contemporary critics of 'System of the Heavens'. What I do wish to consider, however – and indeed where I depart somewhat from Smith's reading – is how De Quincey defends and develops his initial remediation of the Orion Nebula in the revised text of 'System of the Heavens' which he prepared for *Selections Grave and Gay* in 1853.

When it came to it (again, as Smith notes), De Quincey, despite his critics, retained his controversial remediation of the Orion Nebula essentially unchanged in the revised text of 'System of the Heavens'. Indeed, De Quincey was even more explicit about the composite nature of his imagining of the nebula, describing, in pseudo-Biblical language, 'the stages of a solemn uncovering by astronomy, first by Sir W. Herschel, secondly by his son, and now finally by Lord Rosse [...] like the raising one after another of the seals that had been sealed by the angel in the Revelation'.[47] However, De Quincey did marshal a defence of that remediation in two additional footnotes. These notes, I want to argue, reveal not only De Quincey's sense of the purpose of his article in remediating for the reader of *Tait's* the astronomer's encounter with the 'natural sublime', but also the achievements and limitations of this commoditisation of the sublime as a cultural text.

The first of these footnotes was added, by De Quincey, to the title of the essay. In it, he sets out to clarify the relationship between his own essay and Nichol's *Thoughts*, 'the text to which this little paper refers, and about which it may be said to hover'.[48] De Quincey emphasises that his essay ought not to be considered a 'formal', 'grave' or 'scientific' 'review' of Nichol's work, and that he had never 'designed it for discharging such a function'.[49] 'My purpose', De Quincey continues, 'was humbler, but also higher':

> from amongst the many relations of astronomy – 1. to man; 2. to his earthly habitation; 3. to the motions of his daily life; 4. to his sense of illimitable grandeur; 5. to his dim anticipations of changes far overhead, concurrently with changes to earth – to select such as might allow of a solemn or impassioned, or of a gay and playful treatment.[50]

Here, then, De Quincey draws an explicit distinction between a scientific treatise, or even a work of popular astronomy like Nichol's, and an essay like his, the purpose of which, he argues, is exactly to remediate (to 'select') for the reader the 'solemn or impassioned' or 'gay and playful' elements of scientific discourse. Again, the distinction is equivalent to that which De Quincey elsewhere draws between the 'literature of knowledge' and the 'literature of power'. That De Quincey wishes to present the 'humbler, but also higher' purpose of 'System of the Heavens' as being thus to remediate for the *Tait's* reader the astronomer's encounter with the natural sublime is evident from the conclusion of this first defensive footnote. 'If, through the light torrent *spray* of fanciful images or allusions', De Quincey continues:

> the reader catches at intervals momentary glimpses of objects vast and awful in the rear, a much more impressive effect is likely to be obtained than through any amount of scientific discussion, and, at any rate, all the effect that was ever contemplated.[51]

Here De Quincey both acknowledges and rejects the criticisms of his 'fanciful' handling of the Orion Nebula by arguing that such 'images' are more conducive to the magazine reader's vicarious experience of the astronomical sublime ('momentary glimpses of objects vast and awful'), that is, more conducive to conveying 'impressive effect', than 'any amount of scientific discussion' could be.

Taken on its own terms, there is some value in De Quincey's argument: his remediation of the Orion Nebula does indeed offer the non-specialist reader of his essay, for better or for worse, an 'impressive effect', albeit at the cost of the attention to scientific accuracy which such a reader might have expected, and would have found in the many other extant representations of the nebula, such as those by Herschel which Nichol reproduces in his *Thoughts*. In other words, De Quincey's essay successfully commoditises the astronomical sublime by remediating it as rhetorical effect, by making it available for consumption by the non-specialist reader. The problem, however, is that De Quincey has really only side-stepped the main criticism of his essay here, which had attacked the extent to which his handling of the Orion Nebula was not only unscientific in tone, but actually incompatible with scientific understanding of the nebula. In other words, De Quincey seems still to place the commodity value of his sublime product above its value as an accurate reflection of astronomical knowledge. It is this criticism which De Quincey sought to address in his second footnote, which he appended to his description of the nebula itself.

'In reply to various dissenting opinions which have reached me on this subject from different quarters', De Quincey begins, 'it has become necessary to say a word or two upon this famous nebula in Orion.'[52] 'All such appearances', De Quincey says in defence of his particular resolution of the nebula, 'whether seen in the fire, or in the clouds, or in the arbitrary combinations of the stars, are read differently by different people.'[53] Hence, he continues, 'I cannot complain of those who have not been able to read the same dreadful features in the Orion nebula as I myself have read.'[54] Far from assuaging the doubts of those who had attacked his remediation of the Orion Nebula for its lack of scientific rigour, then, De Quincey's initial defence of the passage seems better calculated to strengthen those misgivings by retreating even further into the very subjectivity of perspective which had drawn fire from the critics in the first place. Nor does De Quincey improve the situation by continuing immediately to criticise those who could not accept his imagining of the nebula because they 'have not taken the trouble to look at Professor Nichol's portrait of this *nebula* in the right position: for it happens that, in the professor's book, it is placed upside down as regards the natural position of a human head'.[55] So far, so unconvincing, at least, one assumes, from the point of view of De Quincey's critics.

The second strand of De Quincey's argument is ostensibly no more successful as a rebuttal of the accusation that his handling of the Orion Nebula was unscientific. However, it does demonstrate not only De Quincey's sense of the role of his essay in remediating the sublime, but also both the manner in which the 'natural sublime' is commoditised in his essay and the wider cultural implications of such commoditisation.

In the second phase of his footnote to the Orion Nebula passage, De Quincey goes on to 'complain of others, whose sole objection is, that the earliest revelation of this nebular apparition by Lord Rosse's telescope has by the same telescope been greatly modified'.[56] Here, in other words, De Quincey seeks to address those critics, including Nichol, who had pointed specifically to the fact that the most recent observations of the Orion Nebula revealed a rather different appearance to the one on which De Quincey had based his extemporisation: the sketch by John Herschel given as Plate VIII in Nichol's *Thoughts*. De Quincey, at this point, deflects attention away from the fact that his remediation of the Orion Nebula is in fact, as we have seen, a *composite* image, comprising details from a sequence of observations.[57] Rather, De Quincey rejects altogether the idea that more accurate observational data has any relevance to his remediation of the nebula. 'What of *that*?', De Quincey asks of the modified data:

> Who doubts that it would be modified? It is enough that once, in a single stage of the examination, this apparition put on the figure here represented, and for a momentary purpose here dimly deciphered. Take Wordsworth's fine sonnet upon cloud mimicries [De Quincey quotes from 'Sky-Prospect: From the Plain of France', sonnet 23 from Wordsworth's *Memorials of a Tour on the Continent* (1822)] – would it have been any rational objection to these grand pictures that the whole had vanished within the hour?[58]

De Quincey performs, here, a number of rhetorical sleights-of-hand. First, the claim that his resolution of the Orion Nebula was based on 'a single stage of the examination' by astronomers, when we have seen – and when De Quincey himself admits – that this was not the case. Second, the idea that the nebula took 'the figure' which De Quincey gave it, and which he admits that others might not see, for the 'momentary purpose' of imaging Death. And third, the elision of the difference between variations in the technology of the observer (astronomers looking at a nebula through increasingly sophisticated telescopes) and variations in the phenomenon observed (Wordsworth looking at ever-changing clouds).

If we pass over all these difficulties, however, the essence of De Quincey's claim is that his remediation of the Orion Nebula ought not to be judged by any comparison with the *real* nebula. To do so, he insists, is to make a kind of category mistake. 'He who fancies *that*', De Quincey concludes, 'does not understand the original purpose in holding up a mirror of description to appearances so grand, and in a dim sense often so symbolic'.[59]

De Quincey's outright rejection of the idea that his handling of the Orion Nebula ought to be governed by reference to any *actual* nebula, of which his representation is supposed in some sense to be a copy or *re*-presentation, clearly looks forward to post-structuralist ideas about the textual or linguistic basis of the real. Within the more immediate historical, cultural and commercial context of 'System of the Heavens', however, De Quincey's claim arguably illustrates a key dynamic in the emergence of disciplinarity, although the essay is of course not unique in so doing: this is the process by which the boundary between artistic and scientific engagements with the 'natural sublime' comes to be drawn in such a way as to facilitate the commoditisation of 'impressive effect' at the expense of scientific accuracy. It is a dilemma which continues to mark the 'popular science' industry to this day: striking the balance between accessibility, appeal, accuracy and commercial value.

Whether we view the transition that De Quincey's remediation of the Orion Nebula enacts as a positive or a negative development in the history of European representation, we surely cannot pass over it quite so lightly as De Quincey himself does here. After all, is it not this very divorce of representations of the 'natural sublime' from the thing itself which recent developments in ecological criticism have identified as one of the more pernicious aspects of the Romantic engagement, in the West, with ideas of 'nature' and 'the natural'? More broadly speaking, if it was the remediation and the commoditisation of the various species of 'natural sublime' that were discovered during the eighteenth century and Romantic period that marked the beginning of our contemporary attitudes to the wild places of the world, is there not now an urgent need to re-examine the dynamics of that remediation, its gains and its losses, at a moment when the commoditisation of the natural as a resource (agricultural, industrial, aesthetic, lifestyle) threatens to an unprecedented extent the very thing it ostensibly prizes? We are reminded of Wordsworth's dismayed reaction to the success of his *Guide to the Lakes*: how do we celebrate the 'natural sublime' without commoditising it, without *re*presenting it? And once we set off down that path, do we agree with De Quincey that in the quest after 'impressive effect' and/or saleable product, signs need bear no resemblance to things?

Such fundamental and wide-ranging questions about the future of our remediations of the 'natural sublime' clearly fall outside the scope of my discussion here. I hope, however, that in pointing to their place in De Quincey's essay, I have shed new light not simply on the complexities of De Quincey's engagement with 'the sublime', but also drawn attention to one more strand of that 'romantic ideology' which has become sublimated within our perceptions of 'nature' and 'the natural', and which we should continue to interrogate – whilst the wheels of NASA's *Curiosity* rover begin their journey across the surface of Mars to discover the 'classic ground' of the future.

Notes

Introduction

1. The success on both sides of the Atlantic of BBC natural history spectaculars like *Frozen Planet* (2011), which explored the Arctic and the Antarctic, might be cited as the latest evidence of this continuing fascination.
2. Hence, for example, the global success of Hollywood blockbusters such as *The Day after Tomorrow* (2004) and *2012* (2009).
3. The TV documentaries and publications of Brian Cox are just the latest example of this genre of popular (theoretical) physics, but Cox has numerous predecessors in recent years, including Bill Bryson, James Gleick and Michio Kaku, and this subgenre of popular science, in its late twentieth-century incarnation at least, might be traced back to Stephen Hawking's *A Brief History of Time* (1988).
4. I have placed the term 'Romantic' in quotation marks here (and here only) in order to signal that it is a label whose meaning, implication and usefulness have long been subject to scrutiny. Although I do not engage directly with any of those debates here, much of the ground which I do cover in this book has significance for our understanding of what is and has been meant by the terms 'Romantic' and 'Romanticism'. For this reason, I have throughout this book preferred to use the term 'Romantic period', by which I refer to the years 1780–1830, rather than to a supposed set of cultural practices, granting that this, too, is a somewhat arbitrary label. The ongoing cultural importance of Romantic-period ideas about the 'natural sublime' might also in this respect be adduced as a prime example of what Jerome McGann described in 1983 as 'the romantic ideology': the 'uncritical absorption' of Romantic ideas by popular culture and academic discourse alike. See Jerome McGann, *The Romantic Ideology* (University of Chicago Press, 1983), p. 1.
5. See, for example, Gavin De Beer, *Early Travellers in the Alps* (London: Sidgwick and Jackson, 1930) and *Alps and Men* (London: Edward Arnold, 1932).
6. There is now, for example, at least one monograph examining the place of 'the sublime' in the works of each of the so-called 'big six' Romantic poets.
7. I am of course aware that the use of the term 'popular' to distinguish particular forms of cultural productivity or activity from other such forms has a considerable and problematic history in Romantic-period thought, and beyond. Here I mean to use the term, with as little pre-judgement as possible, to signal cultural productivity or activity which is accessible to non-specialists. For a recent exploration of the problematics of popular culture in the Romantic period, see Philip Connell and Nigel Leask (eds), *Romanticism and Popular Culture in Britain and Ireland* (Cambridge University Press, 2009).
8. The reissuing of Nicolson's work in 1997 is testament not only to its continued relevance, but also to its relatively unique status in the canon of academic studies of 'the sublime'.

9. Throughout this book, I draw on the development of the terms 'genre', 'mediation' and 'remediation' as a technical vocabulary for articulating cultural production and exchange, by Clifford Siskin in *The Historicity of Romantic Discourse* (Oxford University Press, 1988) and Clifford Siskin and William Warner (eds), *This is Enlightenment* (University of Chicago Press, 2010), and by Mary Poovey in *A History of the Modern Fact* (University of Chicago Press, 1998) and *Genres of the Credit Economy* (University of Chicago Press, 2008).
10. Addison's essays were published in *The Spectator* (numbers 411–22) in 1712 (quoting number 420, for 2 July 1712).
11. Adam Smith, *Essays on Philosophical Subjects*, ed. Joseph Black and James Hutton (Glasgow, 1795), p. 3.
12. Martin Rudwick, *Bursting the Limits of Time* (University of Chicago Press, 2005), p. 10. Rudwick's study has also, amongst its many other achievements, entirely revised the commonplace view of a tension between religion and geology in the eighteenth century and Romantic period with a sense of 'how religious and scientific practices and knowledge claims have interacted, in ways that have varied widely according to place, time, and, above all, social location' (p. 6), a revision to which I shall often have recourse in this book.
13. Noah Heringman, *Romantic Rocks, Aesthetic Geology* (Ithaca: Cornell University Press, 2004), p. 9. See also Noah Heringman (ed.), *Romantic Science: the Literary Forms of Natural History* (Albany: State University of New York Press, 2003).
14. Ralph O'Connor, *The Earth on Show: Fossils and the Poetics of Popular Science, 1802–1856* (University of Chicago Press, 2007), p. 13.
15. Thompson's analysis of course parallels O'Connor's description of the popular(ising) geologist as part natural philosopher, part littérateur and part showman.
16. O'Connor, *The Earth on Show*, pp. 21, 15.
17. For an examination of the extent to which the sublime is embedded in a range of genres of writing and areas of enquiry during the late eighteenth century and Romantic period, and of the role of the sublime in the emergence of disciplinarity at that time, see Cian Duffy and Peter Howell (eds), *Cultures of the Sublime: Selected Readings, 1750–1830* (Basingstoke: Palgrave Macmillan, 2011).
18. See, for example, the writings about economics or crowds discussed in *ibid.*, pp. 47–92, 151–78.
19. For a useful, recent overview of the place of the sublime in Lacan's thought, with particular reference to his *Ethics of Psychoanalysis* (1986), see Philip Shaw, *The Sublime* (London: Routledge, 2006), pp. 131–7. A confrontation with the sublime emerges from Lacan's ethics as central to the psycholinguistic construction of self and other.
20. One consequence of this is that I have relatively little to say here about engagements, within the genre of philosophical aesthetics, with the so-called 'rhetorical sublime', or the sublime as a property of writing. Following the rediscovery, and the making available of translations, of Longinus's *Peri Hypsous*, investigations of the 'rhetorical sublime' became an important strand of the eighteenth-century genre of British philosophical aesthetics.

As will become apparent, however, my concern is less with these technical descriptions than with the extent to which other genres (such as expedition narrative, or popularising essay) generate sublime effects for the purposes both of adequately remediating to the reader the impression of the landscapes of the sublime and of creating a commercially viable product.

21. Peter de Bolla, *The Discourse on the Sublime: Readings in History, Aesthetics, and the Subject* (Oxford: Blackwell, 1989), p. 2. De Bolla draws a distinction between this analytical 'discourse on the sublime' and 'the discourse of the sublime': 'a discourse which produces, from within itself, what is habitually termed the category of the sublime' (*ibid.*).
22. See Andrew Ashfield and Peter de Bolla (eds), *The Sublime: a Reader in British Eighteenth-Century Aesthetic Theory* (Cambridge University Press, 1996), pp. 2–5; Duffy and Howell (eds), *Cultures of the Sublime*, pp. 1–15 *passim*; and Cian Duffy, *Shelley and the Revolutionary Sublime* (Cambridge University Press, 2005), pp. 1–6, 9–12.
23. See Giuseppe Micheli, *The Early Reception of Kant's Thought in England, 1785–1805* (London: Routledge, 1993), p. 1. According to Micheli, Kant's *Critique of Judgement*, which contains the 'Analytic of the Sublime', was first available in English translation, in John Richardson's edition, in 1799 (p. 12).
24. De Bolla, *Discourse of the Sublime*, p. 23.
25. Duffy and Howell (eds), *Cultures of the Sublime*, p. 8.
26. For a cultural history of the British experience of the Grand Tour in the eighteenth century and early Romantic period, see Jeremy Black, *The British Abroad: the Grand Tour in the Eighteenth Century* (London: St Martin's, 1992).
27. Joseph Addison, *A Letter from Italy* (London, 1701), ll. 9–16.
28. Duffy and Howell (eds), *Cultures of the Sublime*, p. 4.
29. Percy Bysshe Shelley and Mary Shelley, *History of a Six Weeks' Tour through a Part of France, Switzerland, Germany and Holland* (London, 1817), p. v.
30. Carl Thompson, *The Suffering Traveller and the Romantic Imagination* (Oxford University Press, 2007), p. 11; cp. also Marjorie Hope Nicolson's perception that travellers to the Alps at the end of the eighteenth century 'self consciously anticipated the "sublime" experience' (*Mountain Gloom and Mountain Glory: the Development of the Aesthetics of the Infinite* (Ithaca: Cornell University Press, 1959), p. 372).
31. See, for example, Edmund Burke, *A Philosophical Enquiry into the Origin of our Ideas of the Sublime and the Beautiful* (Dublin, 1757), Part II, Sections III, VI and VII.
32. Thompson, *The Suffering Traveller*, p. 153.
33. Ashfield and De Bolla, *Reader*, pp. 3, 4.
34. O'Connor, *The Earth on Show*, p. 446.
35. My feeling, in this respect, is that Martin Rudwick's decision to focus 'on the activities of the scientific elite, among whom those claims [about the history of the earth] were shaped most effectively, rather than on the beliefs and opinions of the literate public as a whole' – although it serves its purpose well – risks imposing a boundary arguably as arbitrary as many of those which Rudwick dismantles (*Bursting the Limits of Time*, p. 4).
36. Heringman, *Romantic Rocks, Aesthetic Geology*, p. 28.
37. Immanuel Kant's 'Analytic of the Sublime' plays, of necessity, a somewhat lesser part in this process of exchange, however, since it was not widely

known in Britain until well into the nineteenth century. See J. H. Stirling and F. A. Nitsch, *Kant's Thought in Britain: the Early Impact* (London: Routledge, 1993), which includes a reprint of René Wellek's seminal *Immanuel Kant in England* (Princeton University Press, 1931).
38. De Bolla, *Discourse of the Sublime*, pp. 33–4.
39. For a brief sample of Humboldt's and Barrow's encounters with the 'natural sublime', see Duffy and Howell (eds), *Cultures of the Sublime*, pp. 195–200. Nigel Leask offers an extended consideration of the aesthetics of Humboldt's *Personal Narrative* of his travels to South America, and of the difficulties of disinterested aesthetic response, in *Curiosity and the Aesthetics of Travel Writing, 1770–1840: 'From an Antique Land'* (Oxford University Press, 2002), pp. 243–98.
40. O'Connor, *The Earth on Show*, p. 13.
41. Thompson, *The Suffering Traveller*, p. 11.
42. Rudwick's *Bursting the Limits of Time*, for example, makes only passing mention of Carbonnières and Brydone.
43. *Ibid.*, p. 8; original emphasis.
44. O'Connor, *The Earth on Show*, p. 446.
45. *Ibid.*, p. 2.
46. Samuel Holt Monk, *The Sublime: a Study of Critical Theories in Eighteenth-Century England* (Ann Arbor: University of Michigan Press, 1960), p. 4; Thomas Weiskel, *The Romantic Sublime* (Baltimore: Johns Hopkins University Press, 1976), p. 196.
47. Monk, *The Sublime*, p. 22.
48. See, for example, Nicolson, *Mountain Gloom and Mountain Glory*, pp. 392–3.
49. In a similar vein, Peter de Bolla points out that the focus on religious responses to the 'natural sublime' in Nicolson's account comes at the expense of neglect to the rise of interest in subjectivity in discussions of the sublime which took place alongside the demise of religious certainties (De Bolla, *Discourse of the Sublime*, pp. 5–6); Rudwick, *Bursting the Limits of Time*, p. 6.
50. See, for example, Nicolson, *Mountain Gloom and Mountain Glory*, pp. 213–18, 271–323 passim.
51. The contours of the discovery of 'deep time' have been extensively documented by Rudwick and others, and I have no intention to rehearse that narrative in any detail here. See also Paolo Rossi, *The Dark Abyss of Time*, transl. Lydia Cochrane (University of Chicago Press, 1984). The phrase 'deep time' was coined by John McPhee in *Basin and Range* (New York: Farrar, Strauss, Giroux, 1980), p. 20.
52. George Gordon, Lord Byron, *Byron's Letters and Journals*, ed. Leslie Marchand, 12 vols (Cambridge, MA: Harvard University Press, 1973–82), iii, p. 179.
53. O'Connor, *The Earth on Show*, p. 25.
54. Christian Frederick Damberger, *Travels in the Interior of Africa* (London, 1801), p. iii.
55. Francis Spufford, *I May Be Some Time: Ice and the English Imagination* (London: Faber & Faber, 1996), p. 6. In this respect, I agree with Eric Wilson's suggestion that the Romantic generation 'are among the first poets, essayists, and novelists to embrace ice', although I will part company with Wilson's interpretation of the contexts for and contents of that 'embrace' (Eric Wilson,

The Spiritual History of Ice: Romanticism, Science, and the Imagination (London: Palgrave, 2003), p. 5).
56. Spufford, *I May Be Some Time*, p. 7.
57. In *The Suffering Traveller*, Carl Thompson argues that it was Mungo Park's account of his travails in Africa which 'inaugurates a hugely influential rhetorical tradition in British exploration, a tradition whereby defeats and setbacks in the field can be almost as triumphant as victories' (p. 182). The claim to have discovered origins is always perplexed and difficult, however, and my examination of writing about the polar sublime here makes it seem likely that this undeniably 'influential [...] tradition' of writing about exploration was generated in a variety of genres.
58. Richard Holmes devotes his fifth chapter to Park's search for the Niger (see *The Age of Wonder: How the Romantic Generation Discovered the Beauty and Terror of Science* (London: Harper, 2008), pp. 211–34), while Thompson discusses Bruce and Park in the context of the persona of the Romantic-period explorer (see *The Suffering Traveller*, pp. 146–85).
59. Percy Shelley, *The Poems of Percy Bysshe Shelley*, ed. Kelvin Everest, Geoffrey Matthews *et al.*, 3 vols to date (London: Longman, 1988–), i, p. 306.
60. See, for example, Alex Murray, 'Vestiges of the Phoenix: De Quincey, Kant, and the Heavens', *Victoriographies* 1/2 (November 2011), pp. 246–60, and Jonathan Smith, 'De Quincey's Revisions to "System of the Heavens"', *Victorian Periodicals Review* 26/4 (Winter 1993), pp. 203–12.
61. O'Connor, *The Earth on Show*, p. 2.
62. *Ibid.*, pp. 10, 12.
63. See, for example, Ashfield and De Bolla's argument that the enquiry into the sublime in eighteenth-century British philosophical aesthetics contributed to 'an emerging new understanding of the construction of the subject', and that 'the aesthetic', in the period, 'is not *primarily* about art but about how we are formed as subjects, and how *as subjects* we go about making sense of our experience' (*Reader*, p. 2).
64. Immanuel Kant, 'Analytic of the Sublime', in *The Critique of Judgement*, ed. and transl. James Creed Meredith (Oxford University Press, 1992), p. 104). For a discussion of the place of enquiries into subjectivity within the eighteenth-century genre of British writing about the sublime see, for example, De Bolla, *Discourse of the Sublime*, pp. 1–23. Shaw, *The Sublime*, pp. 131–47, provides an overview of the place of the sublime in the work of Lacan.
65. Thompson, *The Suffering Traveller*, p. 148. For discussions of these various aspects of travel and travel-writing during the eighteenth century and Romantic period, see, for example, James Buzzard, *The Beaten Track: European Tourism, Literature, and the Ways to 'Culture', 1800–1918* (Oxford University Press, 1993); Chloe Chard, *Pleasure and Guilt on the Grand Tour: Travel Writing and Imaginative Geography* (Manchester University Press, 1999); and Leask, *Curiosity and the Aesthetics of Travel Writing*. On the development of 'scientific travel', see Barbara Stafford, *Voyage into Substance: Art, Science, Nature, and the Illustrated Travel Account, 1760–1840* (Cambridge, MA: MIT Press, 1984).
66. Holmes, *The Age of Wonder*, p. xvi. By 'Romantic science' Holmes intends not just enquiries in natural philosophy during the Romantic period, but also a specific conception of science as 'Romantic'.

67. O'Connor, *The Earth on Show*, pp. 2–3.
68. Thompson, *The Suffering Traveller*, pp. 8, 17.
69. *Ibid.*, p. 15. See also, for example, Leask's discussion of James Bruce's reconstruction of his travels (*Curiosity and the Aesthetics of Travel Writing*, pp. 54–101).

1 'We had hopes that pointed to the clouds'

1. Louis Ramond de Carbonnières, 'Observations on the Glacieres and the Glaciers', transl. Helen Maria Williams and published as an appendix to her *A Tour in Switzerland; or, A View of the Present State of the Governments and Manners of those Cantons: with Comparative Sketches of the Present State of Paris*, 2 vols (London, 1798), ii, p. 348. As Williams explains, 'the Glacieres are central mountains, on which the snow first collects itself; the name of Glaciers is given to those ramifications of ice which branch from that centre' (*Tour in Switzerland*, ii, p. 279n.).
2. Unless otherwise indicated, quotations from *The Prelude* are from the revised (1850) text, as given in Jonathan Wordsworth (ed.), *The Prelude: the Four Texts* (London: Penguin, 1995).
3. Alan Liu, *Wordsworth: the Sense of History* (Stanford University Press, 1989), p. 4. Wordsworth and his companion, Robert Jones, crossed the Simplon Pass on 17 August 1790.
4. Monk, *The Sublime*, p. 231; Weiskel, *The Romantic Sublime*, p. 196. Cp. M. H. Abrams's claim that Book VI of *The Prelude* is the 'epitome' of 'a century of commentary on [...] sublime Alpine landscape' (*Natural Supernaturalism: Tradition and Revolution in Romantic Literature* (Oxford University Press, 1971), p. 106).
5. Monk, *The Sublime*, p. 4.
6. Liu, *The Sense of History*, pp. 3–31.
7. Jean-Jacques Rousseau, *Julie, or, the New Héloïse: Letters of Two Lovers who Live in a Small Town at the Foot of the Alps* (1761), transl. William Kenrick (London, 1761), p. 114.
8. Henry Coxe, *The Traveller's Guide in Switzerland* (London, 1816), p. iv; emphasis added.
9. M. J. G. Ebel, *Traveller's Guide through Switzerland*, transl. Daniel Wall (London, 1818), p. 376.
10. *Ibid.*, pp. 1, 10.
11. Shelley and Shelley, *History of a Six Weeks' Tour* (1817), p. v.
12. I discuss some of Pococke's experiences of the desert in Chapter 4.
13. William Windham, *An Account of the Glacieres, or Ice Alps, in Savoy. In Two Letters; One from an English Gentleman to His Friend at Geneva; The Other from Peter Martel, Engineer, to the Said English Gentleman* (London, 1744). Martel visited Chamonix in 1742, after having read Windham's original letter to 'his friend at Geneva', the painter Jacques-Antoine Arlaud. Martel sent Windham a description of this journey on his return, which Windham subsequently included in his *Account*.
14. Windham, *Account*, pp. 1, 8. For an indication of the extent to which this refrain has become conventional by the early nineteenth century, compare

Percy Bysshe Shelley's letter to Thomas Love Peacock of 22 July 1816, from Chamonix: 'how shall I describe to you the scenes by which I am now surrounded. – To exhaust epithets which express the astonishment & the admiration [...] is this to impress upon your mind the images which fill mine now, even until it overflows? I too had read before now the raptures of travellers. I will be warned by their example. I will simply detail to you, all that I can relate, or all that if related I could enable you to conceive of what we have seen or done' (*The Letters of Percy Bysshe Shelley*, ed. F. L. Jones, 2 vols (Oxford: Clarendon, 1964), i, p. 495.
15. Windham, *Account*, pp. 10, 25.
16. Ibid., pp. 1, 11.
17. Nicolson, *Mountain Gloom and Mountain Glory*, p. 372.
18. Wordsworth, *The Prelude*, vi, ll. 526–8.
19. Williams, *Tour in Switzerland*, i, p. 57.
20. William Hazlitt, *The Complete Works of William Hazlitt*, ed. P. P. Howe, 21 vols (London: Dent, 1930–34), x, p. 189.
21. I discuss Saussure's celebrated ascent later in this chapter.
22. Windham, *Account*, p. 12.
23. Ibid., p. 26.
24. John Playfair, *Illustrations of the Huttonian Theory of the Earth* (Edinburgh, 1802), p. 110. Diverse aspects of this conflict between various responses to the Alpine landscape are considered in Heringman, *Romantic Rocks, Aesthetic Geology*, O'Connor, *The Earth on Show*, and Rudwick, *Bursting the Limits of Time*.
25. C. M. de La Condamine, *Journal of a Tour to Italy*, transl. anon. (London, 1763), p. 166.
26. Marc Théodore Bourrit, *A Relation of a Journey to the Glaciers in the Dutchy of Savoy*, transl. C. and F. Davy (Norwich, 1775).
27. Ibid., p. ii.
28. Ibid., pp. 116–17, 243–4.
29. Ibid., p. 116.
30. Ibid.
31. Ibid., p. 117.
32. Ibid., p. 65.
33. Ibid., pp. 8–9.
34. Ibid., p. 92.
35. Ibid., p. 112.
36. Ibid., p. 114.
37. Ibid., pp. 114–15.
38. Ibid., p. 116.
39. Ibid., p. 211.
40. Ibid., pp. 8–9.
41. Ibid., p. xvii.
42. Ibid., p. 68 and n.
43. William Coxe, *Travels in Switzerland, and in the Country of the Grisons: in a Series of Letters [...] A New Edition*, 3 vols (Basil, 1802), ii, p. 41.
44. Ibid., p. 48.
45. Ibid., p. 115.
46. Ibid., i, p. 3.

47. Louis Ramond de Carbonnières, *Lettres* [...] *sur l'État Politique, Civil et Naturel de la Suisse; Traduisse de l'Anglois, et Augmentées des Observations faites dans le Même Pays, par le Traducteur*, 2 vols (Paris, 1781).
48. Quoted from Williams, *Tour in Switzerland*, ii, p. 348.
49. *Ibid.*, p. 303.
50. *Ibid.*, p. 280. This opposition between the view from the valley and the view from the summit is very important, and I consider it in detail later in the chapter.
51. *Ibid.*, pp. 282–4.
52. *Ibid.*, pp. 347–9.
53. For a detailed factual history of the various early attempts on Mont Blanc, see Thomas Brown and Gavin De Beer's excellent and entertaining account in *The First Ascent of Mont Blanc* (Oxford University Press, 1957).
54. Coxe, *Travels*, pp. 100, 118.
55. See, for example, Brown and De Beer, *The First Ascent of Mont Blanc*, pp. 145–6.
56. John Ruskin, 'Evening at Chamouni', in *The Poems of John Ruskin*, ed. William Collingwood, 2 vols (London, 1891), i, pp. 161–2 (ll. 1–3, 22–3).
57. Rudwick describes Saussure's achievements in the context of the history of the science of geology in *Bursting the Limits of Time*, pp. 15–22.
58. Saussure's Alpine narratives were also included in John Pinkerton's popular *General Collection of the Best and Most Interesting Voyages and Travels in all Parts of the World*, 17 vols (London, 1809–14).
59. Saussure, *Relation*, quoted from Pinkerton (ed.), *General Collection*, iv, p. 700.
60. *Ibid.*
61. *Ibid.*, p. 691.
62. *Ibid.*
63. *Ibid.*, p. 688.
64. Alessandro Volta, quoted from Stuart Peterfreund, 'Two Romantic Poets and Two Romantic Scientists "on" Mont Blanc', *The Wordsworth Circle* 29/3 (1999), p. 157 (ll. 11, 29–30).
65. For an interesting recent account of the development of the sport of Alpinism in tandem with the rise of Alpine tourism, see Jim Ring, *How the English Made the Alps* (London: Murray, 2000).
66. John Auldjo, *Narrative of an Ascent to the Summit of Mont Blanc, on the 8th and 9th of August, 1827* (London, 1828), pp. 1–2.
67. Ebel, *Traveller's Guide*, pp. 378–9.
68. Martyn, *Sketch of a Tour*, p. 91.
69. Thomas Glover, *A Description of the Valley of Chamouni* (London, 1819). See also d'Ostervald's popular *Picturesque Tour in the Valley of Chamouni, and Round Mont Blanc* (London, 1825).
70. Glover, *Description*, p. 34.
71. Hazlitt, *Complete Works*, x, p. 291.
72. Saussure, *Relation*, iv, p. 691.
73. Nicolson's *Mountain Gloom and Mountain Glory* remains the seminal history of the religious response to the 'natural sublime' in the eighteenth century.
74. See Burke, *Philosophical Enquiry*, Part II, Section III.
75. Quoted from Samuel Taylor Coleridge, *The Complete Poems*, ed. William Keach (London: Penguin, 1997) (ll. 3, 75–7). Unless otherwise indicated,

quotations from Coleridge are from this edition. Thomas De Quincey was the first to point out that Coleridge had adapted his 'Hymn', without acknowledgement, from a German poem by Frederika Brun. For a detailed discussion of the relationship between the two texts, see Elinor Schaffer, 'Coleridge's Swiss Voice: Frederike Brun and the Vale of Chamouni', in *Essays in Memory of Michael Parkinson*, ed. Christopher Smith (Norwich: University of East Anglia, 1996), pp. 67–76.
76. Williams, *Tour in Switzerland*, ii, pp. 16–19.
77. Bourrit, *Relation of a Journey*, p. 66; Saussure, *Relation*, iv, p. 677.
78. Alaric Watts, *Poetical Sketches*, 3rd edn (London, 1824), p. 48 (l. 6).
79. Thomas Whalley, *Mont Blanc: an Irregular Lyric Poem* (Bath, 1788), ll. 12, 479–82. In a note to line 480, Whalley observes: 'When this poem was written, no human foot had ever attained either of the summits of Mont Blanc; but, after many fruitless attempts, Mr. Bourrit relates, that a peasant of the valley of Chamouny has at length mounted on one of the lower domes; but the pure snows of the highest still remain involate' (p. 37n). In a further footnote, to the final line of the poem, Whalley says that he only learned of Saussure's ascent 'when the last sheet of this poem was printing' (p. 57n).
80. Glover, *Description*, p. 24.
81. Percy Shelley, 'Mont Blanc', l. 97; *Letters*, i, p. 499.
82. George Gordon, Lord Byron, *Manfred* (London, 1817) I i, ll. 29, 32–3. Unless otherwise indicated, Byron's poetry is quoted from *Byron: a Critical Edition of the Major Works*, ed. Jerome McGann (Oxford University Press, 1988).
83. Ruskin, 'Evening at Chamouni', ll. 22–3; emphasis added. Ruskin himself subsequently came to regard high-altitude Alpine climbing as an invasive practice, detrimental to an aesthetic appreciation of the mountains. In his discussion of 'Mountain Beauty' in volume four of *Modern Painters* (1855–56), Ruskin suggests that we should 'divest [...] ourselves, as far as may be, of our modern experimental or exploring activity, and habit of regarding mountains chiefly as places for gymnastic exercise', and embrace the 'truths and dignities' only truly available, he argues, in artistic representations of the Alps. 'The aim of the great inventive landscape painter', Ruskin claims, 'must be to give the far higher and deeper truth of mental vision, rather than that of the physical facts.' John Ruskin, *Modern Painters*, ed. David Barrie (London: Deutsch, 1987), pp. 441, 446, 481–2.
84. Whalley, *Mont Blanc*, ll. 48–59.
85. Coxe, *Traveller's Guide*, pp. 40–1; original emphasis. Coxe's gendering of the Mont Blanc massif as female is relatively unusual in contemporary engagements with the Alpine sublime, though not, as we shall see, in other areas, such as the Arctic and Antarctic.
86. Edmund Burke, *Reflections on the Revolution in France* (London, 1790), p. 119.
87. Hazlitt, *Complete Works*, x, p. 291.
88. Coxe, *Traveller's Guide*, p. viii.
89. George Keate, *The Alps* (London, 1763), ll. 167–74, 181–91; original emphasis.
90. Windham, *Account*, p. 25; Glover, *Description*, p. 10.
91. G. W. Bridges, *Alpine Sketches, Comprised in a Short Tour through Parts of Holland, Flanders, France, Savoy, Switzerland and Germany, during the Summer of 1814* (London, 1814), p. 120.

92. Byron, *Manfred*, I ii 49–50.
93. Williams, *Tour in Switzerland*, ii, pp. 210, 212–13.
94. Coxe, *Travels*, ii, pp. 64–5.
95. Shelley, *Letters*, i, pp. 480–1.
96. Williams, *Tour in Switzerland*, ii, p. 187.
97. Samuel Taylor Coleridge, *France: an Ode* (London, 1798), l. 77.
98. *Ibid.*, ll. 65, 66, 69, 75.
99. William Wordsworth, 'Thoughts of a Briton on the Subjugation of Switzerland' (1807), ll. 4, 7, 2, 8. Unless otherwise indicated, Wordsworth's poetry is quoted from *The Poetical Works of William Wordsworth*, ed. Ernest de Sélincourt and Helen Darbishire, 5 vols (Oxford University Press, 1952–59).
100. Coleridge, *France an Ode*, ll. 71, 73.
101. Williams, *Tour in Switzerland*, ii, p. 215.
102. *Ibid.*, pp. 270–1.
103. *Ibid.*
104. Saussure, *Relation*, iv, p. 691.
105. Quoted from Byron, *A Critical Edition of the Major Works*, pp. 144–5.
106. Quoted from Williams, *Tour in Switzerland*, ii, p. 280.
107. Hazlitt, *Complete Works*, x, pp. 190–1.
108. *Ibid.*, p. 191.
109. The ambivalence of Hazlitt's ostensibly favourable account of Napoleon's 'vast' Alpine achievements is further signalled by the comparison with Rob Roy. The protagonist of Scott's eponymous 1817 novel, at least, which Hazlitt praised for showing 'that there is no romance like the romance of real life', is an ambiguous blend of revolutionary and opportunist. Hazlitt offers a more sober appraisal of Napoleon's crossing of the Alps in his *Life of Napoleon Bonaparte*, 4 vols (London, 1828), ii, pp. 442–50. For a detailed account of Hazlitt's conflicted attitude to Napoleon, see Simon Bainbridge, *Napoleon and English Romanticism* (Cambridge University Press, 1995), pp. 183–207.
110. Hazlitt, *Complete Works*, x, p. 190.
111. *Ibid.*
112. *Ibid.*
113. Williams, *Tour in Switzerland*, ii, pp. 55–6.
114. *Ibid.*, pp. 56–7. Williams's phrase 'terrestrial region' of course echoes both Rousseau's *Julie* and Carbonnières's 'Observations'.
115. Questions were asked almost immediately about the authenticity of the Ossian poems (by David Hume and Samuel Johnson, for example), but the debate rumbled on until 1805, when a *Report of the Highland Society* concluded that McPherson's 'editing' of his supposed source had been rather liberal.
116. Keate, *The Alps* (1763), ll. 2–3, 27–30; emphasis added.
117. *Ibid.*, ll. 418–20.
118. *Ibid.*, ll. 73, 32.
119. Whalley, *Mont Blanc*, ll. 483–91.
120. James Montgomery, *The Alps: a Reverie* (London, 1822), ll. 9–16.
121. Saussure, *Relation*, iv, p. 682.
122. Montgomery, *The Alps*, ll. 49–54.
123. George Gordon, Lord Byron, *Childe Harold's Pilgrimage: Canto the Third* (London, 1816), ll. 639, 642–3.

124. *Ibid.*, l. 1049.
125. *Ibid.*, ll. 397–405; original emphasis.
126. George Gordon, Lord Byron, *Don Juan*, i, ll. 1737–40.
127. Byron, *Childe Harold III*, ll. 599–600.
128. *Ibid.*, ll. 601–2.
129. *Ibid.*, ll. 1017–21.
130. *Ibid.*, ll. 1028–30.
131. Wordsworth, *The Prelude*, vi, l. 333.
132. Buzzard, *The Beaten Track*.
133. See C. N. Coe, 'Did Wordsworth Read Coxe's *Travels in Switzerland* before Making the Tour of 1790?', *Notes & Queries* 195 (1950), pp. 144–5.
134. William Wordsworth, *Descriptive Sketches. In Verse. Taken During a Pedestrian Tour in the Italian, Grison, Swiss, and Savoyard Alps* (London, 1793), p. 28n. Wordsworth's phrasing suggests that he is referring to Carbonnières's *Lettres*, but it is possible that he refers to the English translation of the 'Observations' published in the 1789 edition of Coxe's *Travels*. There is no record of his having read the Williams translation, but that seems likely.
135. *The Letters of William and Dorothy Wordsworth, Volume IV: The Later Years. Part I. 1821–1828*, ed. Ernest de Selincourt, rev. Alan Hill (Oxford University Press, 1978), p. 234. Wordsworth also recommends Carbonnières to Henry Robinson in a letter of 28 November 1828 (*ibid.*, p. 674).
136. Quoted from Williams, *Tour in Switzerland*, ii, pp. 350–1. The original French reads: 'tout concourt à render les meditations plus profondes, à leur donner cette teinte sombre, ce caractere sublime qu'elles acquierent, quand l'ame, pregnant cet effort qui la rend contemporaine de tous les siecles, & co-existante avec tous les êtres, plane sur l'abyme du temps' (Carbonnières, *Lettres*, ii, p. 138).
137. Wordsworth, *The Prelude*, vi, ll. 532, 538–9.
138. Quoted from Williams, *Tour in Switzerland*, ii, pp. 351–2. In the original French: 'En vain alors la raison voudroit compter des années. La solidité de ces masses énormes oppose à l'accumulation de leurs ruines, l'épouvante & confond son calcul. L'imagination s'empare de ce que la raison abandonne, & dans cette longue succession de periods, elle croit entrevoir une image de l'éternité [...] C'est ainsi que nos idées les plus vastes, que nos sentiments les plus nobles, ont pour origine les seductions de l'imagination: que penserions-nous de grand, que ferions-nous de remarquable, si elle ne transformoit sans cesse le fini en infini, l'étendue en immensité, les temps en éternité, & des lauriers éphémeres en couronnes immortelles' (*Lettres*, ii, p. 139).
139. Cp., for example, Hume's discussion of the imagination in his *Treatise of Human Nature* (London, 1739–40) I iii.

2 'A volcano heard afar'

1. The quotation in the title is from Percy Bysshe Shelley's poem *The Mask of Anarchy* (l. 363), which Shelley composed in September 1819, in the wake of the Peterloo Massacre.
2. Patrick Brydone, *A Tour through Sicily and Malta. In a Series of Letters to William Beckford, Esq. The Second Edition, Corrected*, 2 vols (London, 1774), i, pp. 23–4.

3. John Dryden, *A Voyage to Sicily and Malta, in the Years 1700 and 1701* (London, 1776), p. 25.
4. This tradition inspired Friedrich Hölderlin's play *Tod des Empedokles* (1798, 1800, 1826), and Matthew Arnold's poem 'Empedocles on Etna' (1852).
5. John Auldjo, *Sketches of Vesuvius, with Short Accounts of its Principal Eruptions, from the Commencement of the Christian Era to the Present Time* (Naples, 1832), p. 1.
6. Brydone, *Tour*, i, p. 163; Joseph Addison, *Remarks on Several Parts of Italy* (London, 1705), p. 143.
7. Burke, *Philosophical Enquiry*, p. 107.
8. Rudwick, *Bursting the Limits of Time*, p. 2.
9. Ibid., pp. 15, 3.
10. Ibid., p. 3.
11. Ibid., p. 6.
12. John Playfair, 'Biographical Account of the Late Dr. James Hutton', *Transactions of the Royal Society of Edinburgh*, v, part iii (1823), p. 73; the paper was first read to the society on 10 January 1803. Buffon, in his *Époques de la Nature*, had suggested that the earth might be seventy-five thousand years old, a 'dark abyss of time'.
13. Rudwick, *Bursting the Limits of Time*, p. 10.
14. Heringman, *Romantic Rocks, Aesthetic Geology*, p. 9; O'Connor, *The Earth on Show*, pp. 10, 445, 15.
15. O'Connor, *The Earth on Show*, p. 25.
16. William Hamilton, *Observations on Mount Vesuvius, Mount Etna, and Other Volcanoes*, 2nd edn (London, 1774), p. 56.
17. Henry Swinburne, *Travels in the Two Sicilies*, 2nd edn, 4 vols (London, 1790), iv, p. 146. Swinburne might have been drawing on Oliver Goldsmith's adapted translation of Buffon in his *History of the Earth and Animated Nature* (London, 1774), which tones down some of the Frenchman's more controversial hypotheses.
18. Dryden, *Voyage*, p. 25.
19. Ibid.
20. Ibid.
21. Swinburne, *Travels*, iv, p. 156.
22. Brydone, *Tour*, i, p. 187.
23. Dryden, *Voyage*, p. 29. Cp. Hamilton, *Observations* (p. 59) on Catania, which had been devastated by an eruption of Etna in 1693: 'I do not wonder at the seeming security with which these parts are inhabited, having been so long witness to the same near Mount Vesuvius. The operations of nature are slow: great eruptions do not frequently happen; each flatters himself that it will not happen in his time, or, if it should, that his tutelary saint will turn away the destructive lava from his grounds; and indeed the great fertility in the neighbourhoods of volcanoes tempts people to inhabit them.'
24. Dryden, *Voyage*, pp. v–vii.
25. Rudwick, *Bursting the Limits of Time*, p. 4.
26. Coleridge seems to have made two ascents to the summit of Etna in August 1804, although no record of either is extant in his correspondence or journals. See Richard Holmes, *Coleridge: Darker Reflections* (London: Flamingo, 1999), pp. 21, 359.

27. Brydone, *Tour*, p. 97.
28. *Ibid.*, pp. 163, 97.
29. *Ibid.*, p. 163.
30. Hamilton, *Observations*, p. 92.
31. *Ibid.*, p. 161.
32. *Ibid.*, p. 92.
33. *Ibid.*, p. 160.
34. Brydone, *Tour*, p. 97.
35. *Ibid.*, p. 109.
36. *Ibid.*, p. 97.
37. *Ibid.*, pp. 160–1.
38. *Ibid.*, p. 163.
39. *Ibid.*, pp. 19–20.
40. *Ibid.* p. 22.
41. *Ibid.*, p. 23.
42. *Ibid.*
43. *Ibid.*
44. *Ibid.*, pp. 23–4.
45. *Ibid.*, p. 24.
46. *Ibid.*, p. 29.
47. *Ibid.*, pp. 29–30.
48. *Ibid.*, p. 32.
49. *Ibid.*, pp. 112–13.
50. *Ibid.*, p. 190.
51. *Ibid.*, pp. 114–15. This 'very singular event' was presumably a lahar, or volcanic mudflow.
52. It was also Recupero who dissuaded Henry Swinburne from attempting to ascend Etna (*Travels*, iv, p. 140).
53. Brydone, *Tour*, p. 140.
54. *Ibid.*
55. *Ibid.*, p. 141.
56. *Ibid.*
57. *Ibid.*, p. 147.
58. James Hutton, *The Theory of the Earth* (Edinburgh, 1788), p. 96.
59. Brydone, *Tour*, p. 141.
60. *Ibid.*
61. *Ibid.*, p. 142.
62. James Boswell, *The Life of Samuel Johnson*, ed. J. W. Croker, 2 vols (London, 1833), i, pp. 195, 45.
63. Unless otherwise indicated, quotations from 'System of the Heavens' are from the text published in *Tait's Edinburgh Magazine* (September 1846, pp. 566–79) as reprinted in Grevel Lindop (gen. ed.), *The Works of Thomas De Quincey*, 21 vols (London: Pickering & Chatto, 2000–3). Quotation here vol. 15 (ed. Frederick Burwick), p. 395 and note.
64. Brydone, *Tour*, p. 196.
65. *Ibid.*, p. 212.
66. *Ibid.*, p. 196.
67. *Ibid.*
68. *Ibid.*, p. 198.

Notes to Chapter 2

69. *Ibid.*
70. *Ibid.*, p. 199.
71. *Ibid.*
72. *Ibid.*
73. *Ibid.*, p. 215.
74. *Ibid.*
75. *Ibid.*, p. 216.
76. *Ibid.*, pp. 217–18.
77. *Ibid.*, p. 218.
78. *Ibid.*, p. 203.
79. *Ibid.*, p. 202.
80. *Ibid.*, p. 204.
81. *Ibid.*
82. *Ibid.*, p. 212.
83. By the end of the eighteenth century, the term 'enthusiasm', used in this sense, had become, within a range of different genres, at least in part a term of disapprobation, signifying irrationality, and linked with superstition and political violence.
84. Richard Hoare, *A Classical Tour through Italy and Sicily; Tending to Illustrate Some Districts which have not been Described by Mr. Eustace, in his Classical Tour*, 2 vols (London, 1819), ii, p. 324.
85. *Ibid.*, p. 327.
86. Brydone, *Tour*, i, p. 230. The key word here is *accessible*: Brydone appends a caveat affirming that he is 'persuaded that there are many inaccessible points of the Alps, particularly [Mont Blanc] that are still much higher than Etna' (*ibid.*).
87. *Ibid.*, p. 265.
88. *Ibid.*, p. 24.
89. Addison, *Remarks*, pp. 143–4.
90. *Ibid.*, p. 144.
91. Swinburne, *Travels*, i, pp. 82–3; Thomas Martyn, *A Tour through Italy* (London, 1791), p. 300.
92. Addison, *Remarks*, p. 145.
93. Joseph Forsyth, *Remarks on Antiquities, Arts, and Letters, during an Excursion in Italy* (London, 1813), p. 292.
94. La Condamine, *Journal*, pp. 79–80.
95. For a discussion of these see, for example, O'Connor, *The Earth on Show*, pp. 263–364.
96. Addison, *Remarks*, p. 145.
97. Pliny the Younger, *The Letters of Pliny*, transl. W. Melmoth, rev. W. Hutchinson, 2 vols (London: Heinemann, 1961), I, vi, xvi, p. 475.
98. *Ibid.*, p. 478.
99. *Ibid.*, p. 477. Pliny offers an essentially accurate explanation of the 'strange' shape of this towering column of ash and gas, now known, in his honour, as a 'Plinian column': 'I imagine a momentary gust of air blew it aloft, and then failing, forsook it; thus causing the cloud to expand laterally as it dissolved, or possibly the downward pressure of its own weight produced this effect' (*ibid.*).

100. *Ibid.*, pp. 477–8.
101. *Ibid.*, p. 479.
102. *Ibid.*, p. 481.
103. *Ibid.*, pp. 481–3.
104. John Chetwode Eustace, *A Classical Tour through Italy*, 4th edn, 4 vols (Livorno, 1817), ii, p. 62.
105. Forsyth, *Remarks*, p. 329.
106. Mariana Starke, *Letters from Italy*, 2nd edn, 2 vols (London, 1815), ii, p. 10. Cp. Eustace, *Classical Tour*, ii, p. 70: 'This scene of a city raised from the grave where it had lain forgotten during the long night of eighteen centuries, when once beheld, must remain forever pictured on the imagination; and whenever it presents itself to the fancy, it comes, like the recollection of an awful apparition, accompanied by thoughts and emotions solemn and melancholy.'
107. The 60 illustrations to the *Campi* and its *Supplement*, by the Italian painter Pietro Fabris, constitute a remarkable blend of scientific and scenic representation, and have been identified as marking the moment when geological illustration begins to become distinguishable from conventional landscape painting. See Joachim von der Thüsen, 'Painting and the Rise of Volcanology: Sir William Hamilton's *Campi Phlegraei*', *Endeavour* 23/3 (1999), pp. 106–9.
108. William Hamilton, *Campi Phlegraei: Observations on the Volcanoes of the Two Sicilies* (Naples, 1776), p. 9.
109. William Hamilton, *Supplement to the Campi Phlegraei: Being an Account of the Great Eruption of Mount Vesuvius in the Month of August 1779* (Naples, 1779), pp. 9–10.
110. Hamilton, *Campi Phlegraei*, pp. 31–2.
111. Hamilton, *Supplement to the Campi Phlegraei*, p. 12.
112. N. Brooke, *Observations on the Manners and Customs of Italy [...] also Particulars of the Wonderful Explosion of Mount Vesuvius, taken on the Spot at Midnight, in June, 1794* (Bath, 1798), p. 181.
113. *Ibid.*, p. 190.
114. *Ibid.*, p. 188.
115. *Ibid.*
116. *Ibid.*, pp. 178–9.
117. *Ibid.*, pp. 182–3.
118. Burke, *Reflections on the Revolution*, p. 106.
119. See, for example, O'Connor, *The Earth on Show*, pp. 102–4; see also Ralph O'Connor, 'Mammoths and Maggots: Byron and the Geology of Cuvier', *Romanticism* 5 (1999), pp. 26–42.
120. Eustace, *Classical Tour*, iii, p. 39; Shelley, *Letters*, ii, pp. 62–3.
121. Auldjo, *Sketches*, pp. 10–11.
122. *Ibid.*, p. 10.
123. Hamilton, *Campi Phlegraei*, p. 12.
124. Addison, *Remarks*, p. 143.
125. *Ibid.*, pp. 143–4.
126. Eustace, *Classical Tour*, iii, p. 39.
127. Shelley, *Letters*, ii, p. 62.

128. Eustace, *Classical Tour*, ii, pp. 48–9.
129. Felicia Hemans, *The Records of Woman and Other Poems* (Edinburgh, 1828), p. 307n.
130. Eustace, *Classical Tour*, iii, pp. 61–2.
131. Hamilton, *Campi Phlegraei*, p. 5.
132. Byron, *Letters and Journals*, iii, p. 179. For a detailed consideration of the place of 'the sublime' in eighteenth-century and Romantic-period enquiries into the nature of the human mind, see Duffy and Howell (eds), *Cultures of the Sublime*.
133. O'Connor, *The Earth on Show*, p. 104.
134. Coleridge to Cottle, quoted from Holmes, *Darker Reflections*, p. 21.
135. Madame de Staël, *Corinna, or Italy*, 5 vols, transl. D. Lawler (London, 1807), iii, p. 224.
136. *Ibid.*, p. 207.
137. *Ibid.*, pp. 209–10.
138. Cp. Saussure's similar comparison of physical and moral vertigo in his *Relation Abrégée* (which I have discussed in Chapter 1).
139. Staël, *Corinna*, iii, pp. 207–8.
140. *Ibid.*, p. 209.
141. *Ibid.*, p. 210.
142. Brydone, *Tour*, i, p. 148.
143. *Ibid.*, pp. 148–9.
144. *Ibid.*, pp. 62–3.
145. Mona Ozouf, *Festivals and the French Revolution*, transl. Alan Sheridan (Cambridge, MA: Harvard University Press, 1998); Mary Ashburn Miller, '"Mountain, Become a Volcano": The Image of the Volcano in the Rhetoric of the French Revolution', *French Historical Studies* 32/4 (2009), pp. 555–85.
146. Miller, 'Mountain', p. 567.
147. *Moniteur Universel*, 6 January 1792; quoted from *ibid*.
148. Miller, 'Mountain', pp. 580–1.
149. Geoffrey Matthews, 'A Volcano's Voice in Shelley', *ELH* 23 (1957), pp. 191–228; Duffy, *Shelley and the Revolutionary Sublime*, pp. 149–86 *passim*.

3 'The region of beauty and delight'

1. The chapter title is taken from the would-be polar explorer Robert Walton's description for his sister of what he hopes to find at the North Pole, in the first letter of Mary Shelley's *Frankenstein, or, The Modern Prometheus*, 2 vols (London, 1818), i, p. 2.
2. James Cook, *A Voyage towards the South Pole and Round the World*, 2 vols (London, 1777), ii, p. 243.
3. Unless otherwise indicated, references are to the 1798 text of *The Rime of the Ancyent Marinere*, published in *Lyrical Ballads* (Bristol, 1798, pp. 15–63), and to the 1818 text of *Frankenstein*.
4. Peter Kitson (ed.), *The North and South Poles*, vol. 3 of *Travels, Explorations and Empires* (London: Pickering & Chatto, 2001), p. vii.
5. See, for example, Burke, *Philosophical Enquiry*, Part II, Sections III–V.
6. Wilson, *The Spiritual History of Ice*, p. xiii.

7. Shelley, *Frankenstein*, i, pp. 2–3. For a useful survey of classical, medieval and Renaissance myths about the Antarctic, see Wilson, *The Spiritual History of Ice*, pp. 143–52. Wilson opens this survey with the observation that 'the virginal ices covering the poles have for centuries stimulated robust visions, serving as blank screens on which men have projected deep reveries' (p. 141). Once again, the story which I mean to tell in this chapter is that of the failure of the eighteenth century and Romantic period successfully to accomplish just such imaginative projection.
8. Wilson devotes one chapter to European and American engagements with the polar regions. Spufford is concerned mainly with nineteenth-century and twentieth-century English engagements, but also offers some retrospect over the Romantic period in the first chapter of the book.
9. Thompson, *The Suffering Traveller*, p. 153.
10. Cook, *Voyage towards the South Pole*, ii, p. 243.
11. Kant, *Critique of Judgement*, p. 106.
12. Wilson, *The Spiritual History of Ice*, p. 5; original emphasis.
13. Richard Holmes, for example, does not consider engagements with the polar regions in *The Age of Wonder*.
14. Spufford, *I May Be Some Time*, pp. 6, 7.
15. Wilson, *The Spiritual History of Ice*, p. 168. Wilson arguably misses the point, somewhat, in that it is exactly not against 'the Antarctic whiteness' that the Mariner acts; moreover, Wilson's view of the poem as essentially a psychological or 'spiritual' narrative does not (is not intended to) register the wider cultural-historical context of contemporary interest in the polar regions.
16. Johann Reinhold Forster, *History of the Voyages and Discoveries Made in the North*, transl. anon. (Dublin, 1786), p. iv.
17. See, as only the most recent example, George Soule, 'Coleridge's Debt to Shelvocke in "The Ancient Mariner"', *Notes & Queries* 50/3 (2003), p. 287.
18. *The Letters of William and Dorothy Wordsworth, Volume I: The Early Years, 1787–1805*, ed. Ernest de Selincourt, rev. Chester Shaver (Oxford: Clarendon, 1967), p. 211.
19. George Shelvocke, *A Voyage round the World by Way of the Great South Sea* (London, 1723), pp. 72–3.
20. John Livingstone Lowes, *The Road to Xanadu* (Boston: Houghton Mifflin, 1927), pp. 141–52; Jonathan Lamb, 'The Rime of the Ancient Mariner: a Ballad of the Scurvy', in *The Pathologies of Travel*, ed. R. Wrigley and G. Revill (New York: Rodopi, 2000), pp. 157–77; Sarah Moss, 'Romanticism on Ice: Coleridge, Hogg, and the Eighteenth-Century Missions to Greenland', *Romanticism on the Net* 45 (February 2007).
21. Shelvocke, *Voyage*, p. 71. Cp. 'The Argument' to the *Ancyent Marinere*: 'How a Ship having crossed the Line was driven by Storms to the Cold Country towards the South Pole', and stanza 12 of the poem itself.
22. Shelvocke, *Voyage*, pp. 71, 72.
23. *Ibid.*, p. 73.
24. Again, see by way of representative example, Burke, *Philosophical Enquiry*, Part I, Section XI: 'Society and Solitude'.
25. Wilson, *The Spiritual History of Ice*, pp. 143–68.
26. Pytheas of Massalia, one of the sources used by Strabo in his *Geography*, had explored north-west Europe and the southern Arctic as early as *c.* 325 BC.

Pytheas's account of this journey (which is no longer extant) contained the earliest recorded description of the Arctic ice and is usually credited with introducing the idea of *Thule*, the most northerly landmass, to European culture.

27. See Wilson, *The Spiritual History of Ice*, pp. 143–5.
28. In France, both Buffon and Charles de Brosses also argued for the existence of the *terra australis incognita*; the latter, prompted by the former, in his *Histoire des Navigations aux Terres Australes* (1756).
29. Alexander Dalrymple, *An Account of the Discoveries Made in the South Pacific Ocean* (London, 1767), pp. 88–9.
30. *Ibid.*, p. 91.
31. Alexander Dalrymple, *An Historical Collection of the Several Voyages and Discoveries in the South Pacific Ocean*, 2 vols (London, 1770–71), i, p. xxi.
32. *Ibid.*, p. xxviii.
33. Anon., review of James Cook, *A Voyage towards the South Pole, and round the World*, 2 vols (1777), in *The Annual Register* (1777), p. 234.
34. Quoted in Alexander Dalrymple, *A Collection of Voyages, Chiefly in the Southern Atlantick Ocean* (London, 1775), p. 33. Halley's allusion is to Horace, *Ode* 1.22, 17–20: 'put me in barren fields where no tree is refreshed by a summer breeze, a corner of the world which clouds and bad weather oppress'.
35. Dalrymple, *Collection of Voyages*, p. 35.
36. *The Annual Register* (1777), p. 235.
37. Dalrymple reprinted these letters in his *Collection of Voyages* (1775), pp. 1–19 (p. 4).
38. *Ibid.*, pp. 13–19.
39. See Bernard Stonehouse (ed.), *Encyclopaedia of Antarctica and the Southern Oceans* (Chichester: John Wiley, 2003), p. 154; see also L. P. Kirwan, *A History of Polar Exploration* (Harmondsworth: Penguin, 1962), pp. 79–80, and Wilson, *The Spiritual History of Ice*, p. 158.
40. Trémarec was subsequently released, and included an account of the whole affair in his *Relation de Deux Voyages dans les Mers Australes et des Indes, Faits en 1771, 1772, 1773, & 1774* (Paris, 1782).
41. Dalrymple, who was a fellow of the Royal Society, had himself hoped to be given command of this expedition.
42. *The Annual Register* (1777), p. 236.
43. Cook's record remained unbroken until 20 February 1823, when James Weddell reached 74°15'S.
44. *The Annual Register* (1777), p. 236.
45. James Cook, *The Journals*, ed. Philip Edwards (London: Penguin Classics, 2003), pp. 237, 239. Cook's journals are also testament to the charming vagaries of nautical orthography.
46. *Ibid.*, p. 257.
47. *Ibid.*, p. 241. Cp. John Ross's account of his crew's first sight of an iceberg, discussed later in this chapter.
48. *Ibid.*, p. 247.
49. *Ibid.*, p. 244.
50. *Ibid.*
51. *Ibid.*, p. 249.
52. *Ibid.*, p. 331.
53. *Ibid.*

54. Thompson, *The Suffering Traveller*, p. 182.
55. Cook, *Voyage towards the South Pole*, i, p. 267.
56. Cook, *The Journals*, p. 331.
57. *Ibid.*; *Voyage towards the South Pole*, i, p. 267.
58. Cook, *Voyage towards the South Pole*, ii, p. 230.
59. *Ibid.*, p. 231.
60. Kant, *Critique of Judgement*, p. 104.
61. A German edition, *Dr Johann Reinhold Forster's und seines Sohnes Georg Forster's Reise um die Welt*, was published in Berlin the same year.
62. Johann Reinhold Forster, *Observations Made during a Voyage round the World* (London, 1778), pp. 69–70.
63. *Ibid.*, pp. 86–7.
64. Anders Erikson Sparrman, *A Voyage to the Cape of Good Hope, towards the Antarctic Polar Circle, and round the World* (London, 1785), p. 86.
65. *Ibid.*, p. 85.
66. *Ibid.*, p. 86.
67. *Ibid.*, p. 92.
68. *Ibid.*, p. 93.
69. Dalrymple, *An Historical Collection*, i, p. xvii.
70. *The Annual Register* (1777), p. 236.
71. *Ibid.*
72. *Ibid.*, pp. 236–7.
73. Anna Seward, *Elegy on Captain Cook* (London, 1780), p. 6 (the text is not numbered).
74. *Ibid.*
75. *Ibid.*, p. 7.
76. *Ibid.*, pp. 7–8.
77. Cook, *A Voyage towards the South Pole*, i, p. 269.
78. Coleridge, *The Rime of the Ancyent Marinere*, ll. 49–60. In the text of 1817, Coleridge amended line 49 to 'And now there came both mist and snow'; the gloss which Coleridge added to these lines describes 'The land of ice, and of fearful sounds where no living thing was to be seen'.
79. See Moss, 'Romanticism on Ice', for a discussion of Coleridge's potential borrowings in the poem from eighteenth-century writing about Greenland.
80. For the history of this familiarity see, for example, James Romm, *The Edges of the Earth in Ancient Thought: Geography, Exploration, and Fiction* (Princeton University Press, 1992).
81. For Pytheas's description of Thule, see Strabo, *Geography*, Book IV, 5.5.
82. Byron, *A Vision of Judgement* (London, 1822), ll. 215–16.
83. For a brief account of Egede's influence on eighteenth-century and Romantic-period writing about the Arctic, see Moss, 'Romanticism on Ice'. Egede's *Description* was first published in Danish as *Det Gamle Grønlands Nye Perlustration* (Copenhagen, 1729).
84. Shelley, *Frankenstein*, i, 2–3.
85. *Ibid.*, p. 3. Walton's proposed 'celestial observations' of course recall one of the key objectives of Cook's first voyage in 1768–71: to observe the transit of Venus from Tahiti, with a view to determining the precise longitude of the island. The determination of the location of the magnetic North Pole was one of the objectives of John Ross's polar expedition in 1818, which

was being prepared in the run-up to the publication of *Frankenstein* (see p. 184, above).
86. *Ibid.*, p. 4.
87. Holmes, *The Age of Wonder*, p. xvii.
88. For a detailed account of *Frankenstein*'s relationship with this debate, see Sharon Ruston, *Shelley and Vitality* (London: Palgrave, 2005).
89. Jessica Richard, '"A paradise of my own creation": *Frankenstein* and the Improbable Romance of Polar Exploration', *Nineteenth-Century Contexts* 25/4 (2003), pp. 295–314 (p. 296). Richard's essay is one of the most important recent pieces of scholarship on the cultural contexts for *Frankenstein*, and seeks to redress the fact that 'only the briefest attention has been paid to the historical resonance of Shelley's resort to a narrative of polar voyage' as a framing device (p. 296). My own reading here is indebted to Richard's on a number of points, although I also come to a different conclusion about the novel.
90. Shelley, *Frankenstein*, i, pp. 2, 5.
91. Barrington would also play a role in the publication of James Bruce's *Travels to Discover the Source of the Nile* (1790), a key text within the eighteenth-century and Romantic-period genre of engagement with the sublime of the desert (see Chapter 4).
92. Daines Barrington, *The Possibility of Approaching the North Pole Asserted*, ed. Mark Beaufoy (London, 1818), pp. 21, 25, 37.
93. Peter Pindar, *Peter's Prophecy, or, The President and the Poet* (London, 1788), p. 39.
94. Shelley, *Frankenstein*, i, p. 2.
95. Barrington, *The Possibility of Approaching the North Pole*, p. 51 and note.
96. In Walton's defence, we might note that his theory about an Arctic paradise was far from the only, or even the most outlandish, of contemporary speculations about the North Pole. Both Edmond Halley and William Paley had proposed that the earth might contain apertures at the North and South Poles, through which sea water and atmospheric gases could flow, and in 1818, the year *Frankenstein* was published, the American John Cleves Symmes began to propagate his 'hollow earth' theory, which also proposed apertures at the North and South Poles which granted access to the interior of the planet's surface. We might mention, too, those who attributed the operation of the compass to a supposed enormous iron mountain located over the Pole, etc., etc.
97. William Lisle Bowles, *The Spirit of Discovery* (London, 1804), v, pp. 60–74.
98. Barrington, *The Possibility of Approaching the North Pole*, p. 94. Byron might have agreed with Barrington on this, since he had little time for Lisles's poem!
99. Another such factor, also noted by Richard, is the late date of Walton's departure for the North Pole – in July, when the Arctic summer would be already drawing to a close ('"A paradise of my own creation"', p. 299).
100. *Ibid.*, p. 307.
101. John Ross, *A Voyage of Discovery, made under the Orders of the Admiralty, in his Majesty's ships Isabella and Alexander for the purpose of exploring Baffin's Bay and enquiring into the possibility of a North-West Passage* (London, 1819), pp. 123–34.

102. Olaudah Equiano, *The Interesting Narrative of the Life of O. Equiano, or G. Vassa, the African* [...] *Written by Himself*, 2 vols (London, 1789), ii, pp. 257, 259–60, 261.
103. David Cranz, *The History of Greenland* (London, 1767), p. 25; original emphasis.
104. Ross, *A Voyage of Discovery*, pp. 29–30.
105. Eleanor Anne Porden, *The Arctic Expeditions: a Poem* (London, 1818), ll. 1–4. Porden married John Franklin in 1823.
106. *Ibid.*, ll. 83–90. Porden refers in these lines both to the aforementioned theory of apertures at the earth's poles and to the idea that any ship containing metal parts might be held fast if it approached too close to the magnetic North Pole.
107. *Ibid.*, ll. 91–3.
108. *Ibid.*, ll. 189–91, 196, 199.

4 'The lone and level sands'

1. Mungo Park, *Travels in the Interior Districts of Africa; Performed in the Years 1795, 1796, and 1797* (London, 1799), p. 157.
2. See Shelley, *Poems*, ii, pp. 308–9 for a summary of the links that have been proposed between Shelley's sonnet and both contemporary and classical travel-writing about Egypt. Everest also corrects the long-standing but mistaken belief that Shelley's sonnet was inspired by the bust of Ramses II, acquired by Henry Salt in 1816, but not exhibited in the British Museum until 1820.
3. Horace Smith, 'Ozymandias', ll. 3–4, quoted from Shelley, *Poems*, ii, p. 307. For a discussion of the relationship between the two sonnets, see *ibid.*, pp. 307, 309.
4. Nigel Leask discusses the composition and publication of James Bruce's *Travels to Discover the Source of the Nile* in relation to the controversy about authenticity which enveloped Bruce after he returned to London with extraordinary anecdotes about his time in Africa (see *Curiosity and the Aesthetics of Travel Writing*, pp. 54–102); Richard Holmes provides a mini biography of Park against the backdrop of growing European interest in and involvement with West Africa (see *The Age of Wonder*, pp. 211–35); Carl Thompson examines the contribution made by Bruce and Park to the emergence of the persona of the 'Romantic' explorer (see *The Suffering Traveller*, pp. 146–85).
5. Christian Frederick Damberger, *Travels in the Interior of Africa* (London, 1801), p. iii.
6. John Leyden's *Historical and Philosophical Sketch of the Discoveries and Settlements of the Europeans in Northern and Western Africa* was published in 1799. Hugh Murray (1779–1846) expanded and revised the text for a posthumous, second edition, which was published as *An Historical Account of Discoveries and Travels in Africa* in 1817; the quotation is from Murray's preface (p. vii).
7. M. de Saugnier and Pierre Raymond de Brisson, *Voyages to the Coast of Africa, by Mess. Saugnier & Brisson* (London, 1792), p. iv.

8. Herodotus, *Histories*, III, 26. Cp. Strabo, *Geography*, 17, i, 54.
9. See Diodorus Siculus, *Bibliotheca Historica*, III, iii. The attempts which Diodorus makes to offer and assess rational explanations for such aerial phenomena do little to detract from the sublime spectacle which he describes.
10. Damberger, *Travels*, p. iv.
11. Murray in Leyden, *Historical Account*, p. 6.
12. *Ibid.*, pp. 28–9.
13. *Ibid.*, p. 29.
14. *Ibid.*
15. *Ibid.*, pp. 29, 32–3.
16. *Ibid.*, p. 33. Murray also notes of the native inhabitants of the oases which dot the Sahara that they 'are sometimes isolated for ages from the rest of mankind. Having never seen any people but their countrymen, nor any other part of the earth except the sands by which they are surrounded, they consider themselves as the only nation in the world, and think the boundary of their land that of the universe' (p. 265). Cp. John Ross's account of a similar belief amongst the Greenland Inuit in his *Voyage of Discovery* (discussed in Chapter 3, above).
17. William Howitt, *The Book of the Seasons; or, The Calendar of Nature* (London, 1831), p. 138. Howitt also notes 'the affecting mention of the influence of a flower upon his mind in a time of suffering and despondency, in the heart of the same savage continent, by Mungo Park', which, Howitt says, 'is familiar to everyone' (*ibid.*). Evidently the trope had become ubiquitous by the 1830s.
18. François Le Vaillant, *New Travels into the Interior Parts of Africa*, 3 vols (London, 1796), iii, p. 151.
19. Diodorus Siculus, *Bibliotheca Historica*, III, iii.
20. Burke, *Philosophical Enquiry*, pp. 130, 132.
21. Le Vaillant, *New Travels*, iii, pp. 58–9.
22. *Ibid.*, pp. 43ff.
23. *Ibid.*, p. 60.
24. Sparrman, *A Voyage to the Cape of Good Hope*, ii, pp. 249–50.
25. Le Vaillant, *New Travels*, iii, pp. 120–1.
26. *Ibid.*, pp. 121–2.
27. Thompson, *The Suffering Traveller*, p. 153.
28. Le Vaillant, *New Travels*, iii, pp. 138, 143.
29. *Ibid.*, pp. 142, 138–9.
30. *Ibid.*, pp. 142–3.
31. *Ibid.*, p. 151.
32. John Barrow, *An Account of Travels into the Interior of Southern Africa, in the Years 1797 and 1798* (London, 1802), pp. 83, 11, 81.
33. Burke, *Philosophical Enquiry*, Part II, Section IX; Barrow, *An Account of Travels*, pp. 91, 86.
34. Barrow, *An Account of Travels*, p. 93.
35. *Ibid.*, pp. 93–4.
36. Howitt, *Book of the Seasons*, p. 138.
37. Ludamar, in the south-western part of the Sahara region, encompassed parts of modern-day Mali and Mauritania.
38. Holmes, *The Age of Wonder*, pp. 214, 216, xvi.
39. Thompson, *The Suffering Traveller*, p. 171.

40. *Ibid.*
41. Holmes, *The Age of Wonder*, p. 219; Thompson, *The Suffering Traveller*, pp. 179, 180.
42. Park, *Travels*, p. 168.
43. *Ibid.*, p. 145.
44. *Ibid.*
45. *Ibid.*, p. 146. James Bruce had written of his time at the source: 'The marsh, and the fountains, upon comparison with the rise of many of our rivers, became now a trifling object in my sight. I remembered that magnificent scene in my own native country, where the Tweed, Clyde, and Annan rise in one hill; three rivers, as I now thought, not inferior to the Nile in beauty; preferable to it in the cultivation of those countries through which they flow; superior, vastly superior to it in the virtues and qualities of the inhabitants' (*Travels to Discover the Source of the Nile*, 5 vols (Edinburgh, 1790), iii, p. 640.
46. Park, *Travels*, p. 177.
47. *Ibid.*
48. *Ibid.*, p. 157. The quotation Park gives is from the version of his travels which Edwards had prepared for the *Proceedings of the African Association*.
49. Charles Sonnini, *Travels in Upper and Lower Egypt*, transl. Henry Hunter, 3 vols (London, 1799), ii, pp. 128–9, 133.
50. Constantin François de Volney, *Travels in Syria and Egypt, during the Years 1783, 1784, and 1785*, 2 vols (London, 1787), ii, p. 268.
51. *Ibid.*, p. 183.
52. Laurence Goldstein, *Ruins and Empire: the Evolution of a Theme in Augustan and Romantic Literature* (University of Pittsburgh Press, 1977); Ann Janowitz, *England's Ruins: Poetic Purpose and National Landscape* (Oxford: Blackwell, 1990). The relationship between engagements with ruin and engagements with 'the sublime' has also been well documented; see, for example, Nicolson, *Mountain Gloom and Mountain Glory*, pp. 331–45.
53. Dominique Vivant, Baron de Denon, *Travels in Upper and Lower Egypt in Company with Several Divisions of the French Army, during the Campaigns of General Bonaparte in that Country*, transl. Arthur Aikin, 3 vols (London, 1803), ii, p. 49.
54. *Ibid.*
55. Volney, *Travels*, ii, pp. 183–4.
56. William Richard Hamilton, *Remarks on Several Parts of Turkey: Aegyptiaca, or, Some Account of the Ancient and Modern State of Egypt* (London, 1809), pp. 152–3.
57. Sonnini, *Travels in Upper and Lower Egypt*, p. 133.
58. Carsten Niebuhr, *Travels through Arabia and Other Countries in the East*, ed. and transl. Robert Heron, 2 vols (Edinburgh, 1792), i, pp. 150–1. Niebuhr's travels were first published, in German, in 1772, as *Beschreibung von Arabien*.
59. Denon, *Travels*, i, p. 344.
60. *Ibid.*, p. 345.
61. *Ibid.*, p. 370.
62. *Ibid.*, p. 373.
63. *Ibid.*, p. 374.
64. Shelley, 'Ozymandias', ll. 13–14.
65. Volney, *Travels*, ii, p. 278.
66. *Ibid.*, p. 282.

67. *Ibid.*, pp. 282, 283.
68. Constantin François de Volney, *The Ruins; or, a Survey of the Revolutions of Empires*, 3rd edn (London, 1796), p. 3.
69. *Ibid.*, p. 5.
70. *Ibid.*, p. 9.
71. *Ibid.*, p. 12.
72. Shelley, *Alastor*, ll. 106–28. For a detailed discussion of the relationship between these lines and Volney's *Ruins*, see Duffy, *Shelley and the Revolutionary Sublime*, pp. 76–8.
73. Smith, 'Ozymandias', ll. 9–14.
74. Wordsworth, *The Prelude* (1805), v, ll. 71–5.
75. Wordsworth, *The Prelude* (1850), v, ll. 71–4.
76. Wordsworth, *The Prelude* (1805), v, ll. 76–8, 82–3.
77. Wordsworth, *The Prelude* (1850), v, ll. 81–3.
78. Wordsworth, *The Prelude* (1805), v, ll. 80, 64, 90.
79. *Ibid.*, ll. 135–8.
80. *Ibid.*, ll. 44–8.
81. *Ibid.*, ll. 50, 52.
82. Geoffrey Hartman, *Wordsworth's Poetry 1787–1814* (New Haven: Yale University Press, 1964), pp. 228–32. See also Jane Worthington Smyser, 'Wordsworth's Dream of Poetry and Science: *The Prelude*, V', *PMLA* 71 (March 1956), pp. 269–75; and Theresa Kelley, 'Spirit and Geometric Form': the Stone and the Shell in Wordsworth's Arab Dream', *Studies in English Literature, 1500–1900* 22/4 (Autumn 1982), pp. 563–82.
83. Wordsworth, *The Prelude* (1805), v, l. 59.
84. *Ibid.*, ll. 81–3.
85. Sonnini, *Travels in Upper and Lower Egypt*, p. 128.
86. *Ibid.*
87. Niebuhr, *Travels*, p. 196.
88. Wordsworth, *The Prelude* (1805), v, ll. 141–2, 160.
89. *Ibid.*, ll. 142–52.
90. Dorothy Wordsworth, *Journals*, ed. Ernest de Selincourt, 2 vols (London: Macmillan, 1941), i, pp. 364–5.
91. See Leask, *Curiosity and the Aesthetics of Travel Writing*, pp. 54–102. Daines Barrington (whose support for the exploration of the North Pole is discussed in Chapter 3 of this book) was amongst those who urged Bruce to publish his *Travels* in order to counter allegations that he had fabricated many of his stories.
92. Robert Southey, 'Review of James Bruce's *Travels*', *Aikin's Annual Review* 4 (1805), p. 10.
93. Liu, *The Sense of History*, pp. 3–4; Bruce, *Travels*, iii, pp. 640–1; Wordsworth, *The Prelude* (1805), vi, ll. 452–6.
94. Liu, *The Sense of History*, p. 4.
95. Thompson, *The Suffering Traveller*, pp. 163, 164.
96. Wordsworth, *The Prelude* (1805), vi, l. 548; Thompson, *The Suffering Traveller*, pp. 214–15.
97. Thompson, *The Suffering Traveller*, p. 218.
98. *Ibid.*, p. 219. A putative relationship between the two texts is also hinted at, on different grounds, in Graeme Stones, 'Upon a Dromedary Mounted

High', *Charles Lamb Bulletin* 104 (October 1998), pp. 145–8, and David Chandler, 'Robert Southey and *The Prelude*'s "Arab Dream"', *Review of English Studies* 54/2 (May 2003), pp. 203–19.
99. With that mention of 'history' and 'the canon' it might be worth our while briefly to remember that, in the early decades of the nineteenth century, Bruce's *Travels* were widely known across Europe, whereas only a handful of people had even heard of *The Prelude*.
100. Bruce, *Travels*, iv, p. 532.
101. *Ibid.*, pp. 555, 560.
102. *Ibid.*, p. 552.
103. *Ibid.*, p. 558.
104. *Ibid.*, pp. 568, 595.
105. *Ibid.*, p. 584.
106. *Ibid.*, p. 553.
107. Burke, *Philosophical Enquiry*, Part I, Section XIV; Bruce, *Travels*, iv, p. 554.
108. Bruce, *Travels*, iv, p. 554.
109. *Ibid.*
110. *Ibid.*, p. 556.
111. *Ibid.*, p. 561.
112. *Ibid.*, pp. 555, 563.
113. *Ibid.*, p. 563.
114. Herodotus, *Histories*, III, 26.
115. Hamilton, *Remarks*, pp. 314–15.
116. Park, *Travels*, p. 131; Le Vaillant, *New Travels*, iii, p. 271.
117. Saugnier and Brisson, *Voyages to the Coast of Africa*, pp. 104–5.
118. William George Browne, *Travels in Africa, Egypt, and Syria, from the Year 1792 to 1798* (London, 1799), p. 282.
119. Bruce, *Travels*, iv, p. 563.
120. Volney, *Travels*, ii, p. 41.
121. *Ibid.*, pp. 41–3.
122. Denon, *Travels*, ii, p. 183.
123. *Ibid.*, pp. 183–4, 185.
124. *Ibid.*, p. 185.
125. Mountstuart Elphinstone, *An Account of the Kingdom of Caubul and its Dependencies* (London, 1815), p. 140.
126. Bruce, *Travels*, iv, p. 557.
127. *Ibid.*
128. *Ibid.*, p. 558.
129. *Ibid.*, p. 582.
130. *Ibid.*, p. 581.
131. *Ibid.*
132. *Ibid.*, p. 564.
133. *Ibid.*, pp. 583–4.
134. *Ibid.*, p. 582.
135. *Ibid.*, p. 585. Samuel Taylor Coleridge, *Religious Musings* (London, 1794), ll. 276–9.
136. George Gordon, Lord Byron, *The Giaour* (London, 1813), l. 282 and note; *Don Juan* IV, ll. 244–5.
137. Wordsworth, *The Prelude* (1805), vi, ll. 96, 94–5, 97–9.

138. Bruce, *Travels*, iv, p. 597.
139. *Ibid.*
140. *Ibid.*
141. *Ibid.*, p. 598.
142. For a detailed examination of the controversy surrounding Bruce's claims, see Leask, *Curiosity and the Aesthetics of Travel Writing*, pp. 54–102.
143. Bruce, *Travels*, iv, p. 598.
144. *Ibid.*
145. *Ibid.*, pp. 598–9.
146. Wordsworth, *The Prelude* (1805), v, ll. 102–3.
147. The Italian traveller Ludovico di Varthema had already performed the Hajj during an extended journey around the Middle East in 1503, publishing his account of it in his *Itinerario de Ludovico de Varthema Bolognese* (1510).
148. We might also take as indicative of this problem of originality the fact that Burton's title seems evidently indebted to the translation by Helen Maria Williams of Alexander von Humboldt's *Personal Narrative of a Voyage to the Equinoctial Regions of the New Continent, during the Years 1799–1804*.
149. Richard Francis Burton, *A Personal Narrative of a Pilgrimage to El-Medinah and Meccah*, 3 vols (London, 1855), i, p. 217.
150. *Ibid.*
151. *Ibid.*, pp. 219, 217–18.
152. *Ibid.*, p. 217.
153. *Ibid.*, p. 218.
154. *Ibid.*
155. *Ibid.*, p. 218.
156. Burton frequently alludes, for example, to Bruce's ordeal, noting at a later stage an encounter with 'those pillars of sand so graphically described by Abyssinian Bruce. They scudded on the wings of the whirlwind over the plain – huge yellow shafts, with lofty heads [...] and on more than one occasion camels were overthrown by them. It required little stretch of fancy to enter into the Arab's superstition. These sand-columns are supposed to be genii of the waste' (*ibid.*, pp. 312–13).
157. *Ibid.*, p. 219; emphasis added.
158. *Ibid.*
159. *Ibid.*, p. 220.
160. *Ibid.*
161. *Ibid.*
162. *Ibid.*, pp. 220–1.
163. For a discussion of this 'impossibility' in relation to Alexander von Humboldt's travels in central and southern America, see Leask, *Curiosity and the Aesthetics of Travel Writing*, pp. 243–98.

5 'My purpose was humbler, but also higher'

1. Smith, *Essays*, p. 40.
2. *Ibid.*, p. 3. 'Wonder, surprise, and astonishment' had been key terms associated with the sublime by eighteenth-century British thinkers since at least Joseph Addison's seminal essays on the 'Pleasures of the Imagination'.

3. See, for example, Nicolson, *Mountain Gloom and Mountain Glory*, pp. 130–8, 143, 213–15 and *passim*.
4. Holmes, *Age of Wonder*, pp. 60–124, 163–210.
5. De Quincey, *Works*, vol. 15, pp. 393–420. In preparing a revised text in 1853 for *Selections Grave and Gay*, De Quincey responded to criticisms which had been levelled at the original version of the essay, and also made a number of stylistic improvements. I discuss some of these changes in more detail later. See also Smith, 'De Quincey's Revisions'.
6. De Quincey, *Works*, vol. 15, p. 403. As Burwick notes in his edition of 'System of the Heavens', De Quincey's allusion is to the opening line of Anna Laetitia Barbauld (neé Aitkin), 'Hymn IV', in *Hymns in Prose for Children* (London, 1781).
7. De Quincey, *Works*, vol. 15, pp. 178, 176.
8. De Quincey was introduced to Nichol in March 1841 and spent two weeks as his guest at the Glasgow Observatory. See Grevel Lindop, *The Opium-Eater: a Life of Thomas De Quincey* (Oxford University Press, 1985), pp. 342–3. Jonathan Smith quotes George Gilfillan's description of Nichol as 'the prose laureate of the stars', 'an accomplished mediator, [...] an Aaron to many an ineloquent Moses of astronomy' (Smith, 'De Quincey's Revisions', p. 203).
9. See Joseph Hillis-Miller, *The Disappearance of God* (Cambridge, MA: Harvard University Press, 1963), pp. 22, 65–7 (subsequent editions of this book appeared in 1975 and 2000); Robert Platzner, '"Persecutions of the Infinite": De Quincey's "System of the Heavens as Revealed by Lord Rosse's Telescopes" as an Inquiry into the Sublime', in *Sensibility in Transformation*, ed. Sydney Macmillan Conger (Rutherford: Fairleigh Dickinson University Press, 1990), pp. 195–207; John Barrell, *The Infection of Thomas De Quincey* (New Haven: Yale University Press, 1991), pp. 104–25; and Robert Lance Snyder, '"The Loom of the *Palingenesis*": De Quincey's Cosmology in "System of the Heavens"', in *Thomas De Quincey: Bicentenary Studies*, ed. Robert Lance Snyder (London: University of Oklahoma Press, 1985), pp. 338–59.
10. See Jonathan Smith, 'Thomas De Quincey, John Herschel, and JP Nichol Confront the Great Nebula in Orion' (1992), at www.personal-umd.umich.edu/~jonsmith/orion.html (accessed August 2012); and Murray, 'Vestiges of the Phoenix', pp. 243–60. De Quincey's engagement with Richter, which I consider in detail later, was first described in Frederick Burwick, 'The Dream-Visions of Jean Paul and Thomas De Quincey', *Comparative Literature* 20/1 (Winter 1968), pp. 1–26 (pp. 16–19).
11. O'Connor, *The Earth on Show*, p. 2.
12. De Quincey, *Works*, vol. 15, p. 168n.
13. See Lindop, *Opium-Eater*, p. 213, and De Quincey, *Works*, vol. 1, pp. 289–92.
14. O'Connor, *The Earth on Show*, p. 2.
15. De Quincey develops his distinction between the 'literature of knowledge' and the 'literature of power' in his 'Letters to a Young Man whose Education has been Neglected' (1828) and 'The Poetry of Pope' (1848). The 'literature of knowledge' is fact-based and consequently 'provisional': 'let its teaching be even partially revised, let it be but expanded, nay, even let its teaching be but placed in a better order, and instantly it is superseded' (*The Works of Thomas De Quincey*, 16 vols (Edinburgh, 1862), viii, p. 8). The 'literature of power', conversely, is 'immortal': it enables the reader to 'feel vividly, and

with a vital consciousness, emotions which ordinary life rarely or never supplies occasions for exciting, and which had previously lain unawakened and hardly within the dawn of consciousness' (xiii, pp. 55–6).
16. In this respect, my argument parallels or perhaps supplements that made about De Quincey's *Confessions* by Charles Rzepka in *Sacramental Commodities* (Amherst: University of Massachusetts Press, 1995). For Rzepka, De Quincey's work offers complex (re)negotiations of the relationship between authority and commodity, in which the rhetorical sublime is deployed as at once the guarantor of the authority of the writer and as a commercially viable product.
17. William Wordsworth, 'Star-Gazers' (1807), ll. 5, 21–2.
18. De Quincey, *Works*, vol. 15, p. 403.
19. *Ibid.*, p. 400.
20. *Ibid.*, p. 404.
21. *Ibid.*, p. 406.
22. John Pringle Nichol, *Thoughts on Some Important Points Relating to the System of the World* (Edinburgh, 1846), p. 6.
23. *Ibid.*, pp. 16, 31, 36–7.
24. *Ibid.*, p. 16.
25. *Ibid.*, p. 27.
26. *Ibid.*
27. Rosse's telescope had a 1.8 metre mirror, considerably larger than the 1.26 metre mirror used by William Herschel in his famous 40-foot telescope (40 feet being the focal length), and this was then believed to be the largest possible to attain without compromising resolution.
28. As Jonathan Smith points out, the term 'nebular hypothesis' was actually coined by the Cambridge polymath William Whewell. For a discussion of its place in late eighteenth- and early nineteenth-century astronomy, and of the wider cultural implications arising from it, see Smith, 'De Quincey's Revisions', pp. 204–5 and Simon Schaffer, 'The Nebular Hypothesis and the Science of Progress', in *History, Humanity, and Evolution*, ed. James Moore (Cambridge University Press, 1989), pp. 131–64.
29. Rudwick, *Bursting the Limits of Time*, p. 6.
30. De Quincey, *Works*, vol. 15, p. 401.
31. Barrell, *The Infection of Thomas De Quincey*, p. 124; Platzner, '"Persecutions of the Infinite"', p. 196.
32. Nichol, *Thoughts*, p. 37.
33. Joseph Blanco White, 'Night and Death' (1829), ll. 9–14, quoted in Nichol, *Thoughts*, p. 38. White's sonnet, which was well known and highly regarded in the mid-nineteenth century, was originally dedicated to Samuel Taylor Coleridge.
34. De Quincey, *Works*, vol. 15, pp. 406, 408, 416.
35. *Ibid.*, p. 403.
36. *Ibid.*, p. 404.
37. *Ibid.*
38. Barrell, *The Infection of Thomas De Quincey*, pp. 111–15.
39. De Quincey, *Works*, vol. 15, p. 403.
40. O'Connor, *The Earth on Show*, p. 450.
41. *Ibid.*, pp. 404–5.

42. Hence I disagree, here, with Jonathan Smith's suggestion that 'the reader is left with the impression that De Quincey is describing a drawing by Rosse of the resolved nebula [...] when in fact De Quincey is describing a much older drawing by Herschel on the unresolved nebula' (Smith, 'De Quincey's Revisions', p. 206).
43. De Quincey, *Works*, vol. 15, pp. 403, 404.
44. *Ibid.*, p. 404; Smith, 'De Quincey's Revisions', pp. 206–7.
45. De Quincey, *Works*, vol. 15, p. 404.
46. Smith, 'De Quincey's Revisions', p. 207.
47. Thomas De Quincey, *Selections Grave and Gay*, 14 vols (Edinburgh, 1853–59), vol. 3, p. 182.
48. *Ibid.*, p. 167n.
49. *Ibid.*
50. *Ibid.*, p. 168n.
51. *Ibid.*; original emphasis.
52. *Ibid.*, p. 179n.
53. *Ibid.*
54. *Ibid.*
55. *Ibid.*; original emphasis.
56. *Ibid.*
57. Smith suggests that De Quincey's reference, here, to 'the earliest revelation [...] by Lord Rosse' implies that De Quincey was actually unaware, or had at least forgotten, that the illustration in Nichol's *Thoughts* was not by Rosse, but by John Herschel ('De Quincey's Revisions', p. 207).
58. De Quincey, *Works*, vol. 15, p. 179n.
59. *Ibid.*

Bibliography

Primary sources

Addison, Joseph (ed.), *The Spectator*, 8 vols (London, 1712–15).
—— *Remarks on Several Parts of Italy* (London, 1705).
—— *A Letter from Italy* (London, 1701).
Anon., *The Peasants of Chamouni. Containing an attempt to reach the summit of Mont Blanc; and a delineation of the scenery among the Alps* (London, 1826).
—— Review of James Cook, *A Voyage towards the South Pole, and round the World*, 2 vols, in *The Annual Register* (1777), p. 234.
Auldjo, John, *Sketches of Vesuvius, with Short Accounts of its Principal Eruptions, from the Commencement of the Christian Era to the Present Time* (Naples, 1832).
—— *Narrative of an Ascent to the Summit of Mont Blanc, on the 8th and 9th of August, 1827* (London, 1828).
Barrington, Daines, *The Possibility of Approaching the North Pole Asserted*, ed. Mark Beaufoy (London, 1818).
Barrow, John, *An Account of Travels into the Interior of Southern Africa, in the Years 1797 and 1798* (London, 1802).
Boswell, James, *The Life of Samuel Johnson*, ed. J. W. Croker, 2 vols (London, 1833).
Bourrit, Marc Théodore, *A Relation of a Journey to the Glaciers in the Dutchy of Savoy*, transl. C. and F. Davy (Norwich, 1775).
Bowles, William Lisle, *The Spirit of Discovery* (London, 1804).
Bridges, G. W., *Alpine Sketches Comprised in a Short Tour through Parts of Holland, Flanders, France, Savoy, Switzerland and Germany, during the Summer of 1814* (London, 1814).
Brooke, N., *Observations on the Manners and Customs of Italy [...] also Particulars of the Wonderful Explosion of Mount Vesuvius, Taken on the Spot at Midnight, in June, 1794* (Bath, 1798).
Browne, William George, *Travels in Africa, Egypt, and Syria, from the Year 1792 to 1798* (London, 1799).
Bruce, James, *Travels to Discover the Source of the Nile*, 5 vols (Edinburgh, 1790).
Brydone, Patrick, *A Tour through Sicily and Malta. In a Series of Letters to William Beckford, Esq. The Second Edition, Corrected*, 2 vols (London, 1774).
Burke, Edmund, *Reflections on the Revolution in France* (London, 1790).
—— *A Philosophical Enquiry into the Origin of our Ideas of the Sublime and the Beautiful* (Dublin, 1757).
Burnet, Thomas, *The Sacred Theory of the Earth* (London, 1681).
Burton, Richard Francis, *A Personal Narrative of a Pilgrimage to El-Medinah and Meccah*, 3 vols (London, 1855).
Byron, Lord (George Gordon), *A Critical Edition of the Major Works*, ed. Jerome McGann (Oxford University Press, 1986).
—— *Byron's Letters and Journals*, ed. Leslie Marchand, 12 vols (Cambridge, MA: Harvard University Press, 1973–82).

—— *A Vision of Judgement* (London, 1822).
—— *The Giaour* (London, 1813).
Carbonnières, Louis Ramond de, *Lettres* [...] *sur l'État Politique, Civil et Naturel de la Suisse; Traduisse de l'Anglois, et Augmentées des Observations faites dans le Même Pays, par le Traducteur*, 2 vols (Paris, 1781).
Coleridge, Samuel Taylor, *The Complete Poems*, ed. William Keach (London: Penguin, 1997).
—— *France: an Ode* (London, 1798).
—— *Religious Musings* (London, 1794).
Cook, James, *The Journals*, ed. Philip Edwards (London: Penguin Classics, 2003).
—— *A Voyage towards the South Pole and Round the World*, 2 vols (London, 1777).
Coxe, Henry, *The Traveller's Guide in Switzerland* (London, 1816).
Coxe, William, *Travels in Switzerland, and in the Country of the Grisons: in a Series of Letters* [...] *A New Edition*, 3 vols (Basil, 1802).
Cranz, David, *The History of Greenland* (London, 1767).
Dalrymple, Alexander, *A Collection of Voyages, Chiefly in the Southern Atlantick Ocean* (London, 1775).
—— *An Historical Collection of the Several Voyages and Discoveries in the South Pacific Ocean*, 2 vols (London, 1770–71).
—— *An Account of the Discoveries Made in the South Pacific Ocean* (London, 1767).
Damberger, Christian Frederick, *Travels in the Interior of Africa* (London, 1801).
Denon, Dominique Vivant, Baron de, *Travels in Upper and Lower Egypt in Company with Several Divisions of the French Army, during the Campaigns of General Bonaparte in that Country*, transl. Arthur Aikin, 3 vols (London, 1803).
De Quincey, Thomas, *The Works of Thomas De Quincey*, gen. ed. Grevel Lindop, 21 vols (London: Pickering & Chatto, 2000–3).
—— *Selections Grave and Gay*, 14 vols (Edinburgh, 1853–59).
Dryden, John, *A Voyage to Sicily and Malta, in the Years 1700 and 1701* (London, 1776).
Ebel, M. J. G., *Traveller's Guide through Switzerland*, transl. Daniel Wall (London, 1818).
Elphinstone, Mountstuart, *An Account of the Kingdom of Caubul and its Dependencies* (London, 1815).
Equiano, Olaudah, *The Interesting Narrative of the Life of O. Equiano, or G. Vassa, the African* [...] *Written by Himself*, 2 vols (London, 1789).
Eustace, John Chetwode, *A Classical Tour through Italy*, 4th edn, 4 vols (Livorno, 1817).
Forster, Johann Reinhold, *History of the Voyages and Discoveries Made in the North*, transl. anon. (Dublin, 1786).
—— *Observations Made during a Voyage round the World* (London, 1778).
Forsyth, Joseph, *Remarks on Antiquities, Arts, and Letters, during an Excursion in Italy* (London, 1813).
Glover, Samuel, *A Description of the Valley of Chamouni* (London, 1819).
Hamilton, William, *Supplement to the Campi Phlegraei: Being an Account of the Great Eruption of Mount Vesuvius in the Month of August 1779* (Naples, 1779).
—— *Campi Phlegraei: Observations on the Volcanoes of the Two Sicilies* (Naples, 1776).
—— *Observations on Mount Vesuvius, Mount Etna, and Other Volcanoes*, 2nd edn (London, 1774).
Hamilton, William Richard, *Remarks on Several Parts of Turkey: Aegyptiaca, or, Some Account of the Ancient and Modern State of Egypt* (London, 1809).

Hazlitt, William, *The Complete Works of William Hazlitt*, ed. P. P. Howe, 21 vols (London: Dent, 1930–34).
Hemans, Felicia, *The Records of Woman and Other Poems* (Edinburgh, 1828).
Hoare, Richard, *A Classical Tour through Italy and Sicily; Tending to Illustrate Some Districts which have not been Described by Mr. Eustace, in his Classical Tour*, 2 vols (London, 1819).
Howitt, William, *The Book of the Seasons; or, The Calendar of Nature* (London, 1831).
Hume, David, *Treatise of Human Nature* (London, 1739–40).
Hutton, James, *Theory of the Earth* (Edinburgh, 1788).
Kant, Immanuel, *The Critique of Judgement*, ed. and transl. James Creed Meredith (Oxford University Press, 1992).
Keate, George, *The Alps* (London, 1763).
La Condamine, C. M. de, *Journal of a Tour to Italy*, transl. anon. (London, 1763).
Le Vaillant, François, *New Travels into the Interior Parts of Africa*, 3 vols (London, 1796).
—— *Travels into the Interior Parts of Africa* (London, 1790).
Leyden, John, *An Historical Account of Discoveries and Travels in Africa*, 2nd edn, ed. Hugh Murray (London, 1817).
Longinus, Dionysius, *Dionysius Longinus on The Sublime*, transl. William Smith, 2nd edn (London, 1743).
Martyn, Thomas, *A Tour through Italy* (London, 1791).
—— *Sketch of a Tour through Swisserland* (London, 1788).
Montgomery, James, *The Alps: a Reverie* (London, 1822).
Nichol, John Pringle, *Thoughts on Some Important Points Relating to the System of the World* (Edinburgh, 1846).
Niebuhr, Carsten, *Travels through Arabia and Other Countries in the East*, ed. and transl. Robert Heron, 2 vols (Edinburgh, 1792).
Park, Mungo, *Travels in the Interior Districts of Africa; Performed in the Years 1795, 1796, and 1797* (London, 1799).
Pindar, Peter, *Peter's Prophecy, or, The President and the Poet* (London, 1788).
Pinkerton, John (ed.), *General Collection of the Best and Most Interesting Voyages and Travels in all Parts of the World*, 17 vols (London, 1809–14).
Playfair, John, *Illustrations of the Huttonian Theory of the Earth* (Edinburgh, 1802).
Pliny the Younger, *The Letters of Pliny*, transl. W. Melmoth, rev. W. Hutchinson, 2 vols (London: Heinemann, 1961).
Pococke, Richard, *Description of the East* (London, 1745).
Porden, Eleanor Anne, *The Arctic Expeditions: a Poem* (London, 1818).
Ross, John, *A Voyage of Discovery, made under the Orders of the Admiralty, in his Majesty's ships Isabella and Alexander for the purpose of exploring Baffin's Bay and enquiring into the possibility of a North-West Passage* (London, 1819).
Rousseau, Jean-Jacques, *Julie, or, the New Héloïse: Letters of Two Lovers who Live in a Small Town at the Foot of the Alps* (1761), transl. William Kenrick (London, 1761).
Ruskin, John, *Modern Painters*, ed. David Barrie (London: Deutsch, 1987).
—— *The Poems of John Ruskin*, ed. William Collingwood, 2 vols (London, 1891).
Saugnier, M. de, and Brisson, Pierre Raymond de, *Voyages to the Coast of Africa, by Mess. Saugnier & Brisson* (London, 1792).
Saussure, Horace-Bénédict de, *Voyages dans les Alpes*, 4 vols (Neuchâtel, 1779–96).
Seward, Anna, *Elegy on Captain Cook* (London, 1780).

Shakespeare, William, *The Oxford Shakespeare*, ed. S. Wells, G. Taylor, J. Jowett and W. Montgomery, 2nd edn (Oxford University Press, 2005).
Shelley, Mary, *Frankenstein, or, The Modern Prometheus*, 2 vols (London, 1818).
Shelley, Percy Bysshe, *The Poems of Percy Bysshe Shelley*, ed. Kelvin Everest, Geoffrey Matthews *et al.*, 3 vols to date (London: Longman, 1988–).
—— *The Letters of Percy Bysshe Shelley*, ed. F. L. Jones, 2 vols (Oxford: Clarendon, 1964).
Shelley, Percy Bysshe, and Shelley, Mary, *History of a Six Weeks' Tour through a Part of France, Switzerland, Germany and Holland* (London, 1817).
Shelvocke, George, *A Voyage round the World by Way of the Great South Sea* (London, 1723).
Smith, Adam, *Essays on Philosophical Subjects*, ed. Joseph Black and James Hutton (Glasgow, 1795).
Sonnini, Charles, *Travels in Upper and Lower Egypt*, transl. Henry Hunter, 3 vols (London, 1799).
Sparrman, Anders Erikson, *A Voyage to the Cape of Good Hope, towards the Antarctic Polar Circle, and round the World* (London, 1785).
Staël, Germaine de, *Corinna, or Italy*, 5 vols, trans. D. Lawler (London, 1807).
Starke, Mariana, *Letters from Italy*, 2nd edn, 2 vols (London, 1815).
Swinburne, Henry, *Travels in the Two Sicilies*, 2nd edn, 4 vols (London, 1790).
Volney, Constantin François de, *A New Translation of Volney's Ruins, Made Under the Inspection of the Author*, facsimile of 1802 Paris edition, 2 vols (New York: Garland, 1979).
—— *Travels in Syria and Egypt, during the Years 1783, 1784, and 1785*, 2 vols (London, 1787).
Watts, Alaric, *Poetical Sketches*, 3rd edn (London, 1824).
Whalley, Thomas, *Mont Blanc: an Irregular Lyric Poem* (Bath, 1788).
Williams, Helen Maria, *A Tour In Switzerland; or, A View of the Present State of the Governments and Manners of those Cantons: with Comparative Sketches of the Present State of Paris*, 2 vols (London, 1798).
Windham, William, *An Account of the Glacieres, or Ice Alps, in Savoy. In Two Letters; One from an English Gentleman to His Friend at Geneva; The Other from Peter Martel, Engineer, to the Said English Gentleman* (London, 1744).
Wordsworth, Dorothy, *Journals*, ed. Ernest de Selincourt, 2 vols (London: Macmillan, 1941).
Wordsworth, William, *The Prelude: the Four Texts*, ed. Jonathan Wordsworth (London: Penguin, 1995).
—— *The Poetical Works of William Wordsworth*, ed. Ernest de Selincourt and Helen Darbishire (Oxford University Press, 1952–59).
—— *Descriptive Sketches. In Verse. Taken During a Pedestrian Tour in the Italian, Grison, Swiss, and Savoyard Alps* (London, 1793).
Wordsworth, William, and Coleridge, Samuel Taylor, *Lyrical Ballads* (Bristol, 1798).
Wordsworth, William, and Wordsworth, Dorothy, *The Letters of William and Dorothy Wordsworth, Volume I: The Early Years, 1787–1805*, ed. Ernest de Selincourt, rev. Chester Shaver (Oxford: Clarendon, 1967).
—— *The Letters of William and Dorothy Wordsworth, Volume IV: The Later Years. Part I. 1821–1828*, ed. Ernest de Selincourt, rev. Alan Hill (Oxford University Press, 1978).

Secondary sources

Abrams, M. H., *Natural Supernaturalism: Tradition and Revolution in Romantic Literature* (Oxford University Press, 1971).
Ashfield, Andrew, and De Bolla, Peter (eds), *The Sublime: a Reader in British Eighteenth-Century Aesthetic Theory* (Cambridge University Press, 1996).
Bainbridge, Simon, *Napoleon and English Romanticism* (Cambridge University Press, 1995).
Barrell, John, *The Infection of Thomas De Quincey* (New Haven: Yale University Press, 1991).
Black, Jeremy, *The British Abroad: the Grand Tour in the Eighteenth Century* (London: St Martin's, 1992).
Brown, Thomas, and De Beer, Gavin, *The First Ascent of Mont Blanc* (Oxford University Press, 1957).
Buzzard, James, *The Beaten Track: European Tourism, Literature, and the Ways to 'Culture', 1800–1918* (Oxford University Press, 1993).
Chandler, David, 'Robert Southey and *The Prelude*'s "Arab Dream"', *Review of English Studies* 54/2 (May 2003), pp. 203–19.
Chard, Chloe, *Pleasure and Guilt on the Grand Tour: Travel Writing and Imaginative Geography* (Manchester University Press, 1999).
Coe, C. N., 'Did Wordsworth Read Coxe's *Travels in Switzerland* before Making the Tour of 1790?', *Notes & Queries* 195 (1950), pp. 144–5.
Connell, Philip, and Leask, Nigel (eds), *Romanticism and Popular Culture in Britain and Ireland* (Cambridge University Press, 2009).
De Beer, Gavin, *Alps and Men* (London: Edward Arnold, 1932).
—— *Early Travellers in the Alps* (London: Sidgwick and Jackson, 1930).
De Bolla, Peter, *The Discourse of the Sublime: Readings in History, Aesthetics, and the Subject* (Oxford: Blackwell, 1989).
Duffy, Cian, *Shelley and the Revolutionary Sublime* (Cambridge University Press, 2005).
Duffy, Cian, and Howell, Peter (eds), *Cultures of the Sublime: Selected Readings, 1750–1830* (Basingstoke: Palgrave Macmillan, 2011).
Freeman, Barbara, *The Feminine Sublime* (Berkeley: University of California Press, 1995).
Fulford, Tim, and Kitson, Peter (eds), *Travels, Explorations and Empires, 1770–1835*, 8 vols (London: Pickering and Chatto, 2001).
Goldstein, Laurence, *Ruins and Empire: the Evolution of a Theme in Augustan and Romantic Literature* (University of Pittsburgh Press, 1977).
Hartman, Geoffrey, *Wordsworth's Poetry 1787–1814* (New Haven: Yale University Press, 1964).
Heringman, Noah, *Romantic Rocks, Aesthetic Geology* (Ithaca: Cornell University Press, 2004).
—— (ed.), *Romantic Science: the Literary Forms of Natural History* (Albany: State University of New York Press, 2003).
Hertz, Neil, *The End of the Line: Essays on Psychoanalysis and the Sublime* (New York: Columbia University Press, 1985).
Hillis-Miller, Joseph, *The Disappearance of God* (Cambridge, MA: Harvard University Press, 1963).

Hipple, Walter, *The Beautiful, the Sublime and the Picturesque in Eighteenth-Century British Aesthetic Theory* (Carbondale: Southern Illinois University Press, 1957).
Holmes, Richard, *The Age of Wonder: How the Romantic Generation Discovered the Beauty and Terror of Science* (London: Harper, 2008).
—— *Coleridge: Darker Reflections* (London: Flamingo, 1999).
Janowitz, Ann, *England's Ruins: Poetic Purpose and National Landscape* (Oxford: Blackwell, 1990).
Kelley, Theresa, 'Spirit and Geometric Form': the Stone and the Shell in Wordsworth's Arab Dream', *Studies in English Literature, 1500–1900* 22/4 (Autumn 1982), pp. 563–82.
Kirwan, L. P., *A History of Polar Exploration* (Harmondsworth: Penguin, 1962).
Lamb, Jonathan, 'The Rime of the Ancient Mariner: a Ballad of the Scurvy', in *The Pathologies of Travel*, ed. R. Wrigley and G. Revill (New York: Rodopi, 2000), pp. 157–77.
Leask, Nigel, *Curiosity and the Aesthetics of Travel Writing, 1770–1840: 'From an Antique Land'* (Oxford University Press, 2002).
Lindop, Grevel, *The Opium-Eater: a Life of Thomas De Quincey* (Oxford University Press, 1985).
Liu, Alan, *Wordsworth: the Sense of History* (Stanford University Press, 1989).
Lowes, John Livingstone, *The Road to Xanadu* (Boston: Houghton Mifflin, 1927).
Lyotard, Jean-François, *The Inhuman*, transl. Geoffrey Bennington and Rachel Bowlby (Cambridge: Polity Press, 1991).
Macfarlane, Robert, *Mountains of the Mind: a History of a Fascination* (London: Granta, 2003).
Matthews, Geoffrey, 'A Volcano's Voice in Shelley', *ELH* 23 (1957), pp. 191–228.
McGann, Jerome, *The Romantic Ideology* (University of Chicago Press, 1983).
Mellor, Anne, *Romanticism and Gender* (London: Routledge, 1993).
Micheli, Giuseppe, *The Early Reception of Kant's Thought in England, 1785–1805* (London: Routledge, 1993).
Miller, Mary Ashburn, '"Mountain, Become a Volcano": The Image of the Volcano in the Rhetoric of the French Revolution', *French Historical Studies* 32/4 (2009), pp. 555–85.
Monk, Samuel Holt, *The Sublime: a Study of Critical Theories in Eighteenth-Century England* (Ann Arbor: University of Michigan Press, 1960).
Moss, Sarah, 'Romanticism on Ice: Coleridge, Hogg, and the Eighteenth-Century Missions to Greenland', *Romanticism on the Net* 45 (February 2007).
Murray, Alex, 'Vestiges of the Phoenix: De Quincey, Kant, and the Heavens', *Victoriographies* 1/2 (November 2011), pp. 246–60.
Nicolson, Marjorie Hope, *Mountain Gloom and Mountain Glory: the Development of the Aesthetics of the Infinite* (Ithaca: Cornell University Press, 1959).
O'Connor, Ralph, *The Earth on Show: Fossils and the Poetics of Popular Science, 1802–1856* (University of Chicago Press, 2007).
—— 'Mammoths and Maggots: Byron and the Geology of Cuvier', *Romanticism* 5 (1999), pp. 26–42.
Ozouf, Mona, *Festivals and the French Revolution*, transl. Alan Sheridan (Cambridge, MA: Harvard University Press, 1998).
Peterfreund, Stuart, 'Two Romantic Poets and Two Romantic Scientists "on" Mont Blanc', *The Wordsworth Circle* 29/3 (1999), pp. 152–61.

Platzner, Robert, '"Persecutions of the Infinite": De Quincey's "System of the Heavens as Revealed by Lord Rosse's Telescopes" as an Inquiry into the Sublime', in *Sensibility in Transformation*, ed. Sydney Macmillan Conger (Rutherford: Fairleigh Dickinson University Press, 1990), pp. 195–207.

Poovey, Mary, *Genres of the Credit Economy* (University of Chicago Press, 2008).

—— *A History of the Modern Fact* (University of Chicago Press, 1998).

Richard, Jessica, '"A paradise of my own creation": *Frankenstein* and the Improbable Romance of Polar Exploration', *Nineteenth-Century Contexts* 25/4 (2003), pp. 295–314.

Ring, Jim, *How the English Made the Alps* (London: Murray, 2000).

Romm, James, *The Edges of the Earth in Ancient Thought: Geography, Exploration, and Fiction* (Princeton University Press, 1992).

Rossi, Paolo, *The Dark Abyss of Time*, transl. Lydia Cochrane (University of Chicago Press, 1984).

Rudwick, Martin, *Bursting the Limits of Time* (University of Chicago Press, 2005).

Ruston, Sharon, *Shelley and Vitality* (London: Palgrave, 2005).

Schaffer, Elinor, 'Coleridge's Swiss Voice: Frederike Brun and the Vale of Chamouni', in *Essays in Memory of Michael Parkinson*, ed. Christopher Smith (Norwich: University of East Anglia, 1996), pp. 67–76.

Schaffer, Simon, 'The Nebular Hypothesis and the Science of Progress', in *History, Humanity, and Evolution*, ed. James Moore (Cambridge University Press, 1989), pp. 131–64.

Schama, Simon, *Landscape and Memory* (London: HarperCollins, 1995).

Shaw, Philip, *The Sublime* (London: Routledge, 2006).

Siskin, Clifford, *The Work of Writing* (Baltimore: Johns Hopkins University Press, 1999).

—— *The Historicity of Romantic Discourse* (Oxford University Press, 1998).

Siskin, Clifford, and Warner, William (eds), *This is Enlightenment* (University of Chicago Press, 2010).

Smith, Jonathan, 'De Quincey's Revisions to "System of the Heavens"', *Victorian Periodicals Review* 26/4 (Winter 1993), pp. 203–12.

—— 'Thomas De Quincey, John Herschel, and JP Nichol Confront the Great Nebula in Orion' (1992), at www.personal-umd.umich.edu/~jonsmith/orion.html (accessed August 2012).

Smyser, Jane Worthington, 'Wordsworth's Dream of Poetry and Science: *The Prelude*, V', *PMLA* 71 (March 1956), pp. 269–75.

Snyder, Robert Lance, '"The Loom of the *Palingenesis*": De Quincey's Cosmology in "System of the Heavens"', in *Thomas De Quincey: Bicentenary Studies*, ed. Robert Lance Snyder (London: University of Oklahoma Press, 1985), pp. 338–59.

Soule, George, 'Coleridge's Debt to Shelvocke in "The Ancient Mariner"', *Notes & Queries* 50/3 (2003), p. 287.

Spufford, Francis, *I May Be Some Time: Ice and the English Imagination* (London: Faber & Faber, 1996).

Stafford, Barbara, *Voyage into Substance: Art, Science, Nature, and the Illustrated Travel Account, 1760–1840* (Cambridge, MA: MIT Press, 1984).

Stirling, James, *Kant's Thought in England: the Early Impact* (London: Routledge, 1993).

Stonehouse, Bernard (ed.), *Encyclopedia of Antarctica and the Southern Oceans* (Chichester: John Wiley, 2003).

Stones, Graeme, 'Upon a Dromedary Mounted High', *Charles Lamb Bulletin* 104 (October 1998), pp. 145–8.
Thompson, Carl, *The Suffering Traveller and the Romantic Imagination* (Oxford University Press, 2007).
Von der Thüsen, Joachim, 'Painting and the Rise of Volcanology: Sir William Hamilton's *Campi Phlegraei*', *Endeavour* 23/3 (1999), pp. 106–9.
Weiskel, Thomas, *The Romantic Sublime* (Baltimore: Johns Hopkins University Press, 1976).
Wellek, René, *Immanuel Kant in England* (Princeton University Press, 1931).
Wilson, Eric, *The Spiritual History of Ice: Romanticism, Science, and the Imagination* (London: Palgrave, 2003).
Žižek, Slavoj, *The Sublime Object of Ideology* (London: Verso, 1989).

Index

Addison, Joseph, 52
   and 'classic ground', 8–10, 12, 17, 36
   Letter from Italy (1701), 9
   'Pleasures of the Imagination' (1712), 4, 37, 113, 216n2
   on Vesuvius, 69, 86–8, 93–4
Africa, 20, 135–73
   see also desert; Egypt
Alison, Archibald, 14
Alps, the, 16, 17–18, 28–67, 81, 85, 91, 92–3, 104, 115, 167, 170
Antarctica, 10, 17, 20–1, 22, 26, 102–24
   James Cook's attempts to reach, 11, 103–4, 111–17, 119, 121–4
   and the *terra australis incognita*, 103, 109–12, 114, 116–19
Arctic, the, 10, 16, 17, 20–1, 22, 26, 102–5, 124–34
   expeditions to, 21
   indigenous populations of, 20, 126, 131
ascent, discourse of, 18, 30–2, 34–9, 40–1, 43–8, 55–60, 63–7, 69, 81–3, 172
astronomy, 22–4, 174–90
   and the nebular hypothesis, 180–1, 183–4
   second renaissance in, 22, 174–5, 178–80
   as spectacle, 23–4, 182–4, 186–7
   and the sublime, 4, 22, 174, 176
Auldjo, John, 45, 68, 93

Balmat, Jacques, 42–3, 44
Banks, Joseph, 53, 103, 117, 127, 144, 169
Barents, William, 128, 129
Barrell, John, 23, 175, 181, 183
Barrington, Daines, 128–30, 132, 133, 214n91

Barrow, John, 15, 21, 139–40, 143–4, 146, 147
Black, Jeremy, 193n26
Bonaparte, Napoleon
   and the Alps, 29, 55–8, 59–60, 63, 67
   Egyptian campaign (1798–1801), 149–50, 151, 164
Bourrit, Marc Théodore, 18, 36–9, 40, 42, 48
Bowles, William Lisle
   The Spirit of Discovery (1804), 130, 131
Bridges, George Wilson, 31, 53
Brooke, N.
   Observations on the Manners and Customs of Italy (1798), 89, 91–2
Bruce, James, of Kinnaird, 20, 22, 136, 210n91, 213n45
   in the Sahara, 144, 155, 160–3, 165–9, 216n156
   and Wordsworth's *Prelude* (1805), 137, 154, 158–60, 166–7, 169
Brydone, Patrick, 16, 19, 69, 90, 99
   on the age of the earth, 19, 78–81
   ascent of Etna, 19, 73–86
   Tour through Sicily and Malta (1774), 19, 73, 74–86, 99
Buckland, William, 25
Buffon, Georges-Louis Leclerc, Comte de, 70, 72, 79, 202n12, 202n17
Burke, Edmund
   A Philosophical Enquiry (1757), 7, 10, 17, 20, 24, 30, 37, 48, 69, 102, 113, 120, 121, 138, 140, 141, 143, 146, 150, 161–2, 171, 207n24
   Reflections on the Revolution (1790), 51, 91–2
Burnet, Thomas, 2, 18
Burton, Richard Francis, 22, 169–73
Buzzard, James, 65

Byron, George Gordon, Lord, 19, 56, 92, 96, 98, 99, 166, 210n98
  Childe Harold's Pilgrimage
    Canto III (1816), 63–4, 65
  Don Juan
    Canto I (1819), 64
    Canto XIII (1823), 92, 93
  Manfred (1817), 49–50, 53
  A Vision of Judgement (1822), 126

Carbonnières, Louis Ramond, Baron de, 16, 18, 52, 55, 194n42
  on the imagination, 65–7
  Observations (1798), 28, 40–1, 57, 65–7, 196n1
'classic ground', 8–10, 12, 15, 17, 18, 20, 21, 22, 25, 32, 33–4, 36, 60, 67, 68–9, 75, 83, 85, 103–5, 117, 124–5, 131, 132, 134, 136–7, 138, 144, 163, 170–3
Coleridge, Samuel Taylor, 57, 74, 156, 218n33
  on Etna, 74, 96–7, 202n26
  France: an Ode (1798), 54
  'Hymn Before Sun-Rise, in the Vale of Chamouni' (1802), 48
  The Rime of the Ancyent Marinere (1798), 21, 102, 105–8, 119, 123–4, 131, 132, 209n78
  on the simoom, 166
Cook, James, 16, 26, 53, 127, 128, 130, 169, 209–10n85
  and the Antarctic, 11, 103–4, 111–17, 119, 121–4, 133
  farthest south record, 21, 112, 115, 208n43
  A Voyage towards the South Pole (1777), 102, 112, 119–20
Coxe, Henry
  The Traveller's Guide in Switzerland (1816), 30, 34, 50–1, 52
Coxe, William
  Travels in Switzerland, 39–42, 46, 52, 54, 65
Cranz, David, 106, 131, 132
Cuvier, Georges, 70, 92

Dalrymple, Alexander, 103, 109–11, 116, 119, 121, 123, 125, 128, 130

Damberger, Christian Frederick, 20, 137
De Beer, Gavin, 2, 198n53
De Bolla, Peter, 6, 7, 11, 14, 193n21, 194n49, 195n63, 195n64
Denon, Dominique Vivant, Baron de, 136, 137, 149–50, 151–2, 164
depth
  and space, 69–70
  and the sublime, 19, 69–72, 80, 83–5, 86, 87–8, 98–9
  and time, 19, 69–70, 78–80, 194n51
De Quincey, Thomas, 7, 17, 198–9n75
  and astronomy, 23–4, 175–90
  and Patrick Brydone, 74, 80
  and popular culture, 17, 23–4, 177–8
desert, 10, 16, 20, 21–2, 135–73
  Great Karoo, 143–4
  Kalahari, 139–43, 163
  ruins in the, 135–7, 147–54
  Sahara, 136–9, 143, 144–7, 154, 155, 160–3, 165–9
disciplinarity
  emergence of, 4, 13, 15, 23, 24, 69–72, 73–5, 95–6, 175–6, 184, 186–90, 205n107
  and natural philosophy, 3–5, 15, 16, 17, 18–19, 22, 34, 93, 100–1, 103, 145, 205n107
  and popular culture, 2–3, 5–6, 14, 19, 24, 34, 176–8, 181–4
  and the sublime, 3–4, 5–6, 10–12, 14, 15, 18–19, 26–7, 46, 71, 84–6, 93, 95–6, 97–9, 100–1, 109, 163–4, 175–8, 181
Dryden, John, junior, 68, 72–3

Ebel, Johan Gottfried
  Traveller's Guide through Switzerland (1818), 31–2, 45–6
Egede, Hans, 106, 126, 131, 209n83
Egypt, 135–6, 147–52, 153, 163–4, 169–73
Elphinstone, Mountstuart, 164–5
Equiano, Olaudah, 132
eruption, volcanic, 77–8, 84–6, 87–92
  and the mind, 72, 86, 96–9
  and poetry, 71–2, 86, 96, 97, 98

eruption, volcanic – *continued*
  and political violence, 71–2, 86, 89–92, 99–101
  see also volcanoes
Etna, Mount, 18, 68–86, 90, 92, 96–7, 100
Eustace, John Chetwode
  Classical Tour through Italy (1813), 89, 92–3, 94–5, 202n106

Forster, Johann Reinhold, 105, 117–18, 130
Forsyth, Joseph, 87, 89
Franklin, John, 21, 105, 126, 131, 133, 134
Freeman, Barbara, 26, 121

gender
  and Romanticism, 24–6, 121, 131
  and the sublime, 24–6, 121–2, 199n85
geology, 69–72, 74, 75–6, 77, 79–80, 94, 95, 100–1
  and the sublime, 2, 4–5, 15, 18, 19, 23, 35, 66, 84, 89, 177
Gérard, François
  Corinne au Cap Misène (1819), 98
Glover, Samuel, 46, 49, 53
Goldstein, Laurence, 149
Greece, classical civilisation of, 53, 68, 75

Halley, Edmond, 110, 210n96
Hamilton, Sir William, 70, 72, 75, 77, 79, 95
  Campi Phlegraei (1776), 89–92, 93, 94, 202n23
  Observations (1774), 75–6
  Supplement to the Campi Phlegraei (1779), 89–92
Hamilton, William Richard, 150, 162
Hannibal, 56–7, 59
Hartman, Geoffrey, 156
Hawkesworth, John, 115
Hazlitt, William, 34, 46, 51, 57–8
Hemans, Felicia, 139–41
  'The Image in Lava' (1827), 95
Herculaneum, 68, 86, 88–9, 94, 95
Heringman, Noah, 2, 4, 14, 15, 71

Herschel, John, 175, 179, 180, 184, 186
Herschel, William and Caroline, 22, 175, 178–9, 180, 182, 184, 186
Hertz, Neil, 7
Hoare, Richard, 84–5
Holmes, Richard, 2, 4, 10, 15, 22, 25, 127, 136, 145, 175, 178
Howell, Peter, 8, 9, 13, 27
Howitt, William, 139–41, 212n17
Humboldt, Alexander von, 15, 216n48
Hume, David, 66–7
Hutton, James, 19, 35, 70, 79, 174
Hyperborea, 124–5, 126, 128, 130

ice, 73, 81, 92–3, 102, 104, 110, 112–14, 116, 117–18, 119, 120, 122, 123, 124, 128–30, 131, 132
  see also Antarctic; Arctic, the
imagination, the, 17, 21, 22, 28–9, 34, 38, 39, 60–2, 65–7, 83–5, 87, 102, 103, 104, 113–14, 119, 123–4, 125, 130, 132–3, 137–9, 143, 149–50, 156, 159, 179, 204n83

Janowitz, Ann, 149
Johnson, Samuel, 80

Kant, Immanuel
  on the age of the earth, 176, 181
  'Analytic of the Sublime', 6, 11, 24, 28, 60, 65, 66, 104, 117, 181, 193n37
  influence on philosophical aesthetics, 6, 12, 181–2
  reception in Britain, 6–8
  and Wordsworth, *The Prelude*, 18, 28–9, 33, 39, 65
Keate, George
  The Alps (1763), 52–3, 60–1
Keats, John, 15
Kerguelen Trémarec, Yves-Joseph de, 111, 208n42
Kitson, Peter, 15, 102

Lacan, Jacques, 6, 20, 24
La Condamine, Charles Marie de, 36, 87

Lamb, Jonathan, 106
Leask, Nigel, 25, 136, 158, 173, 194n39, 211n4, 216n42
Le Vaillant, François, 21, 139–43, 146, 147, 155, 158, 163
Leyden, John, 137, 138
Liu, Alan, 22, 28–9, 56, 67, 159
Longinus, 2, 192–3n20
Lowes, John Livingstone, 106
Lyell, Charles, 19
Lyotard, Jean-François, 2, 6, 20, 24

Macfarlane, Robert, 2, 29
Martel, Peter, 32, 35, 40, 53
Martyn, Thomas, 34, 87
McGann, Jerome, 2, 191n4
McPherson, James, 59, 200n115
Mellor, Anne, 26, 121
Miller, Mary, 100
Monk, Samuel Holt, 2, 6, 17, 24, 28–9, 33, 65
Mont Blanc, 18, 28–9, 39, 40, 45, 85
  discovered by Europeans, 18, 31–9
  earliest recorded ascents, 41–5, 48
  as political symbol, 50–9
  as religious symbol, 47–50, 51, 61
  vicarious ascents, 46, 47, 60–2, 67, 176
  see also Alps, the
Montgomery, James, 61–2
Moss, Sarah, 106, 124, 209n79, 209n83
Murray, Hugh, 137, 138–9, 212n16

Naples, 69, 75, 77–8, 90–2, 97
'natural philosophy', 34, 40–1, 48, 55, 57, 60, 69–72, 73, 79–80, 128, 129–30, 132, 141, 180–1
  and disciplinarity, 2–3, 19–20, 74, 84–5, 95–6, 103, 145, 175–8, 181, 184, 195n66
  and popular culture, 2, 17, 18–19, 23–4, 148, 175, 176–8, 182–90
  and the sublime, 3–5, 10, 32, 35, 44, 66, 71, 84–6, 89, 93, 95, 100, 109, 117, 122, 126–7, 148, 159, 163–4, 179–80, 181, 184–5
  see also astronomy; geology

Nichol, John Pringle, 23, 175, 177, 179–81, 182–4, 185, 186, 187, 188
Nicolson, Marjorie Hope, 3, 4, 7, 13–14, 15, 18, 22, 29–30, 33, 47, 50, 70–1, 91, 167, 174, 182, 193n30
Niebuhr, Carsten, 136, 151, 157

O'Connor, Ralph, 2, 4, 5, 11, 13, 15, 16, 17, 20, 23, 25, 71, 92, 96, 176–7, 178, 184
Ozouf, Mona, 100

Paccard, Michel-Gabriel, 42–3, 44
Park, Mungo, 10, 16, 20, 22, 135, 136, 137, 141, 144–7, 155, 157, 158, 159, 163, 195n57, 212n17
Parry, William Edward, 21, 126
Parsons, William, third Earl of Rosse, 23, 175, 178, 180, 184, 185, 188
Petrarch, Francesco
  'Ascent of Mont Ventoux' (*c.* 1350), 30, 44
Phipps, Constantine, 103, 128, 131–2
Platzner, Robert, 175, 181
Playfair, John, 35, 70
Pliny the Elder, 68, 88
Pliny the Younger, 88–9, 204n99
Pocockc, Richard, 32–3, 34, 68, 136, 148
Pompeii, 68, 86, 88–9, 94, 205n106
popular culture, 2, 5, 6, 11, 16, 17, 19, 21, 23, 25, 43, 45–6, 54, 61–2, 63, 86, 87, 89, 92, 97, 105, 112, 119, 144–5, 171, 175–8, 182–3
Porden, Eleanor Anne
  The Arctic Expeditions (1818), 133

Radcliffe, Ann, 48
Recupero, Giuseppe, 78–80, 81
Richard, Jessica, 128, 130, 210n89, 210n99
Ring, Jim, 2, 29
Rome, 64, 90
Ross, John, 20, 21, 126, 130, 131, 132–3, 209–10n85, 212n16

Rousseau, Jean-Jacques, 18, 53
  and the 'discourse of ascent', 30–1
  Julie, ou, la Nouvelle Héloïse (1761),
    9, 30–1, 34, 37, 52, 65,
    82–3, 172
Rudwick, Martin, 2, 5, 15, 16, 18, 19,
    43, 70, 71, 74, 181, 192n12,
    193n35
Ruskin, John, 43, 50, 199n83

Saussure, Horace-Bénédict de, 18, 34,
    36, 39, 41–2, 48, 90, 97, 98
  ascent of Mont Blanc, 34, 43–5,
    46–7, 55, 59–60, 61, 62, 63, 67
Scott, Robert Falcon, 21, 105
Sedgwick, Adam, 25
Seward, Anna
  Elegy on Captain Cook (1780),
    122, 133
Shackleton, Ernest, 21
Shelley, Mary Wollstonecraft, 26, 121
  and 'classic ground', 9
  Frankenstein (1818), 21, 102–3, 119,
    123, 124–34
  History of a Six Weeks' Tour (1817), 9
Shelley, Percy Bysshe, 15, 54, 93, 94,
    196–7n14
  Alastor (1816), 153, 154
  and 'classic ground', 9, 32, 34
  History of a Six Weeks' Tour (1817),
    9, 32, 34
  'Mont Blanc' (1816), 45, 49
  'Ozymandias' (1817), 21, 135–6,
    147, 148, 152, 153, 154
  Queen Mab (1813), 22–3
Shelvocke, George, 105–8, 110
Siculus, Diodorus, 138, 140, 141, 143,
    146, 148
simoom, the, 22, 163–7
Siskin, Clifford, 2, 5, 192n9
Smith, Adam
  Essays on Philosophical Subjects (1795),
    4, 138, 162, 174, 178, 180
Smith, Horace
  'Ozymandias', 136, 154
Smith, Jonathan, 176, 183–4, 185–6,
    218n28, 219n42, 219n57
Sonnini, Charles, 148, 150, 157
Southey, Robert, 158, 164

Sparrman, Anders Erikson, 118–19, 140
Spufford, Francis, 20–1, 103–4
Staël, Germaine de
  Corinna; or Italy (1807), 97–9
Starke, Mariana, 89
subjectivity
  and the sublime, 22, 24–6, 30, 47,
    58, 117, 119, 121, 122, 137,
    142, 144, 145, 147, 148, 154–5,
    158, 160, 163, 166–9, 170,
    194n49
  see also traveller, the figure of the
sublime, the
  as commodity, 2, 11, 14, 17, 19,
    23–4, 46, 61, 62, 64, 89, 147,
    148, 165, 173, 176–8, 182–90
  as culturally determined, 8–12, 20,
    30, 40, 50–1, 58, 60, 66–7, 94,
    118, 124, 143, 154, 169
  and gender, 24–6, 121–2, 199n85
  the 'natural', 1–2, 5–6, 9–10, 67,
    74–5, 80–6, 87–92, 94, 97–8,
    102, 103–4, 110, 113, 116–17,
    119–21, 130, 131, 136, 138,
    141, 146–8, 151–2, 161–7,
    170–3, 174, 177, 182, 187–8
  and natural philosophy, 2–4, 10–12,
    15, 18–19, 32, 35, 44, 60, 71,
    76, 81–2, 83–4, 93, 126–7, 159,
    163–4, 179–80
  and philosophical aesthetics, 6–8,
    12, 13–14, 25–6, 28–30, 33, 37,
    47, 58, 60, 69, 76, 83–4, 102,
    108, 113, 117, 121, 122, 130,
    136, 137, 139, 140, 142, 146–7,
    149, 150, 151–2, 161–2, 171,
    174, 179, 181–2, 183
  and popular culture, 1–2, 5, 6,
    11, 14, 16, 17, 19, 23, 25,
    45–6, 61–2
  and religion, 14, 18, 29–30, 47–50,
    51, 61, 76, 83, 84, 91, 97–8, 99,
    123–4, 138, 153, 162, 167, 182,
    192n12
  and revolution, 55, 57–9, 63, 89–92,
    99–101
  the 'rhetorical', 16–17, 23, 25, 84–5,
    90–1, 147, 152, 163–4, 176,
    177–8, 184–5, 187, 192–3n20

the 'Romantic', 7–10, 14, 17, 25, 26, 27, 28–9, 41–2, 65, 67
Swinburne, Henry, 72, 73, 86, 88, 203n52
Switzerland, 30–1, 33, 34, 39–40, 51–6, 74, 93, 99
  see also Alps, the

Thompson, Carl, 5, 10, 15, 21, 25, 103, 114–15, 136, 142, 145, 159, 165, 169, 195n57
Thule, 124–5, 126, 128, 130
tourism, 1–2, 9, 15, 18, 24–5, 29, 31–4, 36, 39, 40–1, 44, 45–6, 47, 48, 54, 65, 69, 73, 74–5, 84–5, 86, 87, 89, 94, 193n26
traveller, the figure of the, 5, 17, 24–5, 47, 105, 114–15, 117, 119, 120–1, 126, 127, 137, 141, 145–7, 152, 154–5, 157–8, 159, 160, 164–5, 171, 179
Troil, Uno von, 131

Ussher, James, 70, 79

Vesuvius, Mount, 18, 68–72, 77–8, 86–92, 93, 94–5, 97–9, 202n23
volcanoes, 18–19, 68–101, 104
  and the age of the earth, 70–2, 75–6, 77, 78–9, 94
  see also Etna, Mount; Vesuvius, Mount

Volney, Constantin François, Comte de, 136, 138, 162
  The Ruins (1799), 152–4
  Travels (1787), 148, 150, 152, 163–4
Volta, Alessandro, 45, 47

Watts, Alaric, 49
Weiskel, Thomas, 7, 17, 28
Whalley, Thomas Sedgwick, 49, 61, 199n79
White, Joseph Blanco
  'Night and Death' (1829), 182
Williams, Helen Maria, 31, 33, 40, 48, 52, 53–4, 55, 57, 58–9, 196n1, 216n48
Wilson, Eric, 20–1, 102, 103–5, 106–7, 108, 194n55, 207n7, 207n15
Winckelmann, Johann Joachim, 53, 89, 94
Windham, William, 32–6, 40, 68
Wollstonecraft, Mary, 26, 121
Wordsworth, Dorothy, 158
Wordsworth, William, 15, 31, 35, 39, 46, 54, 83, 105, 107, 189, 190
  Descriptive Sketches (1793), 17, 29, 65, 201n34
  The Prelude (1805)
    Book V, 22, 136, 137, 147, 154–60, 166–7, 169
    Book VI, 17–18, 28–9, 33, 41, 56, 65–7, 159
  'Star-Gazers' (1807), 23, 178

Žižek, Slavoj, 2

Printed and bound by CPI Group (UK) Ltd, Croydon, CR0 4YY